KISSES

Erin Pizzey is well known for her work with battered wives and their children. She has had a successful career in magazine journalism and is now a full-time novelist. Her previous novels include *First Lady*, *The Consul General's Daughter*, *The Snow Leopard of Shanghai*, *Other Lovers*, *Morningstar*, *Swimming with Dolphins* and *For the Love of a Stranger*.

ERIN PIZZEY

Kisses

HarperCollins*Publishers*

HarperCollins*Publishers*
77–85 Fulham Palace Road,
Hammersmith, London W6 8JB

This paperback edition 1996
1 3 5 7 9 8 6 4 2

First published in Great Britain by
HarperCollins*Publishers* 1995

All events and persons in this novel are fictional,
and any resemblance to actual events or persons living
or dead is purely coincidental.

ISBN 0 00 647719 4

Set in Linotron Sabon by
Rowland Phototypesetting Ltd
Bury St Edmunds, Suffolk

Printed in Great Britain by
HarperCollinsManufacturing Glasgow

DEDICATION

'*Kisses* is a must for any woman contemplating an affair with a married man.'

Kisses is dedicated to Eddie Bell, my friend and my publisher. My thanks go as always to David Morris, Alan Cohen, John Levy and Christopher Little, my agent. It takes all these men in my life to keep me out of trouble. To Signor Faenzi at the Cassa di Risparmio di Firenze. To Mr Striessnig, the Manager of the Savoy Hotel, where I always stay. All my books are dedicated to Reno: without him, the Savoy's River Room restaurant will never be the same. To Mr Kelly at Fortnum and Mason's and Stella Burrowes at Harrods. They all make my busy life run smoothly. To Graham Harper at Ashgreen Travel, who efficiently rescues me by air, land and sea. To Patricia Parkin, my editor, and Debbie Collings, who takes care of my publicity so efficiently. For John Munday, who does the best book jackets in the business and Jerry Bauer, who takes excellent photographs. To David Young and the whole team at HarperCollins. For a little girl called Erin Mi Mi Longhurst who was named after me. To my village of San Giovanni d'Asso. To Robert Cappelli, the mayor of my village. To Luana and Nicoletta, my friends. For Lia, Mauro and Rocco Machetti. To Ilda Guidotti who takes wonderful care of me and mucks me out. To everyone at British Airways, my favourite airline. To Janine Quick who listens to my tales of woe. To all the crew of *Scimanini* and my skipper Ottavio. For my bar in Bagno Vignoni run by Susan and J.C. and for Beatrice their beautiful daughter. For Ian Murrel and Sharon Brackly, my management team at Lloyds Bank, my grateful thanks. A special thanks to Romano Battaglia, one of Italy's most loved philosophers, painter, poet and writer, in appreciation for his vision of Versiliana, Italy's most major Arts festival. All of July and August we gather in a pine forest every evening to hear him present the cream of Italy's painters, writers, poets, journalists and politicians. I stayed at the Byron Hotel, now my second most favourite hotel in the world. Nicla Morletti a friend and fellow writer who helps at the Arts festival and her husband Maurizio. Not forgetting Vilma, Romano's wife and Josi Polacci also on the Versiliana team. Above all Elizabetta, Danicle, Rocco and Letizia who run Agro Tourism in Bagnacci. There among the pretty cottages they have a huge pre-Etruscan mineral baths where I swim all summer with their guests. Finally for Mr Nolan and Miss Christine and their family and Mrs Annie Walton in my home, the Cayman Islands.

San Giovanni d'Asso, February, 1994

Life breaks most of us in the end
but afterwards some of us are strong in the broken places

HEMINGWAY

One

❧

'You know, Edwina, I'm really worried about my pregnancy. How long did it take you before you found out that you were pregnant with Tarquin?'

'Gee, I don't really remember, Madeleine. I guess about three months. I was nauseous all the time, but I blamed that on Scott; he was having an affair with his secretary and being such a bastard to me.'

Madeleine finished her glass of white wine and gazed lovingly at her two friends. The three of them were sitting at their favourite bar, Virginia's on Delancey Street. Germaine sat blinking, hamster-like, in the strip of New York sunlight that filtered through the gap in the net curtains, which otherwise shrouded the bar in a twilight gloom. Good, solid, practical Germaine. Once she was fleetingly married to a fellow archaeologist, but now she preferred to remain terminally virginal. She smiled at Madeleine.

'Why do you ask, honey?' Germaine felt a proprietorial interest in Madeleine's pregnancy.

'Well, it's really odd, you know. Syracuse decided when he hit forty that he really wanted to be a father. I wasn't too keen; after all, I'm thirty-two now, and I've always liked kids when you can give them back to your friends. Still, I imagined that I was still young enough to get pregnant without a problem, but the months went by and nothing happened. Syracuse was getting frantic: he consulted all the best gynaecologists in New York. I spent my life with my legs in the air while strange men poked and prodded around inside me. Syracuse had to perform into little glass test-tubes.' Madeleine paused. 'At least he didn't have much time for his women.' Germaine put a hand out to comfort Madeleine. Madeleine smiled at her. 'Actually, Germaine, as you know, I came to terms with that side of our marriage a long time ago, thanks to you.

'No, what's so odd was that the final doctor we consulted suggested that we go to Lisbon. Apparently it's the latest place to screw for babies. There was this one magical night when we'd been swimming and we made love later. Bingo! I knew I was pregnant. How about that?'

Edwina moved her exquisite profile slightly to the left. There was a very handsome man watching her with interest two tables away. Edwina allowed a small, intimate smile to play on her lips. 'How very interesting, Maddie,' she breathed.

Edwina unclipped her long PVC purse and took out a packet of multi-coloured cigarettes. She flipped open her Dunhill platinum lighter, and then, after running the tip of her little pink tongue across her full lips, she slipped the cigarette into her mouth and sucked gently on the end. She lazily flicked her long blonde hair over her face, and then gazed at the bemused man. Her blue, sea-washed eyes stared at him intently.

'Edwina.' Madeleine was laughing. Germaine looked at the two women she loved most in the world. What a foil they were for each other, she thought. Edwina the cool, risk-all blonde, and Madeleine. Madeleine was a tall, slim chestnut tree, her hair thick on her shoulders and her big brown eyes watchful and shy. 'You haven't been listening to me, Edwina.' Madeleine turned round to follow Edwina's gaze.

'Oh, Edwina, won't you ever stop?'

'Nah,' Edwina grinned. 'It's the only recreational

sport I enjoy, Maddie. Anyway, it's so good for my skin. It's my only exercise. Go on, I'm listening. You felt a sudden ping or bing and then what happened? I bet Sy was relieved?'

'He was, actually,' Madeleine admitted. 'We bought one of those pregnancy kits, and when he saw the ring he was thrilled. When we were at the bar that night, he told everybody that I'd have a boy. In Portugal they say that your water's weak if you have a girl.'

'Huh, how can he even think like that, Madeleine?' Germaine leaned forward. 'Your husband is the last of the male dinosaurs.'

'Second only to mine.' Edwina lowered her long, pale eyelashes and blew a plume of smoke through her nostrils. 'Count to ten, Maddie, and I bet the guy comes over.'

'No dice, Edwina. I know he'll come over and then what'll you do?'

'While my husband is away, this mouse is going to play. Why should men have all the fun?' Edwina stretched sensuously. Her eyes were dancing with excitement. 'Oh look, he's getting to his feet and coming over. Seven, eight, nine, ten.'

The stranger had very big brown eyes and a lot of chest hair. 'Would you lovely ladies like to have a drink on me?' he enquired.

'We're just leaving,' Madeleine said firmly. 'Come along, Germaine.'

'Indeed,' Germaine agreed. 'We really must be going, Edwina. We have an appointment with Madame Winona on Beeker Street. Madeleine and I think we could do with some good advice.' Both women rose to their feet, picked up their jackets and purses, and fled.

The sun hit Madeleine's face as she walked out of the bar. She gazed pensively at herself reflected in a plate-glass window across the road. After the first euphoria of the news of her pregnancy had worn off, Syracuse had said, 'I suppose you're going to get fat and cow-like?' His words still haunted her. Well, today she didn't look fat.

It was June in New York. The city was at its most beautiful. The trees supported tender, bright green leaves, and the people who hurried by were smiling and relaxed. Madeleine also smiled, and put her hand on her stomach. She was tall, with a thick head of unruly black hair. Her skin was very white. She knew she would never be as slim and desirable as the other women in Syracuse's life, but she had married him for better or for worse and she at least would keep her end of the bargain.

'Are we really going to visit a fortune-teller, Germaine?' She knew Germaine had always taken an interest in the arcane. She told fortunes with her own Tarot cards, and she swore she would have made a living out of it in her beloved Libyan desert.

'Yes, Madeleine, I've discovered this wonderful woman in Beeker Street, she does everything. I'm nuts about her.' Germaine enthusiastically flagged down a cab. Her small, dumpy, square-bottomed figure was dancing with excitement. Standing next to Madeleine's tall, dreamy presence, Germaine was aware that they made an odd couple.

Germaine had inherited money from her father's trust. She had preferred to give most of it away. She bought her clothes from the Salvation Army and St Vincent de Paul shops. What was left went on her frequent trips to the Libyan desert. Today she was wearing an old pink bonnet tied under her chin with a ribbon, and a dark green velveteen dress with yellowing lace around the neck and arms. Her hands were encased in white cotton

4

gloves, and she carried an enormous, battle-scarred handbag.

As a cab pulled up and they both climbed into it, Madeleine watched with amusement the expression on the cab driver's face. She was used to Germaine's bag-lady act. She also knew that Germaine had a stash of money in her purse that she handed out to the poor and the needy of New York. No mugger would bother with Germaine. Her mousy face and her little sunken grey eyes gave the impression of a prematurely old lady. Despite this and the fact that she was only four foot nine tall, both Madeleine and Edwina knew that Germaine was perfectly capable of knifing a man if she had to. In her adventurous life she had indeed done serious damage to an Arab camel thief; she was also an excellent shot. In the same bag she always carried a dainty little pearl-handled derringer.

'Where to?' the cab driver barked. Two New York kooks, he decided.

'Madame Winona's on Beeker Street, please.'

The cab driver deposited both the women outside the little white clapboard walk-up. Even in the sunshine, Beeker Street was dingy, but the sounds of jazz floated out of the bars that lined the street. The sounds were hot and sweet and set Madeleine's feet tapping. Germaine followed Madeleine out of the cab and stuffed some bills into the man's hands. He inspected the notes suspiciously. 'Hey,' he yelled. 'Where's the tip?'

He glared at Germaine and then he saw a shadow cross her face. 'OK, OK,' he backed off. 'Lesbians,' he muttered as he drove off with a screech of tyres. 'Fuckin' lesbian ball-breakers. New York's full of 'em.' Nevertheless, he was unnerved by the look the old woman had given him. She had the evil eye all right.

The bell made a sound of protest when Germaine

pushed open the door. Madeleine followed nervously. 'Madame Winona, are you ready for us?' Germaine called.

'Just a minute. I'm finishing a long distance Tarot reading. I'll be with you in a minute. Sit down.'

The voice was cracked. It sounded like an old Bakelite record from the forties. Madeleine looked around the filthy little room. There were two garden chairs spotted with dried food. A small rickety table painted white stood drunkenly on three legs; the fourth corner was propped up by a chair. Above the table hung a long electric cable with a naked lightbulb dangling on the end. A door opened and Madame Winona hurried in.

Madeleine tried not to laugh. Madame Winona looked exactly like Judy of the Punch and Judy theatre, which she had watched on Hampstead Heath when she'd visited England as a child. Madame Winona had a long, curved witch's nose, two bright brown, ferret-like eyes, and a perfectly huge wart that hung off her forehead. She had an enormous, comfortable bosom, and a matchingly big behind. She wore an old black fustian dress covered with a dirty pinafore.

'Ah,' she said in a deep, twangy voice. 'You must be Madeleine. And where is the other party?'

'I'm afraid she is otherwise engaged, Madame Winona. She sends her apologies.'

'Huh.' Madame Winona sat down heavily on one of the chairs. 'Come, dear,' she patted the chair beside her. 'Sit you down.' Madeleine sat down. She felt her heart racing. 'What is it you want? Tarot, palm-reading, channelling, table-tapping?' She pulled a lengthy list out of her pinafore pocket. 'You choose.'

Madeleine looked helplessly at Germaine. 'Choose the channelling, Madeleine. Madame Winona is really good at that.'

6

'All right, I'll choose the channelling, whatever that is.'

Germaine leaned against the wall. 'Just watch, Madeleine, and don't say anything,' she advised.

Madame Winona took a deep breath. Suddenly her head fell back and all Madeleine could see were the whites of her eyes. 'Oh, Germaine, is she all right?'

'Shhh, Madeleine, she's in a trance. Don't disturb her, it could be dangerous.'

Madame Winona began to breathe laboriously. Then she began to make sobbing sounds. A voice came out of her mouth but it certainly wasn't Madame Winona's voice. 'Hello, Madeleine, I am Dr Stanislaus and I have been trying to contact you for the last three months.'

'You have?' This piece of news made Madeleine very nervous. She clasped her hands together very tightly. Her knuckles were white.

The voice had a cultured, gentle sound. 'I lived in Vienna in my last manifestation. I was a paediatrician. It is important for you to know this,' the voice continued. 'All I want to tell you for now is that you are going to have a little baby girl. She will have green eyes, like the jade buddha in Bangkok, and hair like the wild strawberries you find in the woods.'

'A girl? Oh no, that's impossible. Syracuse will be so disappointed.'

'No, he won't, my dear, not after he's seen the child. I promise you that. This is all I am allowed to tell you for now, but three days after you've given birth I shall visit you. I must ask that you call the child "Allegro".'

'But, Dr Stanislaus, I was going to call a baby girl Joanna, after my grandmother.'

'No, it is very important that you call her Allegro. That is to be her name in this manifestation.' The voice

7

became stern. 'You will do that for me, won't you, dear?'

'All right, if you insist.' Madeleine comforted herself that, once she was out of this little house and on the telephone to Edwina, they would both find all this stuff screamingly funny. For the moment it seemed better to humour whoever this was giving orders. She wondered vaguely how Edwina was getting on with the man with the gold chains and the chest hair.

Madame Winona shook for a few seconds, cleared her throat and then opened her eyes. Germaine recounted the events and then said, 'Didn't you find that fascinating, Madeleine?'

'Yes, I suppose so,' Madeleine replied dubiously. 'But I'm not sure what any of this means.'

'It means, dear.' Madame Winona took one of Madeleine's hands, turned it over and gazed at it. 'There, you see,' she said, tracing a line from her wrist up to the middle finger. 'You have a deep line of destiny. It is unbroken all the way up from the wrist. It crosses your head line which is excellent. Nice and straight. No depression, no suicides. Very good, my dear.

'The guardians could not have chosen a better host for their baby. Now, you remember to keep the faith at all times. You will be well looked after along your path. You are honoured to have been so specially chosen.'

'I don't have a line of destiny on my hand like Madeleine does.' Germaine's voice was mournful. She'd always wanted children herself.

'Some of us were sent to follow,' Madame Winona said briskly. 'You can help protect your friend and her baby. Madeleine,' Madame Winona stood up. 'You can trust Dr Stanislaus. He is a very old soul. This is his last manifestation before he rejoins the light, which is where we all originated. You are surrounded by those who will

8

love and take care of you – and you have Germaine.'

'What about Edwina?' Madeleine couldn't imagine anything happening in her life that would exclude Edwina.

'She is on your path some of the time, dear, but she does tend to be distracted by carnal matters, doesn't she? Your friend Edwina is a very new soul, isn't she? They tend to run around making a bit of a mess of life.'

'I guess so, but I love her anyway. Thank you, Madame Winona. I'd better go. Syracuse is due back from his office and he gets upset if I'm not there to pour him a glass of wine.'

'Bless you, my children.' Madame Winona kissed them both. It was a soft, whiskery kiss.

Madeleine hugged Germaine goodbye and caught a cab. If Syracuse hadn't been such a jealous bastard about her friends, she would have invited Germaine to come and live in her enormous house. As it was, Germaine was even now on the subway to her tiny apartment on the Lower East Side.

Idly Madeleine put her hand on her stomach. 'Hello, Allegro,' she practised. She swore she felt a little flutter. It reminded her of the fluttering of a trapped butterfly.

'Syracuse,' she said later in bed. 'I felt our baby move this afternoon.'

'Don't be silly, it's much too soon. It must have been indigestion.' Syracuse was in a bad mood because Madeleine had refused to have sex with him. 'I'm much too tired,' she said dismissively. But, given the resounding sulk that always ensued when she refused Syracuse, Madeleine had decided not to make matters worse by telling Syracuse of the adventures she had had with Madame Winona. She'd tell him tomorrow, when he was in a better mood. She fell asleep, dreaming of owls in Central Park.

Two

Syracuse was getting very bored in Frankfurt. Griselda, his mistress, was taking too long to recover. 'Frankly, Griselda,' he said, smiling his most charming smile, 'why on earth would you want a baby at your age?' He remembered after he'd said the words that Griselda's age was a matter of great concern to her. Her lower lip trembled and her big blue eyes filled with tears. When she was in one of her lachrymose moods, Syracuse wanted to kick her. 'Darling,' he said, kissing her gently on her blue-veined eyelids. He probed her mouth experimentally with his tongue while looking at himself in the mirror that hung over the bed. Syracuse liked to see himself in mirrors at all times. Now he watched carefully to see the expression on his face. Yes, it was just as he'd hoped: sincere and anxious. A little sexy, but not too much, given the circumstances. He admired his patrician nose and his sleek cap of black hair that was tinged with a few grey hairs. Not bad for forty-two, he congratulated himself. He smiled. No wonder women fell for him. He was beautiful. Griselda was not responding to his kiss. She heaved a sigh. 'We can't yet,' she said.

Syracuse felt bored and trapped. He had been without sex for a week now, and he felt the tension in his spine. Only sex released that particular tension. He sympathised with Jack Kennedy – he got headaches. He wondered briefly if only he and the president of America suffered, but then thought probably others did: it was just that men never talked as intimately as women did. He was abruptly jolted out of his musings by the telephone. He gestured at Griselda. Rule one, never answer your mistress's telephone.

'For you,' Griselda said, handing the telephone over.

Syracuse put the instrument to his ear gingerly. If the telephone was for him it was usually Mrs Poole, his wife's housekeeper. 'Madam,' she said in her impeccable English voice, 'wishes you to know that you have a baby daughter.'

'Wonderful.' Syracuse tried to sound delighted. He was well aware that Mrs Poole disliked him intensely. The first strike against him was that he was American, and the second that he was part-Italian on his mother's side. That made him both a 'Yank' and an 'Eyetie'. Mrs Poole carried her hatred of foreigners like a battle lance. She was Syracuse's wife's secret weapon, kept well hidden until after their marriage. Mrs Poole made it her business to spy on him and to torment him. A disapproving sniff from her high-arched nose and Syracuse, to his eternal shame, found himself a small boy again.

'Thank you, Mrs Poole,' he said sweetly. 'Tell her I'll be home on the next plane. How is she?'

'Very well, thank you.' As well as can be expected with a husband who is cuckolding her with yet another woman. That sentence went unsaid. Hopefully Mrs Poole didn't know about the abortion, but then she probably did. Syracuse always confessed everything to Madeleine eventually and, like all the women he knew, Madeleine probably briefed her housekeeper. He handed the telephone to Griselda.

'Your wife has had the baby?'

'Yes.' He tried to sound happy, but the idea of fatherhood frightened him, and he had set his heart on a boy.

Having a baby felt like a good idea at the time; after all, Edwina and Scott had Tarquin, or maybe it was

Edwina and Jonathan, her lover. Either way, Scott was silly about his boy, and whatever Scott had, Syracuse acquired. Forty-two years old was not exactly spring-chicken time, but he felt young. Now he was not so sure a baby was a good idea. Why did women endlessly have to reproduce? He felt trapped between his mistress's empty womb and his wife's birth trauma. Men should be excluded from all this messy women's business.

'Was it a boy or a girl?'

'A girl.' Syracuse could see a smile of contempt curl Griselda's lip. Why did women have to be so competitive? Now Griselda would go for another pregnancy and try to have a boy. What a bother he couldn't use condoms any more. Men were stuck when the pill gave women control over their own biology. There was never any thought for the wishes of a mere male. He felt sure that Griselda had tricked him this time. In the good old days before women insisted on taking control of their own bodies, he took care of such things and never had an accident. Still, it was time to pour more champagne. He had been told by Griselda's gynaecologist that champagne was the surest way to avoid post-abortion depression. He didn't mind about her depressions, but he did not want her telephone calls upsetting his wife and his new baby.

What he needed to do now was a lightning bit of calculation. So many dollars translated into German money, and then she could go off shopping. She could buy herself never-ending boxes of chocolates and take her appalling friend Lotti on holiday. If, as he believed, all women made war against men, then Lotti was a marine in the great army of women, and Griselda was a paratrooper. At least they were both first in the battle against men. His wife and housekeeper, he thought, were more like the CIA.

He leaned over and kissed Griselda. He checked himself in the mirror again. Eyes large and slanted, mouth full, neat ears fitting well to the head. Very Michelangelo. 'I'll get you a glass of champagne and then I'm off, darling.' He pulled out his chequebook, enjoying the look on Griselda's face when she saw the amount. He did his inaccurate Humphrey Bogart imitation down the hall. 'Here's looking at you, kid.' He raised his glass to Griselda.

'Huh?' Griselda looked mystified.

Damn, that line belonged to Mei Mei Chow, his mistress in Hong Kong. She was mad about all American pictures.

'Never mind, sweetheart . . . I'll telephone you from the airport.' He skipped out of Griselda's bedroom and collected his suitcase. He ran down the stairs; he wanted to avoid yet another doleful goodbye.

On the main road he put his thumb and his forefinger together and placed them between his teeth. He grinned as a cab, upon hearing the shrill whistle, came tearing towards him. He leaped on board, pretending he was a private detective on a hot case. 'To the airport,' he said, 'and step on the gas.' The cab driver grunted and gunned the engine. Syracuse leaned back in the cab to ease the pain in his back.

Still, during her short pregnancy, Griselda had developed a voluptuous bust. Syracuse liked women with slim hips and big breasts. Big breasts were hard to find in these liberated days when women all tried to look like boys. He spent the rest of the journey remembering breasts he had known. They reached the airport before he was half-way through his list. He grinned shamefacedly at the taxi driver as the man cast a glance at Syracuse's trousers and, laughing, said something in German. Syracuse cursed his weak flesh. A long walk through the airport would get rid of it, he told himself, and carefully positioned his suitcase.

Three

୶୫

'Hello, sweetie.' Syracuse walked into Madeleine's private room in the hospital, hidden behind an enormous bunch of blue roses. In his other hand he carried a big Nehiem Marcus carrier bag.

A little nursing sister came in behind him and took the flowers. 'I saw you coming down the hall, sir. May I take these flowers and put them in water for you?'

Syracuse looked at her demure little face and then at her slender ankles. Why were nurses so treacherously sexy? Was it the uniform that always made him feel that they would take charge of him in his own bed as they did on the ward? He'd had quite a few nurses in his time and he found them to be warm, earthy women. This one looked worth a try. He smiled at her. 'What's your name, honey?'

'Lucinda.' She lowered her eyelashes and then looked back up at him.

'Syracuse,' Madeleine interrupted, 'leave the poor girl alone and come and look at your daughter. She really is rather sweet.'

Lucinda disappeared, but not without a backward glance full of promise. The invitation was not lost on Syracuse.

'I'm coming, darling,' he said to his wife, and put the carrier bag on the bed, leaning over to kiss her. This is the second bleeding woman I kissed this week, he sighed inwardly. Still, he had high hopes for Lucinda.

Madeleine inexpertly picked up the sleeping baby and laid her on the bed. Syracuse looked down at the child.

'I called her Allegro like Dr Stanislaus said.' Madeleine had eventually confessed to him that she'd visited Madame Winona. 'I looked it up and it means light, quick and lively. I want to call her Allegro Amanda Winstanley. What do you think?'

Syracuse, for once in his life, could think of nothing to say. There before him lay a perfect reproduction of himself, only in a female form. The baby had a mop of silky pink hair. Her eyes were closed but they were fanned by a double row of long, blonde eyelashes. Two adorable dimpled hands lay open-palmed by her side, and sticking out of her soft cashmere wrap were two perfectly high-arched feet. 'She looks exactly like me,' he said. His eyes were wide with amazement. He bent down and very gingerly took Allegro into his arms. 'She's the most beautiful thing I've ever seen,' he breathed. He carried the baby over to the mirror on the wardrobe and held her up to his face. 'Look, Madeleine, we could be twins – except my hair is dark.'

Allegro opened her eyes and blinked. She saw her father's face for the first time. A wide smile crossed her mouth. 'Hey, she recognises me, Madeleine. Did you see that? She actually recognised me!' He carried Allegro back to the bed. 'Look at those eyes, they're enormous.'

Madeleine was disinterring the contents of the carrier bag. She pulled out a pale silk négligé and made a face. 'I won't be wearing that for a long while,' she said wistfully.

'Why not – you are all right, aren't you, darling? I mean, it didn't hurt much, did it?'

'No, I was surprised. I'd been to all those exercise classes and did all that breathing and she popped out just like a pip – it was a bit uncomfortable, that's all.'

'My, that's a nice bed-jacket, darling.' Madeleine gazed carefully at the label. 'It's from Hong Kong.' She frowned. 'When were you in Hong Kong, Syracuse?'

'Not for ages, darling. I asked a colleague to bring it back with him. He has such excellent taste.'

'You thank him for me, it's beautiful.' Madeleine leaned back on her pillows.

'What colour would you say her eyes are, Maddie?' Syracuse asked her.

'Jade.' Madeleine was pleased that her husband was using her pet name. It meant that he was thrilled and excited. 'I told you all about her after I'd visited the fortune-teller. You remember, I went with Germaine. I wish you'd listen to me sometimes.'

'I don't believe in all that rubbish, Maddie, and you know it. That old boot of a friend of yours will get you into trouble. It's all a lot of hocus-pocus.'

'You have to admit that Dr Stanislaus is right, though. He said she'd have hair like strawberries and that her eyes would be the same colour as the jade buddha in Bangkok. Even the nurse that's on night duty says that Allegro is an old soul and has been here before.'

Syracuse was still staring at his daughter. As a rule he hated all babies and children. Nasty, noisy, messy things. They disrupted the only things worth doing in life – making love, eating good food and drinking fine wine. Riding, shooting, tennis and yachts served to occupy the time in between.

'Can't I take you both home today?' To his surprise he found himself very reluctant to leave Allegro in the hospital. Maddie's quacking spooked him. He didn't like the thought of strangers like Dr Stanislaus talking about his daughter. He wanted his daughter under his roof where she would be safe and sound and out of all harm's way. 'Nanny Barnes is already ensconced and she's hitting it off very badly with Pooley. Don't you think you ought to come back before Pooley decamps back to England? You know you couldn't do without her.' Syracuse could see the look of alarm in Maddie's face. 'Tell you what, darling, I'll nip outside and have a word with the powers that be, see if I can spring you. Leave it to Syracuse.'

He did his Humphrey Bogart imitation slouch. Thank God the child looked like him and did not take after her mother. Still, Madeleine was a good, uncomplaining wife. She was usually grateful for his sexual attentions, and he dutifully made sure she was satisfied every time. He whistled now as he walked down the surgically-clean-smelling corridor.

He came upon Lucinda in the sluice room. 'I'm sorry, sir, I just have to wash these kidney dishes and then I'll bring your wife's flowers.' She had a lock of blonde hair hanging over her eyes.

Syracuse grinned. He crinkled up the corners of his eyes. 'Are you free this evening for a rather late dinner?'

The girl looked startled for a moment and then she smiled back. 'OK. What time?'

'I want to see if I can take my wife and the baby back home this afternoon. I'll settle them down and be round to pick you up at, let's say, nine thirty.'

Lucinda giggled. 'You work fast,' she said.

'Where do I collect you?' Syracuse hoped she was not too far out of town.

'I live at 34, Washington Square.'

'That's not a bad address.' He was relieved. 'I thought all nurses were paupers.'

'Sure I am, but my mother isn't. She lives with her lover and I have the basement to myself. My mother is away at the moment in Rio, so we have the whole place to ourselves.'

'We do?'

'Why go out? I can fix dinner and then we can play.'

18

Syracuse felt a surge of excitement. *Please*, he urged himself, control yourself. You can't walk into Maddie's room with an erection.

'Listen, you go and find the doctor and get permission for us to leave, and I'll take the vase of flowers back to the room.'

He looked up and down the corridor furtively. No one in sight. He leaned forward and kissed Lucinda on the mouth. For a second she looked surprised and then she opened her mouth and took in his tongue. They separated, and Syracuse was left in the hall watching Lucinda's pert little bottom gyrate up the hall. 'I wonder what kind of games you play?' He spoke to her retreating back. She did not turn round.

Four

A few hours later, Syracuse found himself hanging over Allegro's fluffy white cot. Nanny Barnes was in control of the nursery, and she had already drawn the battle-lines at the door of the room. 'Wash your hands, sir, before touching my baby.'

'I didn't know you had a baby, Nanny Barnes.' Syracuse decided to try and charm the woman. Nanny Barnes had the biggest pair of calves Syracuse had ever seen on a woman, and looked as though she ate rugby players for breakfast.

'I don't want my precious to pick up any filthy germs.'

Obviously Nanny Barnes had been gossiping with her arch enemy, Mrs Poole. When they were not at each other's throats, they were united in mutual disapproval of Syracuse. At least, that's what he felt. Really, he should have put his foot down with Madeleine and chosen the housekeeper and the nanny himself. Something elfin and Japanese like Mieko, his mistress in Japan. He really appreciated the way she got down on her knees to serve him his dinner. Maybe a large, busty French girl for a nanny. Instead, Madeleine picked these two frights, who were going to see to it that they gave him a bad time.

He put his newly washed finger into Allegro's tiny hand. She wriggled ecstatically at him. Her whole body radiated joy at seeing him again. Syracuse scolded himself. 'It's only a baby,' he reminded himself. But then again, it was *his* baby. His little tiny Venus. Her hair, set against the very white skin and the gorgeous colour of her eyes, startled him. As a lover of women he could see that she was going to be stunning. A fierce rage blinded him as he leaned over the cot. 'No man is going to harm my daughter,' he said through clenched teeth. All men were beasts when it came to women.

Allegro was getting sleepy; her long lashes closed and her little pink mouth fell open as she began to snore tiny, baby snores. Syracuse tiptoed away, a broad smile on his face. It was nine o'clock and Madeleine was safely tucked up in bed.

'Going out again, Mr Winstanley?' Mrs Poole was standing by the front door, her thin arms folded, as if praying would keep Syracuse out of Lucinda's bed. He suspected Mrs Poole had X-ray eyes; he felt that somehow she had seen him making an appointment with the little nurse.

'Just for the next few hours. I have an appointment – business, you know.' He hated himself when he apologised to his own housekeeper. Why couldn't he just yell, 'Shut your fucking mouth, you old bitch'? He couldn't, he just couldn't. Even arguing with Madeleine gave him a headache. Why couldn't women just lie down and shut up? God had given the human race the best recreational sport possible, and all they could do was bitch. 'Goodnight, Mrs Poole. Please don't wait up.'

Of course she would. Mrs Poole took grim satisfaction in sitting in her rocking chair behind her lace curtain and waiting for Syracuse to come in. He had tried staying out until all hours, but sleep did not seem to be one of Mrs Poole's requirements. She would be there when he opened the front door. Now he automatically looked up to see that the light in Mrs Poole's room was no longer on. Sometimes Mrs Poole made Syracuse so nervous he couldn't perform. Usually he muttered excuses. Life was so damned unfair to men. A woman could always fake orgasm, but a man was on the line. Before Mrs Poole, he'd never had a problem. He would have to do something about the woman, but quite what, he had no idea. Madeleine adored her, and she in turn deified Madeleine, and that was the last thing Madeleine needed, in his opinion.

He hurried on out to his Alfa Romeo. He raced the engine and didn't bother to look up. Mrs Poole didn't start her vigil until after she had dinner with Nanny Barnes. He cruised downtown to an all-night store where he bought a traditional bunch of roses and a posh box of chocolates. He liked the smell of his eau-de-cologne, Givenchy. Madeleine always bought it for him every birthday and Christmas. He was wearing a fawn cashmere also bought by his loving wife. He checked his reflection in the window of the store and then sucked in his stomach. Recently he'd doubled his work-out time: he was worried about his thighs. He was comforted by his German mistress, as she was already showing signs of ageing. There were little frilly bits under her armpits, and a slight tendency for her breasts to wrinkle when she leaned forward. Lucinda had such smooth, creamy skin. She ought to have pink nipples, Syracuse decided, with that fair colouring. He felt his groin bulge in pleasant anticipation.

When Lucinda opened the door to her basement apartment, Syracuse was taken aback. Gone was the little demure girl in a nurse's uniform; instead Lucinda was dressed in a little black dress that barely covered her bottom, and very little else, as far as he could see. She certainly was not wearing a brassière. Even so, her breasts wobbled a friendly greeting.

'So you've decided to come?' Lucinda smiled. She reached out and removed both the flowers and the chocolates from his grasp. 'You dear old-fashioned thing, you.' She turned and walked into her apartment.

Syracuse had never been called old, or old-fashioned, and the words hung uncomfortably in the air. 'I didn't know what sort of chocolates you liked,' he mumbled into the empty space.

Lucinda had gone ahead of him and had turned the corner. He followed her down the hall to where she was standing in the kitchen. 'Beats the sluice room, doesn't it?' she said cheerfully, taking down a green vase from the shelves stocked with crockery.

Syracuse looked around the kitchen. It was a big square room. Against one wall was a bank of cooking equipment. In the centre of the room was a black steel wrap-around kitchen counter. Down the centre of the counter lay hobs for gas and for electricity.

'Are you a serious cook?' he enquired.

Lucinda nodded. 'It's what I like to do best in the world; after fucking, of course.'

Syracuse took a deep breath and decided that it was up to him to assert himself now and take control of the situation. 'Whatever happened to the demure little nurse back in the hospital?'

Lucinda giggled. 'That was the hospital. This is my territory. Let's get down to business. I make a really mean Martini. This is English gin, it's so much better than the sweet stuff you get in New York.'

Syracuse took the proffered glass and sipped. Martinis were too strong for him; he much preferred to drink wine, and maybe a good glass of The Macallan after dinner with coffee. 'Wonderful,' he said, hoping she was not going to ply him with more than one drink.

Lucinda tore off the lid of the box of chocolates. She rummaged about in the box and pulled out a square chocolate with a rippled top. 'I do hope it's a caramel;

I'm mad about caramel.' She bit down on the chocolate and then spat it out. 'Nope, not that one.' She threw back her Martini and absently poured herself another drink. 'You ready for another?' she asked, still picking out chocolates and discarding them. Soon the kitchen counter was littered with brightly coloured wrappers. Finally she pounced on one of the few remaining chocolates and gave a grunt of satisfaction. 'That's it. What a buzz.' She grinned at Syracuse. There was chocolate all over her mouth, but Syracuse found himself thinking how adorable she was. Unlike so many of his other women, she seemed so unconcerned, so very open. Maybe it was her age.

'When's your birthday?' That was always a good opening line. Followed by the star sign. Most women couldn't resist astrology.

'February,' Lucinda said. She poured another Martini. 'I'm twenty-four years old and I'm an Aquarius. It's my birthday next week.' She smiled at Syracuse and, for the first time, he felt she really was looking at him. There was something rather intimidating about her gaze. Her eyes were very blue and they stared at him without blinking. He felt as if she were drinking him down to the very last drop of blood in his veins.

He shook himself and attempted to disengage her stare. 'Why are you looking at me like that?' he enquired nervously.

'Because next you are going to say that you want to read my hand.'

'How did you know that? Are you a mind-reader?' Really, what with Nanny Barnes and Mrs Poole and now this little slip of a girl, it really was not his day – or night. He struggled to gain the upper ground. 'Do you think I could have a glass of wine, Lucinda? I'd like to sit down and catch my breath.'

'Have you left your poor wife tucked up in bed all by herself?' Lucinda's tone was mocking. She pulled a chair out and made a gesture for Syracuse to sit down. 'Here, I have a really good bottle of Les Amoureuses for us to drink.' She poured out a glass and held it under her nose appreciatively. 'Wonderful body.'

She passed the glass to Syracuse, who nodded. As the wine went down to his stomach he realised it was very empty. His stomach growled back.

'Oh dear, I'd better feed you.' Lucinda busied herself at the stove. She took out a wok and began to throw things into it. 'I'm cooking a Chinese duck soup, and then we're having grilled curried prawns and noodles. Does that sound OK?'

'That sounds marvellous. This is a great place you've got here.' Somebody had a lot of money. He wondered if it was the mother or the lover.

'Mom's last husband left her a bunch of money, so she invested in real estate. She has houses all over New York. My mom is a character, but she has a bad habit of always marrying her men. Not like me. I don't ever want to get married and I don't want children. Ugh!'

'What do you want, Lucinda?' Syracuse was curious. Most women these days loudly announced their need for freedom, but Syracuse found, and often to his cost, that they didn't mean a word of it; after a year or two they began to make nesting sounds, which was when Syracuse moved on.

'I think,' Lucinda said, biting her bottom lip, 'I think I want to have several lovers and live a totally reprehensible life. So far I haven't done too badly.'

'What do you mean by that?'

'I was seduced by my uncle when I was fourteen, and really haven't stopped since. You know,' she said, pulling up a chair after splashing what seemed to

Syracuse like an awful lot of rice wine into the wok, 'you don't really know a guy until you've known him sexually.'

'I suppose that's true.' Syracuse found himself feeling uncomfortable. He felt as if he were being auditioned.

Lucinda began to lay two places. She passed behind Syracuse and then leaned over and kissed him. He could see her two small round breasts like puppies as she leaned forward. He tried to hold her for a moment but she pulled away. 'You'll have to wait,' she said, 'I'm hungry.'

Syracuse sighed. Maybe he should stick to older women; they didn't give orders like Lucinda. He dutifully took a spoonful of soup. It was good, very good. In Syracuse's experience a woman who cooked well was also good in bed. If his theory was anything to go by, Lucinda should be superb. He ate his soup with relish and he lifted his glass of wine. 'To my new baby daughter.' He felt happy, really happy.

Five

It was nearly eleven o'clock by the time Lucinda had finished eating. Syracuse watched her smoking her cigarette. She smoked with a black ebony cigarette-holder rimmed with jade. 'I don't like the smell of cigarettes,' she said. 'This holder keeps the smoke away from the front of my hair.'

'Have you always smoked?' Syracuse was now making polite conversation. He wanted to get into bed with Lucinda, make love to her and then go home. He tried not to look at his watch too obviously. Pooley would be getting ready for her night's vigil. He imagined her locking into his head for the next few hours. Then he quickly unimagined her. He mentally turned off the light-switch in his brain so Pooley would have to sit in the dark. He noticed that Lucinda's hands were small and wedge-shaped, and that she bit her nails. That gave him a slight sense of satisfaction; she was not nearly so in control as she pretended to be. He waited.

Lucinda also watched Syracuse. She knew she had him on edge, because the right-hand corner of his jaw was twitching. He was one of those men who would go running back to his wife after sex, which suited Lucinda. Once she was satisfied sexually, she wanted a man out of her bed. Men, first thing in the morning, were always a gruesome sight. Lucinda had long ago decided that women were fine in the morning, even quite ugly ones, but men struggling to escape from their night-time terrors seemed to spend the first ten minutes of their waking hour trumpeting and spitting. She hadn't always felt like that about men. Sebastian, the great love of her life, was as fastidious as she was, but then he was also a ten-carat shit. Lucinda reckoned that Syracuse was probably an eight-and-a-half-carat shit. It was too early to say. He wittered on about his new baby, but soon he would be in her bed and in her body on the baby's first night home.

She stretched and then looked at Syracuse. 'Let's do it,' she said in a flat voice. Syracuse stood up. 'Follow me,' she said to him.

Lucinda left the dishevelled table and walked to the door of the kitchen. Syracuse wondered if he should try and kiss her at this stage. It all seemed so completely cold-blooded. Maybe things between men and women had changed far more than he realised.

The same corridor seemed longer and darker now that he had swallowed several glasses of wine. The Martini was also making itself felt. Damn, he'd left his antacid pills at home. Lucinda turned right into an open door-way. The room was dark. Syracuse tried to make out the objects in the room, but it was almost pitch black.

'Come on, take off your clothes.' Lucinda's voice was firm. 'I'll lead you to the bed.'

He felt her hand in his as she pulled him quite vigor-ously. He felt the bed against the calf of his right leg. He heard a rustle of material, and when he put his arms around Lucinda, he realised immediately that she was naked. Her skin felt like silk. 'Your skin is so soft,' he exclaimed, and continued to run his hands up and down her body. In the darkness his fingertips found their way around her breasts and then down to her vagina. He felt a surge of lust, a sensation so intense it was almost painful.

Lucinda pulled at his belt and then unzipped his fly.

'Don't bother to take off any more clothes,' she said. 'I want to straddle you.'

She pushed him on to the bed and sat across his knees. Going into her was ecstasy. Her immediate, uncomplicated demands satisfied his week-long need. His mind now obliterated, he lunged under her light body. She held him fast. He could hear her gasping breath and then a long, drawn out sigh. He hadn't finished yet, and she waited for him. When he finally shuddered to a halt, she rolled off him and switched on the bedside light. He could see she was smiling.

'Was that all right for you?' he asked anxiously.

'You'll have to come faster than that,' she said. 'I'll get bored – I get bored easily.'

'Do you always come that fast?' Syracuse now felt very unsure of himself. No one had ever complained about his technique before. Often it was he who had to exercise patience. In all the reading he'd ever done about sex, it was women who took their time and had to be coaxed.

'Yeah, usually, unless I'm very tired or I've had too much to drink.'

Syracuse watched Lucinda lying languidly on the bed. She lay with her legs splayed out in front of her. Her feet were wedge-shaped like her hands, but her toenails were painted a childish pink. She was flushed with a post-orgasmic flush which made her blue eyes shine brightly. He could see a patch of damp between her legs and he smiled. He'd had her and he'd enjoyed the event.

'Would you like to make love again?' she said.

'I can't for a while,' he confessed.

Lucinda shrugged. 'It's so much better for women; we can come all the time.'

'I know.' Syracuse was penitent. 'Life sucks for men.

I've got to get back. I'm sorry I can't stay, but you know how it is.'

'Sure.' Lucinda looked at him. Her eyes were level. 'I know exactly how it is.'

Syracuse felt uncomfortable. Damn the girl, how on earth did she become such a cynic? It was a strange quality in one so young.

He sat up and pulled Lucinda into his arms. 'Darling,' he said, 'don't be so angry. I really have to get back. You knew I was married. I haven't tried to hide anything from you. I've really enjoyed this evening and I'd like to come back and see you next week for your birthday. I'll take your telephone number and give you a call.'

'I'll believe that when I hear from you.' Lucinda wiggled out of his reach. 'Don't call me darling. I'm not your darling.'

She lay flat on the bed, her knees looking very white and defenceless. Syracuse got to his feet. He hated this bit. He much preferred it when the lights were off and he could creep into his clothes and glide away. Now he was conscious of the unforgiving light beaming on his middle-aged blemishes. He wished that he did not have a varicose vein running down his left leg. He tried to pull on his underpants without bending too far over. He tucked his behind in as far as he could without falling over.

Lucinda burrowed into the duvet under the silken counterpane. She wished he'd just hurry and go. Finally, after giving him her telephone number, he leaned over her and kissed her gently on the forehead. She waited for him to leave by the front door and then she switched out the light. She lay back on her pillow and her eyes filled with tears. It hurt, it still hurt, and she supposed it probably always would. Sex took the pain away for a few minutes, but then it was back. She wondered if you could die from a broken heart. She rather thought she could. Sleep stole across the bed and held her in its comforting arms. Sebastian. She wondered where he was now.

Six

Syracuse doused the car lights as he slid into his own front drive. He checked his Rolex. The green numerals stated coldly that it was a quarter to two in the morning. A bitter frost gripped the oak trees in the front garden. He looked up and he saw a tall shadow flit across the window. Mrs Poole, of course. Her light went off. Still, in the heat of his love-making with Lucinda she'd not been able to intrude.

He climbed out of the car and then locked it before pulling out his door-key. His front door possessed two solid brass doorknobs. Syracuse had never told Madeleine that he chose those big brass door-knockers because, for him, they represented courage. Why couldn't I tell her that they reminded me of my own balls? he wondered. Maybe because Madeleine doesn't think of me that way. She doesn't know I'm shit-scared most of the time and I need symbols like the doorknobs and my car and my Rolex to comfort me. In fact, most days before he slid his key in the big mortice lock, he gently rubbed the surface of the brass door-knockers. Now he rubbed them for a blessing for the new life in the house, then he put the key in the lock and listened for the sound of the mortice releasing its bite. Yes, he admitted, entering his own house was always a sexual high. Standing replete from his encounter with Lucinda, he was aware that he did not carry with him his usual dose of guilt. Why? Maybe it was because Lucinda had taken an equal part in the love-making. There had not been a long chase followed by persuasion. With other women, coming home was like re-entry from outer space. Tonight he found himself smiling as he climbed the stairs. There was something so clear about Lucinda. She seemed to know what she wanted out of life; but then Syracuse remembered the short bitten fingernails, and he felt a pang of fondness for the girl. He would see her again, and soon.

As he passed the nursery he put Lucinda out of his mind and quickly pushed open the door. He could hear Nanny Barnes snoring. Huge hectoring sounds emanated from her room next to the nursery. Syracuse moved quietly across the thick white carpet to bend over the cradle and gaze at his new daughter. A small nightlight illuminated the baby's flushed face as she lay sleeping. Her pink hands were tightly curled into fists and her hair was damp against her head. Her mouth moved as she sucked rhythmically in her sleep. Syracuse, to his embarrassment, found his eyes filling with tears. He stood by the cradle, feeling as if the ground were swelling under his feet. He put his forefinger gently on the side of his daughter's face. He was conscious of the furrows and the thickening of the skin on his finger. By contrast his baby's skin was soft. She looked innocent and so pure. That, he realised, was what made him want to cry. It had been a long time, such a very long time in his misspent life, that Syracuse had almost forgotten what innocence was. His baby was perfectly formed and wonderfully beautiful and she was his creation. Madeleine, he decided as he stood vigil over the child, only housed Allegro. She was his great work of art. He had created this beautiful creature and, from now on – he addressed God, not sure of his existence – I'll take good care of her, he promised.

Nanny Barnes stirred in her sleep. Syracuse experienced a moment of sheer terror. Suppose Nanny Barnes discovered him in her private sanctuary at five minutes past two in the morning? Would she cry 'Rape', or accuse him of abusing his own daughter? Mrs Poole would believe her. He hurried from the room.

Twenty minutes later, having showered, he slipped into the matrimonial bed. In the laundry basket lay his shirt and underclothes. No need to check for lipstick marks; Lucinda hadn't been wearing make-up. He breathed deeply and patted his wife affectionately on the arm. He very much wished the bed had not been bought for them by his mother-in-law. Dolly was such an old harridan, and a bed from her didn't feel quite decent. At times Syracuse had to restrain himself from hanging upside down and peering under the bed. He wouldn't put it past Dolly to bug him for evidence. Dolly had cursed the marriage from the beginning. Now, of course, he had produced the family's first grandchild. Dolly had better treat him well from now on. He stretched. The tension in his back was gone and he had a new interest in life. She was five foot two and thought she knew all about men. Well, he – Syracuse – would show her a thing or two.

The next morning, Syracuse took the day off work. His father-in-law was most understanding, and promised to be around for dinner to hand out the cigars. The old man was now in his seventies. English by birth, America was his country by choice. Dolly, his wife, was a good twenty years younger. Without make-up she was a witch. Once the make-up had been applied she looked as if she were preserved in aspic. Her face reminded Syracuse of a grouper fish's. He had been on his honeymoon with Madeleine in the Bahamas. They had spent days just soaking in the sun and swimming along the reefs that protected the big sandy beaches. He had forgotten – well, almost forgotten – all the unpleasantness that had led up to the wedding. He'd rounded a corner and come face to face with a monstrous fish that had big pouting lips and protruding, cold eyes. They'd faced each other for a moment; then Syracuse had swallowed a lot of water as he'd snorted with laughter. 'It's your mother, darling,' he'd spluttered. Madeleine, who took her snorkelling very seriously, had been angry. 'Don't be so rude, Syracuse. After all she's done for us.'

Dolly was no friend of his, though, and tonight she would be here for dinner to dribble over the baby. She had two passions in life, did his mother-in-law: one, shopping, which she had passed on to her daughter with a vengeance; and the other dieting. That she had failed to pass on to Madeleine, who lived on chocolates and pastries. Come to think of it, so did many of the women he pursued. What on earth had happened to women with appetites? Lucinda was a refreshing exception.

He awoke in a good mood and put his arm around Madeleine. 'How are you, darling?' he asked, hoping she would give no gynaecological answers at this hour of the morning.

'My stitches hurt,' she said, blinking at Syracuse. 'I gotta go sit in some salt water.'

'You do that.' Syracuse rose out of bed in one fluid movement. Once Madeleine got going on such intimate matters, there was no stopping her and, after last night, Syracuse was going downstairs to order a big breakfast.

On the way down he put his head around the nursery door. Nanny Barnes was holding his baby. He walked across the carpet. 'Good morning, Nanny Barnes.' He sounded as confident as he could on an empty stomach. 'Let me hold Allegro for a moment.' He put out his arms.

'She has just been fed, sir, and we wouldn't like our

little pet to spit up all over your clean shirt, would we?' Nanny Barnes turned a forbidding back on Syracuse.

Syracuse was amazed to find himself angry with the woman. That was his daughter, and no one was going to refuse him access to her. He caught Nanny Barnes by the arm and swung her around to face him. 'Give her to me,' he said firmly. To his surprise, Nanny Barnes relinquished her charge and left the room. No doubt to summon help in the shape of Mrs Poole, but for now he had Allegro in his arms. Her eyes were very wide and she contemplated her father's face with her deep green eyes. Pleased with what she saw, she wrinkled her nose and yawned. Syracuse saw an expanse of pink gums and a tiny pink tongue. He felt she was so fragile that he was afraid of harming her. He rather wished Nanny Barnes would come back. But then the baby waved her little fists, and he stood there, turned to stone with the force of his love.

'I'll take her now, sir.' Nanny Barnes was back with Mrs Poole hovering behind her. Syracuse bowed and then he handed the baby back to her nurse.

'I'll be back to see her at lunch-time,' he said. 'See that she is ready for my visit.'

Syracuse left the room, triumphant. Two fried eggs, sunny side up, and a sliver of bacon. Just what he needed to kick-start the day.

Madeleine was in a half-dream when she heard a tapping on her bedroom window. Idly she opened her half-closed eyes then, tired, she closed them again.

Tap, tap, tap. The noise was incessant. She turned her head towards the window and was startled. She closed her eyes very firmly. The face she had seen in the window was of a very old man. He had a long white beard. He reminded Madeleine of a small barn owl. His eyes were brown and round. His nose was hooked and the tip was buried in a big, fluffy moustache. The voice said, 'You remember me, don't you, Madeleine?'

Of course! Madeleine's brain stopped running around in frightened circles – Dr Stanislaus. This was exactly the same voice she'd heard at her seance in Madame Winona's fly-blown front parlour. 'Now do you believe me, Madeleine? I got it right, didn't I? Your baby has green eyes and hair the colour of wild strawberries, doesn't she? Good girl. Madeleine, I hear you've called her Allegro. Her guardians are very happy. All our plans for Allegro's future are under way now.'

Plans for Allegro's future? Madeleine was nonplussed. Was she wondering if this thing in the window was all in her imagination, stoked by her session with the old fortune-teller? Or maybe childbirth had driven her mad? She very much hoped that Germaine would arrive very soon and take charge. She needed a friend very badly; besides, it was Germaine who had got her into this mess in the first place.

Dr Stanislaus sat in the window and didn't seem in a hurry to go. 'Have you any questions for me, my dear?'

'Well,' Madeleine cleared her throat. She was hugely embarrassed at the sound of her own voice. Seeing a vision was bad enough, but actually talking to it seemed even more ludicrous. 'What do you mean when you said these guardians had plans for Allegro's future? She's my baby, isn't she?'

'No, no, no, no, dear girl, that is merely human thinking. Allegro is in your care due to a dreadful accident. Most careless, I'm afraid. You are going to need all the help you can get with her manifestation. In Allegro's last reincarnation she caused no end of trouble. She won't listen to anyone, manifested or unmanifested. Not even myself.' Dr Stanislaus shook his head mournfully. 'Not even me,' he said gently.

Once over the shock of his sudden appearance in her bedroom, Madeleine found herself interested. 'What does manifested and unmanifested mean, Dr Stanislaus?'

'Well.' Dr Stanislaus obviously enjoyed the sound of his own voice. It reminded Madeleine of thick Viennese coffee sipped through cream. 'All creatures are eternal. For your understanding, I will say that your soul, Madeleine, is eternal. Of course, other people have different words for "soul", but it will do for now for the purpose of this discussion. You are a woman in this incarnation and therefore your soul is also female — anima. You are at the stage of your spiritual existence where you are a relatively young soul. A sort of teenager, I would say, in human terms. However, you are slowly evolving along your path, and that is why you can see me today. Most newly manifested humans have their spiritual eyes tightly shut — they can see nothing but what is in front of them. They are all sleepwalking.'

It all sounded a bit Alice-in-Wonderlandish to her, but she had to admit that Dr Stanislaus was sitting at her window and she was talking to him. She pinched herself hard on the arm. 'Ow.' She must be awake: it hurt.

'Did you know, Madeleine, that you were a Celtic wise-woman in your last life?'

'Really?' Madeleine was surprised. 'I was always told by my father that his people were originally French.'

'No, sorry about that. In your last manifestation you were born in a little town outside County Kerry in Ireland. You were very much loved and revered but you behaved very badly, I'm afraid.' Dr Stanislaus sighed. 'You ran off with a young prince who was entrusted into your care.'

'I did?' Madeleine was shocked at her former self. 'It

38

doesn't sound like anything I'd do today. I lead a blameless life, unfortunately,' she added, feeling rather sorry for her present self.

'Of course you do now, my dear girl. You still bear trace memories of your horrible death in your DNA.'

'DNA, what's that?'

'There is no modern education these days,' Dr Stanislaus hooted gently to himself. 'DNA is coded information that is carried by all creatures. So far humans have only realised that DNA carries information about the physical evolution of man. They understand its uses for medicine and the like, but those of us who are more evolved know that DNA carries also the history of the whole universe. So within you is, if you like, a record of everything that has occurred since the Light first shone on the Void.' He said the words 'Light' and 'Void' with an almost religious fervour. 'Anyway, to get back to you. You were stoned to death, I'm afraid. That was the punishment for women who committed adultery, and you were a married woman. However, rest assured you died very bravely.'

'I did?' Madeleine was beginning to like her former self quite a lot. Running off with a prince and being stoned to death sounded a far more exciting life than sitting in bed with stitches. 'What happened to my prince?'

'Oh, it was all right for men to make love to married women. He mourned your death for a while and then he married a princess and had six children.' Dr Stanislaus was beginning to fade.

'That figures. Men! Nothing changes, does it, Dr Stanislaus?'

'Not if men can help it, but that brings me to my central problem. You see, Allegro didn't want to be manifested as a woman again. She caused havoc when she was a woman last time. Her guardians and I had planned a completely different manifestation for her. We were going to give you a nice, plain little girl-host for Allegro so that she couldn't use her great beauty to manipulate her way through her new life. Firstly, Allegro redesigned the host body without us knowing and then she switched her sex six weeks after she had inhabited your womb.'

'You don't mean that she's going to be a –'

'No, no, no, my dear, that's a completely different manifestation and we all spend lives as men/women and women/men. If only she is we would be lucky. No, Allegro is the most dangerous of all manifestations. *Puer aeternus* – the eternal boy-child. Peter Pan is a well-known example.

'You see, Allegro insisted that she did not want to be a woman because women don't have power. That's the problem. Allegro intends to grow up to be the most powerful woman in the world. Even worse, she intends to lead other women out of what she sees as their slavery to men. She did it before with disastrous results. She was a Greek queen called Hippolyte with her marauding band of Amazons; then she was Boadicea, that terrifying nightmare of a woman for men. She held men to sexual ransom when she was Lysistrata, and then, of course, there was her never-to-be-forgotten performance when she decided to be Joan of Arc. She got herself burned at the stake for that one. I'm afraid I thought it served her right. As much as I adore her, she went too far.'

'If all that you're saying is true, Dr Stanislaus, you've made me very nervous of my baby.'

'Don't be nervous, dear, once I've gone you won't remember a thing I've said. If you did, you wouldn't have to learn your lessons the hard way like all humans do. You know,' he smiled and twinkled at Madeleine, 'humans are arrogant enough to think they are more evolved than animals and insects. Bah, what nonsense! Insects are the most evolved beings on the earth, followed by animals, and then plants, rocks, stones, and finally humans.'

'Really, Dr Stanislaus, you surprise me.'

'Oh dear, I must go, I'm being summoned by the unmanifest guardians. I can feel my photons dispersing. You'll hear from us from time to time. When I am in this world you often see me in your garden. I am a barn owl. Look out for me, I have a withered right claw.'

Dr Stanislaus was gone. Madeleine shook her head. She heard a knock on her door, and called, 'Come in.' She couldn't wait for Germaine to arrive, she had so much to tell her. Madeleine frowned. What did she have to tell her? She couldn't remember. Something about the baby. It was gone.

Seven

Madeleine sipped her coffee in her big bed. Edwina sat on a chair beside her.

'I've got a lousy hangover.' Edwina had made a face. Edwina had been born beautiful. Sometimes Madeleine wondered if that was why she loved her so much. She'd met Edwina when she had first been dating Syracuse. Edwina was part of a hell-raising crowd that centred around Weldon Art College just off Times Square. Madeleine had been very shy, and felt intensely privileged just to know people like Edwina and her friends. It was Edwina who had taught Madeleine how to dress. On her first visit to Dolly and Ronald's magnificent mansion off Central Park, Edwina had turned up dressed in a scruffy pair of tight black pants and a torn T-shirt. She'd bounced through the big front doors and warmly shook the footman by his white gloved hand.

'What a great place, Maddie.' She'd hugged her new friend. 'You never said you were loaded.'

Maddie knew that her mother, upon hearing voices, would descend from her first-floor sitting room. Nothing escaped her mother's notice. Dolly had stood at the top of the stairs, one hand poised on the brass rail that ran all along the art-deco staircase. 'Who is it, honey? A little friend of yours? How nice.' Dolly had applied her diamond-studded lorgnette to her protuberant eyes. Madeleine had sensed her relief. Although mother made endless jokes about Madeleine's girlfriends, they were harmless. At that time Madeleine had had no boyfriends, and was beginning to believe she never would have a boy in her life because he would have to survive her mother's selection procedures. Ronald, Madeleine's father, had, through insurance broking, become a self-made millionaire, whereas Dolly's family were rich Floridians. She was a Daughter of the American Revolution and had married beneath her. She would only consider someone from one of the Ivy Leagues for her daughter.

Now, sitting in bed on her five stitches, Madeleine found a smile beginning to surface. Whatever kind of bastard Syracuse was now, he'd been a hell of a handsome guy then, and the most eligible bachelor of the whole group. His credentials were impeccable. Dolly, in the early days before the engagement, had adored him. Now, however, after several financial and sexual débâcles, Dolly loathed the sight of her only son-in-law. She made her feelings perfectly clear. Now she had a grandchild, though, and try as she would to ignore Syracuse's part in the production of Allegro, Syracuse and her mother would have to come to the peace table.

Eight

~๛

'Edwina. You told me about stitches, but I never guessed they'd hurt like this.' She paused. 'Mom's coming for dinner with Dad and the whole thing is bound to be a nightmare. Germaine is coming for lunch, I ordered a whole heap of Italian *dolci*, and I have a bottle of Italian San Gimignano to go with them.'

'Who does the baby look like, Maddie?'

'She's really pretty, Edwina. Sort of like Syracuse but with green eyes and this funny-coloured hair. I told you that Dr Stanislaus predicted all this and it's real spooky because it's all come true. I'm just going to ring the bell for Nanny Barnes to bring her up.'

Madeleine slid down into her soft bed and put an elegant finger on the brass bell beside her bed. With Nanny Barnes in the house, Madeleine felt very British.

When Nanny arrived, slightly breathless, her pendulous bosom shaking with the effort of walking briskly up the long hall, she put the baby in her mother's arms. 'What a pretty sight,' she exclaimed as she stood back to watch them.

Madeleine searched the baby's face, as if looking for handling instructions. Allegro gazed back at her mother with a slightly, 'I've seen all this shit before' look. To be stared at by a slightly supercilious baby threatened Madeleine.

'Is she OK, Nanny Barnes? I mean, she isn't sick or something? I thought babies of this age were supposed to howl and spit up. In my baby book it said they couldn't concentrate their eyes until they were six weeks old. Allegro is staring straight at me, as if she recognised me or something.'

'Well, dear, every baby is a little sunbeam in its own right. You can't go making predictions about babies. You young mothers think just because you read something in a book, it's all fact.' She snorted. 'My little precious is the cleverest little diddums in the world, aren't you, my darling?' She leaned over the bed and pulled Allegro out of her mother's arms. She handed Allegro to Edwina. 'Now we must go back to the nursery. We don't want our baby to catch a cold, do we?'

'Er, no, Nanny Barnes. You're quite right, that would be awful.' Madeleine consulted the empty space where her daughter had snuggled. She wished she still held her. Her breasts still ached with milk in spite of the injection. Syracuse had assured her that breast-feeding was death to nipples; somehow he'd managed, without actually saying the words, to convince Madeleine that women who breast-fed their babies ended up with breasts like withered udders. The idea had horrified Madeleine, but now she wasn't so sure he was right – and anyway, he was usually so busy with all his other women, she might as well have developed two cow's udders and enjoyed feeding her baby. It was too late now, though. Nanny Barnes had a firm hold on the bottles, and was not going to give up her little charge without a fight.

Madeleine lay back on her pillows and tried to tell herself that childbirth was a woman's greatest achievement. However, nobody told you that you had sore nipples, swollen breasts, and a cunt that felt as if it was going to take two years to recover. That is what the books did not tell you – and no wonder. No woman in her right mind would ever have a baby if she really knew what lay ahead.

Nine

Germaine was the next to arrive. Syracuse's opulent life-style always infuriated Germaine. She never for a moment questioned Madeleine's hand in the spending of the money. After all, Germaine reasoned with Edwina, the money all belonged to Madeleine's family. Still, as she brushed past Syracuse on her way up the stairs, she had to admit that he sent a thrill up her ordinarily straight-backed spine. What was it about the rat? she wondered as she walked down the long, blue-carpeted corridor. She arrived at the door and stood for a moment to clear her head of a delightful sexual thought. She had a momentary vision of herself lying on a blanket in the Libyan desert, her favourite place in the world, with Syracuse poised on his hands, about to enter her. Germaine was not very clear about the details of sexual activity. She had been married once, a long time ago, to a man who turned out to prefer the company of her camel-bearers. Their honeymoon had been spent in a tent in Egypt, and their only physical encounter foundered in a flurry of sand and creased sleeping-bags. Germaine had been so put off by the several aborted attempts, that she had let it be known to her husband that they should no longer pursue the sexual side of the marriage. Except for the odd one-night stand at parties that added little to her knowledge, she remained celibate. Her camel-loving husband had taken off with a Nigerian hunter, and Germaine had remained cocooned from members of the opposite sex. Long ago she made her life around Edwina and Madeleine.

She pushed the door open and peeked at Madeleine and Edwina. Madeleine, seeing her old friend, tried to smile. Germaine had a square head, a pudding-basin hairstyle and no neck. She was short and dumpy, and at this moment in time, Madeleine definitely felt she needed Germaine's company. 'Do come in, Germaine.' Madeleine tried to hoist herself up on her pillows. She made an agonised face. 'Bloody stitches, they're worse than the labour pains.'

'Was it too awful, darling?' Germaine tried not to wince in sympathy. She remembered how she'd suffered each pang in the retelling of Edwina's ordeal of childbirth. 'The things we do for men,' Germaine sighed, and put a small parcel into Madeleine's hands. 'Praline,' she said, 'your favourite.' She bent and kissed Madeleine's scented cheek. As she touched Madeleine's flawless skin, she could not help but reflect that the rich smelled so much better than the rest of humanity. Other hands made the beds, scrubbed the floors, and plunged into hot, detergent-laden water. She sighed and looked at her own worn hands. Far away, sometimes early in the morning, she left her tiny apartment on the outskirts of New York to come to see her old friends.

'Are you tired, darling?' Madeleine looked at Germaine with genuine affection. In the years that she'd been married to Syracuse, she had come to love this woman. Edwina might be closer in that they could discuss sex, or their lack of sex, together, but Edwina was available only when she was either in-between men or settled into a long-term relationship. Germaine was there always. It was Germaine who held her hand on the first heartbreaking few days of discovering yet another woman in Syracuse's life. It was Germaine who counselled her and pointed out that she had to make a clear-cut decision: either she throw Syracuse out, or recognise that he would never change. 'A philanderer is a philanderer, my mother used to say. My mother always had a pearl, as she called them, for every occasion.' Germaine shrugged. 'My mother needed a whole string of pearls – my father was just like Syracuse. He was a rat with women.'

Now Madeleine rang the bell for Nanny Barnes. Edwina took the baby from her arms and banished her firmly. The three women bent over Allegro. 'She is the most extraordinary little girl I've ever seen, Madeleine.'

Madeleine held Allegro in her arms. 'Yes, she really is quite something, isn't she? I feel really proud of myself. Don't you think it's strange how Dr Stanislaus told us she would have green eyes and this odd-coloured hair?' Madeleine kissed the top of Allegro's head. 'Germaine, I've been thinking, would you like to be Allegro's godmother? With Syracuse as a father, she's going to need all the common sense she can get.'

'I don't think Syracuse will be all that pleased to have me as a godparent for his daughter, Madeleine. After all, we don't get on that well.'

Madeleine smiled. 'I've already thought about that, but at the end of the day, Syracuse is quite frightened of you. If we both say "No" to one of his hare-brained schemes, we have a chance of stopping him dead in his tracks.'

'Go for it, Germaine. Keep Syracuse in order.

'Wow, Madeleine, that baby of yours is spectacular.' She put a bejewelled hand on Allegro's stomach. Allegro waved furiously at the lights shining on the emeralds on Edwina's hands. 'Look, darling,' Edwina was entranced, 'she loves me already.' Edwina leaned forward and tickled Allegro under the chin. 'Coochie-coochie-coo.' She was wreathed in a cloud of Opium, her favourite perfume. 'When you're older I'll take you shopping, darling, and we'll buy beautiful clothes and jewels for you.'

'Are you in pain, Madeleine?' Germaine asked anxiously.

'Awful. How long does this go on for, Edwina?'

'For ever. I had a friend who was stitched up too tight. They had to take her back to hospital and unravel her like an old sock.'

'No!' Madeleine gazed at Edwina wide-eyed.

'And then,' Edwina was warming to her subject, 'all those baby books say that your husband can demand sex after six weeks, and it feels like doing it with a brillo pad. Nah, I reckon it takes two years to get over the shock of the whole revolting business. Jonathan reckons it took him three months to even get an erection.'

'Did it really bring you closer, like you said?'

'Well, when a guy gets to see your fanny swell up like a balloon and he doesn't take off instantly, I guess you could say it brought us closer. He certainly loves Tarquin like his own. In fact, I've often wondered if Tarquin is his child anyway – I was having them both at the same time.'

'Weren't you, um, taking care of things?' Germaine didn't really like to ask such personal questions, but she did want to register the fact that one must be very sensible about taking precautions, even though she had no need to worry herself.

'Germaine, darling, I do have one of those awful contraptions that shoot across the floor and fling goo all over Jonathan's ankles, but I'm afraid, in the heat of the moment, I don't usually get round to it; or, if I do, I'm too drunk to remember where I'm supposed to put it, and if I do get it in it's inside out or upside down or whatever. Anyway, it's nice for Tarquin to have two fathers who think he belongs to them. Here, Maddie, have a look.' She thrust a photograph of Tarquin into Madeleine's hands. 'Isn't he just too divine?'

'He is, Edwina, and he looks the spitting image of you.' Tarquin had inherited his mother's aquiline features and her very blue eyes. His hair was cut in a pageboy and he was wearing a black velvet suit with a white lace collar.

'Just imagine, Madeleine, when both our children are older, our houses will be full of juicy young teenagers. I'm going to be a dreadfully lecherous old woman and chase Allegro's boyfriends all over your front garden. How about lunch, now we've discussed our children? Isn't it marvellous, Maddie, now we can add our children to the list of fascinating topics to discuss over the white wine and the *dolci*? Did I tell you about Paolo?'

'No, I don't think so, Edwina.' To tell the truth, Edwina seemed to meet so many men in the oddest places that Madeleine couldn't really remember. 'What about Paolo?'

'I met him last year in Siena. We had one of those hot, passionate, afternoon flings under the eaves of his house. He had a wonderful study up there, and his wife was out. I met him when I was sitting on the Campo after a shopping trip to Mafe to get myself some stuff for riding horses. Anyway, I was resting my feet when he walked by and smiled at me. He spoke perfect English. He bought me a drink. Well, several actually. His wife was in Florence for the day, so I thought, why not? And we proceeded up the road and then fell into bed. It was wonderful, Madeleine. Anyway, he's popped up over here for the next few weeks. When you're out of bed he can take us out to lunch. You'll like him, Germaine, he's an inveterate traveller and he loves the desert. He says that the Arab women he's had in Beirut are some of the best lovers in the world. He says I'm pretty good as well.'

'How can you even discuss sex when I'm in such pain, Edwina?' Madeleine pushed the bell. Allegro was soundly asleep when Nanny Barnes came to get her. 'Could you tell Mrs Poole that we will have lunch up here, please.'

'Very good, madam.' Nanny Barnes lifted the baby into her arms and left the room.

'Lunch was, as usual, excellent.' Germaine removed her napkin which she had tucked under her chin. 'Now I'm over fifty I feel I can do anything I want,' she said with a sigh of satisfaction. 'Put my elbows on the table, belch and tie my napkin round my neck. You know,' she smiled at her two friends, 'I think getting older just gets better and better. I have my job in the bank. That's secure for the next ten years. I am beholden to no man, which is more than either of you can say for yourselves, and I can spend my holidays however I want. No, I think I've got the best of both worlds, and now I can be a godmother without all the worry and fuss of motherhood. It would take an exceptional man to take all that I have away from me.'

'How about if you met a man who could add to what you have?'

'Men can't add to a woman's life, Madeleine. Tell me or show me one example where you feel that a couple that we know are honestly in an equal relationship.'

'It sometimes starts off equal, I suppose,' Edwina furrowed her brow, 'but in my case you either have to keep slapping the bastards down or they start sitting on their arses and expect you to do all the work. Jonathan's quit work again.'

'Why don't you just tell him to get lost, Edwina?'

51

Germaine never could quite work out why Edwina needed so many men in her life.

'I don't know. I guess I don't feel whole if lots of men don't lust after me. If I settle down with one I get bored and want adventure.' She sipped the wine in the bottom of the glass.

'You should be married to my husband. I have all I can handle with Syracuse. The idea of another man in my life doesn't tempt me at all.' Madeleine took a bite out of her chocolate. 'Ahhhh,' she murmured, '*Baci* – kisses. Let me see what my fortune says.' She pulled a little slip of paper from the blue wrapper. '"Life is for living lightly." Well then, once I'm out of here, maybe I'd better look around.' She grinned. 'I've been a good girl for far too long. It might bring Syracuse to heel if I have an affair.'

'It might,' Edwina agreed. 'Scott was furious the first time I confessed. He threatened to kill my lover. After all the secretaries he's screwed, I couldn't believe it.'

Edwina lit a cigarette. 'I guess the problem is that we tend to think of them as our providers,' she continued. 'They are central to our lives. Scott takes care of me. He mends fuses, changes tyres, chops the wood and pays all the bills. I'm well kept, warm in winter, air-conditioned in summer, and can eat any time I feel like it. He has affairs always with his secretaries. He says it's cheaper that way – he pays them anyway. He loves me in his own way. He says the sex he has with other women makes me more desirable because what he has at home is the best. He's probably lying, but the idea of me having other men scares the shit out of him, because he's afraid of losing me. I would never leave Scott, though, you know.'

'I know. You're lucky in a way. Syracuse doesn't mend fuses. He tried to chop wood and cut his leg. He knows nothing about cars. He works for Dad because nobody else would employ him. I've never thought of leaving him, but then I was a virgin when I married him.'

Germaine finished her coffee. 'You and me, Madeleine. The only two in New York.'

'Maybe having a baby will make him grow up.'

Edwina blew a smoke ring. 'Don't count on it,' she said.

Ten

❧

'Daddy, I love you.' Allegro beamed at both her mother and her father, but her eyes were fixed on her father's face and had been since the moment she first saw him.

'And I love you too, honey. Say it again.'

'Allegro loves her daddy.' She thumped the apron of her armchair for emphasis. 'Who's Daddy's best friend?'

'Allegro.'

She was wearing a jade-green dress with a lace collar. The dress matched her eyes. Her face was alight with the excitement of finding words that drew her father's undivided attention. 'Dad, Dad, Dad,' she cooed.

Syracuse sat back in his dining chair and contemplated his creation with relish. 'Atta-girl, Allegro, she's a genius at four years old. A regular chip off the old block, aren't you?' He stood up, dropped his napkin on the table, lifted his daughter from her chair and carried her to the window. 'Look,' Syracuse pointed at the pigeons circulating around the trees and the old-fashioned gas-lamps that lined the cobbled streets. 'Pigeons,' he said. 'Say "pigeon".'

Allegro shook her head and pouted. 'OK, then.' Syracuse now knew better than to argue with Allegro. He was well aware that she could throw the most awesome rages. Syracuse hugged her and smiled as he felt Allegro snuggle into his neck and yet again into his heart. She smelled so good, so unlike women when they grew older and began to smell of other things; but he didn't want to think of that now. He was leaving for Hong Kong and Mei Mei tomorrow. These moments with his daughter were the times when Syracuse realised that he experienced unalloyed happiness.

'Come on, darling.' He threw Allegro up into the air and caught her as she descended into his arms, squealing with delight. 'It's time for our walk in the park.'

When Syracuse left with Allegro, Madeleine was conscious of the stillness of the room. It was so quiet that the silence assailed her ears like blows. It was as if, too, he carried a lamp with him, and that, even though it was a bright, sunny day, something had gone out. Wherever he was, Syracuse filled the space with his energy. That was one of the many things she had come to love about him. He could walk into a theatre, a restaurant or a party, and the conversation would dry up. People stopped talking and turned to stare at him. 'Syracuse has charisma,' is what all her friends said of him. 'Yes, he does.' She was always grateful for any form of conversation or attention. Beside him, Madeleine felt drab, and now, after Allegro's birth, which had left her – even four years on – with a stomach like a flaccid hot-water bottle and thighs mottled with stretchmarks, she felt positively ugly.

She walked to the window and gazed down at the gas-lamps that lined the streets. Most of the houses had been made into apartments, but her house had been left intact. The fact that the house was in her name was not a subject that was discussed between the two of them. She knew it rankled Syracuse, as did the fact that he was employed by her father as an insurance agent. Syracuse only did business with his well-heeled friends. He brought with him to the marriage little other than his blue-blooded connections. His work consisted mainly of days spent in clubs and dining rooms talking with people. Syracuse could talk. Madeleine smiled ruefully as she stood in the window. Syracuse could charm the ticks off sheep, sell razor blades to Sikhs and deodorant to skunks. She watched him walk down the drive with Allegro astride his shoulders. She was wearing a navy-blue fitted coat with a black velvet collar. Together they were a startlingly beautiful couple. The man and his girl-child. Madeleine wished she had a camera to hand. She stood still with her hands tucked into her armpits as she needed the warmth of her own body. Syracuse seemed to have taken the heat out of the room when he left. Madeleine felt a chill now. 'I'm feeling bereft,' she whispered. These days she had begun to discuss her feelings with herself. There was no point in trying to discuss feelings with Syracuse. He would listen politely if they'd just made love, but she felt he was bored by her confessions and worries. Slowly, over the years, she had withdrawn from any intimate conversations. She watched Syracuse and Allegro until they moved out of her sight. She walked slowly towards her bedroom. Time for her morning bath now.

Lying in the bath, contemplating her unpainted toenails, Madeleine's mind went back to the events of last week.

'Paolo,' she whispered. The forbidden word hung in the steam. Paolo Boletti. P.B. She drew the initials on the side of the bath. She had met him at Edwina's.

'This is Paolo.' Edwina had pulled Madeleine forward. 'Paolo, meet my very best friend, Madeleine Winstanley. My second best friend, Germaine, will be here quite soon.'

Madeleine had stood shyly staring at Paolo, remembering Edwina's story of her hot and heavy love-making in Siena. She loved Edwina's apartment. The windows overlooked the Hudson River. The apartment was in downtown SoHo. Scott and Edwina had bought the run-down warehouse before SoHo had become wildly fashionable. Edwina had bullied Scott into letting her loose with his chequebook. 'My style is pure Elinor Glyn, and if he's very generous I'll let him make love to me on the tiger skin in front of the fire.'

Now, with the sun pouring through the windows, Madeleine smiled. Edwina's style could be considered vulgar, but because she was able to pull the whole thing off, it was really very elegant. The floors were covered in various animal skins. The walls were hung with dead creatures shot by Scott. The paintings were of fish in their death throes. All the furniture was severely tubular, the bookcases shelved with glass. It took Madeleine quite a while to discover that Edwina bought books by the yard. They were made of wood painted blue, and the titles were embossed in gold. The only real books were on fly-fishing and hunting, Scott's main rec-reations. 'We don't read, honey. Anyway I'm a Sybarite, you know: lusts of the flesh, and all that.'

Now, standing in Edwina's large sitting room, Madeleine felt overcome with embarrassment. It was such a long time since she'd been alone in a room with a strange man. Paolo, sensing her discomfort, smiled quizzically at her. He took her right hand and bent his dark head and kissed her fingers. 'I have heard so much about you from Edwina,' he said.

Madeleine flinched at the touch of his lips on her hand. Since the birth of Allegro, Madeleine had felt no real desire to make love to Syracuse. She'd wondered if she would ever feel that wonderful, burning surge of desire that made her face flush and the blood run hot in her veins. Maybe childbirth killed it for ever. Somehow, giving birth seemed to have changed her completely. Maybe it was the knowledge that now she was no longer simply a woman married to a man. She had created a tiny, vulnerable, delicate other being, and they would be inseparable all their lives. Now, what she was desperately trying to avoid, was the knowledge that, from the moment she had seen Paolo in the room, she had wanted him. The thought shocked Madeleine. Not just because it was disloyal to Syracuse, but also because he was Edwina's lover, and therefore not available to her. The hair on the nape of his neck curled attractively into his collar. She smiled at him. 'Edwina says you live in Siena?' She regretted the glint of his gold wedding ring.

Paolo nodded. 'I have a flat in New York so I can do business selling wine, here, but my heart is always in Siena.' His big brown eyes shone. She noticed that he had eyelashes all round his eyes. Though his eyes were essentially brown, there were deep gold streaks that reminded Madeleine of the gorse in the autumn on the downs above the sea in Charmouth. 'I love Siena; I think of it as the most beautiful city in the world.' He took her hand in his and walked her to the big picture windows.

'Even though the climb up Edwina's stairs is strenuous, the views when you get up here are worth it. Magnificent.' Paolo stood still, apparently unaware that he still had Madeleine's hand in his.

Madeleine withdrew her hand gently. 'Where did you learn to speak such good English?' Madeleine felt she was on safe ground.

'My wife, she is half-Sienese, half-English.'

Madeleine realised that here was a man who could speak of his wife quite openly while standing in his lover's apartment. Madeleine often wondered how people could have affairs and not die of guilt or embarrassment. The mere thought of any man other than Syracuse seeing her without her clothes on made her skin crawl, especially now when, even four years on, she still carried the marks of childbirth.

'Gin and tonic, Maddie?' Edwina bustled into the room.

'Thanks.' Madeleine took the drink gratefully.

'How about a vodka, Paolo? I've got some of the real Russian stuff.'

'No thank you, Edwina, I only drink wine.' Paolo smiled at Madeleine. 'We Tuscans tend to stick to wine or grappa. Also, we usually prefer to eat when we drink. I know it makes us bad guests, but Tuscans are sticklers for tradition. I'm glad to say that, around the corner from my apartment, there is an Italian *forno* – bread shop – where I can get unsalted bread. From when I was a little boy, I was taught by my mother that no meal was complete without unsalted bread.' He laughed and his slightly oriental brown eyes glinted. 'Do you find that odd?'

'No, not really. I miss things about England like that. I went to school there, and my father is English. I find I'm very English, even though I've lived in America for such a long time. Sometimes I feel so different it hurts.' Madeleine looked at the busy tug-boats bossing their way around the freighters. 'I miss things like clotted cream and raspberry jam. Of course, you can get all that here, but it's not the same as sitting in the sunshine in an English garden, with the smell of a newly mown lawn, and the bleating of English sheep in the distance.' A shadow crossed her face. 'I don't know why it's different. It is just different. Besides, English sheep are different to any other sheep in the world. They are round and beautifully woolly. Oh dear, I probably sound terribly childish.'

'Paolo, honey, Germaine has just arrived and I want you to meet her. She's travelled all over the world.' Edwina pulled Paolo from the window towards the front door. She glanced back at Madeleine and winked.

Madeleine smiled back weakly and followed them. She was glad Germaine had arrived. Now maybe, in her sensible presence, everything would go back to normal.

Even with Germaine sitting across the dining table, Madeleine felt the world had not yet returned to normal. Just what was so abnormal about the situation remained inside her head. She tried very hard not to look at Paolo, but it was difficult. Paolo seemed determined to direct most of his conversation towards her. 'What was your school like in England?' he asked with great interest.

'Well, it was a girls' school. I mean there were no boys,' Edwina interrupted. 'No dating, no nights at the prom with the best-looking boy in the class. No petting either. Really, Maddie, it's all most abnormal.'

'I don't think it's abnormal, Edwina. I'm glad I had all those years where I was able to devote myself to things I loved, like books and music.' Madeleine was beginning to feel attacked. Edwina had a way of teasing her that made her feel uncomfortable. There was a mocking tone in Edwina's voice that made Madeleine feel provincial and unsophisticated.

'Don't pay any attention to Edwina, Madeleine. She's just jealous of you.' Germaine smiled and Madeleine smiled back uncertainly. 'Why on earth would Edwina be jealous of me?'

There was a moment's silence and then Paolo said gently, 'Maybe she envies something in you, Madeleine.'

Edwina sat upright in her seat, her eyes narrowed. 'And what might that be, Paolo?'

He shrugged. 'Oh, I don't know, *cara*. Maybe a certain innocence that you lost a long time ago.'

'You're one to talk, Paolo.'

'Now, now, let's change the subject, everyone,' Germaine interrupted. 'It's impolite, my mother always told me, to chew with your mouth open, for a gentleman to

60

discuss sex or politics at the table, and to leave the lavatory seat up.'

'Anyway,' Edwina was determined to have the last word, 'how could I be jealous of such a goody two-shoes?'

Madeleine felt her cheeks catch fire and her face flushed. Paolo leaned forward. 'You look so beautiful when you're cross, Madeleine. Did anyone ever tell you that?'

For a moment Madeleine was startled. 'No, actually, I don't think anyone ever has.' She gazed at Paolo as if she were seeing him for the first time, which she realised in a way she was. For all her married life, the only man she had ever looked at with love and affection was Syracuse.

She had been a virgin when she'd met him, and on her wedding night she'd been grateful to him that he'd made love to her gently and expertly. As the years had gone by and he'd pursued other women, she'd hidden the hurt and continued to respond to his sexual demands. She did recognise that some of the joy and spontaneity had gone out of her sex life with Syracuse. Often she lay there, making the right noises, while Syracuse pursued his own satisfaction. Now she knew she would never reclaim that simple warm trust that she had given to Syracuse from the start. Sitting opposite this stranger, she toyed with her ravioli, pushing the plump little white cushions around with her fork. Edwina, she knew, had guessed she was attracted to Paolo, and that was why she was cross. Edwina was unused to any of her men having eyes for anyone else but her.

'Tell me more about your schooldays, Madeleine. The English school system is unique: that's why you produce so many eccentrics.' He smiled and his face was kind. Madeleine felt he was genuinely interested in what she had to say. Even if she was a bit of a country bumpkin.

Edwina stood up abruptly. 'I'll clear the plates,' she said loudly, looking at Paolo. He gazed at Edwina and Madeleine laughed. 'Edwina, Paolo is an Italian man. European men don't help around the house like American men.' With the exception of Syracuse, she reminded herself. He couldn't even boil water.

'Well, it's time he learned. Germaine, will you give me a hand?'

'Certainly.' Germaine rose to her feet. All this sex flying around the table was disconcerting. Why, Germaine asked herself, had the gods designed sex the way they had? Surely, just like animals, women should mate once every six months or so, and then spend the rest of their lives getting on with living. Now even Madeleine – dear, sweet, faithful Madeleine – was bitten by the bug. Must be the time of the year. She trotted down the corridor after Edwina.

'Madeleine,' Paolo's voice was urgent. 'We really must see each other again.' He leaned across the narrow glass dining table. His big eyes beseeched her.

'No, we can't, Paolo. I'm a married woman and I also have a child.'

'Madeleine, I can see you're married and I know about your little girl. Her name is Allegro and Edwina says she's beautiful. An affair with me won't hurt your marriage. I just have this urgent desire to hold you in my arms and to kiss you until you are breathless.'

Madeleine hoped she was not going to blush. His face was close to hers and he reached over and put a hand on her shoulder. Straining across the table, he put his mouth on hers. She sat still as a stone. Her lips tightly shut. The kiss was light, undemanding, questioning, but she was not ready for an answer. He knew that, and he let go of her shoulder and sat back in his chair.

'You're such a beautiful, interesting woman, Madeleine.'

'Do you really think so?' Madeleine was surprised. Occasionally Syracuse told her she looked good, but the word interesting never passed his lips. Anyway, how could a life that was devoted to taking care of a house, a husband, and a small, four-year-old child ever be described as interesting? 'Just a boring housewife', is how she described herself whenever anyone asked her what she did. 'Oh, really, how interesting', was the stock reply and, if the enquirer was not another boring housewife, they left, usually muttering that they must find another drink. Syracuse, for the last few years, had not found her interesting. Funny ha-ha, perhaps, when she dropped things or fell over, but not interesting like Griselda, his German mistress. Griselda had a degree in Fine Art from Berlin University. Madeleine had two 'O' levels: one in Domestic Science and the other in English Literature. No wonder he didn't find her interesting.

Syracuse usually took his telephone calls from his women in the library. Business calls, they were known as. One day, Madeleine had found herself listening to a phone call from Griselda on the extension in the dining room. She'd felt guilty but she had had to listen. 'How absolutely fascinating you are, my darling . . .' Syracuse's voice had been light and warm with admiration. It had been years since Madeleine had heard those tones in his voice to her.

Now she was sitting alone in a room with a man who was saying the things she most wanted to hear said by her husband. 'I went to a convent school – although my family weren't Catholic: it was just the best school in the area. I loved my boarding school.' This was a safe topic. 'I liked riding horses and playing cricket. I loved games of all kinds.' She smiled. 'I liked hockey the best, I suppose.'

'Don't hide from me, Madeleine. I warn you I shan't let you go. I'm a patient man and I can wait. See.' He put one hand on the table, and turned it over to expose a wide, deeply lined palm. 'Look there,' he pointed at his hand, 'that's my heart line. Look at that break in the middle of the line: that's you. I've been waiting for you all my life.'

'You ought to visit Madame Winona on Beeker Street. She reads palms.'

'Maybe I ought,' Paolo agreed.

'. . . and I had a really good English teacher, her name was Mrs Durrant.' Damn, she could hear Edwina's stilettos tapping their way back to the dining room.

'Are you still on about your boarding school, Maddie?'

'Yes, I'm afraid I am.' Madeleine was aware that there was a little flare of triumph alive in her heart. She had been called interesting by a very handsome man.

When it came time to say goodbye, Paolo kissed Germaine first, and then he pulled Madeleine to him. There was an intensity in his manner that touched her. She felt his mouth on her cheek and then a waft of the smell of him. His hands were trembling. '*Au revoir*, Madeleine. We shall meet again soon.'

Madeleine stared at him. 'That would be nice.' She kept her voice noncommittal.

'You're going to the Parmiters' party next week, aren't you, Maddie?' Edwina's eyes were like slits.

'I think so. I know Syracuse wants to go.' She made a face. 'I don't like their parties; there are usually far too many people for me.'

'Paolo knows the Parmiters, don't you, Paolo?'

Edwina put her hand possessively on Paolo's arm.

'I do, and I must say I feel like Madeleine. But,' he grinned, 'if you girls are going to be there, so shall I.'

Eleven

After a lonely supper in the library, Madeleine waited for Syracuse's evening call. When he was away he always called to say goodnight. She supposed at first it was because he missed her, but after the first few affairs she realised that it was his way of getting rid of the guilt – if she believed that guilt was an emotion suffered by Syracuse. Maybe it was just a way of checking on his possession. The telephone rang and Madeleine picked up the receiver beside the chair. 'Well, you've certainly made a conquest.'

'What do you mean, Edwina?'

'You know damn well what I mean. I was all set to have a long sexy afternoon with Paolo when he put on his coat and said he had to go. Really, Maddie, the last thing I'd ever expect from you is that you'd pinch my lover.'

'I haven't pinched your lover, Edwina. I've no intention of having an affair with anyone. Paolo is a married man with children, anyway. Maybe he didn't feel like sex?'

'Paolo, not feeling randy: chance would be a fine thing. No, dear, he wanted to know what perfume you liked and your favourite flowers. I know when a man's hooked. Paolo's the persistent type; you'd better watch out.'

'Don't be silly, Edwina, you know I'd die of fright first. Anyway, my stomach still looks like an old hot-water bottle. I'm expecting a phone call from Syracuse, he's in Hong Kong.'

'With another of his women, Maddie?' Edwina's tone was sharp. 'At least Scott doesn't make a practice of setting up house with his women.'

The tone of Edwina's voice cut Madeleine; she felt a drop of blood spill from the wound. 'I know . . . Syracuse says he can't stand hotels but, worst of all, it's my money that's paying for it all. Does it ever go away — the pain, I mean?'

'Only when you get the bastards back. Wake up and smell the coffee, Maddie, you're a big girl now.'

'I suppose I am. I just don't feel very grown up, Edwina.'

She put the telephone down and went up to the nursery where Nanny Barnes was getting Allegro ready for bed. The child was sitting up in her bed looking at a book.

'I'll just read Allegro a story, Nanny.' Madeleine wished she didn't have to supplicate the woman.

'Righti-ho, I'll just pop out and iron some of her clothes.'

Madeleine took the book from Allegro's hand. She wasn't sure if she should lift Allegro on to her lap. She had been so pushed and poked and pulled by her own mother and her friends when she was little that she was diffident about invading Allegro's little world. Allegro just smiled at her mother, and when Madeleine sat down, Allegro climbed out of her bed and curled into her mother's lap. The child's hair tickled Madeleine's chin, and a soft feeling of warmth and contentment filled Madeleine's heart.

'One day, Humphrey lost his mother . . .' She looked down at the big, adoring eyes that were fixed on her face. She felt a pang of guilt for her time spent with a man other than her daughter's father. Eventually she tucked Allegro up and kissed her forehead. 'Goodnight, darling, sweet dreams.' She wandered downstairs in the big, dark house and poured a gin and tonic. The phone rang.

'How was your day, darling?' Syracuse sounded cheerful. Good, everything must be going well for him. Many times, if business was bad or possibly a mistress was acting up, it was Madeleine who sat on the end of the telephone listening to Syracuse justifying himself.

'I had lunch with Edwina and her lover, Paolo.' She realised she'd have to mention Paolo as they would be meeting him at the party next week. 'And Germaine was there.'

'What's the lover like?'

'Oh, he's Italian, his name is Paolo Boletti.' She kept her voice light . . . And he told me I was beautiful and interesting, she very much wanted to add; but that would be dangerous. 'I've just been reading Allegro a story. You know she's coming up for five. She can read really well now; it's amazing.'

Syracuse couldn't wait to tell her his news. 'Your father is going to be very pleased with me. I've done a big bit of business with the Hong Kong and Shanghai Bank. I patted the nose of one of the huge lions that crouch outside the front door and everything went swimmingly. I'm off to celebrate now.'

'Oh, and who are you celebrating with?'

'Oh, just an old schoolfriend. We're going out to Cold Storage. I'm desperate for a hamburger and a milkshake. All this Chinese food is getting me down.'

Madeleine heard the slight pause in his voice as he fluently lied to her. This time she didn't mind so much; she had something to hide herself.

'Goodnight, Syracuse,' she said.

'Goodnight, sweetheart. You go out and buy anything

you like to celebrate my new business. Goodnight, you funny old thing. I miss you, Maddie.'

'I'm not a funny old thing.' Madeleine was talking to her old school hot-water bottle. Pooh Bear stared back at his mistress very seriously. 'Of course not,' he said, 'you're a rich, beautiful, interesting woman.'

As Madeleine climbed into bed she remembered Edwina's words. You don't know a man until you've had him sexually. Anyway, it was something like that. I'm going to throw out all my old underwear and buy a new dress for the Parmiters' party. I need a new me, she told herself.

Twelve

Madeleine knew that she was taking Allegro to the zoo in Central Park as an act of contrition. How convenient it would be if I were a Catholic, like Germaine. A confession followed by six Hail Marys and my soul would be pure again. Anyway, she reminded herself as she walked past the big iron bars that housed the gorillas, I've committed adultery in my heart already.

'Look, darling.' She tried to sound enthusiastic. 'See that mummy gorilla over there; she has a little baby gorilla.'

'Where?' Madeleine lifted Allegro up and put her on her shoulders. Madeleine didn't want to talk. She was back in her teenage years. She remembered the hours that she lay in her bed aflame with desire. Her legs shook uncontrollably and waves of sensual pleasure assailed her aching body. She was blessed, she felt, with the ability to have vivid Technicolor sexual dreams that ended in orgasm. Edwina, whom she consulted on the subject, said she was not so lucky. Madeleine refrained from discussing her night-time orgies with Germaine: it was not the sort of thing they could discuss.

Still, at a time like this, when she had been spiritually unfaithful to her husband, it was nice now to be able to co-opt Paolo into her dreams. She'd endowed him with a much bigger penis than Syracuse. Edwina had informed her many years ago that you could tell the size of a man's prick by the size of his nose. She hadn't been in possession of that piece of news when she'd first met Syracuse. His nose was short and, she thought, very sexy. Still, the problem of making up love scenes was that on occasion reality wasn't anything like as good as her fantasy life. Already she'd had several intense conversations with Paolo in her head. What she really ought to do is to write it all down and give Paolo the script so he couldn't disappoint her. But then maybe she'd be a disappointment to him. After all, she had no experience at all. Syracuse seemed to favour only the missionary position after the first few years of marriage; the only time she'd tried to roll on top of him he had pushed her off. 'Maddie, you've been seeing too much television. Don't you become an American ball-breaking bitch.' She felt so humiliated by his comment that she'd returned to being an obedient partner in bed ever since.

'Look, Mommy, the baby's down.' Mother and daughter watched the tiny baby gorilla swing from its mother's arms and climb the big mesh fence that separated the cage from that of a big male who was sitting on his haunches, staring fixedly at Madeleine. His eyes were all too human. They were a deep amber with brown specks around the iris. The gorilla drew back his lips and exposed a great deal of pink gum. He leered at Madeleine and then took the shaft of his penis in his hand. There was a gasp of horror from the audience.

'I said bigger, but not that big.' Madeleine giggled and led Allegro away from the gorilla cage. It was almost as if he read her mind. She swung Allegro down from her aching shoulders. Syracuse was sleeping off jet-lag but would be awake and ready to party when she got back.

In her wardrobe hung a long black dress with a sunburst of coloured beads at the neck. The dress was tight-fitting and cut low. Childbirth had improved the size of her breasts. The rings around her nipples had not darkened to an unattractive brown like Edwina's had. Edwina was threatening to have breast surgery to lift her breasts, but had decided to wait for her fortieth birthday and give herself a present of a face-lift as well.

Now Madeleine had to run after Allegro. They were approaching the bird-cages. At least the birds won't do anything too gross. Madeleine didn't want any more shocks. People turned to stare at Allegro as she ran past. Allegro hopped and skipped away from Madeleine's grasp. Her long hair blew in the fresh wind and her eyes blazed with mischief. Mothers, aunts, uncles and lovers wandered around on this hot, sunny day. Madeleine realised that she too wanted the excitement of being in love. What had happened between herself and Syracuse was that she'd grown stale. He no longer made her heart skip and jump.

The zoo smelled of her favourite smells. Ice-cream, wet sawdust and stale lion's dung. The smell took her back to her first visits to the London Zoo with her father. The two essentially private things that bound them close together for ever were their ritual visit to the Changing of the Guard at Buckingham Palace, and the zoo. They would leave her mother glued to the telephone in their fourth-floor suite at the Savoy. Her father would take her hand in the doorway of the hotel and summon the doorman to flag a passing black London taxi. Madeleine always chose to sit on one of the foldaway chairs. She remembered the day she realised that both her feet could touch the black rubber matting that carpeted the floor. London taxis smelled like rich men. Of English bank-notes and cigars and oysters sharpened with the juice of a lemon. As the taxi pulled out of the cul-de-sac, Madeleine would look back at the huge canopy that welcomed tired travellers. It reassured her that her mother was in good hands while her daughter shared a guilty feeling of excitement that she and her father had escaped from her mother's world for a few hours. Ahead of them was their secret adventure. Her father, in her childlike presence, would forget that he was a millionaire and a businessman and became the friend and companion he had always been.

Ronald, her father, was a man of few surface emotions. He coped with his nagging wife by nodding sagely and withdrawing to his place of work. He was much loved by all his staff. Everything he had and all he would ever have was laid at the feet of his daughter Madeleine. Other women tried to attract his attention, but Ronald, the big, affable boy from Ealing, never looked at another woman. Once he'd married Dolly and she'd presented him with a daughter, he had fallen in love for life. In Madeleine he'd found an ideal companion. She, as a little girl, listened to his stories and to his worries. Dolly was largely immersed in her huge circles of New York friends. She had little time in those early years for her husband, and even less for her daughter. The houses got bigger, the cars more numerous, and a vast army of servants was hired to keep the household running smoothly. Dolly was as efficient in her household as she was in bed. 'There's a good boy,' she would exclaim once Ronald had achieved his weekly orgasm. She handed out an orgasm to her husband once a week in the same way that she handed her daughter a bar of candy on a Friday night. 'A place for everything and everything in its place' was a maxim she lived by.

Sometimes Ronald wanted to shout and to swear and to scream, but he'd left all that behaviour behind him. Instead he immersed himself in his little girl. Dolly had rescued him from a life as a junior insurance salesman, and swept him into her bigger, glamorous world. Just sometimes he wished he could sit in his little Ealing childhood home, opposite the fireplace with Joanna, his mother, knitting her eternal knitting that grew into clothes just for him. Joanna had died in a car accident, which is why and when he had left England to begin a new life. No, he would never shout at Dolly. His mother had been a quiet, gentle woman, and England had lost much of its meaning for him once she died.

Madeleine desperately wished she could talk to her father nowadays. Her mother she knew was a lost cause. Her mother's only advice about sex and marriage was that sex was a boring duty to be discharged as quickly as possible. 'Men,' she would say with an air of mystery, 'want it all the time. A woman can use sex to get what she wants. Always use it to your advantage. A clever woman knows how to manipulate her man.' After this piece of sage advice, she would smile like a shark and consult her big diamond engagement ring.

Fortunately Syracuse had been an experienced lover, and Madeleine had found the whole initiation delightful. 'What about women who want it all the time?' she'd asked her mother.

'Don't be disgusting, darling. Really, the things you say. It must be that dreadful friend of yours, Edwina. She's not well bred, you know.'

'She does her best.' Madeleine had tried not to smile. Irony was completely lost on her mother. Scott, Edwina assured Madeleine, was a complete pig in bed. 'He rolls on top of me, grunts a few times, and then falls off, snoring. Thank goodness for lovers, but then he keeps me well, so I have the best of both worlds.'

As she and Allegro passed the last big bird-cage at the zoo, Madeleine caught sight of a small owl. The bird regarded her calmly and then lifted up a claw. 'Dr Stanislaus, I presume?' Madeleine felt a surge of happiness. 'Would you approve of my taking a lover?' she asked the bird. The owl stared back and then slowly its left eyelid dropped. The wink sealed Madeleine's fate.

On the way home she stopped the car in front of her favourite toy-shop. She loved toys. For so long she had had to pretend she was buying presents for a series of nieces and nephews; now she had Allegro as an excuse. Unfortunately Allegro hated dolls and doll's-houses. She wanted toy trucks and guns. By now the child had a whole arsenal of firearms which she insisted on taking with her to the various children's parties.

Madeleine wondered as they climbed the front stairs to her house how Allegro had grown to become quite so aggressive. She was into biting these days. She bit Tarquin so regularly that the boy only had to see Allegro and he would run for his mother's skirts. Allegro ran inside the house waving yet another sub-machine gun. 'It's not natural,' Nanny Barnes sniffed at Mrs Poole. 'Not natural at all.'

'Well,' Mrs Poole's long nose quivered, 'things are changing in this house, I can tell you.' She nodded, her long neck waving backwards and forwards like a mongoose about to strike at a snake. 'Madam came in the other day from shopping. I had to help her carry in bags and bags of clothes. I had to check her wardrobe to see if anything needed dry-cleaning,' and she paused for maximum effect. 'Madam has bought a pile of silk underpants and brassières. Most unsuitable for a married woman. More like a woman about to take a lover.' The look of disapproval on Mrs Poole's face would have withered granite.

'Do you really think she's going to . . . ? Ohhhh, how romantic.' Nanny Barnes seemed oblivious to Mrs Poole's disapproval.

Mrs Poole swept out of the room. Nannies are all the same everywhere: childish, like their charges, Mrs Poole sniffed.

'Nosy old bitch.' Nanny Barnes hurried away to find Allegro. 'No business poking about in Madam's wardrobe anyway.'

'You look as if you've been at the wine-decanter, darling.' Syracuse was amused. Madeleine had two bright red spots on her cheeks and she was smiling at him. Usually, the thought of yet another party at the Parmiters' house made her tense and unhappy.

'It's the carpets, they make me sea-sick, all those squiggles, and the smell of deodorant everywhere. I don't know which smells worse: the bathroom or Sunny Parmiter.' Tonight she was skipping about the bedroom, humming to herself.

Syracuse watched his wife remove her clothes in order to get into her bath. She was still beautiful, he realised with a start. Lucinda's young smooth body excited him and made him feel young himself, but there was something so very sensual about the way Madeleine's long back fitted into her swelling hips. She was twice the size of Lucinda, but her breasts were still satisfyingly round and the nipples surprisingly pink. He walked up to his wife and put his arms around her bare waist. He pulled her close to his body and then inhaled her well-remembered sweet smell. She smelled of sandalwood. 'Hmmm, darling,' he nibbled at her ear, 'you're so sexy.' He wished that there was such a thing as an anonymous knee-trembler with his wife. A quick in and out without speech or consequences. He pushed his fingers in between her thighs in order to slide his hand into her delicate crevices. He was surprised when Madeleine stood coldly silent. No welcoming intake of breath, no slight arching of the muscles on her back. He removed his hand and stared at her. 'What's the matter, honey? Are you OK?'

'Sure I'm OK, Syracuse, I just don't feel like sex at this moment.'

'Not you as well.' Syracuse immediately regretted this last sentence.

'Why, Syracuse, have you been propositioning anyone else recently?' Madeleine swung her body away from him and sauntered off to the bathroom.

'Well, actually, now that you mention it, yes.' He addressed the big brass bedpost. Madeleine might as well have taken a leaf out of Lucinda's book: she refused him regularly as well. He had a date for dinner with her the night after the party. Really all men wanted was sex without complications, and these days all men got was complications without the sex. He kicked the bedpost – it hurt.

Madeleine always wondered what it would be like to make love in the bath. It always seemed such a shame that Syracuse refused to join her. For a man that seemed to spend his life chasing women, he was remarkably prudish. Or maybe the fault was hers because she couldn't take sex as a serious pastime. Idly she wondered if she should bring herself to a climax. The water was hot and the bath-oil sensuous. If she did climax she remembered she would lose that hugely sexual tingle she always felt before she wanted to make love. Maybe if she took Paolo as her lover, she would have a more satisfactory love-life. For so long she had been subordinate to the demands of her husband, and now she was beginning to wonder if there was more to life than sex with Syracuse in their matrimonial bed, paid for by her mother.

She lay in the bath, contemplating the big gold taps. So far her life had been uneventful. She'd been born, loved her parents, went to school, came to New York and then got married. She now had her baby. She shifted her position in the water and watched a ripple of foam break over her stomach. Thirty-six years old. The same age as Edwina and twelve years younger than Germaine. She was aware of a yearning for adventure. Germaine had travelled all over the world. Edwina had taken many lovers. Madeleine had nothing to offer: she only travelled cocooned by Syracuse. Her only memories of foreign parts were her schooldays in England. There had been trips with her mother and father to Chapel Hill, where her grandmother had a huge, whitewashed mansion, and the servants, all black, wore white gloves to serve at meals. Dolly didn't like going abroad. Madeleine knew she herself had also led a very cloistered life. So far she had accepted that, but in this, her thirty-seventh year, she felt she was left with unanswered questions. The biggest one of them all was, 'Is this all there is to my life?'

The question popped into her head and stunned her. She rose dripping from the bath and walked across the thick carpet to stand in front of the marble washbasin and stare desperately into the gilt mirror. 'Is this really all there is to the rest of my life? I sit and watch my husband chase other women. I take care of Allegro. I watch the wrinkles on my face grow deeper and liver spots rise on my hands until they look like the back of the toads that live in our garden. I'm in a trap. It may be a mink-lined trap, but I feel trapped anyway.'

'Hurry up, Maddie, I want my shower.'

'Take a shower in one of the other bathrooms, Syracuse.' There were three other bathrooms for him to choose from, but Syracuse was bored if he had to spend any time on his own. He obviously wanted to talk. Sometimes Madeleine felt that part of her resentment was that, since the birth of Allegro, she had outgrown Syracuse's infantile behaviour.

78

'Let me in, Maddie, I want my shower in my own bathroom.' He shook the door impatiently.

'Go away, Syracuse. You can't come in, I'm busy.'

Madeleine took her powder-puff and liberally applied powder all over her body. The powder fell in loose drifts all over the floor. Behind her were wet footprints across the carpet. Her big, thick bath towel lay crumpled behind her on the chair by the bath. The chair was for Syracuse to sit in while she bathed, and then for her to sit in while he bathed. In the early years they had had so much to talk about it seemed such a natural way for two people to spend their time. Slowly, as the talk remained centred around Syracuse and his life, she found herself wishing she could have the bathroom to herself and now, far too late, she was trying to find some peace and silence for herself. Whatever it was that was nascent inside her, born of a chance meeting a week ago, it needed a chance to flower in peace.

That she even considered Paolo, a married man, as a lover was shocking enough. That he had made love to her best friend, which made the thought of making love to him rather incestuous, didn't really bother her. After such a virtuous life, she argued with herself, she seemed to be jumping in at the deep end. But then maybe sometimes it was wise not to dither on the edge of life, but just to hold your nose and jump. She didn't want endless amounts of men in her life like Edwina, neither did she want to live an emotionally stunted life like Germaine. She just wanted to recapture the days in her life when she first met Edwina and Syracuse and each day was a new adventure. Syracuse seemed to be fast settling into a very premature middle age, and Madeleine did not want to stay and share it.

'Fuck you.' She heard the sound of Syracuse kicking the door, and then the bedroom door slammed. Syracuse was going to use the other bathroom. She smiled a tiny smile of triumph.

Because Syracuse had been orphaned at an early age, he had appealed to Madeleine's compassionate nature. He had never known his mother: she had died in childbirth. He had been brought up by two very strict aunts in Boston. Aunt Frannie and Aunt Denny. All the ills of his life, Syracuse laid at their richly shod feet. They died just after Madeleine married Syracuse. He never talked about them except with anger. They had left him nothing in their Will. All the money had been left to the local cancer society. Why, Madeleine often wondered, did Syracuse expect these two old ladies to leave him anything when he so obviously hated them and gave them such a hard time? To Syracuse she said nothing: she had learned very early in their marriage that Syracuse was perfect, and any attempt to question his behaviour was met with a terrifying emotional tantrum, when he was liable to jump up and down like a three-year-old and hit the furniture.

Madeleine sighed. She opened the bathroom door and went to her wardrobe. She pulled out her new long black silk dress with the jewelled neck, and collected her bra and underpants from the tallboy. She slipped her legs through the underpants and enjoyed the hiss of the silk on her legs. She pulled on a pair of black silk Paris tights, and then slipped her arms into her black matching brassière. She fiddled with the clasp at the back, rather wishing Syracuse was there to help her, but then he would be sulking and Syracuse sulking was a black cloud. She didn't want anything to spoil her evening. She was aware of a small residue of resentment like the green whiskery fungus on a piece of stale bread. It rankled her.

The thought of the party, and the fact that he'd be

meeting Lucinda the next night, put Syracuse in a better mood. He let the hot water wash over him, remembering the tepid showers he had endured in his aunts' stone-faced house in Boston. They had saved money like they saved their virginity. They were so successful in both cases that no man dared ever ask, and they had gathered a great deal of money from their real estate that dotted downtown Boston. Still, the fact that they had cheated him of his inheritance angered him. Women were definitely not to be trusted, any more than he ever trusted the processions of women who were paid to take care of him and keep him out of his aunts' way. He'd made short work of all of them except for Florrita, a huge woman from Florida who had masturbated him to sleep every night. She'd suited him nicely. She'd continued to do it when he was perfectly capable of doing it for himself. He grinned at the memory. He'd enjoyed lying back on his bed while she laboured. She was so uncomplaining, so compliant. She serviced his needs in silence and without question. Maybe that was why he was so attached to Griselda and to Mei Mei. They were both willing women, unlike Lucinda. He soaped himself under his arms. Now Madeleine, his wife, seemed to be becoming a problem. She had actually locked him out of his own bathroom. He began to get angry again, but then he reasoned it was better to stay calm and charm Madeleine out of her obstreperous mood. Women were unpredictable creatures at the best of times. Charm always got them every time; especially his.

Together they made their nightly pilgrimage to say goodnight to their daughter. There was always the hope that Allegro might be lying peacefully asleep on her pillow, but so far it was a hope not born of any experience. Allegro didn't need sleep. Nanny Barnes and Mrs Poole took it in turns to stay up and play with her. Now she wanted books to be read to her too. Both women looked worn out. Allegro was waiting for them, sitting up in her bed.

'I swear she knows when you are coming to see her. She really is a strange child.' Nanny Barnes these days seemed uneasy. 'I am sure that child is a changeling,' she often said to Mrs Poole when they were lunching together. She never any more said anything in front of her charge. Allegro seemed to understand everything she said. In many cases Nanny Barnes felt she only had to think a thought and Allegro would run to execute the action. 'The other day I wondered if I ought to put more wood on the nursery fire. I was sitting in my chair and Allegro was playing with her toy soldiers behind me. The next thing I knew, she had run up beside me and picked up a piece of wood. I must say, Mrs Poole, it did give me quite a turn.'

'There's something not quite right, and that's a fact.' Mrs Poole's voice was sour. 'Mrs Winstanley seems to be in a world of her own. I suppose living with Him's done her in. She was so bright and so beautiful when I first came. Now she looks so pale and so sad. Pity, really.'

'Goodnight, darling.' Madeleine leaned over the bed and kissed Allegro's curly head. Allegro regarded her mother with a cool stare, and Madeleine shivered. She felt as if Allegro had just filleted her secret wish to see Paolo from her brain, and now the secret lay on the pillow of her bed.

Allegro reached up to her father. 'Daddy, Daddy,' she whined. 'Go for a walk.'

'Not now, darling, Daddy's got to take Mummy out to a party.'

'Wanna come too, Daddy.' Tears were welling in Allegro's eyes. Both adults winced as they braced their shoulders. Seeing that the tears were not going to bring her results, Allegro reached up and bit Syracuse on the hand.

'Ouch,' he shrieked. 'Nurse Barnes,' he yelled, holding his hand. Nurse Barnes came running into the room. 'Your bleeding child just bit me.'

'I'm so sorry, sir. I don't know what's got into her these days.' She felt in her capacious pocket for a tube of ointment. 'Here, let me put some Germolene on the wound.'

'I'm lucky she didn't amputate my finger.' He noticed a bandage on the nurse's hand. 'You too, Nanny Barnes. Allegro bit you as well?'

'It's a stage she's going through, that's all.'

By now Allegro's shrieks were ear-splitting. Syracuse pulled Madeleine by the hand. 'Come on,' he ordered, 'let's get going. She's giving me a headache. You don't suppose they have shrinks for four-year-olds, do you?'

'I don't know,' was Madeleine's uneasy reply.

The sounds of the party flitted over the lawn. Big wide french windows were open, and people were bending over a big open barbecue.

'Hi, Syracuse.' Jack leaned into the window, grabbed him, and enveloped him in a big bear-hug. Syracuse shook himself free. Madeleine knew he was cross: Syracuse hated to be touched by anyone except the fair sex.

Sunny, Jack's wife, came running up to the car. 'Darling,' she simpered, 'tonight you look exceptionally beautiful.'

'Thank you, Sunny.' Madeleine was pleased because she knew it was true. She did indeed look wonderful, and for once she felt wonderful; maybe a life of perversity and guilt would make a new woman of her. She climbed out of the car and left Syracuse to take it off to park.

'I've been waiting for you, darling.' Edwina swung her long fair hair forward in a conspiratorial manner. 'You know who's here, don't you? And he's clutching a bouquet of your favourite flowers. They must be for you; he didn't offer them to either Sunny or to me.' She pouted. Edwina conceded defeat gracefully. 'You must tell me what he's like in bed.'

'Oh Edwina, I've no intention of sleeping with him. I'm a married woman, remember?'

Edwina laughed. 'You sound like a nun saying her Hail Marys. He's a married man,' she mocked.

She saw Syracuse entering the house ahead of her. He usually took off at a party, and didn't bother with her until he was ready to go home. 'No point hanging off each other at parties when we see each other every day. You go and meet the kind of people you like, and I'll find mine.' After a while that made sense. Syracuse seemed to attract a whole raft of people with personal, sexual and financial problems. 'She had her Alsatian dog,' he reported after the last party.

'Please don't tell me the details, I don't want to know,' was Madeleine's reply. No doubt he was off in search of his Alsatian woman for another week's worth of details.

'Come on.' Edwina pulled Madeleine's now reluctant body into the crowd.

I shouldn't really be doing this, was Madeleine's only feeling at this point.

Up in a tree, a small barn owl hooted softly, putting its head to one side to listen for the answering chorus. The guardians were about their business tonight, and everything was still going according to plan.

Madeleine fervently wished she had a pair of dark glasses. She was always amused by Edwina, who scarcely ever took hers off. Obviously if she were to decide to take to a life of perverse pleasure, her next acquisition after her last shopping spree must be a pair of dark spectacles.

Now she tried to gaze at the floor. Edwina's impatient elbow crooked under her own. She felt like a fish hooked by Edwina's impatience. 'Come, get out of the way will y'all?'

'Edwina, we're not in a rush. I've only just arrived.'

'Well I'm in a rush, I wanna see Paolo's face when he sees you.' She paused dramatically. 'Besides, darling, he's fabulous in the sack.'

'I didn't want to hear that, Edwina.' Madeleine tried to purse her lips. Pursed lips in novels always signified disapproval. Mrs Poole was a master of lip-pursing. She felt the muscles around her mouth bunch.

'What are you doing, Maddie? You already look as if you're going to kiss the guy.'

'I do wish you'd shut up, Edwina.'

Edwina gave a raucous shriek of laughter. 'There he is,' Edwina's voice rose. 'Paolo, darling, here we are.' A further jet-like thrust of Edwina's elbow into Madeleine's side, and she fetched up in front of a beautifully made pair of soft brown Italian shoes. She stood with her head down, staring at the neat shoelaces with their matching tassels.

'Aren't you going to look at me, Madeleine?'

She felt long slim fingers slide under her chin. He raised her head with his fingertips. She finally was forced to gaze into his eyes. Paolo was smiling. Gently he turned her face to the right and kissed her cheek; then, brushing his lips lightly across hers, he turned her head again and kissed the other cheek.

'I am so pleased to see you again, Madeleine,' he said. His voice was deep and resonant. He lifted his other hand. 'Here,' he said, 'I hope I have been reliably informed that these are your favourite flowers.' He handed her a bunch of yellow jonquils. They were wrapped in Cellophane, tied with a pale pink ribbon and surrounded with a cloud of white baby's breath.

'Oh thank you.' Try as she might, Madeleine could not avoid blushing. Damn, she thought, there I go, looking like a complete idiot again.

'You really shouldn't have,' she murmured, casting an anxious eye around the room in case Syracuse was around. You really shouldn't, she heard her brain mimic her heart. How original, shrieked her brain. Well, I haven't had much practice at this sort of thing. How often did Syracuse bring me any flowers? her heart replied, stung.

'A beautiful woman like yourself should be given flowers every day of the week, Madeleine, and twice on Sundays. Now I am really very, very hungry. Would you like to accompany me to the garden to forage for food?' Madeleine looked for Edwina but she had gone. 'Come along, Madeleine, I've been in Boston all day and I just caught the train in time to get here.'

'Boston? Oh yes, that's where my husband comes from. He grew up with his two old aunts in Beacon Street. You know those lovely old streets: all cobbles and gas-lamps.' She realised that she must seem like a frightened animal caught in the headlamps of a runaway car. Her heart pounded and her palms were sweating. Paolo seemed to sense her confusion. He put a reassuring hand in the small of her back and steered her out of the sitting room into the garden.

It was a very dark night. Intermittently stars twinkled. The air was soft and balmy. Madeleine could smell jasmine in the wind that curled around her body and lifted her silk dress in gentle, billowing folds.

'You look so beautiful tonight, Madeleine.' There was a wistful tone in Paolo's voice. Madeleine wondered if he was remembering the early days in his marriage when he was first in love with his wife. She remembered now how she had felt when she'd first fallen in love with Syracuse and everything had felt so new and so sharp and clean. Maybe they were still in love, she didn't know; but she did know he'd had an affair with Edwina, so things couldn't be that happy.

'What would you like to eat, Madeleine? I can smell steak and, of course, the great American hamburger.'

'Do you like the food here in America, Paolo?' This seemed a safe enough subject.

Paolo nodded, 'I do, but I prefer the food from my country. On my *podére*, that means farm, I make my own salami and mortadella. We grow our own vegetables, and so I am spoiled. I find it difficult to eat the vegetables here because there is no taste, but then maybe I'm just prejudiced.' He laughed. There was a boyish sound to his laughter. Madeleine realised that Syracuse seldom laughed involuntarily. He laughed *at* someone, usually herself. Maybe it was because he was used to the sound of canned laughter from his television set or the radio. She found herself enjoying Paolo's very real hunger. 'I feel like a really big juicy American T-bone steak. Then a hamburger followed by a baked potato, with lots and lots of mayonnaise.'

'My goodness, Paolo, aren't you on a diet?'

'Never,' he said. 'I don't do diets and I won't work out either.'

'Good heavens, you must be the only person in America apart from myself who doesn't do either. I'm in awful trouble with my husband. He always says I'm too fat.'

'Does he really, Madeleine? How very cruel. You're

not fat at all. You are marvellously beautiful.' Although Paolo's accent was very English, there was still the soft Italian flattening of the consonants. He made the words sound like water running across pebbles.

'I must learn Italian,' Madeleine offered as they walked towards the barbecue pit.

'Yes, you must,' Paolo's mouth was close to her ear, 'and I will be the one to teach you.'

Thirteen

❧

'Well, and how was your party, Maddie? I caught a glimpse of you talking to a dark-haired man. Who was he?'

'Oh, just a friend of Edwina's. He's Italian and Edwina asked me to keep an eye on him.' Madeleine realised that this was the first time she'd ever lied to her husband. She didn't really want to talk to Syracuse. She wanted to staunch the gaping wound she felt in her body long enough to get home and climb into a steaming hot bath. Then she could try and discover how it was possible to meet someone for the second time in her life and hand over such an important thing as a heart.

'You know, Maddie, I've seen and done some things in my life, but Rhoda, she's something else. She really takes the biscuit, or should I say the dog biscuit?' Syracuse was quite drunk, Madeleine realised. This was going to be the next endless conversation: Rhoda and her damn boring dog. Madeleine blanked out Syracuse's voice and just said 'Yes, dear' and, 'No, dear.' She'd learned to do that many years ago. It kept the peace between them, but the acquiescence required gave Madeleine heartburn.

The car turned into the drive and Madeleine nursed the sense of loss she'd felt when she'd watched Paolo leave the party. She had so much wanted to run after his tall, loping figure and put her hand in his and leave to be with him for the rest of their lives. 'I must go,' he'd said after they had sat in aching silence over their many coffees. He put his long fingers under her chin.

89

He kissed her once again, lightly brushing her lips. She felt a great blast of heat from his body. So this is what desire feels like; she had never felt that heat from Syracuse. 'I shall miss you.' He smiled down at her. 'I will ask Edwina to arrange for us to have lunch together next week. Would Wednesday be a good day for you?'

'Any day would do for me.' Madeleine was aware that she sounded like an eager child, but she didn't care. She very much wanted to see Paolo again, and she was so glad he had set a day and time so now she could at least exist and dream about the next time.

Syracuse cut the engine. He didn't look up. Pooley didn't keep vigil on the few occasions that he went out with his wife. 'You're unusually quiet, Maddie. Cat got your tongue?'

'No, I'm just tired, Syracuse. I've got a headache. I'll take an aspirin and have a hot bath.' She realised that she hoped that by the time she slid into the bed, Syracuse would be asleep. When he'd had too much to drink it took him ages to come, and Madeleine didn't feel like dealing with another sulk at this time of the morning.

'OK, I'll close up the house and see you later.' Syracuse rushed inside. Madeleine smiled a tired, strained smile. Syracuse lived believing they were always on the edge of disaster. He was sure that without his constant surveillance the house would catch fire or fall down. In his omnipotence he walked around the rooms every night, removing all plugs from their sockets. He checked every window and then, for good measure, he looked up the chimney. Of course, it was further proof of what a good father and husband he was. Once Madeleine tried to vary the nightly routine. She seduced him, but even then, after he thought she was asleep, he tiptoed out of bed. She shrugged as she climbed the stairs. She had not married a man, she'd married a frightened child.

What woman hadn't, though? That's what happened when you slip a gold wedding ring on a man's finger. He got you nailed to the kitchen and the bed, and you got him tied to your apron strings with a dummy in his mouth.

As she wandered up the staircase to the bedroom, Madeleine realised with a pang that she no longer loved her husband.

How can I fall out of love so quickly with a man I thought I adored for twelve years? This is the man I promised to love and to live with for the rest of my life. The man I think I love is almost a complete stranger. She didn't know the answer.

Lying in the bath looking at her recently painted toes, Madeleine tried to sort out the muddle in her head. The first symptom of her new-found love was the fear and pleasurable apprehension she'd felt when she'd known she was going to see Paolo at the Parmiters' party. Once she had felt like that about Syracuse. The second symptom was the way her heart lurched when she'd first seen Paolo standing in the sitting room full of people and he had handed her the bunch of flowers. She had left the flowers at the Parmiters', as she didn't want to try and explain them to Syracuse. Then there were the three hours of intense pleasure she had felt in his company. They had spent their second meal together surrounded by all the other guests, but they were secure in their own little bubble of happiness. She wondered if he felt the same way as she did, or if she were childishly making all this up. He was so used to seducing women like Edwina that this was just an enjoyable preliminary move for him. Well, we'll see.

She washed away the smell of nicotine from her body. How lovely to slip into bed clean and fragrant. Then she realised with a start that she had subconsciously made the decision to sleep with Paolo from the moment she first met him. Whew, I'm going to be an adulterous woman. A woman taken in adultery. Oh dear. She put down the soap. Why does he have to be married? She got out of the bath feeling fragile and insecure. She knew that when Paolo left her side after kissing her, he had walked off with her heart, and she very much wanted it back again.

She felt so empty. She missed his brown, laughing eyes, his head of black, unruly hair and his even white teeth. She even missed the glossy silk sheen of his tie. She slipped into her nightdress and walked quickly towards the bathroom door. She put the light out and then opened the door very carefully. She breathed a sigh of relief. Syracuse seemed to be asleep. She climbed into the bed and lay still. She lay rigid, but then she felt Syracuse's hand slide between her legs. He lifted himself on to his elbow. She could see his head outlined in the darkness.

'Let's make love, darling,' he said in a tense, hoarse voice. 'I haven't felt I've wanted you so badly for a very long time. Don't say no, Maddie, please don't say no.' He leaned over her and kissed her passionately. She felt his tongue flailing wildly in her mouth, and his hand prising her legs apart. He sprung his body on top of hers and then, with a practised ease, he hooked his feet under hers and swung her legs open with a scissor-like motion. For a moment he paused. She felt the tip of his penis at her entrance. Oh shit, she thought, I'm going to sleep all messy. Because she was unaroused, she knew he would hurt her, but out of guilt she also knew she must respond. She gasped with pain as he entered her, and then obediently, as she had done so many times before, she moved rhythmically in time with his mounting urge to climax. She heard his breathing accelerate and the muscles in his back tighten. She waited for the sound of his panting to mount until the moment he was ready to ejaculate. How many women, she wondered – and not for the first time – must be lying under some man waiting for him to orgasm. Probably millions, she thought as she moved her hands lower down his back. She started to count: one, two, three, four, five. Get *on* with it, she wanted to scream, but she knew the wine was holding him back. Finally Syracuse flopped on top of her.

'Was it good for you, Maddie?' he whispered.

'Yes, thank you, darling,' she whispered back.

He lay, a dead weight across her body. She pushed him gently away from her and he fell back on to his own side of the bed. The sudden cold as she moved the sheets and the duvet made itself felt in the wet patch on her nightgown.

'Oh, Syracuse, what's going to become of us?' she wondered out loud. There was no answer: Syracuse was fast asleep. Tears coursed down Madeleine's face.

In all the novels Madeleine read, the heroines fell in and out of love. There were great descriptions of beautiful-looking men and women. Sometimes she was sexually stirred by descriptions of the love-making, but she could not remember any of her favourite modern heroines describing or feeling moments of terrifying guilt.

Ever since she'd first seen Paolo, every waking thought of him brought with it these black trailing plumes of anxious regret. Guilt, she realised, was a highly complex emotion. Edwina seemed to feel it only in very occasional circumstances. 'Usually when Scott finds out I've been with another man, and then he gets all teary. It's not the man that bothers me, but I hate to see Scott upset.' That description bore very little relationship to what Madeleine was feeling now. So far nothing had transpired between Paolo and herself, except in her highly active imagination. Even so, she shielded her usually translucent gaze from Syracuse as if by looking into her eyes he could see that she had betrayed him. Their relationship had hit the hard shoals and the hidden reefs that seemed to bedevil most other couples after ten or so years of marriage. Many, she knew, would survive the rents and lacerations caused by the coral that tore apart the planks that had once held the couple together. Maybe, she tried to reason with herself, this infatuation of mine will fade away, and Syracuse and I will come closer together as a result. She knew that was not to be true. Somewhere along the way, she had left Syracuse alone on a small atoll, and she had sailed away with not so much as a backward glance. Perhaps it was having her baby in hospital. Those moments when Germaine and Edwina were with her, but when she'd fiercely felt she should have had the man she loved and who had created this new life there to hold her hand. And, after the last agonised, gasping push, she had known and could no longer lie to herself. Syracuse, her husband, would never be there for her.

Madeleine sat holding a gin and tonic in one hand and an unread novel in the other. She could hear Allegro riding her small tricycle around the big square main hall. She tried not to wince as Allegro rammed her bike into yet another wall. The hall was pockmarked with Allegro's attempts at demolishing the house. Where does she get it from? Madeleine was baffled. She put down her book and carried her drink into the hall.

'Darling,' she said brightly, 'what would you like to do now that we are alone?'

'Play wolves.' Allegro's eyes widened. She threw her bike on the ground and crawled on all fours across the floor. 'Grrrrr,' she growled, crawling steadily towards her mother. Madeleine stared down at her little daughter. For a moment she was mesmerised by the authenticity of the sound of her growling. She took a nervous sip of her gin and tonic.

'Allegro,' she said sharply, and then she paused, unsure of what she'd just seen. For a split second Madeleine had thought she'd seen the image of a young wolf's head superimposed upon Allegro's face. It must be the gin, she thought weakly. She blinked away the apparition and then she saw Allegro on her feet, smiling at her mother.

'Come along, Allegro.' Madeleine was feeling very silly. 'Let's go to the kitchen and we can make supper together.'

She passed a hand weakly across her face and glanced down at Allegro, who was holding her other hand with such complete trust and confidence. 'Tell me about the wolf,' Allegro demanded.

'What do you want me to tell you about the wolf, darling?'

'Tell me about the wolf in the park,' she repeated. Her little face had a determined look.

'Well, just behind the children's zoo is a big wolf. He has enormous eyes and a terrible big mouth.'

'Say he wants to eat Allegro all up.'

Why, her mother wondered, does the child need to live in a constant state of terror? Not only did she thrive on dreadful tales of disaster, but she frightened poor little Tarquin to death. 'You've given birth to a monster, Maddie.' That was Edwina's last telephone call. 'Tarquin is in my bed howling with fear. Your daughter has been scaring him with stories about a dinosaur with big teeth.'

'I'm so sorry, Edwina; she does seem to revel in all

this. Syracuse and I have been thinking of taking her to a shrink. Do you know anyone who might take on a child like Allegro?'

Of course, she couldn't take Allegro to Dr Lovejoy, the paediatrician, any more. Madeleine had telephoned Dr Lovejoy to ask if it was normal for a toddler to enjoy eating raw minced meat. Allegro had first tasted steak tartare off her father's plate in a restaurant. She'd always been a difficult child to feed, and they'd been so delighted that she'd enjoyed the dish that they had let her finish it, only to find that it was all she was prepared to eat, other than mounds of chocolates and ice-cream.

Dr Lovejoy had laced his fingers together and wondered how Madeleine would feel beneath her clothes. Such a pity that a pretty woman like Mrs Winstanley had to be married to that bastard Syracuse. Both men belonged to the same racquet club, and Syracuse was known to cheat at tennis.

Dr Lovejoy particularly liked the way Mrs Winstanley's shapely breasts strained against her cashmere sweater. 'Well.' He'd glanced at Allegro who'd gazed back at him with hooded eyes. 'I don't think that we can judge Allegro by normal standards.' Nothing about her had been normal since her birth. He should have strangled the little monster the first time he'd set eyes on her: now it was too late. He gazed at a crescent-shaped scar on his finger. Perhaps it was as well she'd taken to eating red meat instead of sinking her teeth into innocent passers-by. In fact it might be a great improvement. 'The child is certainly very advanced for her age.' He had beamed at Madeleine. 'Let's hope time will bring an improvement in her behaviour.' Allegro had slipped off her chair and crawled under the desk. Dr Lovejoy had instinctively crossed his legs.

'I don't think we should worry about Allegro, Mrs

Winstanley. She's a healthy little thing with an excellent pair of lungs on her.' Usually Allegro screamed from the moment she entered the consulting room until the moment she left. He was glad he was free of her pale-green staring eyes. He'd got up from his desk and stood behind Madeleine's chair, putting his long white fingers on her shoulders. The cashmere sweater had felt soft and springy under his fingertips. 'Now, bend your head forward, Mrs Winstanley, and let me relieve the tension in your neck. Remember my maxim – a tense mother is a guilty mother – and you've got nothing to feel guilty about.'

Madeleine had exhaled. 'Oh, thank you, Dr Lovejoy. I've been feeling so awful lately.'

Dr Lovejoy had expertly massaged away the knots of muscles in Madeleine's neck. He'd wished very much that he could relieve his own building tensions. Madeleine was not one of his many mothers who could be persuaded to enjoy a little consulting-room sex. Now, her friend Edwina was quite a different kettle of fish. He was soon lost in reverie, thinking of Edwina's shapely bottom gyrating under him on the examining table behind the screens at the far end of the room. Tarquin, her son, was such a placid little boy; he always amused himself so well playing with the cars that Dr Lovejoy kept in the bottom drawer of his desk.

'Ah,' he'd said, 'what have we here? Does that hurt?'

Madeleine had winced. Dr Lovejoy had closed his eyes and thrown back his head. A frown had creased his brow. 'What's that smell?' He'd sniffed sharply. 'I smell something burning.' He had removed his hands from Madeleine's neck and stridden over to his desk. The smell of burning suffused the room. 'You've set fire to my carpet, you little bitch.' He'd grabbed Allegro by the arm and hauled her out from under the desk. Allegro had hung grimly on to his cigarette lighter. She let out piercing screams. 'Let me go, you bad man. Mommy, Mommy.'

'Fire,' Dr Lovejoy had yelled, 'help!' The nurse and the receptionist had come running into the room. 'Fire!' Dr Lovejoy had screamed again. The nurse had headed for the big fire-extinguisher hanging off the wall. She'd released the trigger, and foam had covered the doctor, the desk and the floor. 'Under the desk, you fool!' Little flames were waving their way across the floor. Allegro clung to her mother. Madeleine had surveyed the wreckage and decided that a hasty retreat was the only answer.

When Syracuse had got the bill for the damage he'd been outraged. 'That cheating bastard can rebuild the whole consulting suite with this amount of money.'

'The damage was really quite extensive.' Madeleine had tried to placate Syracuse. 'Anyway, he said it was OK for Allegro to eat as much raw steak as she wanted.'

'She should have drunk his blood instead of setting fire to his consulting rooms – it would have been cheaper.'

Now, standing in the kitchen, Madeleine found herself smiling at that remark. They had not seen Dr Lovejoy since then. What Allegro needs, she lectured herself as she ground the steak, was a little play-group of children of her own age. Nice, normal little children; but then she had to admit, when she sat opposite her daughter who was slurping up the blood-soaked mince, that maybe Allegro was not a nice, normal little girl.

Later that evening, she lay in bed alone. Syracuse was in Boston, trying to winkle money out of his aunts' estate. He telephoned at ten. 'Sleep well, darling. I'll be home around two o'clock.'

'Why don't you stay the night in Boston, Syracuse?'

'I want to be with you, Maddie; besides I like the train journey in the early hours of the morning.'

Madeleine had rather hoped for a night on her own. 'You are peculiar, Syracuse. I can't imagine why you should want to spend the night on a train.'

She heard the click of the telephone and she made a face. His telephone call made the guilt come flooding back.

Lying on his back on Lucinda's bed, Syracuse waited for her to come out of the shower.

'Saying goodnight to wifie?' Lucinda was grinning as she walked across the carpet naked.

'Come here, Lucinda, and mind your own business. Anyway, how did you know who I was calling?'

'They all call their wives, darling.'

Syracuse pulled Lucinda down on to the bed. 'How do you know so much about men, Lucinda? You're far too young.'

Lucinda rolled her eyes. 'A girl's got to take care of herself these liberated days. Men certainly don't any more.'

'And whose fault is that?' Syracuse urgently wanted to make love to Lucinda, but he knew that she insisted on these discussions.

'All men are bastards,' she whispered into his ear.

'I know,' Syracuse agreed as he slid into her slim, supple body. 'That's what's so marvellous about living now.'

Fourteen

'You know, Edwina, I feel as if the whole world has changed. I walk around with this silly smile on my face, and inside I feel I'm fizzing like a bottle of soda pop.'

'Why's that, Maddie? Have you decided to join the rest of us sinners? Or are you suffering from PMS?'

'I don't suffer from PMS, Edwina, and you know that. Don't be unkind. No, the problem is that I ought to feel guilty about being unfaithful to Syracuse but I don't, so I feel guilty about not feeling guilty. The problem with going to a Catholic boarding school is that all good Catholic schoolgirls have Reverend Mother sitting permanently on their left shoulder. She's been whispering chastisements down my ear all day and I haven't even done anything yet. But then of course she'd say I'd already committed adultery in my heart, and that's just as bad. You can't win with Reverend Mother, you know.'

'Thank God I went to a good normal school with lots of boys and no Reverend Mother. Just think what I'd have missed if I'd been bundled off to a convent. Why feel guilty for wanting to screw Paolo? You know Syracuse has never been faithful.'

'I know, but I always have. I guess I'm scared of complications. I mean, I'm married and so's he. I don't know what Syracuse would do if he ever found out.'

'Oh, he'd want to kill you or Paolo or both of you. It's different when a man screws about, but if their woman does then it's the end of the world. Scott always has a fit.'

'But then you always confess, Edwina. I never really understand that about you.'

'Madeleine, you don't understand anything about anything, darling. I think an affair with Paolo would do you the world of good. Come on, you've been a sleeping beauty for far too long.'

'But what about my stomach?'

'What about your stomach?'

'You know, Edwina, it looks awful. It hasn't recovered from Allegro's birth. What about his wife?'

'Listen, Maddie, you're in the best position. You can both screw like rabbits and it can't get too hot and heavy because you're both married to someone else. Now, take my advice, go and buy yourself something outrageous, get your hair done, and just wait for him to suggest the place and the time. I've never been to his new apartment, but it's somewhere in the Italian quarter. Whatever he does he will do with style. He's really elegant.'

'I know that, Edwina, and I'm not. Every time I think about him I come out in a cold sweat. I've really only made love to Syracuse. I don't know how to take my clothes off in front of a strange man.'

'Get drunk, darling, that's my advice. Just get blind drunk and let him do all the seducing. Men love that. They like to feel they're in charge.'

'But what happens if I bore him rigid? I don't have much experience to offer him.'

'Pretend you're a virgin again and you're doing it for the first time. That's what I always do; it drives them wild. Makes them feel very potent and very masculine. Anyway, Maddie, are you all set for lunch on Wednesday?'

'I guess so. I'll have to buy myself a pair of dark glasses. If I'm going to be taken in adultery, I might as well look sinful. Oh, Edwina, I'm not sure about all this.

Can you make sure that Germaine's there? She gives me so much confidence.'

'Well, OK, but at some point you're going to have to deal with him yourself. You can't cart us about all the time.'

'I know, but I'm too frightened at the moment to think about anything like that, Edwina. I'm so shy. I'll see you at the restaurant. I'll be there about a quarter to one. Don't be late, promise?'

'OK, you idiot. I'll be there with a large gin and tonic for you.'

'Thanks, Edwina, you're a good friend.' Madeleine put down the telephone, picked up her purse and fled the house.

She was choosing her glasses when she realised that she was really very happy. She tried on an enormous pair of wrap-around glasses with reflecting lenses. She gazed at herself in the mirror. Would she ever be able to make love again with Syracuse if she was guilty of sleeping with Paolo? Her reflection stared back. She tried to smile a suitably seductive smile, but she just looked silly. She bought the glasses. 'I'll keep them on,' she informed the girl behind the cash desk. She realised as she groped her way out of the shop that they really were incredibly dark.

Half-way down the street she found a kiosk. It was piled high with New York papers and hung about with T-shirts advertising New York. She smiled: she too was wild about New York. She hunted for a little shirt for Allegro, turning over a pile of T-shirts until she found one. Pink to match Allegro's hair. In a corner she saw a guide-book to Italy and her heart lurched. 'I'll take that T-shirt,' she said, 'and this book.'

The book had a picture of a gondola on the cover. The man poling the gondola had Paolo's black hair and brown eyes. She drew a deep breath and flipped open the book. She ran her finger down the index, then she saw the word 'Siena'. There was a drawing on page one hundred and three. A shell-shaped piazza lined with restaurants. There were rows of little tables and chairs with small, stick-like figures sitting in them. She imagined a blue, blue sky and pigeons wheeling over the tall spire with the clock. The clock was stuck for eternity at a quarter past three. She could feel the sun on her skin and she could smell the strong smell of real Italian coffee.

'Your change, ma'am.' The man's voice made her jump. He watched the woman carefully as she hurried away into the crowd. Big tits, he thought. Beats my wife any day.

'Who ya staring at?' The sound of his wife's nasal whine made him wince.

'Nothin',' he said, gazing at her pinafored figure. Where had she gone, that young girl he once loved to distraction? He shrugged. Well, it happens, he comforted himself, and lit another cigarette.

Allegro looked sweet in her new pink T-shirt. 'Wow, honey.' Syracuse picked her up as he came into the sitting room carrying his briefcase. 'You look great.' He kissed Madeleine absent-mindedly. 'What's for dinner, Maddie, I'm starving.'

'I don't know, Syracuse, you'll have to ask Pooley. Cook's gone to the cinema again.' Madeleine laughed. 'Cook's got Dean Martin on the brain at the moment.'

'Why don't you take the responsibility of organising a daily menu, Maddie? After all, you do nothing all day. I work my fingers to the bone and I'm famished. I got into the office at seven o'clock this morning and you don't even know what's for dinner.'

'I'm sorry, darling. I'll go and ask Pooley right away.'

Madeleine hurried down the hall. He's right, she thought. I really ought to make a weekly menu. She poked her head around the kitchen door. 'What's for dinner, Mrs Poole?'

'Cook left prawn cocktails for a starter, then veal cutlets and a lemon sorbet for dessert.'

'Oh dear, Syracuse doesn't like veal cutlets. Perhaps we ought to try and find something else, Mrs Poole?'

She felt Mrs Poole's back stiffen. 'Mrs Winstanley, there is nothing else. Cook doesn't go to the market until tomorrow.'

'Oh, I see, I'm so sorry, Mrs Poole. Well, I'll just have to go and explain the situation to Syracuse.'

She hurried back to the drawing room. 'I'm very sorry, Syracuse, I'm afraid it's veal cutlets.' She watched his face fall and felt the familiar wretched feeling of failure. Now not only was Syracuse upset, but Mrs Poole was too.

'Come along, Allegro, let's go and find Nanny Barnes.'

Allegro threw herself on the floor and clung to her father's ankles. 'No, no, no,' she screamed. 'Get away from me, you horrid woman.' She was sobbing heavily, great tears rolling down her face. 'Daddy, Daddy, don't let Mommy hit me.'

Madeleine felt outraged. 'I don't hit you, Allegro. I never hit you.'

Syracuse bent down and picked Allegro up. 'There, there, darling, nobody's going to let my baby be unhappy. Daddy loves you. You can have dinner with us.'

Madeleine caught a glimpse of Allegro's triumphant face beaming at her over Syracuse's shoulder. Suddenly she very much wanted to slap her daughter.

Later that night, Madeleine lay in bed waiting for

Syracuse to reach his orgasm. They'd had several bottles of red wine between them, and once again he was taking ages. She felt her eyes fill with tears. This shouldn't be what making love was about. Finally she felt him jolting to an end, and felt grateful when he collapsed on top of her. Maybe sex was like chocolate – too much of it and it just got boring. Their early passionate love-making seemed very far away. Now, she realised she used sex to placate Syracuse.

'Was that all right for you, darling? You're not sore, are you?' he asked anxiously.

'Wonderful,' she said, hoping he'd go to sleep in the next few minutes. She could pleasure herself so much better than Syracuse ever did.

The day of the luncheon party was hot and muggy. 'What are you doing today, darling?' Syracuse asked before he left for the office.

'Oh, nothing much.' Madeleine felt her face flush. 'I'm having lunch with Germaine and Edwina.'

'I see, a cats' convention. You women certainly don't have much to do other than lunch.'

'Yeah, I guess.' So this is what lying about your lover feels like. Madeleine felt immediately uncomfortable. Lying had always been considered such a terrible sin. One small lie and your soul rotted in hell, so now not only had she committed adultery in her heart, she had lied and was in a state of mortal sin. Even all these years later she always ate fish on a Friday. All those years in a convent school had left their mark. The idea, even though she wasn't a Catholic, of facing eternity in hell if a piece of meat passed her lips on a Friday still terrified her. Why do I spend so much of my life shit-scared, she wondered, as Syracuse left the house. She heard the wheels of his Alfa Romeo squeal.

She raced up to the nursery to spend some guilt-reducing time with Allegro, her little daughter, who was soon to have a mother condemned to death by all the hierarchy of the Roman Church. She wondered if Paolo was a Catholic and, if he were, what he did about his conscience. He obviously must have done something, because he's already had Edwina. She resolved at some time to get up the courage to ask him. After all the lurid imaginings, just meeting his eye at lunch-time would be difficult enough.

Later, as Madeleine sat with her back to the door of the restaurant, she watched Edwina's face. Edwina sat opposite her, wearing a lime-green dress. She looked stunning. Why on earth Paolo was interested in her she had no idea. Edwina had all the experience a man could want. She also had firm, taut breasts and fantastic stomach muscles. Maybe Paolo was just teasing her.

Germaine sat at the end of the table and looked concerned. 'Madeleine, don't get involved with this man just to please Edwina.' She leaned towards Madeleine. 'Promise me, Madeleine, you won't make any quick decision about this man. We don't really know him.'

'Oh, shut up, Germaine. He'll do Madeleine the world of good. She's tired of being taken for granted by that selfish bastard of a husband of hers.'

Madeleine saw Edwina's eyes light up. 'Here he comes,' Edwina breathed. 'He looks so adorable.' Madeleine wished the floor would open and swallow her up.

'I'm so sorry I'm late, Madeleine.' He didn't seem to see the other two women. He was carrying another bunch of jonquils. 'Here you are; I had such a time finding these for you.' He smiled down at her and she gazed into his bottomless brown eyes. There was a hint of sunshine in them. They were warm, hinting maybe at a bit of Tuscan sun. He was wearing a plover-coloured jersey with the two wings of his shirt collar tucked inside the neck. She felt breathless; she just wanted to sit quietly and look at him. He was beautiful, she realised. Syracuse was handsome, but his face was spoiled by an almost permanent look of dissatisfaction. Paolo's face had no shadows. He leaned forward and kissed her. Then he kissed Edwina, and even Germaine blushed and received his salutation with a smile.

'Have you ordered drinks yet?' His eye fell on Madeleine's glass. 'What were you drinking? Don't tell me.' He picked up the glass and sniffed it. 'Gin and tonic, how very English; but then you are English, aren't you, Madeleine?'

Madeleine nodded. 'Yes, and my father's mother was French, hence the name Madeleine.'

'It's such a pretty name, Madeleine,' he said, and then he hummed it. 'Madeleine, Madeleine.'

Edwina grinned. 'That's right, Paolo, burst into song and embarrass us.'

'Nothing embarrasses me, Edwina, and you ought to know that.'

There was a very pregnant pause as Edwina registered his remark and then looked embarrassed. 'I do, Paolo, I do.'

Madeleine, faced with the obvious knowledge that they shared a past together, very much wished to call the whole thing off. It just didn't feel right that she should be indulging in an affair with a man who had slept with her best friend. Was he going to try Germaine next? If not, why not? Here was a man who was unfaithful to his wife. He probably had no morals at all, and she was risking her marriage, her husband and her child. No, this way had to lead to madness. She quietly took a knife and cut his vine out of her heart. She would not be seduced by Paolo, that was her new decision. Germaine had been right.

Gazing at Madeleine, Paolo registered her internal resolution. 'Don't mind my teasing Edwina, Madeleine. We've known each other for a long time.'

'I know you have, Paolo,' Madeleine inclined her head. 'You've been lovers.'

There was a sharp intake of breath. The barman's arrival broke the silence. 'What would the ladies like to drink?' he asked. 'A gin and tonic for Mrs Winstanley,' Paolo instructed. 'For you, Edwina, a vodka on the rocks.' Germaine ordered a beer. 'I'll wait until we eat,' Paolo added.

Well, at least it's out and he knows it's over for us, Madeleine thought as she listened to him. She felt a sharp pain in her heart. She wondered why she wanted to cry.

'Well, I'd like lobster.' If she was going to get rid of Paolo, he could at least buy her a decent lunch. She looked at Edwina, who gazed back at her with an uncomprehending smile. Something was wrong with her friend and she didn't know what.

Paolo leaned over Madeleine. 'Darling,' he said softly, 'don't be a child. After all, we are all grown-ups here.'

'You may be,' Madeleine was angry, 'but I'm not.' She pushed back her chair and fled the restaurant. Oh shit, she thought as she ran down the pavement, pushing away the oncoming people. I've really gone and done it. He'll think I'm mad.

As she ran she tripped; the pain forced her to hobble to a stop. She felt a pair of arms swing her into the air. 'Madeleine, don't run away from me. I love you.' Paolo kissed her very gently on the mouth. 'Please, Madeleine, don't ever run away from me again.'

She lay looking up into his face and then she knew

this was inevitable. 'I won't, Paolo,' she promised, 'never again.'

'Come, *cara*, I'll carry you back to the restaurant, and you shall have your lobster.'

As she lay contentedly in his arms, she watched the faces of the passers-by. They stared at the tall figure of a man carrying a woman up the street. She knew they looked odd and out-of-place, but she didn't care. 'Ah! *leve-toi soleil*,' Paolo sang in a light baritone.

'Gounod,' she said, helpfully.

'I know.'

Madeleine snuggled deeper into his arms. Syracuse couldn't sing. 'Do you like to dance?' she asked shyly.

'All the time, darling, all the time,' and he waltzed his way back into the restaurant.

Madeleine didn't hear from Paolo for a few weeks after they had lunched with Edwina and Germaine. 'I don't know if he's gone off me, Edwina,' she said on the telephone.

'Oh, don't be so silly, Maddie, he's probably got to go to Italy on business. Men are like that. You'll hear from him in due course. Anyway, he can't ring you at home, he'll have to contact you through me.'

A week later, Edwina telephoned. 'I have a postcard from Siena for you. Do you want to come and get it?'

'Oh, yes,' Madeleine let out a sigh of relief. 'I'll come over right away.'

'Leave your little beast of a child with your nanny. Tarquin still has a black eye from her last visit.'

'OK. I could do with a break from her, really. Sometimes she's not like a child at all. Talking to her, I sometimes wonder if she's not a changeling. She says such odd things. She says she has a fairy under her bed and she insists there is a lion under her chair. But it's more than just childish imagination: she so believes in what she sees, that sometimes I think she really *can* see things that other people don't see.'

Later, Madeleine sat at Edwina's kitchen table. Edwina was warming to her theme.

'It's time you told Syracuse to piss off, Maddie. You let him take much too much control over your life. You let him bully you into the ground. I think you'll have a wonderful time with Paolo; he'll put a smile back on your face in no time.'

'I'm sure he would, Edwina, but what happens if Syracuse finds out?'

'He won't, because you're not going to tell him. Husbands and wives should keep part of themselves to themselves. It keeps a mystery in a marriage. After all, you don't know half of what Syracuse gets up to, do you?'

'Yes I do because he always confesses. He's seeing that little nurse from the hospital now. Actually, she must really do something for him; he hasn't taken a trip to Hong Kong or Japan for months. His women out there must be wondering what's happened.'

Madeleine had the postcard in her hand. On the back in Paolo's square, beautifully written script she read it again. 'One day,' it read, 'we will be here together and eating white truffles at my favourite restaurant. The wine will be Brunello and you will be mine.'

Madeleine gave a snort of amusement. 'I haven't even decided whether I'm going to sleep with him or not, and he seems already to have made up his mind. Huh, he seems pretty sure of himself, doesn't he?'

'He has every right to be sure of himself, Maddie. You're so vulnerable at this point in time it will be like taking candy from a baby.'

'You know, ever since I met him, I've been feeling indecently randy. Everywhere I go I see couples kissing and I wish it was me. Does that sound ridiculous?'

'No, not at all. Syracuse was your only relationship and he grew into an old man overnight. He takes all the fun out of things with his crabby ways. Both Scott and Syracuse are American spoiled brats. Paolo is different. Maybe Italian mothers' boys know a thing or two about women; they certainly know how to woo a woman.' Edwina laughed. 'Germaine says even she feels jealous. He is so beautiful to look at, isn't he?'

Madeleine nodded. 'He certainly is. It's his eyes and his mouth. He has such beautiful teeth. Oh Edwina, I can't wait to see him again. I have to put up with Syracuse's boring conversations all about himself every evening, unless he's out womanising. Funnily enough, I couldn't care less how many women he has, as long as he leaves me alone. I'm totally happy dreaming about Paolo. In a way, I'm scared for this romance to end up with us getting into bed together in case it is ruined. It's so much more romantic like it is now. All these yearning feelings and waiting to hear from him. The days and weeks fly by. He says he'll be back in two weeks.' Madeleine shrugged. 'I'm going swimming every day of the week to get my stomach back into shape. I'll take Allegro with me.'

'Why don't you drown her while you're at it, Maddie?'

'Oh, Edwina, she's not that bad.'

'Yes she is, she's terrible.'

Madeleine left Edwina's apartment and walked down the road. She had her postcard in her handbag, and the world was full of wonderful people rushing past her to go home to someone they loved. She felt at peace with everyone. She stopped at a patisserie and bought some *Cantuccini alla Mandorla* biscuits. They also had blue-topped jars full of *Baci* chocolates. She bought those for good measure, and opened one to see if there was a slip with her fortune on it. 'Trust your heart, not your head.' Madeleine laughed. She knew what her heart wanted, even if her head said no.

'What's all this Italian stuff, Maddie?' Syracuse was in a bad mood.

'Oh, I just bought it on a whim on the way back from Edwina's apartment. I was in SoHo, and I thought you might like some chocolate.'

'I've got to go out later on, so I'll take some to nibble in the car, if that's OK.'

'Sure thing, Syracuse. I'm going to have an early night tonight, so don't wake me, I'm really tired. Tomorrow I'm going to take Allegro to the swimming baths and teach her to swim.'

'OK.' Syracuse got to his feet. 'I'm going to the library to read the *Wall Street Journal*.' He bent over Madeleine and kissed her. 'You know, there's something going on, Maddie. You're changing. You don't have your eye on another man, do you?'

'What on earth do you mean?' Maddie felt her body stiffen, and wondered if Syracuse had been searching her bag. As soon as he left the room, she raced upstairs to the bedroom and removed the postcard. Oh dear, having an affair was going to be difficult. It seemed to involve so many different things. Telling lies, making arrangements. This all seemed to come naturally to Syracuse, but Madeleine found it difficult to lie and to connive. She told herself, 'I can learn.'

She listened to the sound of the owls hooting in the dusk of the garden. The future lay stretched out in front of her for miles. Hopefully a happy future, filled with fun and laughter. It was such a long time since she had laughed with abandon. Maybe marriage was not for her. The ceaseless nights with the television booming away in the background. Or the gramophone blaring out Syracuse's music. She now had no music of her own. They only listened to what he wanted to listen to. Syracuse always flipped the television so that he could switch from channel to channel. She rarely ever saw the end of a programme that she wanted to watch. Syracuse watched endless amounts of football. He lay back in his chair, shouting at the players and throwing his empty cans of beer at the set. Edwina said Scott behaved the same way. Syracuse was not always like that, but he had degenerated and now was running to seed. Men like Syracuse seemed to grow old overnight.

She sighed an impatient sigh and went to the nursery to kiss Allegro goodnight. Allegro lay in her bed, her green eyes shining.

'Goodnight, darling.' Madeleine leaned over the cot.

'Blue fairy, Mommy.' Allegro pointed at the wardrobe. 'And there, big, big wolf. Going to eat me all up?'

'Darling, I don't think the wolf is going to eat you at all. Why don't you make friends with the wolf?'

Madeleine felt a shiver crawl up her spine. Allegro's love-affair with the wolf was so very real. She remembered the time she thought she'd seen a wolf face superimposed on Allegro's face. She shook herself.

'Goodnight, darling,' she said, and left the room.

'Come here, wolf.' She heard Allegro's voice in the darkened room. She could almost swear that she heard the sound of a big animal padding in the room she had just left, and smelled a whiff of carrion-meat.

Don't be so silly. Go and get another gin and tonic. She went downstairs and sat by the dying fire, dreaming of Paolo and his soft, gentle kisses.

Fifteen

'Paolo is back, Madeleine, and he wants to see you alone.' Madeleine could hear the excitement in Edwina's voice.

'Do you think that's wise, Edwina? Anyway, I don't know how I'm going to arrange that. I mean, it will involve a lot of planning, won't it?'

'You idiot, Maddie, that's the whole point of affairs. All that sneaking about and planning and nearly getting caught. That's what makes it all so intense and so much fun.'

'Is it really? It all sounds like one big headache to me. I hate lying and sneaking about. Even having to hide Paolo's flowers and his postcard makes me feel quite ill. I don't like being devious. I don't think convent girls are good at breaking the rules. After all, there is always that awful fiery furnace and years and years in purgatory.'

'Maddie, you're not even a Catholic.'

'I know, that's what makes it worse. I'm doomed by association. My father lapsed years ago, and I spent my childhood praying for his eternal soul. Now, if I go ahead and become an adulteress, I'll have to pray for mine as well. Oh, Edwina, I think it might be much better to just leave it all in my imagination. I think to actually have an affair, really do it; take off my clothes in front of a stranger . . . Well, it takes the romance out of everything. I'm used to Syracuse. If he farts, for instance, which he does endlessly, it just makes me laugh — but with another man I'd be horribly embarrassed.'

'Maddie, you'd get used to it – and think of the fun you can have. Paolo has lots of money and he's very generous. You need a bit of real romance in your life, anyway. You don't have to go to bed with him. You can just have lunch.'

'By myself? I wouldn't know what to say. You do all the talking for me.'

'It's you he wants to take out to lunch, darling, not me. Maddie, you're going to have to grow up and join the real world, darling. You can't go on living behind your front door with only Allegro for company. I'm going to telephone Paolo and tell him you'll be delighted to have lunch with him. He suggested our bar because he knows you'd be comfortable there. He wonders if you are free the day after tomorrow.'

'Yeah, I guess I'm free. I'm free all the time. That's my problem – I don't have enough to do. OK, I guess we can give it a whirl.'

'Good girl. I'll telephone you this evening to confirm, and if Syracuse is home, he can think we're having one of our usual lunches. That way he won't get suspicious.'

'I don't know about that, Edwina. He's noticed that I've changed. I suppose I went out and bought that sexy dress and all that underwear. He's already asked if I'm interested in another man. Still, he's very caught up with his nurse. I have a feeling she gives him quite a hard time. He comes home looking quite depressed at times.'

'Serves him right. He deserves a lot of grief. He's hurt enough women in his time.'

Madeleine put the telephone down and wandered off into the drawing room. Its cold formality appealed to her. For the moment she felt the stillness of the room and the deep brown shine of the shelves that held rows of books. These were the overflow from the library. Syracuse very rarely read a book; most of these belonged to Madeleine. She walked over to the shelf that held her books from childhood. *Winnie-the-Pooh*, a present from her father. *The Wind in the Willows*, *The Tales of Beatrix Potter*. She held the three books in her hands and sniffed the musty covers.

She opened *The Wind in the Willows*. Ratty and Mole's dear faces stared back at her. She closed the book; now she was secure again in the memory of sitting beside her father at night while he read her bedtime stories. When she was away at boarding school, these were the moments that she missed the most.

Eeyore without his tail. His drooping head begging for pity. She knew how he felt. She had lost her safe, warm perspective; what lay ahead seemed to her to be dangerous. I never even considered an affair with another man, let alone a married man, she agonised. What happens if his wife finds out? What happens if Syracuse finds out?

At least she wouldn't lose her home. That belonged to her. But would Paolo belong to her? Would his wife put her hands on her hips and make him pack his bags and leave their house in Siena for ever?

She remembered the description of Paolo's house. Edwina had made love to Paolo in the eaves of the house. They met on the Campo and then walked up the cobbled streets. Could she really go to bed with a man that had picked up her best friend like a fallen woman? Given her a few drinks and then illicitly made love to her while his wife was in Florence?

She saw Nanny Barnes come in with Allegro. She rang the bell for Mrs Poole. According to her new regime she must now order the meals for the rest of the week. Lunch for herself would be missing on the Friday. That was the day she was to have lunch with Paolo. 'I will be lunching on Friday with Edwina, Mrs Poole. Allegro can have lunch in the nursery.' She felt herself blush. Darn it; she would have to learn to control her feelings. She rather doubted if she ever could.

The rest of the day was spent worrying about her decision. Should she go ahead and allow herself to be seduced by Paolo? Certainly, he would have to seduce her. She really had no idea of how one went about these things. At times she felt quite excited by the idea of a man who had sufficient experience to make her feel like a real woman. Syracuse made her feel like a middle-aged mother. The more she thought about it, the more she realised that, for many years now, that was exactly what she had been. She had been a wife, a mother and a housekeeper. She had been good at all three roles, but slowly over the years her femininity had been eroded.

She no longer bothered to wear pretty dresses or high-heeled shoes. Syracuse didn't really seem to notice what she wore and, in the face of his indifference, she felt herself fading like a sunflower at the end of a hot summer.

In the beginning of their marriage, she had blossomed under the fierce glow of Syracuse's attention. He was her sun and, as she bloomed, she realised that his approval meant everything to her. He moved around her like a planet, and slowly became the arbitrator of her whole existence. He commented on everything. He did not like her to wear bright lipstick. He did not like her in high heels. In fact, now she came to think about it, the little nurse with her scrubbed face and her flat nurses' shoes was just what he'd tried to create in her. At some point, though, she had subconsciously rebelled, and it was this tension between the two of them that was slowly surfacing.

'I've had a hard day.' Syracuse came through the front door at eight o'clock. 'What's for dinner, Maddie?'

'Your favourite: fried chicken and french fries.' She smiled, and guilt gripped her throat with a raddled hand. 'Gee, thanks.' Syracuse moved towards Madeleine and kissed her. He pushed the tip of his tongue into her mouth and waited. They both knew the signal. If she responded, it would mean they would make love later that night. She knew she must respond. She felt the slight intake of breath as Syracuse now knew that there would be love to be made between them. Maybe, she thought as she walked through to the dining room, he considered what they did love – but for her it was no longer enough. She was bored by him and his attempts at making love.

'So I explained to Scott that, if he practised his overhead smashes, he could one day beat me. Put him in one hell of a temper. The tennis pro says I'm getting better, though I think I need to change my racket, Maddie. The grip is OK but the head is too small. There's a new one out that'll improve my play.'

'Mmmmm.' Madeleine watched Syracuse's face in the harsh light of the big chandelier that hung over the table.

'Maddie, you're not really listening, are you?'

'I am, darling, I really am, but I don't play tennis, so it doesn't mean much to me. If you want a new tennis racket, go ahead and order it.'

'Great. I'll go on my way to work tomorrow.'

Syracuse was like a small child when he was spending money, Madeleine thought as she stood up upon hearing the telephone. It would be Edwina with her built-in lie. Madeleine found her heart pitter-pattering. I'm like a small child about to tell his or her first fib. Well, maybe he gets his new tennis racket and I get to have lunch with a married man. Sort of even-Stevens. She was aware as she reached the sideboard that the two thoughts bore no relation to each other. 'Maddie.' There was laughter in Edwina's voice. 'Is he there?'

'Of course.' Madeleine tried to make the 'of course' sound conversational.

'Maddie, I've checked, and Friday lunch would be fine for Paolo.'

'Great, I'd love to have lunch with you. Will Germaine be there?' She glanced at Syracuse, who was busy eating. 'So it'll just be me?' she asked hesitantly.

'Absolutely, Madeleine. I'm a bit bored trying to get you together with the poor man. After all, he's known you for months now and he's scarcely been alone with you.'

'All right,' Madeleine put on a cheerful, loud voice. 'I'll see you at a quarter to one in the usual place.' She paused for a moment. 'You're not cross with me, Edwina, are you?'

'No, darling, just don't be such a goose!'

'Why should Edwina be cross with you, Maddie?' Syracuse's face was alight with mischief. 'Just what have you been up to? You've been mooning about a lot these days. Have you two got a secret? Should I come to lunch with you and see what you and Edwina have been plotting?'

'Sure, honey.' Her heart was thumping now. 'Edwina and I are going to discuss our winter wardrobes and then go shopping. You're welcome to come.'

'In that case I'll give it a miss. I'll lunch Scott and show him my new racket. I must get a new headband and a leg brace. I also need a wrist brace for my left wrist.'

Madeleine smiled indulgently. Syracuse dressed up to play tennis looked like the walking wounded. She heaved a sigh of relief and promised herself she'd take up yoga. When she was around Syracuse, she tended to hyperventilate, and Edwina said it was death to the complexion.

Last time she and Edwina had shared a yoga session, Edwina had told her she was studying anal retention as a yogic art-form. She resolved to discover more next time they met.

She heard Nanny Barnes's heavy footsteps coming along the corridor, and Allegro screaming, as usual. 'No, no, no,' and then a loud scream from Nanny Barnes. 'Don't bite me, Allegro, please don't bite me.'

Nanny Barnes erupted into the room with Allegro hanging on to her arm, her teeth sunk firmly into Nanny Barnes's hand. 'Oh, Allegro.' Madeleine was on her feet at once. 'Let go, darling! That's awful! Oh, poor Nanny, you've hurt her. Look, she's going to cry.'

Allegro gazed at her mother and ran her tongue over her bloodstained teeth. 'Nanny Barnes bad to Allegro,' she grinned. 'Sorry, Nanny Barnes.' Allegro ran to her mother and buried her head in her skirt.

'Are you really sorry, Allegro?' Syracuse leaned forward from his chair. Allegro lifted her head from Madeleine's skirt, leaving a patch of blood.

'Really sorry, Nanny,' she said penitently.

'Come here, Allegro.' Syracuse spread out his arms and Allegro jumped into them. She snuggled down on his lap.

'Allegro loves Daddy,' she said, smiling.

'Daddy loves his Allegro.' He made a gobbling sound and pretended to nibble Allegro's shoulders.

'Daddy's going to eat me all up like the big bad wolf.'

'You take Allegro up to bed, Nanny, and I'm going to take a bath.' Madeleine knew that Syracuse liked to read the newspaper after dinner. This might restrain him from invading the bathroom and talking.

'OK, you do that.' Syracuse gave his wife permission to have some peace and quiet. 'I'll go off and read the *Wall Street Journal*.'

There was a tacit agreement between the two of them that Madeleine would never point out that Syracuse was incapable of understanding the *Wall Street Journal* even if he could be bothered to read it. He needs to feel he can run our family life, she comforted herself as she left the room. Like he needs to feel I am a bad driver. I guess that's what makes men feel masculine. Incompetent women – and we play up to it.

Later that night, they lay in bed together. Syracuse was snoring slightly. Madeleine wondered, not for the first time, that when love and lust died in a marriage, why did the formerly loved one even smell different?

No longer was she turned on by the smell that she had found so attractive when she had first met Syracuse. Now she found that he smelled faintly rancid. Rather like the stale french fries that he so loved. She wondered briefly, as she fell asleep, if he felt the same about her? The thought that she might smell bad made her uncomfortable. Maybe I'd better buy a new deodorant tomorrow, she thought.

Sixteen

❦

'Edwina.' It was Madeleine on the telephone, and it was one o'clock in the morning. 'I'm sorry to wake you, Edwina, but please, please just have lunch with us, will you? I won't be able to go if you don't. I'm too frightened. I'm lying here shaking with fright. Thank goodness Syracuse is fast asleep.'

'Oh, Maddie. OK, if I have to. Now go to sleep and I'll meet you at the restaurant at a quarter to one.'

Madeleine put the telephone back on the hook. Whew, she thought. She'd been awake since eleven, and by now her brain seemed to be running around like a dog without a leash. But Edwina hadn't let her down, and finally she drifted off to sleep.

Madeleine decided to take a cab to the restaurant. This time she was going to do most of the talking. Last time she had been almost dumb with fright. She applied her make-up very carefully. Checked that her stockings had no holes. 'How odd,' she murmured at her reflection in the mirror. 'To be dressing for a man other than one's husband.'

For a husband you could put off shaving your legs for another day, or allow a comfortable amount of growth of hair in the armpits, but for a man you barely knew the preparation time was enormous.

She very carefully chose a black silk chemise from Paris so that, if she did decide to go to bed with Paolo, hopefully she could hang on to the chemise and hide her awful stomach. Sitting in the taxi, she felt her face growing red with guilt, and then white with desire. Today she noticed New York seemed to be especially full of fuckable men. Since she had lost all desire for Syracuse, she was quite shocked by the lust that seemed to have consumed her soul. Everything made her feel randy.

The taxi drew to the kerb and interrupted her thoughts. The cab driver smiled at her. 'Meeting some special guy?' he said.

Madeleine blushed. 'Yeah, actually I am.'

'Won't be your old man, would it?' The cab driver gave a loud guffaw of laughter and drove off. My goodness, does it show that much? She was embarrassed. She pushed open the swing doors and then she took a deep breath. Remember Edwina's advice. Ten deep breaths from the stomach when you're nervous. Edwina had discovered some guru who was giving her yoga lessons. 'Hi, Maddie. I ordered you a double gin and tonic.'

'Thanks, Edwina,' Madeleine slipped into a chair. This time she faced the door. It's no good avoiding him, she told herself while she waited for her drink. I'll just tell him I'm not going to have an affair with a married man. We can say goodbye and that's it.

'Tell me about your guru, Edwina.' Madeleine was anxious to distract herself. She took a big slurp of her gin. It was very strong, and she coughed. 'Well,' Edwina warmed to her favourite subject. 'It's very good for you. He teaches you to tighten all your anal muscles; if you fall into water and remember to tighten the anal muscles, you don't drown like everybody else. Also he says, if you are dying and don't feel ready to plutz, you bunch your muscles together and you don't die yet. He says some people he's known even get better right away and live for yonks.'

'How on earth do you do it, anyway?'

'Well, you sort of think about your anus and then visualise it in your mind. I can do it easy-peasy, and it's supposed to do wonders for your love-life.'

'Oh, Edwina, you're so clever: wherever did you find this guy?'

'He's a strange guy. He looks rather like an owl. He has a funny little beaky nose and a big fluffy beard. He's really rather weird: he sort of materialises whenever I'm in Central Park and tells me things. Like he knew I was going to have lunch with you. He described you perfectly.'

Madeleine nodded. 'Huh, that's Dr Stanislaus. I know him too. He is mysterious. He was the voice that came through Madame Winona. Does he know about Paolo?'

'Yes, he said to tell you to relax and have fun.'

'You're not just kidding that he said that, are you, Edwina?'

Edwina's eyebrows were raised. 'No, honestly I wasn't. That's what he said. He also said I'm stuck with Scott in this lifetime. What a bummer. He says if I get rid of him now I'll just have to come back and do it all again.'

Madeleine looked up and she saw Paolo's tall figure threading its way through the chairs. He was smiling. In his hand he held a huge bunch of jonquils. 'They're for you, *cara*,' he said. He bent over and kissed Madeleine lightly on the lips. She blushed a deep, dark red. Paolo's eyes lit up in amusement. Blast. Madeleine felt as if she'd lost control of the situation. She had so much wanted to be cool and calm.

Paolo kissed Edwina on both cheeks. '*Ciao*,' he smiled. 'I'll go to the bar and get some more drinks.' How easily Paolo makes himself at home, Madeleine thought, watching him fondly.

She watched him collect another gin and tonic for

her. This time the gin was a single shot, but she could feel the effect in her head.

She ordered swordfish carpallio and then pasta di cinghiale, after Paolo informed her that cinghiale was the Italian for wild boar.

'Do you have many wild boars in Tuscany?' This seemed like a safe conversation.

'We have loads in America: they're called men.' Edwina lit a cigarette and smiled sweetly at Paolo.

'Oh, Edwina, don't say that! It's not kind,' Madeleine protested.

'Maybe it's not kind, honey, but it's true. Scott and Syracuse have dreadful table manners. Dirty, vulgar men.' She sniffed. Madeleine looked at Paolo. He smiled back at her. He seemed to realise that Madeleine hadn't enjoyed Edwina's personal remarks. She began to relax under his sympathetic gaze. It was such a long time since anyone had gauged her feelings with such accuracy. There was no room in her claustrophobic relationship with Syracuse for her to have any feelings at all. She was only allowed to feel what Syracuse felt, and to talk of the things that interested Syracuse. 'What wine would you like to drink, Madeleine?'

'I know very little about wine, Paolo, apart from the fact that you drink white with fish and red with meat. You choose.'

'*Allora*, let's have a Chardonnay with your fish and a Brunello di Montalcino for the wild boar.' He motioned to the wine waiter who came scurrying over. She noticed yet again that there was such an assurance about Paolo. People took notice of his wishes and his wants. 'I'm afraid you're stuck with Italian wines, Madeleine. I drink no other.'

The waiter arrived and carefully filled the wine glasses with white wine. Edwina raised her glass. She had a plate of swordfish in front of her. '*Salute*, you two,' she said, her voice dripping with meaning.

'*Salute*, Edwina.' Paolo lifted his glass but he didn't drink. Madeleine looked at him, but then remembered him saying that in Tuscany they didn't drink until they had food in front of them. The waiter arrived with Paolo's seafood risotto. 'Ahhh,' Paolo bent his head over the steaming plate of food. Madeleine could see little pink octopus tentacles, shrimp nestling in the pearly rice, and the delicious smell of wood mushrooms. 'This food is good, Edwina. It's a good choice of restaurants. *Complimenti*.' Edwina inclined her head.

Madeleine just watched Paolo. He looked so beautiful, sitting with the sun falling on his shoulders. He had such wonderful glossy black hair, and his eyes were gentle and smiling. She wondered why his wife couldn't stop him from straying, but then acknowledged she hadn't been able to keep Syracuse faithful. Maybe all men strayed? Germaine's husband had taken off with a hunter; Edwina and Scott were never faithful to each other either. Maybe it was time she joined in this other world. This 'real' life, as Edwina called it. Maybe she'd been standing on the sidelines of the football pitch with her finger in her mouth for far too long.

After two cups of coffee and a grappa, Edwina stood up. 'Goodbye, darlings. I must run. I feel a trip to Asprey's coming on. I always feel a trip to a jewellery shop is necessary after a good meal. Goodbye!' She airbrushed Paolo's face with a kiss and then waved at Madeleine. 'Be good, darlings.' She waved her finger again and was gone.

There was a moment's silence. Madeleine was holding her wine glass tightly in her hand. Paolo leaned forward and took her glass, and then put his big, suntanned hand over hers which was now lying helplessly on the table.

'Madeleine, I want you to know that I'd never do anything to hurt you. I do want you to come to my apartment with me now.' His voice was filled with urgency.

Madeleine sighed. It had to come to this moment. How awful that reality was so much more brutal than fantasy. There were no fade-ins and fade-outs in real life. No swirly pink clouds to obscure the uncomfortable moments. Only the question of now going to Paolo's apartment.

'All right, Paolo. But I do think we ought to have a sensible talk. You must promise that you won't. Well, I mean . . . you mustn't. Make a pass at me,' she said in a desperate rush. 'I'd be terribly frightened if you did. I'm not like Edwina. I don't pick up men and I've never been unfaithful to my husband.'

'Don't you think I don't know that?' Paolo smiled. 'I promise you I won't do anything that might frighten or hurt you ever. I love you far too much for that.'

'OK.' Madeleine got to her feet with a sinking feeling in her stomach. Why, oh why had she ducked out on the one thing she most wanted to do, and that was to make love to Paolo?

'Have fun.' She heard the soft fluted voice of Dr Stanislaus.

'Where are you when I need you most?' she whispered.

Seventeen

Madeleine sat beside Paolo in the quiet luxury of his car. Cars are so important, she thought. Syracuse's car was just the right sort for him: red and randy. Her car was a reliable family Volvo. A sort of mumsy car. I'll change it as soon as I can, she promised herself. Being mumsy was no longer her image. She felt glad she was wearing the black silk chemise, and she tried to meditate on the state of her anal muscles. She took deep, soothing breaths.

The streets flew by. They were changing areas. Now they were in the Italian section, and she felt Paolo relax. His hands were lighter on the wheel. He was wearing a broad striped shirt and a lightweight silk Yves St Laurent suit. The silk tie was creamy to match the suit. He always wore the most beautiful shoes. Madeleine was fussy about shoes, and deplored Syracuse's need to wear trainers. Come to think of it, Syracuse and Scott really wore baby clothes.

She was unused to the silence in the car. Syracuse always kept up a steady stream of chatter. It was as if he needed to hear the sound of his own voice to convince himself he existed. His talking had tired her for years, and she found she was enjoying Paolo's competent driving and his silence. She had another go at trying to visualise her anal muscles. She supposed her anus must look rather like the mouth of an octopus without the beak.

'What are you thinking about that makes you look so serious, *cara*?' Paolo's deep musical voice interrupted her endeavours.

'Er . . . um . . . nothing really, Paolo.'

She blushed. She really must try and curb her imagination. If she confessed to visualising anal muscles, he would probably drop her there and then on the kerb, and she would have to take a cab back to her house, and then what would Edwina say to her? She'd be furious. Edwina had always told Madeleine to keep her erratic mind to herself. 'Men don't want to listen to your ideas, Maddie. They just want to talk about themselves and fuck. Just learn that lesson, and everything in your garden will be roses.'

'There aren't any roses in my garden. I'm married to Syracuse. I only have weeds and big dandelions and cow parsley,' had been her reply.

Now she turned to Paolo. 'I was thinking about gardening,' she lied. 'Do you like gardening?'

'I live in a top-floor apartment, but I do have pots of herbs because I love to cook. I bring back basil from Siena and I also get sent parcels from my father. He sends me buristo and his own sausages.'

There was such a note of longing in his tone that Madeleine felt bound to ask. 'You miss Italy, don't you?'

'Yes, I do love being here, but after a few weeks I want to go back. You see, Italian life is so simple compared to here. My family all live in and around Siena. I grew up with everybody around the Campo. Everybody knows everybody. There is no reason for so many psychiatrists like you have here in this country. If I am sad I tell a friend.'

'Or your wife.' Madeleine froze. 'Oh dear, I didn't mean to say that. It's just I'm so used to thinking of people in couples.'

'That's all right, Madeleine. You don't have to apologise. No, I don't talk to my wife. She is very Sienese, my wife. She lives her life and I live mine. Sienese wives are very practical. They put up with a lot from us men, but then in return they wear our mink coats and drive the latest, largest car. Of course this is a generalisation. There are couples who tell each other everything and are very close. This is rare, though. Italian women like my wife don't ask questions and don't expect any questions to be asked of them.'

'Does it make you sad, though, not to share your thoughts and feelings?'

'Not when I have a beautiful woman like you sitting next to me, Madeleine.' She flushed. 'You look so lovely when you blush, do you know that?'

'I'm afraid it's a long time since a man told me I looked anything but overweight and ugly. I can't seem to please my husband whatever I do. And since the birth of my daughter, my stomach looks awful, rather like a hot-water bottle.' She enjoyed the sound of Paolo's ringing laugh.

'*Cara*, none of us is getting any younger. Even I have to remember to suck in my stomach. I have a paunch.' He grabbed his stomach with his hand. 'I'm not one of these men who take exercise . . .' He pulled into the kerb and parked the car efficiently.

Madeleine climbed out of the car and looked around her. The usual New York crowd was pushing past, but there was a babel of Italian voices. Huge barrows filled with fruit. Big, juicy-looking red tomatoes. Giant green and red peppers. The stalls were aburst and ablaze with colours. 'Oh Paolo, I've just realised I left my flowers in the restaurant.'

'Never mind, I'll fill your arms full of flowers. Come to my favourite flower-stall.' He took her by the hand and they walked side by side down the street. '*Ciao, Volga, come stai?*'

'*Sto bene*, Paolo.'

'*Questa è la mia amica*, Magdalena.'

Madeleine watched Volga as she cast swift, professional eyes over her left hand. '*Una bella signora, Paolo. Complimenti.*'

'*È vero.*' He began to pick up sheaves of flowers. Jonquils, brilliant red roses, blue cornflowers. Soon Madeleine's arms were filled, and the perfume of the flowers assailed her nostrils.

'That's enough, Paolo,' she remonstrated shyly. 'I can't carry any more. Besides, I can't take them home: Syracuse would have a fit.'

'Tell him you bought them for yourself.'

'But Paolo, I don't tell lies.'

'Then learn.' He took out his wallet and peeled off some notes. '*Arrivederci*, Volga.' He waved his cupped hand and put an arm around Madeleine. 'Come, *amore mio*, let's go upstairs. It's quite a climb but the view is magnificent. Here, let me take some of the flowers for you.' He swung open a big heavy front door and then they began to climb.

'No wonder you're so slim, Paolo.' Madeleine was puffing when they reached the top of the stairs.

'I'm used to it! All the houses in Siena are tall and thin. As a child I had my bedroom on the top floor. From my window I could see the belltower of the old *comune*, the town hall, in the centre of the Campo.' He paused and fished a key out of his pocket. He pushed open a walnut-coloured front door and motioned her in.

Once inside the door, Madeleine leaned against it for support while she caught her breath. Paolo, his arms full of flowers, leaned forward and kissed her.

Madeleine found her eyes widening with surprise. 'Paolo,' she said. 'You promised.'

'I know I did, but I'm a man who breaks all my promises.' His eyes were sparkling with mischief.

'And you tell lies.' Madeleine was shocked.

'That too,' he agreed. 'Anyway, I've been waiting to kiss you ever since I first saw you. Come into the kitchen and we'll put the flowers in the sink.' She followed him through a large square sitting room. The room was furnished lavishly. The sofas were covered in a soft pink floral material. There was a big fur rug in front of the fireplace, and the lamps were mostly art deco. The floor was of polished wood, and small Persian and Indian carpets lay pleasingly on the floor.

'Paolo, what a wonderful kitchen.'

'Do you like it? I designed the whole thing myself.'

He put the flowers in the sink and removed his coat. 'Here, let me take your coat. I'll be back in a minute.'

Alone, Madeleine gazed about the room with delight. She loved kitchens. Ever since she was a child, she had believed the kitchen to be the most important part of the house. You could tell so much about people by looking at their kitchens.

This was a kitchen where Paolo obviously spent a lot of time. On the marble counters there were bottles of spices. In a terracotta jug by the cooker there was a bright green bunch of parsley. She very much wanted to taste Paolo's cooking.

'What's your favourite thing to cook?' she asked nervously as Paolo came back into the room. He had taken off his jacket and was wearing a light blue wool sweater. His tie was gone and a lock of his black hair fell over his face. Madeleine felt her heart thump. He was so devastatingly handsome.

'Let me see . . . I think I like to make *aglio olio*. You make it with fresh pasta and lots of garlic; extra-virgin olive oil and a pinch of black pepper. It is a very simple dish, but it carries with it the history of Italian olive oil, and the taste of the early spring when the garlic is fresh and very gentle.'

'Do all Italians care as much about food as you do, Paolo?'

'Certainly, Madeleine. Our food and our wine is just as important as our wish to make love to beautiful women.'

He took her hand and pulled her gently to him. 'I won't do anything you don't want me to do, *cara*. Just let me kiss you a little. You need kissing. I can always tell when a woman has not been kissed enough.' He gently pecked at her mouth. Madeleine felt a quite extraordinary feeling invade her body. In his gentleness she found herself able to respond in a way that she had never experienced before.

Syracuse only kissed her when he wanted sex. So his kisses were brutal and demanding. Paolo kissed her as if they had all the time in the world. She found herself moving deeper into his arms. They seemed to her to merge into each other. Madeleine closed her eyes and let the sensual moments flush through her. 'That's marvellous, Paolo,' she whispered.

'I know it is. Come with me,' he said, and he drew her back through the sitting room into a darkened room that she supposed must be his bedroom. Madeleine, by now, felt she would follow him anywhere. He stood with his arms around her and his hand under her chin. 'Making love, *cara*, is not about ever hurting anybody. Making love is a gift from the gods. We must never despoil that gift. Better to remain alone all your life than to make love with someone you don't love or care about. I do love you, Madeleine. I have from the moment I first saw you, and I do truly care about you.'

'Did you feel the same thing about Edwina?' She knew it wasn't a wise question, and she felt him flinch.

'I suppose I should have expected that question. Yes, I do care about Edwina, and I do love her – but in a different way. Edwina's much harder than you are. She is more like the women I am used to in Tuscany. But you are different. Very soft.' He began to undo the buttons of her dress. 'So gentle.' He helped her out of her dress. Now the dress lay on the floor, and Madeleine was very grateful for her silk chemise. Paolo began to lift the edge of the chemise, but Madeleine crossed her arms. 'Don't, Paolo. I'm embarrassed.'

She slipped into his bed and pulled the blankets over her head. She lay there, peering over the edge of the blanket, while he peeled off his clothes. He had broad shoulders and a very long back. He climbed out of his trousers and then hung them neatly over the back of a chair by the bed. He folded his socks and then removed his underpants. She was amazed at how hairy he was. The light from the open bedroom door fell across his shoulders. She stared between his legs and Paolo gazed at her quizzically. 'You know what they say about men's noses?' He was smiling. Madeleine nodded. 'Yes, I do, and Edwina says it's the same for women. Big noses big cunts,' she said by way of explanation.

Paolo bellowed with laughter. 'Madeleine, you're amazing. Here you are, practically a virgin, and your language is awful!'

'I know, us convent girls have filthy minds. Syracuse says I read too many dirty novels.'

'That husband of yours shouldn't be mentioned in my bedroom. Come here.' He climbed into bed next to her and took her in his arms. 'I love the feel of silk,' he muttered. He slid her tights down her legs. 'Kick them off,' he instructed. He slid his hands under her buttocks and opened her legs. His kisses became deeper and more passionate. Madeleine felt she might faint with the pleasure of it all. She felt her back arch and her body fall into rhythm with his. She heard the sound of her own voice gasping and moaning, and then she felt the tidal wave of her orgasm taking her out of her body and into space.

Somewhere so far away. She was flung against a planet. When she came back she felt alone for a moment. Then she heard Paolo's voice. 'You haven't finished,' he said. She tried to push him away. 'Let go, don't fight me.'

She found herself moving involuntarily against his fingers, and then the waves came again and again. This time she was going down deeper and deeper, down into soft blue water. 'This can't be a sin,' she gasped. She was holding on to Paolo as if her life depended upon him. 'Nothing this beautiful could be wrong.'

She realised that she was crying. Really crying, and Paolo held her gently in his arms. 'Cry,' he said. 'You have a lot of crying to do. Don't worry, we have found each other, and I won't let you go. I promise. You can trust me. I have safe arms.'

Madeleine raised her tearstained face to his and she whispered, 'I don't know why, Paolo, but I do trust you. I really do.' He sealed her mouth with a kiss.

Eighteen

Madeleine knew, even as she was drowsing in Paolo's arms, satiated and at peace with herself and the world, that soon she must leave him and go back to her house and her life in the outside world. He helped her dress, his hands kind and steady. He made her feel loved and wanted. 'I never knew love-making could be like this, Paolo.'

'You're naturally good at love.' He smiled at her. 'In Siena we say a man can tell how good a woman is in bed by tasting her *sugo*. Can you make *sugo*?'

'What's that?'

'It's the all-important sauce for pasta. Each man has to find a woman who can make *sugo* better than his mother.' He kissed the tips of his fingers. 'That's what I feel like now. A big plate of pasta and *sugo*. Shall we go to the kitchen and I will cook for you?'

Paolo's eyes were pleading with her to stay. 'I can't, Paolo. I have to get back. If I'm not home to pour a glass of wine for Syracuse, he'll sulk for the rest of the evening. He says he works very hard all day, and he expects to come home to a wife who is waiting for him. He didn't have any parents, you see. They died when he was very young.'

'What's that got to do with you having to be there to pour a glass of wine for him? Surely he can do that for himself occasionally?'

'I suppose so,' Madeleine sighed. 'I guess I've always felt so lucky with my parents. I felt sorry for him and guilty that I've had such a happy childhood. Everybody deserves a happy childhood, don't they, Paolo?'

'Yes, *amore*, but then remember that millions and millions of people have terrible childhoods and recover from them. Yes?'

'Oh dear, I've made my husband out to be an awful beast. He's not really. I think I just need to get back home and think about this situation.' She was standing in the middle of the bedroom looking at Paolo. 'I suppose I ought to think about the plusses and minuses of having an affair with a married man. I guess I'm now an unfaithful wife, aren't I? A woman taken in adultery. It doesn't sound very nice, does it?'

Paolo got off the bed where he'd been sitting. He put his arms around Madeleine's waist and said softly into her ear, 'Madeleine, had you been truly happy and sexually satisfied by your husband, you would not have been the slightest bit interested in me. As it is, you have a lot to learn about pleasure. You are like a beautiful flower that has always been in bud and never flowered. Today you flowered, and it is good for you.

'You have always lived with the fear of God taught to you by nuns. There is another God who is not vengeful. Who will not condemn you for being with me. We have to be responsible, both of us, that we harm no living thing. What we do between ourselves is our business. We must both think of our partners and our children; but what you and I can share between us will, I hope, be unique. Each time you know a person sexually, you are naked in the universe. People can lie to each other. They can present a false self; but when the clothes come off and you are in each other's arms, then there is really no way for a falsehood to continue.

'I knew when I first saw you that our relationship would not just be a passing affair. I have had many of

137

those and pffft . . .' He snapped his fingers. 'They mean nothing. But for us I have hope of great things. Of big happinesses.' He kissed her.

'I must go, Paolo. I'll think about what you said. I promise.'

'I'll come down and call you a cab.' He went off to collect her coat. Madeleine walked to the front door and then turned and gazed back into the sitting room. She was trying to make a mental picture of the room, and then retain the memories of the bedroom beyond.

She felt as if she had taken a huge step and was now not certain of the next move. 'When will I hear from you, Paolo?'

'Ah, that is the curse of this kind of loving. I cannot just pick up the telephone and talk to you. But you can talk to me anytime you like. If you are upset or scared or have questions, telephone me. Promise me that, Madeleine. Even in the middle of the night. I want you to think of me as your friend and lover. Will you do that?'

They were at his front door. 'I will, Paolo.'

'Maybe we could meet for lunch by ourselves,' Madeleine said hopefully.

Paolo laughed. 'Not only can we meet for lunch, my darling, but we can meet *here* for lunch, and then we can make love.' He hugged her. 'Really, Madeleine, you are like a beautiful violin for me. I feel so happy.'

Madeleine was laughing now. He looked so like a little boy with a lollipop in his hand. 'Does sex really mean that much to you, Paolo?'

'Oh, it does, it does,' he said fervently. 'I can't think of anything I like better, and especially with you.' They were on the street. He flagged down a cab. As he put her into the car he whispered, 'I will keep the flowers; their smell will remind me of today.' He pulled the head of one of the pink roses out of his pocket. He put the rose in her hand and curled her fingers around it. 'Keep this in your bag and think of me every time you see it.'

Madeleine smiled at him from the cab window. 'A Stradivarius has to be played regularly,' she observed, grinning. She waved goodbye, and then watched his figure grow smaller and smaller until the cab turned a corner and he was gone.

Madeleine had an hour left before Syracuse came home. Allegro was in the park with Nanny Barnes. She could hear Mrs Poole talking to Cook. She was glad the house was empty, except for the sound of the two disembodied voices. She ran up the stairs and hung her coat on a peg on the back of the bedroom door. She frowned at the pile of toys on the floor of her bedroom. Then she realised that it was useless to think of Paolo ever coming here. He would never see the damage that Allegro's tricycle had done in the hall. Another sad aspect of being lovers but married to other people.

She hurried into the bathroom and stripped off her clothes. She sat up to her neck in steaming water. She scrubbed herself carefully with a loofah, as if to remove all evidence of her love-making. She took her knickers into the bath with her. 'Oh dear,' she thought. 'Is this what Syracuse had to do?'

Probably not. He'd just let Mrs Poole take the dirty washing and put it into the machine. She wondered idly if Mrs Poole was the sort of woman who checked for stains. Then she felt embarrassed. Apart from listening to that one telephone call from Germany, she had never bothered to check on Syracuse. Now no longer innocent herself, her mind seemed to open up another filing cabinet. This one had 'Top Secret' stamped on the front.

Now she had secrets. Before there were none, except for the odd white lie to deflect Syracuse's wrath.

She leaped out of the bath and put the rest of the clothes into the laundry basket. She removed her knickers from the bath and hung them over the shower curtain, where she usually hung her hand-washing. It seemed rather important to her to do everything as she usually did.

She felt as if she were now walking in a strange territory. Instead of the one level of existence she'd shared with Syracuse, she now had two. It was as if they were on a double-decker bus, like the red buses she rode as a child in London.

On the bottom deck of the bus was Syracuse. He was the driver. She was one of the passengers, along with Allegro, her parents, Mrs Poole, Nanny Barnes and Cook.

Upstairs, however (and upstairs on the London buses had always been her favourite place), there was Paolo. He was the conductor, but there was only herself up there, sitting high over the traffic of Hyde Park. 'Ping.' Paolo rang the bell and then looked over his shoulder and smiled at her. 'Where to?' he shouted. 'Anywhere,' she yelled back. 'As long as it's an adventure.'

She was smiling as she walked downstairs, the image of the bus still filling her thoughts. Her spine felt as relaxed as fluid. Her legs moved gracefully. As she looked at her hand on the banister, she remembered where her hand had been. Where it had touched Paolo in the most intimate places. How she had not been afraid but glad to rejoice in his moving body. Yes. Paolo was right. Sex was God's perfect recreational gift to mankind. It had taken Paolo to teach her this. She squared her shoulders as she heard the front door open. 'Honey, I'm home.' The greeting never varied.

'I'll bring you a glass of wine, Syracuse. I won't be a moment.' She moved to the wine pantry. How do I face him? she wondered. She poured two glasses of wine and then carried them in on a silver tray with a small plate of olives and gherkins.

'Had a good day, Maddie?'

Madeleine tried to smile, but merely succeeded in moving her lips. 'Yeah. I had lunch with Edwina; she's in good form.'

'Good. I'm going out later tonight to beat Scott at tennis: I've got my new tennis racket.'

Madeleine handed him his glass of wine on the tray. 'That's nice,' she said, feeling a sense of relief. 'I need to catch up on my reading. I seem to have been so busy lately.'

'Really, Maddie, you need to get your head out of a book and get back into real life.'

'I know, Syracuse. I'm sorry I'm so boring.'

'That's the problem right there, Maddie. You don't have any interests.' Madeleine sipped the wine. It was a white from California. It had none of the mellowness of the red Brunello she shared with Paolo in the restaurant.

Syracuse stared at her, his pale blue eyes flickering. 'Are you OK, Maddie? You're not sick or anything? I know – you're having a period.'

'Yeah, Syracuse, you know me so well.' She smiled weakly back at him.

Nineteen

&

'I don't know what's come over Maddie, Lucinda!' Syracuse was lying on his back in Lucinda's bed. 'She's acting funny, like she's not always here or something. I thought maybe she's having an early menopause. I read about that in the *Reader's Digest* magazine.' He gazed disconsolately at his knees. He wished his knees were less knobbly, his dick were longer, and his balls bigger. Still, it was quality, not quantity, he reminded himself again. He had plenty of quality.

'I need a couple of thousand bucks, Sy. I want to go to Florida with Clarissa and she's broke.'

'Who's Clarissa? And anyway, don't change the subject. I'm talking about Maddie.'

'I don't want to talk about your wife, Syracuse. You complain about her all the time. You say you can't stand her, and then you come round here and can't shut up about her. Why don't you leave her?'

'I can't do that: she's my wife. Really, Lucinda, you do say the silliest things.' He lay there, furious. Time to visit Mieko in Japan, and then go on to Hong Kong for a fling with Mei Mei. He needed both women's oriental concern. It would never cross their minds that he should leave his wife. Women in the East knew their place. 'Anyway, there's Allegro to think about. I can't desert my little girl. I'm the first man in her little life. If I left home she'd feel I'd abandoned her. Think of the psychological damage that would do to her. How could she ever learn to trust a man again?' He was enjoying the virtuous glow that fatherhood had bestowed upon him.

'Maybe she'd be better off knowing from the beginning that all men are bastards – particularly her father? Then she wouldn't have to learn the bitter truth so late in life? Anyway, I want two thousand bucks. Maybe your wife is having a fling with another man?'

'Oh no, Lucinda! She'd never be able to do a thing like that. I can read Maddie like a book. No, it's not that. I think it's Allegro. She's a difficult child. Anyway, that's enough about me, darling. Pour me another glass of wine and let's talk about you.'

'Two thousand dollars, and no shit from you, Syracuse. I'm expensive.' Lucinda was sitting at the bottom of the bed, her legs spread wide open in a yoga pose. Syracuse fluttered his hand at her. He wished she were more modest.

After sex was over, he felt a distinct distaste at the sight of a woman's genitals. Lucinda grinned. 'Two thousand,' she said implacably, and gracefully rose to her feet and picked up his wine glass.

'Why should I pay for your friend to have a holiday?' he grumbled.

'Because your wife is rich, that's why.' Lucinda walked out of the bedroom, carrying his empty glass of wine. Syracuse imagined her in the kitchen, pouring the last of a bottle of Sancerre into his glass. 'You have absolutely no taste in anything, Syracuse.' He could hear her contemptuous voice now. She was always scathing about his attempts to impress her.

In spite of her, he'd chosen this bottle himself. It was an excellent, rather thin wine, with a metallic bite at the end of the first sip. She wanted two thousand dollars. That was a bit steep. How was he going to fiddle that on his expenses sheet? He began to plot. Mrs Spender, his father-in-law's secretary, hated him and checked his expenses rigorously. So far she'd never once caught him out. Syracuse grinned. 'I'll go round and see James at the Criterion Hotel. He'll arrange it for me.'

James had no surname as far as Syracuse was aware. He spent his life squatting like a huge toad behind his office desk. He ran his hotel with a rod of iron, and was famous throughout New York for his ability to fiddle his clients' expenses for them. He would find the two thousand dollars for Lucinda. No one could say that Syracuse was not a generous man to those he loved.

The problem with Lucinda in a nutshell was that she appeared to feel no gratitude. She was good in bed, though. Every time he made her come he felt young and powerful. He forgot his nascent paunch and his varicose veins. She made him feel young again.

He watched her walking into the bedroom, carrying his glass of wine. He felt a surge of lust. Lucinda looked at him, a half-smile playing on her lips. 'For two thousand dollars I'll give you what you want, Syracuse.' She bent down to give him his drink. She let the nipple of her breast tantalise his mouth, and then she bent down and kissed him where he most liked to be kissed.

'You win, honey,' he said hoarsely. He sipped his glass of wine and watched his erection grow.

'Shall I do this?' Lucinda found a spot no one else had ever discovered before. She nibbled on it wetly. Her tongue flickered backwards and forwards. 'Two thousand bucks: you got it . . .' Syracuse was gasping with pleasure.

'I love it when you talk money.' Lucinda smiled and increased the pressure. She watched him writhe helplessly under her mouth. 'Men are so simple,' she reminded herself. 'Feed them and fuck them and you can have anything you want.' She waited until Syracuse had finished.

'I'll bring the money around tomorrow,' he said. He closed his eyes and sank into a deep, satisfied sleep.

Twenty

❧

'One lump or two, dear?' Madame Winona smiled at her nervous client. She remembered Madeleine well. Introduced by Germaine Archer, who was such an aware client. Madame Winona had a cold; she sniffed.

'I decided to come by myself, Madame Winona.' Madeleine was shaking. 'I don't want anybody to know that I'm here.' She knew she sounded inane. She tried very hard to keep her hands still. She didn't know that her knees could actually knock together until today. Hers made a horrid, clonking sound, and she hoped the noise was only in her imagination. 'I desperately need to talk to Dr Stanislaus. Do you think you could find him for me? I don't know where he is, and he won't answer me.'

Dear God, she agonised. Here I am, asking for a creature that exists only in my imagination. Madame Winona is the only person who can help me. Thanks to Dr Stanislaus, I've become an adulteress. A marriage-wrecker. She knew that it wasn't fair to blame Dr Stanislaus for her decision to sleep with Paolo, but then today she felt like making it his problem.

During the days that followed after her love-making with Paolo in his apartment, she was alternately filled with joy and terror. At moments she danced and sang about the house, and played frantically with Allegro, who watched her mother's manic behaviour with suspicion. Then there were days when she watched television, or read newspaper reports about women found in bed with men other than their husbands, and a stab of fear rippled through her. She would run into her bedroom and lie on her bed, gasping with fright.

'You see, Madame Winona, I'm not sure of what to do next. Is one allowed to ask Dr Stanislaus for advice? I mean, is it sort of spiritual etiquette, or is it considered vulgar? I'm not sure of the social code here . . .'

'Oh, it's strict, my dear, very strict. Now you drink your tea and I will have a chat with the other side.'

Madeleine raised the cup to her lips, trying to ignore the filthy brown rim where the tea lapped against the side of the cup. The tea was weak and tasteless, but it soothed Madeleine while she tried to get a list of questions in order in her head. It was no good. She'd get three questions marshalled into some sort of order, and then two more jumped the queue. The first two questions would go scuttling off into the darkest corner of her brain. 'Come back,' she implored but the questions just stamped their feet and sulked.

Madame Winona rolled her eyes and grunted. She cocked her head on one side, and her greasy rolls of grey hair fell over her face. She seemed to be wrestling with something, and then she drew a deep, laborious breath.

'Good morning, my child. I'm sorry I've been unavailable. A spot of bother among the unmanifest. Took some sorting out, I can tell you. Women, of course. On the rampage. Demanding their rights. I see you've come on your own. A very good idea, Madeleine. You are altogether too trusting. Madame Winona tells me you want some advice? Go on then, fire away.'

'I must explain to you that I've had very little experience with men,' Madeleine began. 'In fact, apart from Syracuse, none at all . . . As far as I know, both my mom and dad have been totally faithful to one another. Now, I guess you might know this? A few weeks ago I

'. . . sort of . . . Well, I went to bed with a married man.'

'We expected that,' Dr Stanislaus harrumphed with amusement. 'Did you have fun?'

'Who exactly is *we*?' Madeleine was offended.

'Oh, the guardians. They are souls that have finished their earthly existence. While on earth they were humans who chose to live and to work for the good of mankind. Social workers, probation officers, kindly bank managers – and there aren't many of those, I can tell you. They perform the same sort of functions in the unmanifest world. But do let's get on, dear. I haven't that much time. It's the women again. They want a meeting.' He clicked his beak with annoyance.

'You weren't watching me, were you?'

'Oh dear no, girl. Please, you make us sound like voyeurs. No, not at all. We would only watch if invited to by some of our most perverse clients. We can, of course, join in as well. But I digress.'

'What I am frightened of is that I've done something so awful that I will never be forgiven. I don't know if it's Reverend Mother's version of God who will strike me dead, or your unmanifest light of love or whatever, but I'm scared of failing. I'm so confused at the moment. Sometimes it feels as if Paolo is the best thing that has ever happened to me. At other times I feel as if I've let everybody down. My parents, Syracuse, my child.' As the list grew, Madeleine imagined a thin long trickle of black slime oozing between her legs.

'Don't look down, dear.' Dr Stanislaus's voice was sharp. 'We have an unwelcome visitor in the room.' It was too late. Madeleine had already looked down; there was indeed a black thread of slime coursing down her leg. 'Oh no,' she screamed. She buried her face in her hands.

There seemed to be a furious battle going on in

Madame Winona's old body. She was shaken and bounced on her chair like an old rag doll. Her hair flew all over the place and her hands clenched and unclenched. After a few minutes, the battle abated. 'Huh, that's over.' There was the light of a victory in Madame Winona's eyes. 'She'll not bother you again.' Madeleine opened her fingers. 'Who is "she"?' she said faintly. She risked another peek at the floor. There was nothing there.

'Guess,' Dr Stanislaus chuckled, and Madeleine shook her head, perplexed. 'Reverend Mother,' he told her.

Madeleine was astonished. 'Reverend Mother?'

'Sure thing. Those women are hell to deal with. They don't give up their possessions without a struggle.'

'But Reverend Mother died ages ago . . .'

'Yes, she did, but she's in the unmanifest now. She is where all the people go who say no to the great joys of life. Most of the great teachers were lovers of good wine. They were lovers of life and of children. The greatest of them all, the only one to achieve divinity, changed water into wine.'

'Not according to Reverend Mother. She always said he never made wine but non-alcoholic grape juice. That's what we had for communion.'

'So now she lives in an aspect that reflects her earthly experiences and her own repressions,' Dr Stanislaus went on.

'That sounds awful.'

'It is awful, but it is her choice. She was holding on to you as one of her earthly possessions, but now Madame Winona has forced her to let go.'

'So are you saying that now, without Reverend Mother to make me feel guilty all the time, I'm free to love Paolo?'

'I can't say anything as direct as that. I'm not allowed

149

to interfere with your consequences. If I do there are dreadful long-term penalties attached. I can only give you celestial helpful hints. I'm sort of like your "agony aunts".' Dr Stanislaus sounded very pleased with his role.

'OK. I can live with that. The second question is, would it be an awful big sin if I tried to get out of being married to Syracuse?'

'I will give you two rules. The first is: thought creates matter, if you concentrate or pray. Whichever suits your temperament, you will pull out of the ether what you ask for. Be careful, Madeleine. You will get your heart's desire. Always remember that a mind is a powerful thing. Be sure of what you ask for and why you are asking for it.

'The second rule is: harm no living thing. This is your dilemma now. How you resolve it is your affair. I can only point to your problem. A final thought before I go and deal with this monstrous regiment of women. Remember, when faced with action on the material level – that is, when the real world demands action and you are unsure about what to do – practise non-action. Do nothing, remain passive, and the act of action will resolve itself.

'Remember that you are only the last breath of air you breathed a second ago. Your last breath is all that sustains you in this material world. Go home and learn to breathe properly. Talk to Edwina; she knows how to breathe properly.'

'You got it.' Madeleine took a deep breath and held it while Madame Winona came out of her trance. 'That was a long session, wasn't it, dear?'

'Yes, it was.' Madeleine was beaming. 'I feel much happier, Madame Winona. Thank you for your help.' She stood up and took out her purse.

'That'll be twenty-five dollars, dear.' She grasped the money in her withered little hand and stumbled out of the room. 'Let yourself out, dear. I'm always here when you need me, remember.'

Madeleine practised her breathing all the way home in the cab. By the time she got home, she could hold her breath and retract her anus at the same time. Wait until Edwina hears about this, she thought triumphantly.

'Edwina, you have to teach me to breathe properly.' Madeleine gazed at Edwina, who was filling her glass with vodka in her kitchen.

'Who says?' Edwina lit a cigarette.

'Dr Stanislaus. I was asking him about my affair with Paolo. He can't give me an answer, but he did get rid of Reverend Mother. I feel so much better. Not guilty all the time. Yesterday I ran out of lavatory paper, and God didn't strike me dead. It's such a relief not to live with good Catholic guilt.'

'OK. The breathing is simple. Breathe from the stomach for a count of seven, then hold it for a count of seven, and then slowly exhale. I can't help you with your guilt about Paolo because you won't tell me the details. It's very boring of you, Madeleine.'

'I'm sorry, but it feels incestuous to discuss my sex life with Paolo. After all, you were his lover first. Anyway, it doesn't take much imagination. Making love is a fairly universal pastime.'

'Madeleine, you're such a delightful fuddy-duddy. Maybe that's why Paolo is attracted to you?'

'You mean he wanted to dud some of my fud?'

'Yeah, something like that. All men like to remove the bloom off grapes; you are one of life's innocents. He can't take your virginity – Syracuse did that – but . . .'

Edwina poured another vodka. 'If you won't tell me, that's that. How's Allegro?'

'I'm taking her to a shrink on Friday afternoon. Actually I think we both might need a shrink. Allegro keeps staring at me with those big green eyes. I think she knows about me and Paolo.' She wondered vaguely if it ought to be Paolo and I. It was no use consulting Edwina: she only majored in nail-polish remover. Today her nails were immaculate and painted a deep vermilion. 'Can I have a gin and tonic, Edwina? I find taking a lover increases one's alcohol intake by leaps and bounds. Syracuse has a Far East trip coming up, so I'll be able to spend some time with Paolo. Do you think I could telephone him when we finish lunch?'

'Sure thing. I got to go and pick up Tarquin for his exercise class.'

'Exercise class? Doesn't he get enough of that at school?'

'I don't know about that, but everyone says it's better to have too much exercise than too little. He has friends that work out. They look so cute in their little boxing outfits. Tarquin doesn't want to box, really. He's too sensitive, but Scott insists. Says it'll make a man out of him. Next, of course, it's braces until he's eighteen. Ahhh, it's a bitch of a life, Madeleine, and I don't have a new lover in sight. I can't live without the possibility of a new lust. When I'm with a guy, even Scott is bearable.' She finished her vodka. 'Honey.' Edwina leaned forward. 'I'm scared to tell you the truth. Now, I trust you. I know you don't trust me enough to tell me how you made out with Paolo, but –'

'Edwina, it's not that.' Madeleine felt a real sense of anguish. 'It's not a lack of trust. I just feel some things should be private.'

'Sure you do, and that's how from the beginning men

have ganged up on women. Men talk about women sexually all the time. Scott says there's a new woman in the office who's frigid. He says several of his partners have had sex with her. They are bored of her now. You think your love for Paolo is a private and a sacred matter. If he beckons, you will run. If he tells you something is secret, you will keep it a secret to the grave. Men don't do that for us, Madeleine. You're wasting your time, darling. Anyway, that's enough of that. Tell me the truth: is it time for the big "O"?'

'The big "O"? I thought that's what feminists called orgasms?'

'Not nowadays – we're way past bothering with orgasms. All that stuff did for women was to remove the war from the boardroom – where at least we get paid for our work – to the bedroom. Now we are expected to have not just one orgasm, but multiples, and we are expected to do it for free. No, I mean, is it time for me to out myself and have a nose job?'

Madeleine could see that Edwina was in earnest. It took the oddest subjects to arouse Edwina's emotions. 'You're emoting, Edwina, aren't you?'

'Sure I'm emoting, and for once you used the word right. I'm seriously waiting for your advice.'

'Well, I'm the last one you ought to ask, Edwina. I think you look perfectly all right, but I'm terribly vague about these things. Why don't you ask Paolo?'

'Madeleine, you don't ask a man that sort of question. It's like asking your lover to buy you sanitary towels.'

'Why can't you ask your lover to buy your sanitary towels? You let him buy lavatory paper, don't you?'

'OK, OK. You disappoint me, Madeleine, but I'm sorry I asked.'

'Please, Edwina – not a guilt trip. I get those from Syracuse. I promise you I think you look great. My advice is to save the big "O" for when you find a new man. Or better still, find a new man who doesn't want you to mutilate your body for his sake.'

'I'll die before I meet a man who doesn't want me to go under the knife for the love of him. Remember, honey, we live in New York. The men here are either gay or kinky. It's in the water or the steam from the drains. Never mind, somewhere out there, probably still in diapers, is a man waiting for me.' She glanced at her watch. 'Shit, I'm late. Use the telephone, Maddie, and then let yourself out.'

Madeleine watched her friend run to the mirror in the hall and smear an enormous amount of red lipstick across her mouth. She remembered that she'd read in a book somewhere that temple prostitutes used red lipstick to let their clients know that they practised oral sex. Madeleine grinned as she watched Edwina leave the apartment. Maybe in her past life Madeleine herself had been a temple prostitute. Probably not one of the most senior ones, but a novice. Now, all these lives later, she was learning about sex again. She telephoned Paolo.

Twenty-one

'Don't fall out of the tree, Allegro.' Why, oh why, must Allegro turn the whole of Central Park into an assault course? Madeleine got to her feet wearily. 'Honey, come on down. We'll go and get an ice-cream, OK?'

She gazed down at her daughter's defiant eyes. 'Please, honey, Mommy's tired. Be good to Mommy.'

Tomorrow was the appointment with the child psychiatrist. According to Nanny Barnes, there was no point at all in taking Allegro to a psychiatrist. 'Some children are just born evil,' Nanny had informed her startled mistress. Before Allegro, Nanny Barnes had tried to find a redeeming feature in all her little charges, but Allegro frightened her. She was so strange, so unchildlike. Now Madeleine found they both seemed to have declared war on each other.

Allegro had finished with her biting phase, and was well into the hair-pulling and nose-grabbing. The only person she no longer attacked was her father. Allegro realised quite quickly that Syracuse was infinitely more easily manipulated by charm rather than terror.

Try as she might, Madeleine was aware that her daughter was disliked by almost everyone she met. Madeleine, however, had a sneaking sympathy for Allegro's unrepentant bad behaviour. Maybe it was a projection of her own good-little-girl image that was still rock-solid after all those years in the convent. 'Don't want ice-cream.'

'OK, I'm off to get one for myself.' Madeleine knew

that Allegro feigned an independence she did not really possess. She wandered off with a practised nonchalance over the grass.

The earth already had a late summer hardness. The grass was brown at the tips and the rose bushes that encircled the beds of flowers were wrinkled and past their prime. There was a smell of decay in the air. The big hydrangeas smelled dry and of city dust.

Madeleine watched Allegro covertly as she swung one skinny leg over the branch she was dangling from. Madeleine caught her breath, but she knew better than to interfere. Allegro was one of those children that hurled themselves into space and always seemed to bounce when they landed. There was a loud thump as Allegro hit the ground, and then she came charging across the grass. Madeleine bent down and swept her into her arms. 'I love you, Allegro,' she whispered into her hair. 'I'll always love you, my baby.'

Allegro covered her mother's face with kisses. She wriggled to get down and ran ahead of her mother towards the ice-cream van. Madeleine wandered along behind her.

How dare Nanny Barnes and my friends say such horrid things about Allegro? She knew those were her motherly, protective feelings coming to the fore. Allegro was difficult, but maybe if she were happier, her child would be calmer.

Now, with Paolo in her life, Madeleine realised that much of her existence had been just that – existing. There was no love left between herself and Syracuse. Yes, they had sex when he demanded it, which was rarely. She had long ago stopped trying to please him. His idea of love-making had little to do with love. It took just the first time with Paolo to realise what she had been missing. Then she reasoned with herself that there must be rules to this game of loving a man who was not free to love.

One of the rules she had already learned. There was no spontaneous possibility of his telephoning her at home. Mrs Poole and Nanny Barnes would smell a rat, even if this rat wore Gucci shoes and tiptoed down the telephone line. She knew how much both women disapproved of Syracuse receiving telephone calls from his mistresses whenever he felt like it; Madeleine was sure they would equally disapprove of her liaison with Paolo.

In any case, she did not want her relationship with Paolo to become soiled in the picking-over of the bones of the day. What she had with Paolo, she needed to keep sweet and clean. There was so little in life that kept the golden glow of her well-remembered childhood.

She dead-headed some roses as she passed by the last bed of flowers before they got to the ice-cream van. Today was almost the end of this perfect hot summer. The van stood outlined by the deep blue sky. Children waved their heads, their hair grainy with leaf mould where they'd been rolling on the grass. Their voices sounded shrill in the heat. The acrid smell of hot children's bodies pleased Madeleine.

Allegro was standing at the back of the little crowd, but her ferocity parted the children like the Red Sea, and she elbowed her way to the front. Madeleine reached for her purse. Allegro had no money; besides, she had no business pushing her way through. She fished in her purse for a quarter, but Allegro was already talking to the ice-cream man. He bent down low, listening intently. When he stood up, he looked as if he were in a trance. The crowd of children fell silent. He picked up two ice-cream cones and filled one with chocolate ice-cream and the other with butternut – Madeleine's favourite. Allegro turned and smiled at him as she carried the ice-cream cones triumphantly through the crowd. 'One for you, Mom,' she said, beaming. The man shook his head as if to clear it, and gazed blankly at Madeleine. She realised that there was no point in trying to pay for a transaction which as far as he was concerned had never taken place. She looked down at Allegro who was grinning with mischief.

'Nice man,' she said, and handed her mother an ice-cream.

Twenty-two

Allegro sat on a big squishy seat in front of a funny
little man who had pale blue eyes and gold spectacles.
Allegro was bored, watching his mouth make rings and
flat grimaces as her mother earnestly laid bare all the
problems confronting her. Allegro was bored because
she'd heard it all before. First there had been a report
from Nanny Barnes that had been damning in the
extreme. Then a report from Mrs Poole who had to
stick her oar in. By now her mother was looking very
shaken and about to cry.

Allegro decided to remove the doctor's clothes. One
blink removed people's clothes, and two restored them.
Without his clothes, the doctor looked less frightening.
He had a withered chest covered in grey, wispy hair. It
was not that Allegro was afraid of this man. It was far
more the fear that poured in a constant green stream of
light from her mother. The green light was sticky, and
Allegro tried to rub it off her lap.

'I really don't think you have anything to worry
about, Mrs Winstanley. She looks like a dear little girl
to me.' He gave Allegro a sickly leer. He stood up and
Allegro giggled. The thing between his legs was longer
than her Daddy's. It bobbled as he moved his hands
while he talked. 'Come along, honey, we'll go next door
and play with some toys.'

Allegro gazed uncertainly at her mother. Would her
mother be all right on her own?

'Don't be shy, Allegro. I'm used to little girls. I have
two of my own. Look.' He picked up a picture frame

and handed it to Allegro. 'Those are my little daughters. One is called Annie – she's ten, and the other is Sarah – she's twelve.'

Allegro took the picture frame and gazed at the two girls. She squinted for a moment and they disappeared. She handed the picture frame back to the doctor.

He glanced fondly down at the photograph as he returned the frame to his desk. He frowned and looked puzzled. 'Whatever happened?' He handed the frame to Madeleine. 'The girls have disappeared.' Madeleine stared blankly at the photograph. There were trees and a park but no people. 'How odd.' The doctor rubbed his head. 'How very odd. Come along, Allegro, let's go.'

Allegro took his hand and then lifted her legs and allowed her body to slump. She added two invisible stones to her natural weight. The doctor tried to hoist her on to his shoulders. He pretended to laugh heartily. Allegro caught the glint of a dawning dislike in his eyes, and she smiled. Psychiatrist? He would never get the better of her, she thought. She took a quick look at her mother over her shoulder. Her mother was gazing soberly at her lap. Her head was bent and a black cloud of defeat settled on her shoulders.

Oh well, however long it took. One day her mother would realise that Allegro had no intention of being like everybody else. Until that day she would just have to bear these frequent trips to various psychiatrist's offices. Thank goodness there were millions, if not trillions, of psychiatrists in New York. Edwina said there were good psychiatrists in California too, so if they ran out in New York, she and her mother could always catch a plane. Allegro had never been on a plane and she rather liked the idea.

She obediently let the doctor plonk her on a small kiddie chair in his room full of toys. On the desk in front of her she could see the doctor's name. Dr Steckel. Here she sat, being a girl when she wanted to be a boy. It was enough to make a cat sick. Boys did things and didn't get taken to psychiatrists' offices. Tarquin only went because his mother was jealous that Madeleine kept dragging Allegro around these offices. Tarquin was a wimp. Now she could see the cat. 'Cat threw up,' she said. She gazed at the corner of the room. 'Over there,' she pointed to the animal.

'Eh?' Dr Steckel had his spectacles on the top of his head and was shuffling through papers. 'What's that you said?'

'Cat's thrown up,' Allegro said patiently. Adults were so stupid. She pointed a stubby finger at the cat which was now licking its paws.

Dr Steckel glanced in the direction of the cat. He looked amazed. 'Good heavens.' He pulled his spectacles down over his nose. 'There really is a cat. Shoo,' he shouted, and strode over to it. Allegro made the cat disappear, and the doctor stood staring into empty space. 'It's gone,' he said wonderingly. 'I must be ill. I need a holiday.' He put his hand on the desk and tried not to stagger. 'There was a cat, wasn't there, Allegro?'

Allegro nodded. She left her chair and went over to join him. 'Look,' she said, pointing to a little puddle of sick. Dr Steckel looked down at the wet patch at his feet. 'Oh dear me, yes indeed.' He stood over the puddle. 'But is it cat-sick, dear child? That is the question. How can we have cat-sick without a cat?'

'Cat gone.' Allegro was in a helpful mood, and she enjoyed watching the clouds of confusion swirling around the good doctor.

It was very difficult being nearly five and imprisoned in a child's body. Especially when she had the gift of instant understanding. She had a lifetime ahead of her being a girl, and that made her angry. Bugging this old man was going to be easy. He looked so funny, bending over the wet patch with no clothes on. He had a thin, concave belly and his skin was greeny-white.

Allegro was getting bored now. She blinked twice to re-dress the doctor. She sat and gazed at the wall. She projected a few dinosaurs on to the blank space. One of them roared loudly.

Dr Steckel jumped. 'What on earth was that?'

'A dinosaur,' Allegro said obligingly.

'I think I'd better go home, Allegro. I'm afraid I don't feel too well. I'm sorry, my dear, I'll ask my receptionist to make another appointment for you next week.' Dr Steckel was very white by now, so Allegro gave him a blinding headache just to make sure that things got speeded up and she could go and play in the park with her mother.

Allegro followed Dr Steckel into the waiting room. Madeleine looked up anxiously as she saw them emerge. She checked the doctor's face for signs of dripping blood and nose-grabbing. She was pleased to see him in one piece. 'I'm awfully sorry, Mrs Winstanley, but I have a bad headache. I don't feel too well. Do you mind if I take a rain-check and I'll get my secretary to make another appointment?'

He sat behind his desk and picked up the telephone. Allegro decided to give the daughters a reprieve. 'Good heavens.' Dr Steckel picked up the photograph. 'They're back again. Well I never.' He made the appointment and then he stood up. 'I'm sorry, Allegro.'

He really did sound sorry, but then men always did when they were ill. Allegro took her mother by the hand and escorted her out into the busy New York morning.

Twenty-three

A cold November wind blew around the New York harbour. Madeleine could just faintly make out the tall figure of the Statue of Liberty rising above the fog in solid splendour. She was sitting on the floor of Germaine's apartment and, as she sat wrapping her arms around her knees, she marvelled at Germaine's ability to make herself uncomfortable.

'Want another drink, Madeleine?' Germaine's small body loomed behind her.

'No thanks, Germaine, I've got to dash to collect Allegro from Dr Steckel's office. I seem to spend my time now delivering and collecting from various places. I'm so tired.'

Germaine grinned sympathetically. 'I wish I had your problems. Anyway, how's Paolo?'

'He's wonderful, Germaine. I get to do all those lovely things I was never able to do with Syracuse. We wander around the museums. He knows when to talk and when not to talk. You know, apart from you, I think most Americans talk far too much.'

'I guess so, but then I live alone and I think if you live alone you get used to silence. I think sometimes of silence as a great friend.'

'Funny you should say that. I find now that if Syracuse has the television and his music blaring all through the house, even if Paolo is away, I go to his apartment, slip the key into the lock, lean against the door and just savour the immense noise of absolute silence. I know it sounds silly to use the word noise when I talk about silence, but silence has a huge white noise of its own. It sort of fills my ears and my head with a kind of pure light. And, oh Germaine, I've begun to paint again. I keep it all at Paolo's place because Syracuse just laughs at what he calls "my little interests", but I find it so exciting. I can see over the rooftops and down into the streets full of Italians and other people. I imagine Paolo in Siena.' She made a face. 'I try not to imagine Paolo with his wife in Siena, though, especially not in bed. You pay an awful price for an affair with a married man, don't you?'

'You do, my dear. Indeed you do. I'm afraid there seems to be a very high price in this world on happiness. It's as if the gods resent us mere mortals enjoying ourselves too much, but then I'm pleased to see you looking so well. You have a sort of warm glow about you, Madeleine.'

'I know. Everything about me seems to be alive. You know, I thought I knew about making love from Syracuse; but now I *really* know how to make love, it's completely different. Syracuse can only fuck. He can only satisfy himself because he can only feel for himself. He has no idea of who I am. I'm his wife who has a place at the end of his table and at the end of his prick. Paolo is completely different. He treats me so gently and with such respect. I think that is probably the difference. Syracuse respects only himself. He is convinced he is a genius, and in a way he does get what he wants because he bullies everybody until they give in. Everybody except my mother, that is.'

Madeleine laughed. 'And he's met his match in Allegro. She doesn't take any shit from him.'

'How's it going with Dr Steckel and Allegro?' Germaine carried a can of beer to the sofa and sat down. The sofa protested with a dusty sigh.

'OK, I guess. She goes every week. She doesn't dislike him, but he says he can't really find anything wrong with her except that she has a bad attitude. How you can have a bad attitude at five I don't know, but I guess he's right. I find that she does exactly as she pleases whenever she pleases. Nanny Barnes is covered in bruises, because if she tells Allegro off she finds that almost immediately she falls over. It's weird. I saw it happen yesterday. Nanny Barnes found Allegro's dolls all cut up. She'd taken the kitchen scissors and removed their arms and their legs and their heads. I was quite spooked by the naked bodies. Anyway, Nanny Barnes carried them to me. I asked Allegro why she did it, and she said she wanted to be like Dr Steckel and put them all back together again. I thought that was rather sweet, so I wasn't cross, but Nanny Barnes marched out of the room in a huff. She fell flat on her face over nothing. Don't you think that's odd?'

'I do, Madeleine, but then we both know that Allegro is going to be a very different child. You know, in the desert, the magic man finds a child every year that is to be special. He does many ceremonies and kills a white rooster and a young lamb. Finally he is directed to the tent where the child lives. The child leaves his family and goes and lives with the magic man. He usually has six or seven children living with him. When they reach puberty, they lose their powers. I've seen the children do the most amazing things. At twilight they change themselves into different sorts of animals. I've seen them leap into the air and fly. I often thought I was just hallucinating, but then I don't think I was.

'I was often reminded of the quote from Shakespeare, "There are more things in heaven and earth . . . Than are dreamt of in your philosophy." It always gave me goose-bumps even as a child. The older I get, the more

I respect the worlds that we have within ourselves. I think of myself as an iceberg. Three-quarters of who I am is under the sea. Only a very little bit of me shows. Some people have vast amounts of depth to their lives; others have very little. Mostly I think people don't bother to look inside themselves. They live on the surface of life. Those are the people I don't bother with.'

'That's the trouble, Germaine. I am bored. I'm terminally bored with Syracuse. How do I get away from him? That's my problem.'

'Yeah, honey, that is your problem. But unfortunately we can't just hoist him on to a passing camel and point him in the direction of a Libyan desert . . . Madeleine,' Germaine looked serious, 'you're not bored with Syracuse because in your heart of hearts you want to leave him and eventually marry Paolo?'

'Oh no, Germaine. I was bored with Syracuse long before I met Paolo. No, I know that Paolo will never leave his wife or his children. I've accepted that.'

'Good.' Germaine heaved a sigh of relief. 'I'd hate you to be just another woman deluding herself that eventually she would get her lover to marry her. That doesn't happen, darling. Or rather, only occasionally, and of course in films.'

When Madeleine left the apartment, she bent double against the wind and cursed herself. You're a liar, she accused herself. You lied to your best friend.

Reverend Mother spread her huge black cloak and flapped into the fog, screaming, 'You thought you could get rid of me, but your lies brought me back, my child. You are a liar.'

Hell, hell, hell, screamed the wind.

Twenty-four

Syracuse was in a bad mood. Hong Kong was cold, freezing cold. There was an unusually icy wind blowing in from Canton and Syracuse felt irritable. 'Do get a move on, Mei Mei. I'm really hungry.'

'I'll fix food for you, Syracuse. Anything you like.'

'I don't like, Mei Mei. I feel like a hamburger and a milk-shake. I'm bored of Chinese food.' He knew he ought not to be so angry with Mei Mei, but her submissiveness at times got him down.

Really, he was missing Lucinda. She treated him like shit, but at least she never backed down. There was something challenging in her spirited onslaughts that he missed when he was with Mei Mei and Mieko. There were subtle differences between the two women. Mieko never cried, but she just set her mouth in a firm line and agreed with anything Syracuse wanted.

Mei Mei collapsed if he so much as raised his voice, and that made Syracuse hysterical. 'Why can't you answer back for once, Mei Mei?'

'In my family it is not good for a woman to speak badly to a man. It shows lack of respect.'

'You Chinese have too much respect for everything,' Syracuse grumbled as he got off the bed and headed for the shower. He found the hot water coursing down his body refreshing. He was aware of Mei Mei standing in front of the shower. He handed her a loofah and she began to scrub his back. Usually, after she scrubbed him all over with the loofah and left him feeling all pink and tingly, he took her back to the bedroom and they made love. Today it was too cold, and her Hong Kong apartment was not built to withstand the cold. Mei Mei lived at the base of the Peak. Her apartment was just two rooms and a bathroom, but she had made a very pretty home for herself, and Syracuse liked to be there. 'Come along, gorgeous,' he said, his good humour restored. 'Let's hit Nathan Road.'

'Strewth,' he muttered as they walked down the road. Mei Mei was a lovely-looking woman. She was reed-slim, and today she was wearing a black dress with matching black leather high heels. She was unusually tall for a Chinese woman, and her head was level with his. Of his four mistresses, he mused as they walked along the road, I think Mei Mei is my favourite at the moment. He watched heads turning to monitor their progress. Griselda was the most practical and motherly. He went to her for sound advice and sensible love-making. Griselda was very Teutonic about making love. It was something she felt she had to do to repay Syracuse's kindness, and she did it with brisk efficiency.

Mei Mei was endlessly obliging, but he felt as if he were shooting in the dark. Mieko made love to him with all the grace and experience of her geisha upbringing, but again there was never a shadow on her face.

He remembered last night, when he'd raced to his late-night climax and had lain there, panting, he had had a flash of his coupling with Lucinda. After making love, they both lay dishevelled and satiated. Lucinda had no need to sexually please him. If he was delighted in a moment of passion, she was happy for him, but not unduly so.

Syracuse wondered if it was the fact that women in their twenties were now able to demand more sexual adventure from men? Or were American women becoming more masculine in their demands?

He was hungry now and he hurried along the pavement, breasting against a tide of humanity that surged backwards and forwards in the wide, tram-lined street.

Now he remembered the noise and bustle of Hong Kong. The screaming of insults. The rickshaws darting in and out of the traffic. The trams that swayed perilously along the tracks in the middle of the road, hauling their load of tightly pressed bodies in carriages. The bodies that hurled themselves on and off the trams whenever they had time to slow down.

It was hard not to love Hong Kong. The city reminded Syracuse of the big silver ball that floated down over New York on New Year's Eve. Only Hong Kong celebrated every day of the year with a feast. Now the shops were packed with Christmas presents and decorations. 'I must get Madeleine a gift, Mei Mei. I've promised her something special for Christmas. What do you suggest?'

'I may not choose a gift for your wife, Syracuse. That is not respectful.' Syracuse knew that it made Mei Mei uncomfortable to have to chose presents for Madeleine, but he hated choosing gifts.

'I don't have any idea of what to choose, Mei Mei. You know I hate shopping. You're a woman – you're good at that sort of thing. Don't sulk, darling. Come on, make a choice.'

After he'd eaten two big hamburgers piled high with fried onions and liberally splattered with tomato ketchup, Syracuse felt a lot happier. All around them, Americans sat in their business suits, gorging themselves. Syracuse picked up the tomato-sauce container. It was round and bright red with a green stalk and two imitation tomato leaves. 'Only from America,' Syracuse said with reverence. 'It makes me feel so homesick.' Indeed, he suddenly felt a terrible pang: for his tennis club, for his big house and his bright red car, for his tennis racket, even. Allegro would be asleep now in her bed. 'You know, Mei Mei, I'm worried about Madeleine. She's been acting funny lately.'

'You are always so worried about your wife, Syracuse. Let us try and find something happy to talk about.'

'No, I'm serious, Mei Mei. She's been going out a lot to have lunches with her friend Edwina and that bitch Germaine. She's up to something, I can feel it. She's different, Mei Mei. I mean, even in bed.' He could feel Mei Mei shifting uncomfortably on her chair.

'You show lack of respect to your wife, Syracuse.'

'Damn respect, Mei Mei, I think my wife is having an affair.' Once having voiced his secret concern he found himself feeling very upset. 'That could be it, Mei Mei, couldn't it?'

After lunch, Syracuse shepherded Mei Mei to a jewellery shop. 'What do you think, Mei Mei?'

Mei Mei shrugged. 'You can't make a mistake with a string of pearls, Syracuse.' She pointed a long, pink-nailed, highly manicured finger at a long string of pearls hanging from a fake hand. The string gave off a lovely warm glow. Mei Mei was now interested. Sex did very little for Mei Mei, but in the presence of jewellery her skin flushed with pleasure and her eyes lit up.

'Choose a nice string of pearls for Madeleine, and then you can choose a Christmas present for yourself.' Syracuse rather liked the perversity of his mistress choosing a Christmas present for his wife.

'Oh, thank you, Syracuse, you're so kind!' Mei Mei beamed at him, her wide, doe eyes flashing with happiness. She fingered the first string of pearls. Then she checked the second string against her teeth. 'These are better,' she said. She walked to the door with the pearls in her hand. 'Look, no yellow at all. Very good pearls.' She turned to the man behind the counter and began to haggle in a high, shrill voice. Syracuse stood back and watched them both.

'No wonder I love women so much,' he smiled as Mei Mei's voice rose higher and higher. At one point Syracuse thought she was going to resort to violence. Then, with a sharp click of her heels, she threw the string of pearls on the counter and said, 'Come on, Syracuse, this pig of a man won't give me a good price. We go elsewhere.'

Syracuse was used to this ploy, and was prepared to amble after her. They got as far as the door before the man made little ho-ho-ho sounds of capitulation. Mei Mei grinned in triumph. She picked up a small jade bracelet. 'I'll have this as well,' she said. She slid the bracelet on to her arm.

The shop-owner smiled. 'You drive a hard bargain, Mei Mei,' he said in Cantonese.

'I know, Uncle,' Mei Mei replied likewise, 'but these pigs need to be impressed. What about the one I brought in last week? He spent enough, didn't he?'

'Tell your friend that I've given you the bracelet for free.'

'I will, Uncle. At the end of the week he goes, and I have an Arab friend coming in. He has much money.' She gazed at her uncle. 'This time I want a good diamond.'

'What's he saying?' Syracuse didn't like being excluded.

'Oh, I've just convinced him to give me my bracelet for free.'

'Hey, that's great.' Syracuse was furrowing his brow over the bill. 'That's an awful lot of money for a string of pearls,' he grumbled.

'It will make your wife very happy,' Mei Mei said.

Twenty-five

※

Allegro was waiting for her mother to come home from one of her many lunch dates with her friends. She saw her mother's tall figure arrive through a flurry of snow.

The cobbled streets looked so pretty now. Icicles hung from the gas-lamps. Her mother was not wearing her usual slacks and a warm coat. She was walking up the drive in a pair of very high, spiky heels and wearing a mink coat, which had been a present from her father last Christmas. There were huge flares of red and gold coming off the coat. The lights were so bright that Allegro blinked.

'Nanny Barnes, can you see a light all around Mom?' she asked. Nanny Barnes was ironing in the nursery.

'You know I can't see your lights, Allegro. Nor all those fairies and witches. What happened to your wolf?'

'Oh, he went off into the forest with his new wife. He doesn't want to live in New York any more. He says people try to shoot him. It's not a good place for wolves, Nanny Barnes.'

'I should think not indeed. Do you tell all your fancy talk to your psychiatrist?' Nanny Barnes thought it was an awful shame that Allegro had to go to man like Dr Steckel at all. She had to take Allegro when Madeleine was busy. Psychiatrists were for mad people, and Allegro wasn't mad. Just a little doolally tap, as her old mother used to say. A little short of a shilling. Still, it was the fashion these days. Edwina's little boy, Tarquin, also attended a psychiatrist. No wonder, and him dressed to the nines like a girl. All those floppy clothes and long hair: it was a disgrace. Nanny Barnes thudded down the iron on to Allegro's jeans. 'And another thing, young lady. When are you going to dress like a proper little girl? Mummy ordered all these lovely things from Daniel Neils and Harrods, and you wear these dreadful old jeans and T-shirts?'

'Nanny Barnes,' Allegro ran up to the elderly woman and kissed her on her leathery cheek, 'I'm never going to grow up and I'm never going to wear pretty dresses.' She stood in the middle of the room and pressed her hands together. A shot of blue electricity singed through the room. 'I'm going to tell you a secret, Nanny Barnes. A really big secret.' She held out her hands. 'It's this big.' She spread out her arms. 'Almost too big to show you.'

'All right, child, get on with it. I've got work to do.'

'Nanny Barnes,' Allegro felt her voice trembling with excitement. 'I'm not a girl, I'm a boy.' She said the words very quickly so they couldn't escape into another part of her body and refuse to come out. 'There,' she said, exhaling loudly. 'What do you think of that?'

'Not much, Allegro. You're a girl and you have to get used to the idea that one day you'll grow up, fall in love and get married.'

Allegro saw her lovely blue flame wilt and die. It fell across the floor and the blue faded until there was nothing but a white slash across the carpet. She gently bent down and patted the defeated energy. 'Don't worry,' she whispered. 'It's only Nanny Barnes and she doesn't know about anything.' The flame burned brightly for a moment and then, unloved and unappreciated by Nanny Barnes, it vanished.

'Nanny Barnes, you may never say that I will grow up or that I will get married. I won't ever. I'll never grow up. I'm like Peter Pan. I have my Never-never-land where I live. Only I don't have a Captain Hook. I have my friend called Dr Stanislaus. He looks like an owl and he comes into the garden at night and he talks to me.'

'Get along, Allegro. I'm too busy for all your talk. You've been reading too many books. Dr Stanislaus: now there's a foreign name for you if ever there was one. Of course you'll grow up and get married. Everybody does.'

'You didn't, Nanny Barnes.'

'Course I did, but he died in the war. I loved children, so when he died I thought to myself: Well, Nanny Barnes, you'll never find the likes of him again, so you'll have to look after other people's babies.' She smiled at Allegro. Allegro could see little flickering black tongues around Nanny Barnes's back. Impulsively she rushed up to her nanny and hugged her. 'I'm so glad you found me, Nanny Barnes. I love you.' She planted a big squashy kiss on Nanny Barnes's nose and then ran off to find her mother.

Twenty-six

❧

The days leading up to Christmas were very busy. Madeleine unwillingly held a party for Syracuse's business friends. Awash with guilt, she went out one freezing Monday morning and chose a dark blue cashmere pullover for Paolo. She felt half guilty, but also thrilled. She had never bought such an expensive jumper for anyone in her life before.

She stood at the counter, running the soft, silky material through her hands, and imagined how Paolo would look wearing it. Would he wear it in front of his wife? The question popped unbidden into her head. She banished the thought immediately and pulled out her charge card. Then she thought better of it. How would she explain this charge to Syracuse who so carefully ran the family accounts? No, she would have to pay cash.

How complicated her life had become. She smiled grimly. No doubt somewhere in New York, Syracuse was shopping frantically for his little nurse and his other women. She had no access to his spending habits. If she ever dared to ask Syracuse, he would either scream that she didn't trust him, or maintain an outraged silence. Long ago she'd stopped asking. She just added her signature to the blank cheques.

She had tried to complain to Edwina. She was told she was lucky she had such a good husband. All Scott ever did was to throw his bills at her. Yes, Madeleine reasoned, Scott did do all the work, and it was Edwina who hung about the house doing the odd bit of decorating when she felt like it. Still, Madeleine had withdrawn cash for her Christmas shopping. She peeled off the notes and handed the cash to the woman behind the counter. 'Real nice sweater, madam.' Madeleine smiled joyfully back. 'Yes,' she agreed. 'And it's for a very special person.' She could see her eyes shining in the mirror behind the counter. Falling in love with Paolo had changed her so much. She felt softer, more like a woman. His appreciation of how she dressed and his admiration and constant compliments made her feel soft and pliable. His hands on her body stroked her; after making love she tingled, and the world seemed to be bathed in a special glow. Often, as she busied herself about her day, she heard music. 'Don't be so silly,' she told herself as she pushed her way through the crowded door on to the street.

This time there was music, real music. A small group of children were standing muffled up against the cold on the corner of the block. 'Hark the Herald Angels Sing.' Their young soaring soprano voices wheeled high above the noise and the stench of the traffic. Madeleine stood watching them, cradling her present for Paolo in her arms. This time last year she had been alone in her life. True, she loved Allegro with a passion, but what existed between herself and her husband were the dying embers of affection, and now – even without Paolo in her daily life – they were dead.

In the fireplace that had once blazed with love and passion, there was now only a well-swept hearth. Standing beside the children, she was oblivious to the traffic and crowds. People swept past her in a continuous rush that washed the pavements with thousands of restless feet, all hurrying and scurrying to get to the shops to fill their arms with presents for those they loved. Or just cross and tired people who wanted to get home. To be able to close their front door behind them and to smile and to rejoice.

Madeleine knew she was not going to be one of those rejoicing faces. This Christmas she would wear a mask. Later she would be a good hostess. An obedient and a loving mother. The last role was the only one she could play. She heaved a sigh and beckoned a taxi.

She left Paolo's present in his letterbox. She knew she would not see him again before he left for Siena. Their last farewell had wrung her dry with anguish. Now she needed to concentrate on Christmas and Allegro.

As the dinner progressed, Madeleine watched Syracuse flushed with wine and with the success of the evening. When she was in the kitchen with Cook, she attended to the last-minute decorations for the duck in an orange sauce. Syracuse came in to collect more red wine.

'Excellent dinner, Cook. My compliments to the chef.' Cook flushed with pleasure. A compliment from Syracuse was a rare occurrence. He slipped his arm around Madeleine's waist and she repressed a desire to flinch. Now his touch was repellent to her.

She carried the pretty bowl full of tiny bright green peas into the dining room. There, four couples, all well known to her, sat around the table. By now sufficient wine had been consumed for the majority of the people to have settled into their obsessive recounting of their daily events.

She could hear Scott recounting his titanic tennis battles with Syracuse. 'That mother-fucker got me on his last serve. I smashed it back but it went wide.' Scott's face was livid. Madeleine looked at him and wondered how he managed to avoid a fatal heart attack. His voice filled the room and boomed against the ceiling. Crash, smash, bash, went his sentences. Scott talked loudly and vigorously, as if by filling the room with his sound it would drown all other opposition.

Edwina had learned to handle her husband many years ago. Now she was talking in a subdued whisper to the man on her right, Peter Swanson. Madeleine knew that Peter Swanson was now 'seeing', as their social set put it, Edwina. Peter Swanson's wife Hilary was English. So far, Madeleine had never really spent any time with the woman, largely because she was very shy and mostly looked miserable. Madeleine put the peas down in front of Hilary, and put her hand on her guest's shoulder. 'It must be very hard to be away from your family for Christmas,' she said gently.

'It is, it really is. Our Christmases are so different.'

'Hilary's family go to church. Can you beat that? We all play these childish games until eleven o'clock, and then we pile into their muddy old shooting-brake and go to church. No heating of course, they're English. Then we go back to the house for hot cocoa and home-made biscuits.'

'How quaint,' Edwina was smiling at Peter. 'How absolutely dear.'

Madeleine felt a moment of rage, but it quickly subsided. Usually Edwina stealing other people's husbands enraged her, but now she had no excuse to feel anger. She was guilty now. At least she did not have to sit in the same room as her husband's mistresses, though. Syracuse spared her that. As for Paolo, they never discussed his life in Siena. She did not even know his wife's name. She felt good about that. The less she knew, the less she needed to feel the guilt.

She returned to her seat and, lowering her voice so as not to compete with Syracuse and Scott, she said, 'Hilary, tomorrow I have to take Allegro to her shrink. Would you like me to drop by for a cup of coffee?'

'I'd love that, Madeleine, I really would. My two boys need to find friends. We've only been in town for three months, and I really don't know anybody yet.'

The evening dragged on, deteriorating into a pile of wine bottles, inelegant piles of debris and filled ashtrays. Peter and Edwina were almost in each other's laps. Madeleine watched Hilary's anxious face. Was this all new to Hilary, or had she, like Madeleine, long ago learned of her husband's deceit? Tomorrow Madeleine would find out.

Women, fortunately, have the ability to cling to each other in their hurt moments. That's why they live longer than men. Madeleine had worked that out long ago. They have the ability to staunch each other's wounds and then go back to the battle refreshed.

Unlike Edwina, Madeleine did not savour the battle of the sexes. She would rather wash up on the shores of love in Paolo's arms. Nights like this were such a waste of time.

Before she met Paolo, she had thought of these evenings as theatre. She would plan the menu with Cook, and discuss the linens with Mrs Poole. In the morning she would decant the red wine so that it could breathe. Wine had its special part to play in her theatrical dinner parties. Just before six she would have a hot bath and get ready for the performance. She knew that Syracuse, in his black dinner jacket, would complement her long, formal dinner dresses. Yes, they made a handsome pair. 'A wonderful couple,' all their friends said.

What a lie it all was. The ashes that filled the ashtray filled her heart too. Cigarette butts, gone cold for lack of passion. She would stand looking at the table after all the guests had left. Wine stains like tears on her white tablecloth.

'Don't you think he's scrumptious?' Edwina

whispered now as Madeleine helped her on with her coat.

'I like his wife, Edwina,' and then Madeleine regretted the hurt she'd caused Edwina.

'Don't be such a stuck-up bitch, Madeleine.'

'I'm sorry, darling.' Madeleine hugged Edwina as an act of contrition. 'I'm just missing Paolo. He left today for Siena. I never realised it could hurt so much.'

Edwina hugged her back. 'It does, darling. It hurts all the time if you're stupid enough to fall in love with a married man, and that's what you've done, isn't it?' Madeleine nodded miserably. 'I guess so,' she said. 'I know it's stupid of me, but I don't know any other way.'

Edwina shot a glance at Madeleine, and then they heard Scott coming down the hall. '. . . And then that son-of-a-bitch said, "Your shot, Syracuse," and you missed it!' There was a roar of laughter. 'Your mother, Scott.' Syracuse came into the hall and stopped. 'Well, well. What are you two plotting tonight? Huh?'

'Oh nothing, Syracuse. We're just discussing Tarquin's train set. I've got it hidden in the basement, and Edwina's got Allegro's bicycle in her shed.' How we women lie, she thought. She looked at Edwina. She felt a thin film of disgust forming in her heart. She walked up to Scott and pushed away his hands as they groped for her breasts. She saw them both out to the door and then she walked back into the dining room. 'You go to bed, darling; you have to go to work tomorrow. I'll wash up.'

'Can't you leave it all for Mrs Poole in the morning?'

'You know I can't, Syracuse.'

'OK, I'm tired. I had a busy day.' He came towards her and pulled her into his arms. He fumbled for her lips. She could smell the sour smell of red wine on his breath, and the thought occurred to her that for years

180

she had always insisted on clearing up after their parties so as to avoid his drunken efforts at making love. The day would come when she could leave the dishes and go happily to bed.

That's a promise, she told herself.

Twenty-seven

Allegro watched her mother's face as she lifted her up to light the candle on the top of the Christmas tree. Her father's face was full of red light. He was beaming. But her mother's face was dark and shadowed. Allegro began to cry. 'What's the matter, darling?' Syracuse wrenched Allegro out of Madeleine's arms.

'Mom is sad inside, Dad.'

Madeleine stood watching her daughter. She knew that Allegro was right. To spend Christmas Day away from the man you love was hell. There was no other word for it. It was beyond words like sorrow, pain, suffering. It was just a terrible torment.

She had her map of Tuscany hidden under their mattress. When Syracuse was asleep she pulled it out and crept into the bathroom. Hugging her guilty secret, she stared at her map of Siena.

It was such a small city, but she could see the road that led straight to the Campo. Then there was the little road where Edwina said Paolo had his house. She could forgive Edwina for making love with Paolo. There was still a niggling doubt that her mind would not leave alone. Was Paolo right this minute also standing by his Christmas tree with his wife and children and missing her? Probably not. The hell of it all was that there was no way of knowing. She had not asked for his telephone number on purpose, and he hadn't offered to give it to her: it would be impossible to call him anyway.

So far she'd relied upon Paolo to take her by the hand and lead her through her first love affair. He knew the rules and she didn't. Obviously 'thou shalt not telephone one's lover at his house,' was one of the golden rules. Deprived of the intimacy of long warm gossipy chats with Paolo, she was left with phone calls to Edwina and Germaine. Her visit to Hilary had been cancelled, and she was relieved. Hiding the fact that she knew that Hilary's husband was screwing Edwina would have made her feel unbearably guilty.

'Mom's fine.' She came back to the present to hear Syracuse excuse her pain with a braying laugh. 'Why don't we call Nanny Barnes and you go have your afternoon nap?'

'I don't wanna . . .' Allegro whined, reaching out for her mother.

'Don't be silly.' Syracuse was immediately jealous. 'Here, I'll let you ring the bell.'

'I want Mom.' Allegro began to scream.

'Allegro, shut up. I don't know why we're paying a shrink. Her behaviour is no better.' Syracuse's voice was beginning to rise.

Normally now, Allegro kept her rages and tantrums for the rest of the household, but today she was beside herself. 'Fuck off,' she screamed.

Syracuse went white. 'Where,' he said, 'did you learn that dirty word?'

'Fuck off, fuck off, Daddy fuck off.' Allegro was now delighted.

'No daughter of mine is going to use foul language in my house.' He raised his hand, but Madeleine caught it just in time. She stared strangely at Syracuse and he backed down.

'Firstly, Syracuse,' Madeleine said coldly, 'this is not your house and secondly, you will never raise a hand to my daughter. *Never*, do you hear?' Her voice frightened Syracuse. He felt as if ice was running through his veins.

The words came out like silver-plated bullets and found their mark.

Nanny Barnes came running into the room. 'What's the matter with my precious?' she crooned. 'Has someone been nasty to you?'

'I haven't done anything.' Syracuse was feeling defensive. 'I've only been trying to discipline Allegro. She's become a brat. A spoiled brat. It's you women; you've ruined her.' He glanced at Madeleine and he realised that she was no longer willing to be bullied. She stood there absolutely expressionless. For a moment he felt as if he was lost in space. 'I'm going out,' he said.

He walked into the hall with dragging footsteps. Maybe if he left her alone on Christmas Eve, Madeleine would be forced to beg for him to come back. But there was no deliverance. Madeleine stood by the tree, her arms crossed, and waited. Allegro was now quiet in Nanny Barnes's arms. Her great green eyes evaluated every move her father made.

He pulled on his thick winter coat. As he approached the heavy front door it swung open, as if an unseen hand was helping him on his way. 'Huh,' he exclaimed. A freezing gust of wind pulled him through the door on to the front doorstep. Then the door closed behind him. Madeleine looked at Allegro.

'You opened the door, didn't you?' Nanny Barnes said. 'Well, I never! Gordon Bennett! I've seen everything now. I must tell Mrs Poole.' She flew out of the room.

Madeleine held out her arms to Allegro. 'Come here,' she said. 'You're a little witch.'

'Nicer without Dad?' She looked questioningly into Madeleine's face.

'It sure is,' Madeleine replied, heaving a sigh of relief. Mother and daughter had a cosy Christmas evening meal beside the fireplace in the informal sitting room. Madeleine toasted the bread for the smoked salmon on a long toasting fork. Allegro, with her tongue between her teeth, applied the fresh mayonnaise.

Upstairs, Mrs Poole and Nanny Barnes were celebrating their own Christmas Eve. 'I don't give their marriage very much longer.' Mrs Poole's eyes were hooded with prophecy. 'I don't know,' Nanny Barnes shook her head. 'But that child is a strange one, to be sure. One minute she's a devil, and the next I forget that I was ever angry with her because she's so enchanting.'

Nanny Barnes sipped her glass of wine. 'D'you reckon she's got somebody else?' Mrs Poole was the acknowledged expert on the subject of matrimony.

'I shouldn't be surprised. She comes in looking so happy these days, and you should see her face when her hubby comes home. Downcast, to say the least.'

'I would be downcast if I had to put up with that toad! Ugh.' Nanny Barnes made a face. 'Imagine having him in bed.'

'No, thank you.' Mrs Poole filled up her glass. 'I'd rather not. I say, do you think we're getting rather tiddly, Hilda?'

'Just a little, Marjorie. But a drop at Christmas time never hurt no one, I always say.' Nanny Barnes acknowledged the sudden intimacy. 'To us. Oh yes, and God Save the Queen. God bless 'er.' They both got unsteadily to their feet.

Mrs Poole said a little woozily, 'I think I'll go and lie down.'

'Likewise,' said Nanny Barnes, and she stumbled out of the room.

'You stupid bastard,' was Lucinda's comment when Syracuse telephoned her from a pay-phone. 'No, I don't want to see you. I hate Christmas and I'm spending it in bed with tranquillisers. I don't want to see anybody or hear from anybody until the day after tomorrow.'

'If you don't let me in, I'll have to spend Christmas in a hotel. I can't go to my friends and tell them I walked out on my family on Christmas Eve. Please, Lucinda, please.'

Lucinda was grinning. 'Fuck off.' She put the telephone down.

Syracuse walked out of the telephone booth and climbed back into his car. Time to take refuge in James's hotel. He'd show Maddie. He'd have a hell of a Christmas and he'd find himself a willing woman. He cursed Lucinda and all women as he drove into the night.

Twenty-eight

❧

'Darling, you're looking very white. Is something the matter?' Dolly looked at her only daughter. 'You're not having marriage problems, are you?'

'Oh, Mom, how did you guess?' Dolly had guessed some while ago. She'd sensed the tension in the house on Christmas Day. Syracuse had arrived in the middle of Christmas dinner with a face like thunder. Ron, seeing his face, had chatted amiably, but Syracuse had just stared down at his plate.

'Dad and I have been worried about you for some time, darling. We think what you both need is to take a break. Have a spring holiday. I hear that Italy is lovely in the spring.' Madeleine's eyes widened. Did her mother know about Paolo? No, she decided she didn't. Only Edwina and Germaine knew.

'Mom, I don't really want to go away with Syracuse. We don't need a break together. I hardly see him anyway. Allegro doesn't even miss him any more, he's away so much. She used to sit by the window waiting for him, but she's realised there's no point. She was six in February; she's ready for school. No, if anything I need to go away for a break myself. I feel as if I've lost the person I once was. A happy, carefree woman who laughed a lot. I feel boring and uninteresting. No, I am seriously thinking of taking myself off to a Caribbean island and just lying in the sun.'

'You know there's no divorce in our family? Never has been.' Madeleine sensed a cold warning in Dolly's voice.

'I know, Mom,' she said miserably. 'I'm well aware of that.'

'There's a good girl. Now you take this money and go out and buy something nice. It's just the blues, that's all it is.'

Dolly reached into her handbag and pulled out a wad of notes. Money for Dolly dealt with all feelings. It had always been that way between them. No delicious sharing of intimacies; but then her mother had nothing to share. She was happily married to one man, played bridge, went shopping and monopolised her hairdresser. So no wonder she had nothing to say.

Madeleine jumped into her car and sped away from her mother's mansion. Dad'd be different, but he was away on a business trip. On impulse, on her way to collect Allegro from Dr Steckel's office, she stopped at her travel agent's and booked herself a week's spring holiday on an island called Little Cayman. She saw the photograph of the island in the window. 'Very, very beautiful,' her travel agent informed her. 'One of the last unspoiled places in the world.'

'Would I be all right with my little girl. I mean, on my own?'

'Sure.' Her agent looked at Madeleine carefully. They were friends from way back. 'Madeleine, is something wrong?' When she accompanied her husband to buy tickets she always looked so lost and miserable.

'Yeah, but I'd prefer not to talk about it for now.' She knew she could trust him and tell him anything. He had always been a shoulder to cry on, but for now she felt frozen with misery. She felt as if a frozen bag of peas had been placed straight from the freezer into her heart. Of course I would think of frozen peas. It's all I do all day. Think about what Syracuse wants to eat, or what he doesn't want to eat – which is most things.

She flinched at the thought of going home tonight and breaking the news that she was going away for a week. She had never done that before. He was bound to be angry.

'OK, honey, you're booked. A week on Little Cayman will straighten you out. Just you see.'

Madeleine walked back to the car. Yes, she thought. A whole week with just Allegro and myself. Not being frightened or shaking when he came to the door. The two of us, just by ourselves. She sighed with the pleasure of it all.

On the way home, she decided to pay a surprise visit to Hilary. At least Allegro enjoyed playing with her two boys. She had stopped by on more than one occasion, but had felt weighed down by the woman's sadness. Now she felt positive about her holiday with Allegro, she decided to share some of that good feeling with Hilary; besides, it would give her something to talk about when Syracuse came home. Now, they had so little to say to each other in the evenings. She tended to go to bed early and leave him watching the television. But she could tell Paolo about her holiday when she saw him on Wednesday afternoon.

She was horrified when she saw Hilary's face. 'What on earth is the matter, Hilary? You've been crying.' Hilary's face was swollen and blotchy.

'I know, Madeleine. Come on in. I'm glad you came. The boys could do with someone to play with them. Jonathan, Justin – Allegro's here.'

Both boys came running into the hall and threw their arms around Allegro. 'Let's go and play kick the can in the garden.'

Madeleine smiled. 'That's just what Allegro needs. She's such a bitch to poor Tarquin, Edwina's boy.'

'Come to the kitchen while I make Peter's supper. We

can talk while I cook.' Madeleine followed Hilary into her kitchen. The place was in chaos. 'Please forgive the mess, darling. I'm just too tired to keep up with it all.' Hilary ran a hand through her lank hair.

'Listen, don't apologise to me, Hilary. I have three staff, and even then I don't get anything right, according to Syracuse.'

'I'm making, or trying to make, Peking duck for tonight. Peter has friends; well, they're not really friends because he doesn't bother with that sort of thing. They're business acquaintances, and actually they bore me to death . . . Damn, I can't get the straw under the skin. I've hung the bloody thing up for twenty-four hours. It's dripped fat all over the place and now I'm supposed to shove a straw up its bum and blow.'

'Sounds fairly obscene to me. Why don't you order a take-away and stick it in the oven and say you cooked it. Nobody would ever know.'

'What a very good idea, Madeleine. But then Peter would know. He checks the kitchen if we have guests. Good heavens, I've got to get cleaned up.' Hilary was running around the kitchen lifting plates and forks and then putting them down in the same place.

'Honey.' Madeleine put a hand on her shoulder. 'Something really big is bothering you, and I'm probably the only person you can tell. New York is a bitch of a place to break into. Let's sit down with a cup of coffee and then we'll both do a blitz on the place, OK?'

Hilary burst into tears. Madeleine steered her to a chair and hugged her gently. 'Now, tell me what it is.'

'I think Peter is having an affair.'

'My dear girl, is that all it is? Listen to me, they all have affairs. When I found out about Syracuse I was devastated, but Germaine steered me through the whole thing. Now I know that six months after Syracuse starts an affair, he has to confess to his mommy. That's me. That's what I am to Syracuse. I'm good mommy and he's nice to me, and if I don't give him exactly what he wants then I'm bad mommy and he throws temper-tantrums.'

'Yes, that's what Peter does, and now I'm away from my family, he thinks he can do anything he likes. He's out all the time, and I sit here after the children have gone to bed going spare with boredom. I can't go out by myself – sometimes it's months before I go out. Anyway, I'm not sure about the affair, but he comes home sometimes in the early hours of the morning and I wonder.'

Madeleine cursed Edwina. Hilary was not fair game for a woman like Edwina. She was an innocent, and Madeleine knew what it felt like to be betrayed. 'If he *is* having an affair, what would you do, in my place?'

Madeleine shrugged. 'I'd chuck him out, Hilary.'

'I will.' Hilary looked a better colour now. 'I'm very homesick for the English countryside and my family and our horses. I thought it might work between the two of us, but it can't. There are too many differences. He likes parties and impressing people, and I'm shy and prefer to stay at home. By the time I've cleaned the house, and chauffeured the boys to and fro from school, and then cooked the evening meal, I'm so tired that all I want to do is to go to bed and read.'

'So do I . . . Listen, I'm off on a week's holiday with Allegro. I know I have some serious thinking to do, and I can't do it with Syracuse around. I've got to get myself together and get rid of him.' Why on earth did I say that, she asked herself. I hadn't even thought of getting rid of Syracuse up till now. She grinned. 'I tell you what, we both dump our husbands together and I'll come back to England with you. I've nothing to do until Allegro goes to school. She's bored stiff in New York, and if I have to see another lion or another wolf in the zoo in Central Park, I'll have a breakdown.' She was relieved to see Hilary smiling.

'That's a deal. Sod this duck.' Hilary glared at the dead bird. 'I can't make Peking sodding duck. I'm hopeless.'

'No, you aren't. You've just been trained to think you're hopeless. Look, throw the Peking idea out, and we'll just dump a jar of marmalade on it and throw some soya sauce at it. Lots of garlic, and there you go. I'll make a chocolate mousse for pudding. Now you get me that cup of coffee.'

She could hear the children whooping and yelling in the back garden. She made the mousse, and soon the coffee-pot was fuming gently to itself. The smell of roast coffee filled the room. 'Ummmmm, there's no smell quite like it . . . I have an Italian friend called Paolo who makes wonderful coffee.' She so loved to say his name. She felt guilty, but she knew she couldn't tell Hilary. If she got involved in the subject of infidelity, all sorts of traps lay ahead. After all, here she sat with the wife of her best friend's lover. What a tangled web indeed.

'Here, I'll pour.' Hilary filled Madeleine's cup.

'Hilary, are you serious about getting rid of Peter?' Madeleine asked.

'Yes, I am. I've had a miserable ten years with him. He's mean and bad-tempered and spoiled rotten. I shan't even tell him that I'm leaving him. I'll go home and write to him from there. I don't want to deal with his anger. He yells so.'

'I know what you mean. I don't know how Syracuse will take the news. He can always move in with the nurse he's sleeping with at the moment. She can probably cope with him better than I ever could . . . My real problem is going to be my mother and father. I think Dad will be all right, but Mom will be wild because of the disgrace in front of all her friends. Mind you, most of them are divorced now.'

They sipped their coffee. A conspiratorial silence fell over the two women. Madeleine smiled at Hilary. 'You look better already.'

'I feel better, Madeleine. I'm so glad you came by. I've been needing to make this decision for a long time.'

'So have I. Sure thing I'll send you a postcard from Little Cayman.'

'OK, and I'll write to my mother and tell her we're going to be in England. When do you want to go?'

'For next Christmas. That will give us time to sort ourselves out; our husbands can hang out and console each other.'

Hilary stood up and held out her hand. 'It's a deal,' she said seriously.

Twenty-nine

❧

'You're going to have to stop your affair with Peter, Edwina. Hilary is suspicious, and besides, she is a really nice woman.'

'Not according to Peter she isn't.'

'Yeah, well, Peter is a rat. Anyway, you're not really interested in him, are you?'

'Nah, I was just bored and he was available. He's not much good in the sack, so if it really bothers you, I'll let him go.'

'He's in for a big surprise. Hilary is going to divorce him.' Madeleine leaned forward. 'And I'm going to get rid of Syracuse.'

'No, really, Maddie! You're going to dump your old man?'

'Yeah, really, Edwina. I felt ten years younger once I'd made the decision. He's such a mean little bastard, and I suppose having Paolo as a lover made me realise just how much I was missing. I can't go on putting up with all Syracuse's crap. His awful messy way of living, and all his horrible habits. No, Hilary is going back to England for Christmas, and I'm going with her. I'll take Allegro. She's just the right age to really enjoy London. The Changing of the Guard, and all that.' Madeleine lifted her glass of white wine. 'Here's to my new life, Edwina – *senza* Syracuse.'

'Maddie, you don't somewhere in your secret heart think that because you're getting rid of Syracuse, Paolo will get rid of his wife and marry you?'

'No, honestly, I don't. I know your rules. The first:

never telephone your married lover at home; and the second: married men almost never leave their wives.' Madeleine knew she was lying, but she heard herself fluently protesting the truth. 'I suppose the third rule ought to be that all women having affairs with married men secretly believe that their men will love them enough to leave their wives eventually?'

'That's the fifth rule. The last rule was the fourth. No postcards, remember?' Edwina was picking at her omelette. They were not at their usual restaurant. Edwina had found this little French place off the Rockefeller Plaza. She had been buying summer clothes. Paolo was back in New York, and had made an appointment to see Madeleine at three o'clock. Now she was no longer nervous before seeing him. They had shared enough time together to make their relationship seem substantial. She wondered what he would say when she told him she was going to divorce Syracuse. More to the point, what Syracuse would do when he found out.

'You know, Edwina, I think I'll make an effort and find out where his little nurse lives. If I'm going to get rid of him, I need a good reason. I know he takes her away with him on his weekend business trips. All I need to do is check his hotel. Dad's secretary can do that for me. She can give me the bill, and then I'll have a good excuse to throw him out. The problem with Syracuse is that he pretends to be so perfect. I need an excuse to placate my mother. She doesn't like him, but divorce hasn't happened in our family, and Mom behaves as if it's worse than a venereal disease.'

'I know what you mean. If my Dad ever caught Scott cheating on me, he'd kill him. My Dad, God rest his soul, was a real back-woodsman. He always packed a gun, and Scott was shit-scared of him. They don't make men like my Dad any more. Anyway, honey, I've got to run.'

Madeleine checked her watch. 'OK, I'll go over to Paolo's place and wait for him there. Oh, Edwina, loving a man who is married is terribly complicated. I'm not used to all the lying and sneaking about.'

'That's part of the fun, hun.'

'It's not for me. I don't enjoy any of it. I like life to be clean and simple. Not devious and delinquent.'

'Grow up, Maddie. Remember you're not a little girl any more, and life out there is cruel and evil.'

'I hope I'm not cruel and evil, Edwina; I know Paolo isn't. He's just not very happily married, that's all.'

'None of them are, Maddie. There is no such thing as a man who thinks he's happily married. They're all six-year-olds with big dicks, that's all.'

'Edwina, you're so cynical. Sometimes I wonder how you survive.'

'Don't worry about me, Madeleine. It's you I worry about. You're such a nincompoop!'

Madeleine hugged Edwina and raced for a cab. She waved at Edwina out of the window, and watched the slim, elegant figure of her friend disappear down the road.

She put Paolo's key in the lock of the apartment and took a deep breath. She so much enjoyed being in his apartment when he wasn't there. She wandered around the sitting room, catching up on his invisible life that he did not share with her. New flowers in the vase on the big television. How she wished she could spend her evenings curled up beside him watching the television. No, that pleasure was for his wife. A wife who hardly ever left Siena. Unlike Edwina, Madeleine didn't wish to discuss his wife and children with him – ever. Edwina, she knew, haunted the other woman in any relationship she had with a married man. She followed Hilary all the way to the boys' school. Madeleine had been embarrassed at her revelations. 'But why, Edwina?' she'd exploded.

'It makes it so much more exciting, Madeleine. What's she like? Am I as good in bed? Of course they all say yes. I'm the best they've ever had. Lying bastards.'

Madeleine thought about this conversation as she wandered around the sitting room. She went into the kitchen and checked the pots of herbs. The basil came from Siena. What must Siena be like, she wondered. From Paolo's description it must be a beautiful city. He talked of it with such love. His *contrada* – parish – was that of the dolphin. How marvellous to feel yourself bound by such a beautiful creature. He told her about the fountain where he was baptised. He explained that Siena was subdivided into seventeen slices, like a big pizza; those seventeen slices were the *contrade*. 'All Sienese,' he said solemnly, 'are born, married, live and die for their *contrada*. That is what makes Siena such an exceptional city. Florence is nothing compared to Siena.' Certainly his love for the city seemed passionate enough. She saw an envelope with an Italian stamp. She picked it up. Hurriedly she pulled out the letter. Her heart was hammering. She recognised the word '*cara*'. She was unable to translate the rest of the letter, but the signature ended with the name Beatrice. So that was the name of his wife. At least, she assumed so. She folded the letter back up again and put it in the envelope. She felt dirty and mean. 'I'm no better than Edwina, but at least she is honest.' She spoke the words out loud.

She heard Paolo's step on the stairs. She ran to the door and opened it. 'Darling,' she cried, and buried herself in his arms. She felt guilty but relieved. Paolo would understand her need to leave Syracuse.

* * *

Later, after they had made love and Madeleine had reassembled herself from the far corners of the earth, she said, 'Why is it I can come so hugely with you and not with Syracuse?'

Paolo rolled over and propped himself on his elbows. 'With each person it is different, *cara*. Your husband is like a very shallow pond. There is no depth to him: that is his problem. While you are like a mill pond. You go down deep, and there seems to be no bottom.' He grinned. 'Not that I can find so far.'

Madeleine took a deep breath and sat up. 'Paolo, I have decided to leave Syracuse . . .' She hesitated. 'Not right away. I'm leaving in a few days for a week with Allegro on a tiny Caribbean island. I need time to think about my life. Ever since I had Allegro, everything has become such a rush. I feel as if I've lost myself, and I need to get myself back. Does that make sense?'

'Yes it does, Madeleine. Coming to America did just that for me. I love my wife and my family, but I need to be here to have time for myself. And, of course, I found you. You make me very happy, Madeleine. You know that?'

'Yes I do, Paolo, but do you think we'll be happy like this for ever?'

'There is no for ever, Madeleine. Learn this in your life. We are not masters of our destiny and we can only live and love from day to day.'

'Oh dear, I don't like the sound of that, Paolo. I like things to be secure and safe.'

'Life is not like that, Madeleine.'

'I know.' Madeleine hugged Paolo. 'I must get dressed and go and collect Allegro. She's at Hilary's house.'

Paolo watched her getting dressed. Now she was no longer shy with him, she dressed casually. He loved her modesty and her vulnerability, and he worried for her. Syracuse wasn't going to go that easily.

Madeleine kissed him on the forehead before she left. '*Ciao*,' she whispered. 'I'll see you when I get back.' He watched her tall figure with its tousled hair leave the room, and he lay back in the bed. She's right to get rid of that bastard Syracuse. Madeleine was the one woman who really had found her way into Paolo's heart. At Christmas he'd entered his own front door expecting to leave his other life behind, but all through Christmas he'd found himself missing her. Beatrice, his wife, had noticed his absent-mindedness. 'Another woman?' she'd enquired. He had smiled back at her. She knew better than to expect an answer to that question.

Thirty

Allegro felt as if she'd always lived on Little Cayman. As the plane came down to land on the tiny runway, she laughed out loud. She had an unrestrained belly-laugh that usually caught people unawares and made them laugh as well. Her infectious gaiety put the six passengers in a good mood.

They were all given a rum punch after they'd landed and the door of the little plane had been pushed open. The heat swept into the plane making Madeleine gasp. She was glad of her blue striped cotton dress, and that she had taken off her light summer coat. Allegro was wearing her usual jeans and a T-shirt. She refused to wear anything else, and Madeleine had long ago decided to let Allegro go her own way. Now Allegro kicked the back of her seat and loudly sucked her Coca-Cola through a straw. She finished the drink and heaved a sigh. 'Mom, it's beautiful.'

Madeleine's thoughts were far away. She wondered how Hilary was coping. She loved Peter very much. It was different for Madeleine. Syracuse had been such a pain in the neck for so many years that she knew getting rid of him would hurt, but the pain would be more like a toothache than a heartache. And she had Paolo. For Hilary it would definitely be a heartache. Still, they would be together when the final break came, and for now she resolved to write her a postcard as soon as they got to the hotel.

Madeleine glanced at the four other passengers. Two middle-aged women and a young couple. Probably the young couple were on their honeymoon, she guessed. Well, she too had once been that happy. Sadly it hadn't lasted, but then there had been many good times, she consoled herself as they followed the tour guide into the hotel. Her bag was weighed down with novels, and she had brought a book of Auden's poetry as well to read on the beach. Allegro had a copy of *Swallows and Amazons* with her, and also had an ambition to find herself a Cayman Island parrot, so she could imitate George, her best friend in her Enid Blyton books. Madeleine was glad to see her looking so calm and relaxed.

They changed into their bathing suits and carrying towels, walked down to the beach to swim. Madeleine carried two masks and snorkels. The water was warm and clear. Gently Madeleine sank into the waves. Beside her Allegro lay spread-eagled on the top of the water. Tiny fish encircled their legs. Allegro giggled. Madeleine could hear the sound under water. 'Come here, little fishes, I want to talk to you.'

Madeleine noticed that, within a few minutes, Allegro was surrounded by fish. A quorum of blue and green striped parrot-fish danced around her. Two superior black angel-fish swept by. They were certainly not entranced by a little girl emitting waves of light. Allegro, as she swam, could see all her vital electrical energy discharging into the water. She lay still with her hands and legs outstretched. A moment of utter peace stole over her. So much of her time she felt bored and frustrated, but for now everything was perfect. She raised her head from the water and smiled at her mother. Green eyes blazed into the dark eyes.

She really understands, Madeleine thought wonderingly. Allegro senses everything I think and feel. She reached out in the water and pulled Allegro to her, laughing and splashing.

Later they made their way back to the hotel. Lunch was set out on the patio there. The softly scented wind blew the smell of hibiscus and oleander among the tables. Their table was set with a big pink queen conch-shell in the centre of the table. The waitress was a pretty dark-haired girl. 'We have turtle soup, swordfish steak or coconut-fried grouper.' Her voice was gentle and singsongy.

'I'll try the coconut-fried grouper. How about you, Allegro?'

'Oh, the poor turtle.' Allegro's eyes filled with tears. 'Why do you eat turtle on this island?'

'We only catch a few turtles, just for eating. We protect all our turtles very carefully.'

'Good.' Allegro smiled through her tears. 'What's your name?' she enquired. 'Sarah,' the girl smiled back. 'I have a brother called Dameon. He is your age, I think. Do you want him to come and play with you this afternoon?'

Allegro nodded. 'Yes,' she said beaming. 'Mom, I'm going to like this island.'

'I'm glad, darling. We both needed a break.'

'From Dad?' The question was direct, and Allegro's eyes fastened on Madeleine.

'Yes,' Madeleine said, 'from Dad.' Now the subject was out in the open. It was far too early to tell Allegro of her plan to divorce Syracuse, but at least the ice had been broken and no more lay dangerously covering the pond. As they ate, Madeleine felt the dark water draining away inside her. Her skin was freckled with large crystals of salt. The sun beat down on her back. She felt tired all of a sudden. Only that special tiredness that assaults people who live in a frenetic city like New York. Boston was a different kind of tiredness. London, too. But for now all she wanted to do was to sleep.

Allegro, busy with her new friends, would give her plenty of time to rest. To take a book down to the beach and to lie exposed to the sun like a lover. She wondered what Paolo was doing. He was in Siena for the week. She hoped he was missing her as much as she missed him. But she rather doubted it. On the way to the beach earlier she had bought a postcard for Hilary and one for Edwina. She remembered all too well the rule that you cannot send postcards to a married man. Life for star-struck lovers was full of complications. As she dozed off she could hear the sounds of Allegro and Dameon playing on the beach.

Madeleine awoke to the shrieking of parrots. For a moment she lay confused, wondering where on earth she was. She heard the suck of the sea on the beach outside her window, and then she smiled. Ah yes, she was on Little Cayman. A tiny, remote speck in the Caribbean ocean. She lay for a moment with her hand flung across the double bed, feeling odd that there was no body lying next to her. All those years she had shared the bed her mother had given her with Syracuse. He had gone away for weeks at a time. But this time it was she who had gone away, and she knew it would be permanent.

She rolled over. She was glad of the lazy, swirling fan over her bed. She couldn't hear Allegro; she must still be asleep next door in their little white-washed cottage. A sense of peace lay across the threshold of the cottage. Madeleine luxuriated in the quiet. Often in her own house there was peace with Syracuse away, but then there was the ever-present promise that he would return. Now she had a whole week on her own with Allegro, and no sign of Syracuse anywhere. She sat up and then got to her feet. She pushed open the bathroom door and stepped out of her nightdress. The shower trickled water. They had been warned that water was in scarce supply but it didn't matter because she pulled on her swimsuit instead and headed off for a swim.

'Darling,' she said, scooping up the sleepy little bundle. 'Do you want to go for a swim?' Allegro nodded, her eyes full of the night's dreams. Madeleine helped her into her swimsuit and together they walked across the hot sand and fell into the water.

The waves rolled over Madeleine, and she felt washed clean by the clear blue water. Years of strain seemed to fall away. She came back up from a dive and blew the water out of her lungs. She dived again and again until she was breathless. Beside her, Allegro was paddling furiously. 'Are you happy, Allegro?' She knew it was a ridiculous question, but she worried that Allegro might be missing her father. Allegro grinned and did a duck-dive. Madeleine relaxed. Allegro was happy and that was really all that mattered. Whatever the future held for both of them, for the moment their lives were safe and secure. It was the feeling of security that was the most fragile. For so many years she had lived on the edge of Syracuse's irritation, and now without him there was still that feeling of staring over her shoulder, wondering when the axe would fall. Only there was no axe. No harsh words, just gentle, smiling island people.

'Come on, honey, let's head for breakfast. I could eat a sea-horse!'

Breakfast was deep purple-skinned papaya with small sharp limes. Allegro ordered scrambled eggs with ackee nuts, fresh orange juice and coffee. Madeleine felt the sting of yesterday's sun on her back, and heaved a huge sigh of relief. The young honeymooners were gazing intensely at each other, and for a moment Madeleine felt a pang of regret. All those years ago she had looked at

Syracuse like that on an island not very far away, and now she was running from him. Well, she consoled herself, if you have to leave a man, there are worse ways of doing it. Having money made it a lot easier. The decision had been made and now it was just the fall-out. Come to think of it, leaving your husband was very like a nuclear explosion. Their separation had been mushrooming for several years now, and what existed between them was a big cloud that needed to clear so that they could each get on with their own lives. Quite what her life would be like she had no idea, but Paolo was still there and would always be there, she told herself firmly. Then his voice intruded. 'Madeleine. Nothing lasts for ever.' She jumped from the table and said, 'Come along, Allegro. Let's go and explore.'

The sun was rising higher, and the heat made the sand hot on their bare feet. The water shimmered and the fringe of the palm trees stood silent. The wide white beach was deserted. Madeleine felt she and her daughter were the only human beings inhabiting this world. It was a strange, lonely feeling, but Allegro at her side seemed unperturbed. She was having an intense conversation with a small crab, which stood its ground and waved its claws defiantly at the child.

'A very good day to you, Mr Crab.' Allegro glanced at her mother. 'Let's take Mr Crab home with us,' she said. She picked up the crab and it nestled into the palm of her hand. Madeleine followed Allegro back to the cottage, where she put her crab in her bucket and ran off to find some seaweed. Life was so uncomplicated when you were a child.

Madeleine sat on the doorstep of the cottage, watching Allegro's distant figure. The feeling of aloneness was still there, and she knew in time to come it would get worse. Now she was no longer a couple with her husband. She was amputated from him and, even if it were not yet a physical fact, internally she had cut the bond and she acknowledged that it hurt.

Madeleine made no attempt to make friends with anyone, except the little waitress and her brother, Dameon. The little girl was called Sarah, and she was free after she served the afternoon tea at four o'clock. Madeleine was enchanted at the very Englishness of the island. She enjoyed sitting behind her pretty Victorian tea-pot and watching Allegro tuck into her muffins with English clotted cream. Dameon joined them for all their meals, and by the fourth day Allegro was brown and her eyes burned with pleasure. After dinner, Madeleine usually walked along the edge of the sea, with Allegro savouring the solitude. Bent almost double, she searched for seashells. She collected handfuls of them at a time. She knew she couldn't take them all home, but one she kept. It was a bright pink shell. In her palm, it made her feel as if she held her own heart in front of her. Very thin lines traced their way along the shell; it lay so open and so vulnerable. While Madeleine knew she must now leave Syracuse, a feeling of failure almost overwhelmed her. She who had always been so meticulous about promises and vows was going to break her wedding vows. She had promised to love this man, her husband, until the day he died. She had promised to take care of him for better or for worse. That was the failure. She no longer wanted to take care of him; and he had certainly never taken care of her.

The pain sometimes drove her to roam the island, sometimes riveted her to a chair on her pretty little porch. She let it wash over her like the ripples of the sea. She listened to the cries of the sleepy birds and the hooting of the night-owls. Finally she addressed Dr Stanislaus.

'Am I doing the right thing, Dr Stanislaus?' she asked fearfully. Behind her Allegro was sleeping. Since the first day or two she had not mentioned her father. She had played for hours in the sea and had really enjoyed Dameon's company. He was an uncomplicated little boy who could swim out to the reef with Allegro furiously dog-paddling behind him. 'What do you think, Dr Stanislaus?' She heard the soft hoot of an owl nearby, and then she blinked. The owl was sitting on the chair next to her.

'You have to leave your pest of a husband, my dear. He is no longer in the plan for Allegro. Of course, you will let him see her from time to time. Like most men, he'll find another woman to take care of him, and then you won't hear from him again.'

'Is he going to marry the nurse he's screwing?' Madeleine tried not to feel jealous. After all, she didn't want him, so it didn't much matter what he did with his time.

'I can't tell you that, Madeleine. It's his path and for him to discover. If I let you see into the future, you might alter your path. All I can say is that you can let your marriage go. After all, it has been spluttering to an end for a long time now. When you are near him, the colours you give off are turgid, to say the least. You have your Italian lover and he will comfort you.' Dr Stanislaus twitched his beak. He couldn't tell Madeleine about the pain that lay ahead of her, and that made him feel uncomfortable. Oh, dear human beings, with their insane need to be loved. All such a waste of time, really.

'Will I marry Paolo?' She knew she shouldn't ask, so she bit her lip waiting for the reply.

'You know your own rules, my dear. What is your second rule?'

'Married men don't ever leave their wives. But some must, Dr Stanislaus.'

'Yes,' he agreed. 'Some do, but it is very rarely happy. We men are very poor creatures compared to women. Just look at your aura now.'

'I can't see people's auras like Allegro can. She is always describing people in terms of colours or smells. Can you help me to see my own colours?'

'Certainly, it's the least I can do for you at this very difficult time.' He put his claw on Madeleine's arm. 'There. I have given you the ability to see not only your own colours, but also other people's. When Allegro is asleep tonight, you go for a swim; that will be the beginning of your learning to see properly. Now, I must rush. I have a lot to do.' The old owl with the withered right foot gave a soft hoot and noiselessly took to the air.

Madeleine watched the bird with a now-familiar sense of the absurd. She was still not quite sure if this part of her life was not something purely imagined by her over-active brain.

She tucked Allegro up in her bed, kissed her goodnight and said, 'I'm just going for a swim, darling. I'll be right in front of the cottage, so if you need me just come down to the water's edge.'

She pulled on her bathing suit, and discovered her fingers were twitching with excitement. She ran lightly down the beach and walked into the sea. The night was lit by a vast galleon of a moon. She hung over the sea, sending rays of light into the water. Standing with the warm sea lapping at her toes, Madeleine threw herself into the water. She chose a particularly wide beam of moonlight. Then it happened.

She found herself emitting streams of electric blue lights from her fingers and toes. A bright red stream of light shot from her navel, and there were green flares coming out of her sides. She rolled over and over in the water. The colours spun and chased her. She felt an enormous sense of excitement building inside her and then, as she finally lay on top of the water, she saw a wide pool of gold surrounding her. She lay pulsing with energy and then, quite suddenly, she disappeared. It was only for a swift second but she left her fleshy body and became a particle of the light, a yellow stream of bubbles. She rocked on wave after wave of pure energy, and knew now what bliss was. The closest she'd ever been to this experience before was when she was making love with Paolo. This feeling, though, was beyond all ecstasy. It was spiritual and sensual and also eternal. She came back to earth and saw Allegro standing on the shore. All around her daughter she saw the same flashing lights. 'Allegro,' she called. 'Come and join me.'

Allegro fell into the sea and began to swim. 'I can see your lights, Mom, and now you can see mine.'

'I can, darling, and they are wonderful.' Allegro curled up in her mother's arms, and Madeleine rocked her in the sea. Finally spent with chasing colours, they walked back to the house hand in hand.

Thirty-one

❧

Madeleine almost rather regretted that she could see auras when she walked into her house. She held Allegro's hand for protection. Syracuse was standing in the hall and she could see black and dark violet clouds swirling around his shoulders. His face was amiable and smiling, but she knew that inside he harboured great anger against her. The purple was the give-away clue. She kissed him lightly and said, 'Hello, darling, we've had a wonderful time. Haven't we, Allegro?' The words 'without you' hung between them. The words were ice-cold blue.

'Yes, Daddy.' Allegro hugged Syracuse, but Madeleine could see little patches of doubtful pink around Allegro's face. She realised that Allegro was frightened of Syracuse's moods. For a whole week they had been together without a cross word or a shadow to disturb their happiness. The night before they'd left, Madeleine had stood in the warm water and gazed out to sea. 'I have to do it,' she whispered. 'If not for my own sake, then for Allegro's. Our lives must move on. We can't be stuck in this Syracuse-shaped rut, where nothing happens for days and months on end except that I service him and Allegro entertains him.'

Standing now beside her husband, she realised how very frightened of him she was. For years she had simply absorbed all the bitterness of his fury. Now the break had taught her a great truth. She had the right to live in peace. She had the right to her own feelings and her own words. He had no right to take away her peace or to continually correct her and finish her words for her. Even if she had not talked to anyone on the island except the two children, she had so enjoyed their eager, wide-eyed company. She knew that, had she been there with Syracuse, there would have been no time for the children. Just endless drinks with other Americans, and loud sulks as soon as he didn't get his way. She was trembling with anxiety. She so much wanted to see Paolo.

'Could you take the suitcases upstairs, Syracuse? I must go and see Mrs Poole and Nanny Barnes. I have presents for them both, and one for Cook.'

'Pooley can carry the suitcases. That's what I pay her for.' Syracuse's face was set. 'Anyway, I'm going out and I'll be back tomorrow after work. A sudden appointment. I'm sorry.' Madeleine felt a flash of sadness that things between them had become so bad. She realised in a second that mostly she felt relief. Now she could telephone Paolo this evening from home instead of roaming about the streets looking for a pay-phone.

'OK, have it your way. I'll carry the suitcases.'

'Sure, you're a big girl now. You can carry your own suitcases.' His familiar jeering tone intimidated her.

'Sure I can, Syracuse.' She walked up the stairs feeling the weight of both bags. It's ridiculous to hang on to a husband just because he occasionally carries the groceries and the suitcases for you. She smiled grimly. Well, after he was gone, she'd do all that sort of thing herself, as she was doing now.

'Daddy, we're going to London next Christmas with Hilary and the boys.'

There was a moment of stunned silence, and then Madeleine broke the ice. 'I was going to discuss our trip with you tomorrow, but as Allegro jumped the gun, I'll tell you now.'

'I don't want to discuss anything with you, Madeleine. You've given yourself the right to do anything you want. To go off on holiday without me, and to remove my daughter without so much as a by-your-leave. That's fine by me. I'll spend Christmas elsewhere.' He walked out, slamming the door behind him.

Nanny Barnes and Mrs Poole were in the kitchen when Allegro went running ahead of Madeleine down the long corridor. 'He's off to see his little tart, and Madam's only just come home.'

'Just as well, I think.' Marjorie Poole's face was pink with disgust. 'I'm sick of his awful table-manners. He eats like a pig. Now at least life will go back to normal.'

'Nanny Barnes, Nanny, look what I've brought you!' Allegro threw herself into Nanny Barnes's arms.

'My but you both look so well!' Nanny Barnes hugged Allegro.

Madeleine kissed both women and laughed. 'It was all unbelievably beautiful. I really didn't want to come back.'

'Look at your present, Nanny, I chose it myself.' Allegro pulled off the wrapping paper and deposited a black coral necklace with matching earrings in Nanny's hand.

'How beautiful, darling. Thank you.' Nanny Barnes hugged Allegro.

'I got a Cayman Island T-shirt for you, Mrs Poole.' Allegro pulled out a florid shirt covered in palm trees. 'Lovely, darling.' Mrs Poole was laughing. Madeleine felt glad to be home now. Glad to be with these warm, supportive women. Eager to see Paolo and tonight to hear his voice.

'I'm afraid that my husband won't be in tonight. It will just be us.' She realised that she fooled no one.

'That's all right, madam. I've ordered your favourite

dinner.' Mrs Poole was gracious. Madeleine knew also that, even if Syracuse could no longer hurt her, he could humiliate her, and that was almost worse. It was the pity in both women's faces that she found hard to bear. 'I'll go and find Cook and give her her present.' She spoke lightly, trying to breathe deeply to ease the hurt. Her stomach was churning.

On the way to find Cook, Allegro dashed off to watch television. There had been no television on the island, but neither of them had missed it. 'Cook, I got you an apron with a big grouper on it.' She handed the apron over to Cook, who smiled. 'Welcome back, madam. It was so quiet without the two of you. Mr Winstanley was hardly home at all, except for meals.'

'Yes, I gather he had a lot of business to attend to.' Cook, she knew, was unaware of Syracuse's women, not party to the other two women's knowledge. Madeleine felt comforted by her round, beaming face.

Most women understand sub-texts in a way that men cannot. Women can always read the lines between the lines. Men live only on one level. Not all men, she corrected herself. Paolo was also capable of understanding at a very deep level, but then he was special. Very special, she told herself, as she went upstairs to unpack her bags and to change her clothes. Her island clothes looked so incongruous when they arrived at the airport in New York, but she didn't care. She wanted to keep the island with her until the very last minute.

'Edwina?' It was nine o'clock and Allegro was in bed.

'Have you had a good time?' Edwina's voice was light and teasing.

'It was absolutely marvellous, Edwina. I've got so much to tell you. I've come to a momentous decision. Before I left I thought I *should* leave Syracuse, but now

I know I *have* to. Can I come round for coffee after I've dropped Allegro off for school? Is that OK?'

'Sure, and Paolo telephoned to ask when you were back. He said he'd telephone again tomorrow. I'll tell him you'll be round for coffee.'

'No, it's OK, I can ring him tonight. Syracuse has gone off to sleep with the nurse. I don't like telephoning him from here, but I must hear his voice. I missed him dreadfully. Do you think he missed me, Edwina?'

'Yeah, I expect so, but men tend to compartmentalise their relationships. You know — sort of, out-of-sight-out-of-mind kinda thing.'

Madeleine felt her spirits sag. 'Really, Edwina?'

'Yeah really, Maddie. I told you, stop being such a baby. A week on an island doesn't seem to have done much for your maturity level.'

'No, I spent it with a girl of twelve and Allegro and her little friend. Speaking of little friend, how's Tarquin?'

'He's fine — and Allegro?'

'She was wonderful, no trouble at all. I think she'll settle down once we're on our own. We're both scared of Syracuse; that's what I realised when we had a whole week together away from him.'

When Madeleine put down the telephone, she poured herself a gin and tonic. On the island she had stuck to rum punches served in fresh coconut shells, and wine. Now the gin was gentle on her tongue, and she noticed how long it took for the ice to melt. On the island it melted instantly in the heat. She lifted the telephone with trembling hands. She dialled his number, but there was no answer. She put the telephone down and poured herself another drink. 'Funny,' she thought. 'I used to sit here and cry with loneliness, and now I'm no longer lonely.'

'He's a married man,' ticked the clock. 'Don't set your hopes too high.'

'You know what married men are like. You're married to one yourself,' whispered the big aspidistra. 'Really, woman, you are too silly.' The aspidistra was well aware of its Victorian origins, and didn't approve of this sort of thing at all. Men had affairs with other women, and women stayed home and looked after their children. That, after all, was the proper order of things. Madeleine finished her gin and grinned. She was getting really addicted to the stuff. She wandered woozily off to bed.

Thirty-two

❦

'I guess married women get taken out to lunch by married men. I mean, that is if you're not married to them.' Madeleine knew she wasn't making any sense, but she was feeling gloomy. Syracuse had stayed out as he had promised and she'd woken up feeling alone and insecure. Why was she throwing away a marriage? Was she in the grip of a madness? But then she reminded herself of the week on the island without him. That, she'd told herself that morning as she'd pottered about the bedroom and the bathroom, is really living. Life with Syracuse was about existing. Now she stared at her two old friends.

'Sure,' Edwina agreed. 'Don't you notice that restaurants are always filled with couples talking furiously to each other at lunch-time, and in the evening they are full of people who are not talking to each other? Those are the married couples.'

Madeleine made a face and smiled at Germaine. 'Yeah, I guess I did notice that Syracuse and I are definitely one of the couples who sit in restaurants in the evenings trying to find something to say to each other. When Allegro was a baby we could manage a conversation on her poops, or whether we had our burping routine off-pat, but now ... We can't even manage that.' Madeleine was waiting like a whippet on a racetrack for the telephone to ring.

'Anyway, darling,' Germaine gazed at Madeleine, 'you look terrific. The island sounds wonderful.'

'It was, Germaine. I want to go back with someone I

love. It's the sort of place that lovers should visit, and just walk hand in hand along the beautiful beaches.'

'You're thinking of Paolo, aren't you, Maddie?'

'Yes, I guess so.'

Edwina shook her head. 'You don't get weeks away on Caribbean islands with men like Paolo. He's not like men here, who take risks. If they're American or English, they can always bunk off if their wives find out. Italian couples have different rules, and neither side ever risks getting found out. So you might get a weekend away, but that's about it.'

'Well, I guess I'll just have to be grateful for what I have. Anyway, I decided when I was alone for that week with Allegro that I want to get rid of Syracuse for good.' She hadn't yet told Germaine of her decision. 'I can't go on being this unhappy, Germaine. I know you've said to put up with him for Allegro's sake, but it's not worth it. We're both miserable. When she was younger he spoiled her as long as she absolutely adored him. Now she's six and goes to school and has a life of her own, he gets snappy and nasty to her, just as he does to me.'

Germaine gazed at Madeleine. 'Well,' she said after a pause, 'I guess you know best. And, after seeing what a week away has done for you, I can't say I blame you. I know that I could never share my life again with a man. I'm too set and too selfish now. I love my peace and my quiet. I awake to the sound of the boats and the gulls and I lie in bed just waiting for the moment when my coffee-machine lets out a belch and the wonderful smell of coffee hits the air.'

Edwina let out a dry, rusty little laugh. 'The only thing that belches first thing in the morning in our apartment is Scott. Still, at least he gets up and makes me a cup of coffee. The damn fool thing is I'm so fucking grateful for a cup of coffee in the morning, I put up with him. Why oh why are women such fools?'

'If we knew the answer to that, Edwina—' Germaine wasn't smiling now – 'we could change the world.'

'I think it will take Allegro's generation to get things really changed. We opened the cracks and peered into the can of worms. Now they have got to take the lid off the can.'

'They'll just find bigger worms, darling.' Edwina stood up and then the telephone rang. She grinned at Madeleine. 'Why don't you answer it, honey. Hopefully it'll be Paolo for you.'

Madeleine nodded. She was speechless with fright. What if he didn't love her any more? What if he didn't want to see her? Of course he did, that was why he was ringing.

It seemed to take ages for her to reach the table, and when she finally did, her hand was trembling. 'Hello,' she said uncertainly.

'Is that you, *cara*?'

'Oh, Paolo, is that really you?'

'*Sì*, it is, and I can't wait until I see you again. Oh Madeleine, I really missed you, *amore mio*. How was your trip?'

'It was wonderful, but I didn't send you a postcard because I was afraid someone might see it.'

'You're learning, Madeleine.' The words 'in case a friend of your wife's saw it' remained hanging in the air. 'Anyway, Madeleine, do you want to have lunch with me tomorrow? I can cancel everything and we can lunch here in my apartment?'

'I'd love that, Paolo, I really would. I have a present for you too. Nothing that you have to hide,' she said hurriedly. 'It's just a pretty shell I found, and I thought of you.' She wasn't going to add that she thought of him almost all the time she was there. Nor would she ask how much time he spent thinking about her. Probably not much, but then she was so relieved just to hear his voice, she no longer cared about all the difficulties and complications. She just wanted to lie in his arms and listen to his deep, gentle laugh. She was good at making him laugh, whereas she had failed for so long to even make her husband smile.

She put the telephone down and walked back to the table in the dining room. She sat down and stared dreamily at Edwina. 'So this is what it's like to be in love with a married man.'

Edwina put her hand on Madeleine's arm. 'No, not really. This is what it's like to be in love with Paolo. This is the first time for you and you're very bowled over by the whole thing. Wait until you're a hardened *femme-fatale* like me. You get to know the do's and don'ts. You quit losing sleep and you just take the bastards as they come.'

'Paolo's not a bastard.'

'Honey, before you get badly hurt, just remember all men are bastards. It's in their genes. I've told you that lots of times.'

'Edwina.' Germaine's voice was gentle. 'You know you don't mean that. Not all men are anything of the sort; it's just that if a good, kind, honourable man offered you his hand, you'd bite it off with boredom.'

'Yeah, I guess you're right.' She finished her coffee. 'It's time for us married women to do the school run. I love Tarquin to bits, but all this driving around New York drives me nuts.'

'When he's grown up and has kids of his own, it will all seem worthwhile, Edwina. I'm sorry I didn't have kids. That's the one thing I really miss in my life. Is it

OK, Madeleine, if I come with you to collect Allegro? I haven't seen her since she got back.'

'Sure, and then we can go to Hilary's house. I've got presents for her and the two boys.' She gazed uncertainly at Edwina.

'Don't worry, I dumped him, Maddie.' Edwina stretched. 'I'm seeing Scott's tennis coach. He gets to shout at Scott on the tennis court and to screw me in Scott's bed. Not a bad life, I'd say. I'll talk to you later, Maddie.'

'I expect Syracuse will be there.' Madeleine made a face.

'OK, women's code then.' Edwina grinned. 'Poor Syracuse doesn't stand a chance against us.'

Madeleine realised as she left Hilary's house that she really didn't want to see Syracuse. Normally she would have discussed the matter with Hilary, but Germaine was there and it seemed unfair to have a 'husband discussion' with Germaine present.

Allegro had a ring of jam around her mouth and seemed happy and cheerful. She kissed Germaine. 'I had a lovely time with Mom, Germaine. I didn't want it to stop.' Germaine heard the statement in the child's voice that made her realise Allegro too had found peace and happiness without her father present.

Madeleine discovered that now she was back she was no longer able to see her lights quite so clearly. Just a flicker on a passer-by, but the marvellous aurora borealis was no longer there.

'Can you always see lights, Allegro?' she enquired.

'No, only when I want to. It's like my light by my bed. I turn it on and off. Anyway, today we talked about my island in class and I showed the other children just where it was. Will we go back there one day, Mom?'

'Dr Stanislaus gave me permission to see auras,

Germaine,' she explained. 'It is a marvellous feeling, especially if you can see your own colours.' It was wonderful to know that Germaine understood that strange part of their lives together. 'Honey, I promise we will go back. We'll take Germaine with us too, so she can swim with her colours.' She made the promise easily because she realised that to take Paolo would just be an impracticable dream.

When they got home, Madeleine saw Syracuse's car parked in the drive. 'Damn,' she muttered. She'd hoped to get home first and get changed for the evening. Now he would be in the bedroom waiting to talk to her. More likely to lecture her. She bit her lip and was surprised to find that she must have been unconsciously chewing on the inside of her cheek; it was sore. She stopped the car and leaned across Allegro to open the door.

'Don't be scared of him, Mom,' Allegro's face was anxious. 'Your colour's all gone green.'

'I'll try not to be scared, honey. You go first and put him in a good mood.' She opened the door and Allegro got out.

'Dad, where are you?' Allegro ran up the stairs and Madeleine followed her, stifling the sense of guilt at using her daughter to placate her husband. She followed the child up the stairs and into the bedroom, where Syracuse lay on the bed, fully clothed, with an unsmiling face.

'We're home, Dad.' Allegro flung herself on to her father's chest.

Syracuse put his arms protectively around his daughter. 'Where the hell have you been?'

'I've just dropped Germaine off at the underground station, and we've had tea with Hilary, darling.' Madeleine leaned over the bed and kissed Syracuse on the mouth. His lips trembled with annoyance. 'Well, I hope we have something decent to eat for dinner, Maddie?'

'I'll go down and check with Cook.' Madeleine left the room and ran down the stairs. 'Shit,' she muttered. She'd forgotten to order dinner that morning, she'd been in such a rush to get to Edwina's to wait for Paolo's telephone call. 'What's for dinner, Cook?' she asked breathlessly.

'Jamaican pease and rice, like my mother taught me all those years ago on the islands.'

'Thank goodness, Sentinella. Syracuse really likes that dish. What have we got for dessert?'

'Key lime pie.'

'You're an angel, Sentinella. You've saved my hide.'

Madeleine hurried back upstairs. 'Jamaican rice and pease, darling, followed by key lime pie.'

'That sounds OK.' Syracuse was slightly mollified. He liked it when his wife was flustered on his behalf. Anyway, he wanted to screw her. He rather liked the tan she'd picked up. 'I'll pour you a glass of wine, Maddie. You get changed and join me in the library. And you, little lady . . . Off to the nursery you go. We grown-ups need to spend some time together.'

Allegro watched her mother's aura shoot despairing green flames upon hearing those words. 'Can't I stay up for dinner with you, Dad? I haven't seen you for a whole week.'

'No, off to find Nanny Barnes now. I'll take you out for a hamburger, just you and me, at the weekend. OK, princess?'

Allegro looked over her shoulder as she left the room. She held her mother's eyes and transmitted the thought: Not long and we'll be gone. She knew Madeleine had picked up the thought by the smile on her face. She ran off feeling slightly happier, but later that night, when she tried to pass white, happy light to her mother upstairs in the bedroom with her father, she couldn't succeed. There was a wall against the light, and she knew that the wall had been built by her father.

Thirty-three

By now, making love with Syracuse had just become a matter of allowing him to wrestle with her body. She tried to find some pleasure in the event, but she could find none. The sad thing was that he was beginning to realise that she was bored by his love-making.

'What is it, Maddie? Am I doing something wrong?' he whispered to her as he moved backwards and forwards inside her.

'No, Syracuse, you're not doing anything wrong. I just don't feel like making love, that's all.'

'Well, couldn't you pretend? Most women do.'

'Do they, Syracuse? I'm not most women.'

Syracuse sighed and removed himself from his wife's body. Madeleine felt as if she had been allowed to return to herself. 'You make no attempt to put yourself out for me. Other women want me, you know, Maddie. I don't *have* to stay with you.'

'No, you're quite right, Syracuse. You don't *have* to stay with me.' Madeleine sat up. She could see the white mark where the swimsuit had guarded her breasts from the rays of the Caribbean sun. She stretched out her legs; they were dark in contrast to her belly, which gleamed whitely. Syracuse reached over and stroked her pubic hair. She winced as he stroked her between her legs. 'Don't you feel anything for me, Maddie?'

'I'm afraid not, Syracuse. I haven't for quite a while. I've tried not to say anything, hoping it was just a bad patch such as all marriages go through, but I don't think this *is* just a bad patch. I think our marriage is dead and over.' She was surprised. She had not intended to have this discussion now. Well, she reasoned, I might as well hold my nose and jump off the Brooklyn Bridge. At least I can't drown in bed. She heard a loud gulp, and then she realised that Syracuse was crying.

'Hold me, darling, I'm frightened,' he whispered.

Madeleine obediently put her arms around him, and then she found she was shaking with rage. 'Why should I fucking hold you, Syracuse? You've spent our married life doing exactly what you pleased. You've screamed and shouted, and terrorised me with your moods whenever you've been crossed. It's me that should be crying, not you.'

She pushed Syracuse away. He lay sobbing into his pillow. 'I'm going into the guest room, and I'm going to have a good night's sleep.'

Madeleine was amazed she was still trembling with rage. Clutching her baby pillow, she slammed out of the room and went into the blue guest room. She climbed into the double bed and gave a sigh of relief. From now on, this is where I am sleeping. No more nights being fucked by a man I don't love. And tomorrow afternoon I'll be with Paolo. She was surprised she did not even feel guilty. Usually Syracuse's easy tears raised wells of pity and compassion in her, but no longer. I suppose this is the beginning of a very long, dangerous road out of my marriage. She would have to negotiate with care; but then she had Dr Stanislaus, whereas Syracuse had no one – or had he? He had his women, and with that thought comforting her she went to sleep.

At breakfast Syracuse was in a foul mood. '. . . And you didn't even comfort me. There I was, begging you for understanding, and you threw me away.'

'Syracuse, Allegro is eating her breakfast, and adults

really shouldn't quarrel in front of their children. Remember what Dr Steckel said.'

'I don't care what the expensive bastard said. You're planning to destroy our marriage, and Allegro should know that.'

Madeleine glanced anxiously at Allegro's face. 'Honey, do you want to go up to the nursery? I'll get Cook to send your bacon and eggs upstairs.'

'No, Mom.' Allegro had her elbows on the table. 'I want to listen to what Dad has to say. Why do you say Mom doesn't want to be married to you, Dad?'

'Because your mother is a bad-tempered woman. She is bossy, Allegro. She wants her own way all the time, and in this life everybody has to share. Do you understand that?'

'Sure, Dad, but Mom shares and she doesn't shout like you do. You shout all the time.'

'I know I do, honey, but it's the only way I can get your Mom to listen. If I ask her nicely, she just does her own thing.'

'I think maybe you'd be better off if you got a house of your own, Dad, and Mom and I lived here; then you could come and visit us.'

'Do you really, honey? I can see your mom has been giving you coaching while you've been away from me. You'd never have said a thing like that a week ago, princess.'

'Mom didn't coach me, Dad. We just had such a good time together, and I want it always to be that way.'

Syracuse jumped to his feet and watched his wife flinch. He threw his napkin on to the table. 'I know when I'm not wanted by my wife and my child. I'm going upstairs to pack, and I'm going to move in with a woman who does love me.' He stood there expectantly.

'You mean the little nurse you picked up in the

hospital?' Madeleine raised her eyebrows. 'Do, my dear, by all means go and live with her: she's just about at your level.'

'You bitch,' Syracuse snarled. His face was livid, and both Madeleine and Allegro could see great flashes of black and red lights dancing about his body. He wondered for a moment if he should hit Madeleine. The relief would be enormous, but then he decided it would prejudice his case; he was going to need her as a financial ally. 'Tell your father I'll be in touch, Madeleine. This will break your mother's heart, but then I don't suppose you care, do you?'

'No, not much any more, Syracuse. There's nothing left to care about.' She watched him as he stormed out of the room. 'I think, Allegro, we'll take the day off and go to the zoo. Would you like that?'

Allegro climbed on to her mother's knee and hugged her. She gazed into Madeleine's eyes. 'Mom,' she said, 'Dad will be happy again one day, but not with us. You make him mad.'

'I know, honey. Don't worry, he will be OK and so will we. Anyway, we're going to England for Christmas, and that's something to look forward to, isn't it?'

'Yeah. Let's go and watch television until Dad's gone, and then we can go and see the elephants. Do you have some buns? My elephant knows that I always sneak her a bun.' She grinned, and Madeleine realised that for Allegro life was not ever going to be as difficult as it was for her. Allegro had different standards of guilt and remorse. Allegro was a more secure child than she had ever been.

Thirty-four

Madeleine headed for the elephant house at the zoo. She found herself running and skipping beside Allegro. 'Wait a minute, honey,' she panted. 'Your old mom can't keep up with you.'

'Yes you can, Mom. Come on, it's only over there.' Madeleine could hear the screaming, trumpeting elephants. The noise enchanted her. Then she saw the big, bat-winged ears of a huge elephant. When they got to the bars of the enclosure, the elephant looked at Allegro. Its little pink mouth with its droopy bottom lip slobbered a welcome to her. The long trunk tentatively snaked its way through the bars, and Allegro handed over the iced bun. The elephant put its head back and fed the bun into its mouth; then, taking a small suck of water from the pool at its feet, it sprayed Allegro gently with water.

'Hey, little girl . . .' An officious zoo attendant bustled up. 'You know you shouldn't . . .'

Allegro turned to him and smiled. Madeleine watched as her little face radiated light. Her hair seemed to glow in the sun, and her emerald eyes shone. The zoo attendant came to a halt as if an invisible bar had been placed across his path.

'Well, I'll be darned,' he said, staring at Allegro. 'I've quite forgotten what I wanted to say.'

The elephant rolled back its trunk like the top of a sardine tin, and let out a roar of laughter. The sound floated across the fall-dusted morning. The wolves and the hyenas agreed with the elephant. The zoo keeper was an asshole, but a little human had got the better of him. The parrots in the parrot houses joined in the din, and for a moment it seemed to Madeleine as if the whole zoo had escaped their captivity and were joyfully free. Allegro slipped her hand into her mother's. Suddenly Madeleine felt the need to be liberated too. 'Let's get out of here,' she said.

They got home later than she'd intended. Madeleine realised that she would have to rush to get to Paolo's apartment on time. 'You go to Nanny Barnes, darling. I've got to go out to lunch, and then I'll be back soon and we can hang out together.' While she'd been at the zoo she had managed to block out the reality of Syracuse's desertion. She was desperate to get to Paolo. He would be able to make sense of the cracking-up of her world. He had so much experience and she had virtually none.

Paolo could calm her and advise her in a way that Edwina and Germaine failed to do. Why, she wondered, did she feel this way about Paolo? Was it because he was a man and she was used to the idea that men were practical and women were intuitive? You chose your girlfriends to share the sorrow and the pain, but then you went to a man who told you what to do? That thought startled her. Yes, that was what she thought about men and women. That was one of the major problems of her marriage. She deferred endlessly to Syracuse because he taught her from the very beginning that she was improvident and impractical. Screw that, she thought, I'll talk to Edwina and to Germaine. Particularly Germaine, who had lived and managed for so long on her own. Paolo might know a lot about screwing women, but come to think of it, he had been serviced first by his mother and then his wife all his life.

She decided as she hurried out of the house that she'd

tell Paolo that Syracuse had stamped off, and leave it at that. As she called a cab, she wondered how the news would affect Paolo. Would he be frightened that she might try to cling to him? Rule number five, or was it six? If you try to cling to a married man, you will find that you are a dead vine. He's there to make love to you and to have a good time. Being a vine support is never on the agenda.

'Paolo?' Madeleine was sitting at the kitchen table, dipping her Tuscan bread into a glass of Rosso di Montalcino. She found herself rather nervous about her next statement. 'I guess I'd better just tell you that Syracuse has left me.' She watched as Paolo's hand imperceptibly hesitated as he stirred his sauce for the pasta. 'I'm not surprised, *cara*. You said you were thinking of leaving him. Are you upset?'

'I don't know, really. I don't know what to feel. I didn't intend for us to split this way. I had planned to negotiate in a civilised fashion. Now he's run off, so I don't really know what to do. Part of me is relieved, and the other half is scared. I mean, how will I manage without him? What do I say to Mom and Dad? I don't even know how much we pay Nanny Barnes and Mrs Poole . . .'

Damn, she thought in despair. I'm doing it. I'm whining like a child.

'You have an accountant?'

'Sure, my dad's accountant works for us too.'

'OK, you get him to pay the bills. That's what accountants are for.'

'It's as easy as that?'

'Bah,' Paolo turned, waving his spatula in the air. 'The practical things are easy. It's the things in here.' He made a gesture over his heart with his free hand. 'This is the difficult part. Now the marriage may be dead, but then there were the good times. You Americans are very different from us. You can throw things away like vows and promises. We are not able to do this in Europe. You don't just marry your woman. You marry her family and she marries yours. You have children who have strong ties; and of course divorce is very difficult and very different: it earns the greatest displeasure of your families and your friends. It is not considered normal to divorce. No, marriage is considered like a business transaction, and you find your happiness on the side, if you are lucky – and with you, *cara*, I *am* lucky.'

Madeleine felt tears welling in her eyes. Just the simple act of appreciation by Paolo made her yearn for some sort of permanence with him, but Edwina's voice reverberated in her ears. 'Married men don't leave their wives for their mistresses. If they do they spend the rest of their lives lamenting the loss of the first wife. Men take vows for life. It's the monastery in them.' Madeleine smiled. 'Thank you, darling. I needed to hear that you loved me, Paolo.'

He came to the table and leaned over her with the bowl of pasta in his hand. 'I've cooked your favourite dish: picci.' She felt her heart lurch. He was always so serious about his cooking, and his love-making. Once she tasted the first mouthful of his dishes and deemed them perfect, he relaxed and became the joking, laughing man she so loved. It was the same in bed. Once he had satisfied her and her limp body proved her satisfaction beyond all shadow of doubt, then he teased her and tickled her and made her laugh. It was the intensity of his need to please her that held her so fast. 'How do you make the sauce taste so rich and deep?' she asked. 'When I make it, it's always so thin and so sour.'

'Ah, a trick from my mother. She always put in a

teaspoon of brown sugar; it takes the edge off the bitterness in the cooked tomatoes.'

Paolo's mother was an archetypal Italian mother. He adored her. She was perfect, and all he looked for in a woman were the qualities that she displayed for her only son. Syracuse, on the other hand, had never known his mother, and had been looked after by two crabbed old aunts. Madeleine didn't know which was worse. The dead, idealised mother-figure that Syracuse invented who allowed him to do as he pleased and then deserted him; or Paolo's mother, very much alive, and a fiend in the kitchen and the *casa*. At least Madeleine felt safe from the shadow of his mother in Paolo's bedroom. Or was she? Did Paolo's mother's face loom over them when they made love?

Certainly there was a beautiful painting of the Virgin Mary being crowned by her beloved son. Hopefully the painting spoke of an idealised love between the mother and her son. The same must be true for Paolo; but then Madeleine checked herself. This moment, she told herself firmly, is out of time. I am not going to be a typical American and analyse the moment into the ground until it becomes so much psychobabble. 'Ummmm, Paolo, this is fabulous,' and she concentrated on putting the picci with its thick serrated edges into her mouth. The after-taste of the sauce on her tongue was perfect. Had she engineered dumping her husband to be free to pursue her lover? She sat watching him and found herself dazed with lust. It was not a feeling she had ever experienced before. 'Shut up,' she warned herself.

'Does it make any difference to you if I'm married or not, Paolo?'

She watched a fine line contract between his eyebrows. A place she so loved to kiss. He hesitated before he answered. '*Cara*, if you were any other woman, I'd try to evade the truth, but you know me so well it is sometimes frightening. Yes, it does make a difference. While you are married to your husband –' she noticed that Paolo very rarely used Syracuse's name. 'While you are married to your husband,' he continued, 'I feel very safe for your future. You and I can have these marvellous times together. We can make love whenever we can find time to be together, but if anything happens to separate us I know you are safe and cared for in your own home. If you leave him . . .' he shrugged. 'Well, then I feel bad for you because I know I cannot take that responsibility. I am committed for all my life to my wife and children.'

There was a silence and a breeze blew between them. For the first time, when they made love, she felt a remoteness. Not from him – he was as ardent as ever – but from within herself. If she left Syracuse, even if she had her father and her mother and her daughter, she would be a woman alone. She struggled to concentrate, but she felt none of the usual sensual pleasure she always experienced when she lay in Paolo's arms. Had he let her down somehow? She knew that it was a ridiculous thought. He had always been clear and honest with her; it was she who changed the rules of the game. But then men were very different to women, weren't they? Edwina always said so.

Madeleine sighed and Paolo stopped moving. She could feel him wilt inside her. 'I'm sorry, Paolo, I'm afraid I'm not much fun to be with today. I'm really sorry.' She realised she was frightened.

'Don't be sorry.' Paolo kissed her eyelids gently. 'Your whole world is changing. Your husband has just walked out on you and of course you are sad. It doesn't matter how bad a marriage is, breaking up is always difficult. It wasn't all bad, your marriage?'

'No, I guess not, but looking back I had to do all the giving. He had to have and do anything he wanted, and if I let him he was OK. If I said no to anything then there were terrible frightening tantrums. He battered me with his moods and his impatience. I learned to worry and to scurry when he was home. I used to shake in the kitchen. I told Cook it was just nerves, but I don't think she was fooled. He always made me feel so ugly and useless. It will take time to get my confidence back. If ever.' She gave a hollow laugh. Now Paolo was lying beside her, holding her gently.

'*Cara*, you have a lot to learn about life. You have really been tucked away inside your unhappy marriage for far too long, you know.'

'I know.' Madeleine hated to hear the childlike tones in her voice. 'But I *can* learn, and I *am* learning. I never realised, for instance, that having an affair with a married man could be so complicated. So I am making a list of rules for women who are thinking of having an affair with a married man. Edwina has told me some, and I've discovered others. The first is that married men don't ever leave their wives, and if they do they spend the rest of their lives talking about their wives and making the second wife feel second best. The postcard one I've told you about. No point in birthday presents or Christmas presents because he has to hide them. Married men to take their mistresses out to lunch and their wives out to dinner. What about going away for the weekend, can we do that?' Madeleine was surprised that she'd asked that question. It had just popped up.

'I'd love to wake up one morning beside you, instead of having to sneak back into my house and have a hot bath and change my clothes so I don't smell of your aftershave.'

'Would you really like to go away for a weekend?'

234

Paolo was lying back on the bed with his arms cradled behind his head.

'Sure, I'd love it. What is the tackiest, most mistressy hotel you know in America?'

'Let me see,' Paolo was smiling. 'I think it is the Fontainebleau Hotel in Miami. It is the most amazingly wonderful hotel, and in exquisite bad taste. I love it there.'

'OK, how about you take me there one weekend?'

'It's a deal, honey, as they say in America. We can eat stone crabs in Joe's restaurant.'

'What's a stone crab, Paolo?'

'The fishermen pull out crabs from their nets, tear their claws off, and throw them back in again, and the claws grow back again. They're absolutely delicious if you can forget you've been guilty of amputating the poor things. I can forget very quickly. *Mama mia.*' He kissed the end of his bunched fingers.

'Me too, I expect.' Madeleine was feeling very much more reassured. If she could look forward to two whole days with Paolo, she could bear what was coming next. Her separation from Syracuse. '*Ancora*, Paolo,' she whispered, opening her legs.

'*Prego*,' he whispered back.

Thirty-five

Edwina and Germaine had gathered in their favourite restaurant to discuss the latest developments in Madeleine's life with her. 'The most difficult thing of all is to tell Mom. I'm due to talk to them tonight. When I phoned Mom I said Syracuse had left the house and I wanted to discuss the matter with both of them. I told her on the phone so she and Dad could get used to the idea before I arrived. It seemed kind of gentler than breaking the news over dinner.'

'What did your mom say?' Germaine's voice was gentle.

'She went quiet, but then she was probably rehearsing excuses for her bridge club.'

Edwina snorted. 'My mom was quite straight when I once told her I might be leaving Scott. She said if I did, she'd kill herself. *Quel* guilt-trip.'

Germaine hated to see the look of pain on Madeleine's face. 'At least I only had a few years of the marriage-go-round. My mom didn't want me to get married anyway. She thought marriage was for men only. I think she was right.'

Germaine knew that normally Madeleine's face was alight with laughter. Their lunches were a time together when they laughed at the rest of the world, secure in their own little corner of love and sharing. 'Are you OK, Madeleine? I feel so bad for you. At least you know where he is; he might decide to come back to you after all. He won't get taken care of by his little nurse like you took care of him.'

236

'No, he won't, but then she can give him things I can't. She might be the sort of woman who can lie in front of the television most nights, or go to football games with him. She is trained to listen to long lists of neurotic complaints, and to sympathise if his temperature is one degree above or one degree below normal. Honestly, Germaine, I know you are feeling for me, but apart from the shock of it all happening so suddenly, I know it's for the best. I do feel strange. I guess anybody would when you've been a couple for so long, but in a way I feel as though I've left a mini-concentration camp. I don't mean to sound frivolous, but I often thought my barbed wire was woven with his complaints of me and his dislike of who I was. Every time he tore into me, I ripped a little more, until really I was just a piece of bleeding meat.'

She wrinkled her nose. 'It all probably sounds very dramatic to you, but I realise now with the house empty that I was much more afraid of him than I realised. How can it happen, that, slowly, over all those years, you begin to let yourself slip into trying not to upset or offend a man? Running scared because if you don't get something right it means a pall of silence for the rest of the evening. Any other woman is more beautiful and more talented than you are.' She shrugged. 'It happens to so many women. Hilary says Peter treated her the same way. Anyway, it's blown my plans apart. Tomorrow I'm having the locks changed on the front door, and I've already told Dad's secretary to close our joint account. Thank goodness we have separate credit cards. He's on his own financially now, and I guess I don't have to be frightened of his spending habits any more. Mom and Dad were right when they put the house in my name only. I owe them an apology.' She grimaced. '"I told you so" are hard words to swallow.'

'Sure,' Edwina agreed. 'But at least you're not in the awful crunch so many women are in if they boot their men out. They get half of everything in theory, and mostly nothing of something in real life.'

'Yeah,' Madeleine agreed. 'I want to get a job of some kind. I don't want to be dependent on Dad, and I know Syracuse will be a bastard about maintenance.'

'What does Paolo say about all this, Maddie?'

'He listens, Edwina. He is very comforting, but I don't think men feel things the same way we do, you know. I don't care how much we are supposed to be like men these days, I know I'm not. Paolo can keep things in compartments rather like he keeps his wallet. He has this beautiful brown silky leather wallet. Probably a present from his wife. When he pulls it out and opens it up, everything is neatly placed in elegant order. All his credit cards are stacked down one side. His bills in order of denominations. A hundred dollars takes precedent over twenty dollars, and then the dollar notes and so on. The wallet never bulges. It never looks as if he's hurriedly stuffed notes into it. No, all is quietly and efficiently ordered. I think he lives his whole life like that. I am probably filed in compartment twenty-nine or something. Maybe I come under the heading of "newest woman" in his life, but not *numero uno*. That's obviously his wife, followed by a list of senior mistresses. Maybe if I'm *numero* twenty-nine and he keeps me in New York, there's probably a *numero* twenty-eight in London and a *numero* thirty waiting in the wings. *I* can't behave like that. I'm all over the place when it comes to feelings. I believe you can tell how a woman feels by the state of her handbag. I made a vow the other day that I'm going to buy a little zipper bag to go inside my handbag. I'm tired of pulling out the Tampax when I want to impress the shop assistant with my Access card. I've gone gold, you know?'

'Congratulations, Maddie.' Edwina grinned. 'Credit cards are so sexy. But I don't think you should think of yourself the way you do. I studied the whole business of the war between men and women, and decided the best way to deal with the bastards was to adopt their tactics. If I like a man's body and want to go to bed with him, I do. Just like Scott does with his secretaries. If I want to screw, I don't give a personal fuck about the men or their feelings.'

'Does that really work for you, Edwina?'

'Sure it does, why not?'

'If you only want their bodies, what do you talk about in the between times?'

'You don't, darling. You finish and send them home. Or you do what men do. Say, thanks a lot and I'll see you around.'

'I know you're probably right, Edwina. I really don't want to live like that. I can't.'

'Neither can I, Edwina.' Germaine shook her head. 'I don't think it's a question of women adopting men's strategies for survival. I think that's what's gone wrong for women. Frantz Fanon, the writer, was also a great philosopher. He said that the problem for the oppressed is that they only know the strategies of the oppressor. So when they break free from their tyrants, they tend to become tyrants themselves. You can see that happening in countries all over the world. What are women but oppressed territories? Women, when they do struggle and break free, opt for the quickest route to the top. Tooth and claw, just like the men they escaped.'

'I am woman, hear me roar!' Edwina drew back her lips and opened her mouth wide.

'Don't, Edwina, you scare me when you joke about

being like men. Women civilise men. We've told them enough times now we don't want to civilise them any longer, and that they must do it for themselves. But they won't, and now women are in great danger.'

'How do you mean, Maddie?'

'I mean that men can't civilise themselves. If they have mothers that don't bother to teach them, they never learn and then they are dangerous to women. Not always physically – and anyway, if they are dangerous physically we have laws to protect us from bruises and broken bones. No, it's here in our hearts, where they tear our inner worlds apart. I feel so broken inside. I feel like a vase that has been smashed into so many little pieces that it will take years to mend me again, if ever.'

'You will mend, Maddie. I promise you will.' Edwina smiled at her friend. 'Oh Maddie, why are you so intense about everything? Why can't you just be laid back? Have some fun. Lighten up.' Edwina took out another cigarette. 'You know, you could be right, though. All joking apart, we need to think of another strategy. Playing men at their own game hasn't worked. Maybe Allegro and her friends will have to find the answer. Maybe that's why we ended up in Madame Winona's place.'

'Boy, I'd sure like to think so. Anyway, I'm going to have some fun. I'm going away for a weekend with Paolo.'

Edwina leaned forward. 'Anywhere nice?' she said.

'I don't know yet.' Madeleine wasn't ready to tell anybody about the Fontainebleau in Miami. She just wanted a chance to say Paolo's name out loud, to remind herself that there was life after Syracuse. Tonight wasn't going to be much fun at all.

Thirty-six

'My God, Madeleine, what on earth are you thinking of? You know we've never had a divorce in our family. I'm a Daughter of the American Revolution, and we stick by our men. We did and always have, ever since our ancestors arrived from England. Really, I think this is most inconsiderate of you. After all, Syracuse didn't beat you, did he?' Dolly sat upright in her fat little gilt drawing-room chair. 'I know he cheated on you, but then so do most men; it's nothing to fuss about. You modern women have no idea how to treat a man.' Dolly took a little lace handkerchief out of her reticule and applied it meticulously to her eyes. She glanced sideways to make sure Ron now knew that she was to be officially considered extremely upset.

'Now, now, honey, don't upset yourself.' Ron put an extremely large placating hand on her shoulders. He hoped he could remember his lines. 'There's nothing that a loving family can't get through if we all pull together.'

'We can't all pull together, Ronald. Your daughter has booted your son-in-law out of the front door. We're no longer a happy family. We're, we're –' her voice rose to a wail – 'we're a family facing a divorce. At least if he'd died it would have been respectable.'

'Mom, I could kill him if that would help.'

'How can you be so flippant at a time like this, Madeleine? When you telephoned with your news, I was just eating my Dover sole. I've been waiting all week for that dish. I was too upset to finish it and –'

'I'll get you another fish when I next go shopping, Mom.' She was glad Allegro was at home and didn't have to see her grandmother throwing a tantrum. Though this was a mini effort compared with the tantrums she'd throw when Syracuse's aunts had failed to leave him any money. 'No, he didn't beat me, Mom. He just battered me to death with his bad opinion of me. I needed to get rid of him and his whole lifestyle. Do you understand, Dad?'

She moved from her chair and approached her father. She leaned against his big warm body as she had as a child. She felt the complicit understanding between them from the way he put his arm around her, and he gave her a reassuring hug. 'Well, I know this will make Mommy cross with me, hon, but I think you did the right thing. Syracuse telephoned me this morning and says he wants to keep his job in order that he can do right by you and by Allegro. What do you want me to do?'

'Sure, I don't see why he can't keep his job, though after paying for all his women there was never much left at the end of the month. I always paid all the bills from my trust fund.' She made a face. 'Anyway, after Christmas I want to get a job myself. I don't want his money. I want shot of the whole damn business.'

'There's no one else in your life is there, Madeleine? You're taking all this very calmly indeed.'

'No, Mom, there's no one else, and even if there were, my decision to leave Syracuse was taken years ago. I now realise it was just a matter of time really.' She smiled wanly. 'I guess it will be painful for both of us, but we'll be much happier in the end. He can find himself a woman who can cope with him, and I'll find some peace and quiet.'

'How will you manage without a man in your life?' Dolly's voice was abrupt.

'These days, Mom, women don't *have* to have men in their lives. Look at Germaine, she leads a very happy, independent life without a man. I'd like to be like that.'

Dorothy snorted. 'Your friend Germaine is on her own because no man would look at her. She's a fright. She looks like a bag-lady.'

'She might look like a bag-lady to you, but to me she's my best and staunchest friend. You'd better be careful, Mom, or I'll go to the Salvation Army and get clothes with Germaine, and then we'll both come and visit you when you're having a bridge party, and then what will the DARs think?'

'You wouldn't do that, would you, Madeleine?' Dolly's shaven eyebrows lifted with horror at the thought.

'Not if you calm down and accept that I'm going to divorce Syracuse and that's that. We don't even have to mention the horrible subject again. OK?'

When her mother saw her to the door, Madeleine realised that she was deeply upset. Her father hugged her goodbye in the drawing room, and she knew he understood. 'After all, I work with him,' he said sympathetically. 'Your mother never liked him, but she finds it difficult moving with the times. One day, darling, you'll find a man and be very happy. A man worthy of you.' He hugged her warmly.

'One day, Dad, I'll find a man like you, and then I will be very happy.'

Madeleine suppressed the little voice that whispered that she already had the man she wanted. But he is married, she reminded the voice.

'Are you sure you know what you're doing, Madeleine?'

'I'm sure, Mom, and even if I feel shit-scared every moment I am awake, it's better than living with Syracuse. Anything is better than that.' For a moment Dolly hugged her daughter, and Madeleine saw a blue light flash between them. They were connected again in that second, but when the moment passed, Madeleine felt all the pain and the sorrow that she'd felt when she'd left her childhood and refused her mother's domination.

'OK, honey, you know where I am when you need me. I'll be over Sunday for brunch to see my gorgeous granddaughter. How's she taking all this?'

'With remarkable equanimity, Mom. She hasn't asked after him once, and if I know Allegro, she'll milk her time with him for all it's worth. Don't worry about her, she'll be all right. She's very much looking forward to going to London with Hilary's boys. She particularly wants to go to London Zoo and to the toy department at Harrods. I'm all in favour of a tour of Fortnum and Mason's, and I'll bring you back your English shortbread biscuits, OK?'

'Oh darling, do, and please don't bring back the tin with the plain tartan on it; all my friends have that one. Bring me the one with Bonnie Prince Charlie on the lid. They'll all be so awfully jealous.'

Madeleine left her mother's house wishing that the most important problem in her life was which kind of biscuit tin to choose for a bridge party, but alas, she wasn't that lucky.

Thirty-seven

ॐ

Syracuse became a whining voice down the telephone and a writer of massive missives, which endlessly sought to justify his behaviour. Paolo listened politely to what she had to say in her own defence, but she realised quite quickly that talking about her husband transgressed one of the sacred rules of loving a married man. She had popped out of her compartment and was trying to discuss her life with her husband, which was taboo, like almost everything else in her life with Paolo. For him their life began and ended behind his front door. But now they were going away for two days. Would she remember all the rules? Were there new ones to be discovered? Which side of the bed did his wife sleep on?

She always chose the side nearest the window, away from the door and potential rapists and murderers.

'Darling.' She slid to her knees beside Allegro. 'Mom is going away with a friend for the weekend.'

'Which friend?'

Madeleine sighed. Why do children have to be so uncompromising? 'A friend called Paolo. He's a very nice, kind man, and I need a holiday. Do you mind?'

'No,' she said, staring at her mother. 'Can I stay with Jonathan and Justin?'

'Sure you can. I'll telephone Hilary.'

'Hilary, can Allegro stay with you for a couple of days? I need to go away.'

'Anybody I know?'

'No, it's a man called Paolo. I could do with a break

from Syracuse's whining voice. I'll arrange with Mrs Poole for Syracuse to collect his stuff while I'm away. Then when I come back the house will be mine, if that makes sense.'

'Sure it does. I've got Peter on the doorstep all the time. The trouble is, they make all this fuss about leaving their wives, and when real life hits them between the legs, they want to come back to Mummy.'

'I've told Syracuse that he's somebody else's nightmare now, thank God.'

Madeleine put down the telephone. 'That's all fixed, then.' She sighed with relief. 'Allegro, you will be a good girl, won't you? You won't fight with Justin or pull his hair?'

'Justin's a wimp. I can fight better than he can. Can you buy me a penknife, a big one? You know the kind of knife that I can tie around my waist?'

'OK, but only if you don't fight with either of the boys. Hilary is a very quiet, gentle woman, and I don't want to think of you terrorising her.'

Allegro grinned. The colours around her shoulders flashed with mischievous glee. 'I promise, Mom.'

'Good girl.' Madeleine bent down and kissed her daughter. 'I'm going upstairs to pack. I'll see you at dinner.'

At seven o'clock, Madeleine was sitting in the dining room watching Allegro tuck into a large piece of rare steak. Still, since Syracuse had left the house, Allegro seemed much happier. Maybe it is because I'm much happier and less tense, she reasoned. She watched Allegro and then she smiled. How wonderful to be going off on an adventure with her lover. How very grown-up it was. She knew she didn't know the etiquette. I suppose it is like being at a posh dinner party. 'Posh' was a word Hilary had taught her. It meant very elegant. She remembered the time she had been served little tiny birds in an Italian restaurant with Paolo. She'd watched him nervously, realised that he was crunching all the fragile bones, so had then copied him. That's what she would do this weekend. A dirty weekend, the English called it. Well, she wouldn't be dirty. She would probably take a shower every five minutes. She sat there, dreamily staring into space. 'Mom?' Allegro's voice called her back from the long white Miami beach to reality. 'What's a monstrous woman?'

'What an odd question, Allegro. Where did you hear that word?'

'Last night. My fairy told me I was going to grow up to be a monstrous woman.'

'Oh, I do hope not, darling. A monstrous woman is a bad woman, and you'll never be that.'

'Oh yes I will. I *want* to be bad. I want to be the baddest woman in the world.' Allegro let out peals of laughter. Well, Madeleine thought, joining in the laughter. Your mother is having an affair with a married man, so I guess I'm not much of an example. 'Finish your steak, darling, and then we can watch television together.'

Tomorrow night she would be on the aeroplane with her lover. Monstrous woman indeed; that must be Dr Stanislaus. Later, when she hung out of her window, savouring the New York night air, she called out, 'Dr Stanislaus, do you have your people in Miami?'

'*Certo*,' was the amused reply. Dr Stanislaus had obviously been studying Italian.

Madeleine hugged Allegro goodbye. There were tears in her eyes as she watched her daughter rush out of the house with the boys into their garden. 'I'm going to be Captain Hook,' she heard Allegro shriek.

'Well, it doesn't look as if she'll miss me that much, does it, Hilary?'

'We need our children much more than they need us, Madeleine. You go now, and have a wonderful time.'

'I'll telephone you every night, Hilary, and if she's not OK, I'll come straight back.'

'Don't be such a neurotic mother, Madeleine. She'll be fine. I promise the boys will take care of her and keep her busy. Run along now. Send me a postcard. I could do with a weekend away with a handsome lover. You lucky thing.'

'I'll find you one in England. American men are too childish. What about a real live lord?'

'No thanks, I know a lot of them, and they are mostly spoiled and violent. I'll settle for a nice sexy gamekeeper who keeps ferrets down his trousers.'

'Goodbye, Hilary, and thank you.' Madeleine hugged her friend and got back into the car. She was to meet Paolo at the British Airways ticket counter. She parked in the multi-storey car park and then she pushed and shoved her way into the overseas terminal. As she picked her way through the crowded air terminal, she watched anxiously for Paolo's tall figure. So far there was no sign of him. She glanced at the clock as she reached the British Airways desk. There was still no sign of Paolo. She felt a sense of panic. Maybe he'd changed his mind and wasn't coming after all. She felt tears gathering in her eyes. What would she do if he didn't arrive? Why had she put herself in this position? Why had she deserted her daughter and her safe house and way of life to stand helplessly by a ticket counter wondering if her lover was going to turn up? What was she doing with a lover, anyway – and a married man at that? Surely life had been better with the certainty of her husband.

Had this been Syracuse, he would have been striding up and down the airport, gazing at his watch and cursing all airlines and airways. He hated travelling, and the mere thought of a weekend away would send him into a spinning dervish type of dance. He would make plans and arrangements which would be changed every few minutes.

Usually Madeleine was so exhausted by his behaviour that she preferred to stay at home. Now she fervently wished she *had* stayed at home; then she felt a warm pair of arms around her shoulders. 'Oh,' she exclaimed. 'It's you.'

'Were you worried, *cara*? I'm so sorry about that. I was delayed. You weren't frightened that I might not turn up?'

'How did you know?'

'I know you very well, Madeleine, and you don't trust me yet, do you?'

'I don't trust men in general, Paolo.' She stood on her tiptoes and kissed him gently on the mouth. 'Are we really going away together? This isn't all a dream?'

'No, it's a reality. You'll love the hotel. I can show you from our balcony the suite where Frank Sinatra stayed in the forties and the fifties, and there is a funny old man who knows the whole history of the hotel and he will tell you all of it.'

Paolo put his hand under her elbow. 'Come, follow me. I've got the tickets.' When they got to the plane, Madeleine discovered they were flying first class. 'I've never flown first class before,' she admitted shyly.

'Well, you will with me, *cara*. It's first class all the way in life.' He fussed over her and lifted her luggage into the lockers. 'There you are, *cara*, are you all settled in?'

Madeleine lay snuggled under a soft blue blanket. 'It's wonderful, Paolo. You spoil me.'

'Beautiful women are made to be spoiled.' He called over the flight attendant. 'Champagne for two, please. A bottle of the Boizel. It's such a good Italian champagne. It's excellent for drinking in the morning: it's very light and frivolous.'

The aeroplane took off and Madeleine sipped her champagne. 'You know, Paolo, for a long time I never thought I'd smile again. I realise that I was very unhappy for so long. Why doesn't one know these things? Why did I wait so long to get rid of a man that really was an awful shit?'

'We don't really like to admit we're wrong; and anyway, when we are in love we are truly blind. People all round us can see the truth, but there is a veil before a lover's eyes. You need someone like me to come into your life and just pull it away. Pffff.' He made a tearing motion with his long fingers.

Madeleine lay back in her seat and smiled at Paolo. He was excited by the trip. His eyes were shining and his normally sleek hair was tousled. She longed to take him in her arms and to smooth his hair and kiss him. She loved looking at him. He was so beautiful. He bent over her and kissed her. She felt an irresistible urge to tickle his mouth with her tongue. 'You witch,' he whispered. 'Just you wait.'

'For what?' she replied grinning. 'Until I get you alone?'

She gazed at him, imagining the both of them wrapped around each other in a big double bed. 'All night,' she whispered. 'And it's best in the morning.'

'All weekend,' he replied. 'You don't get to see Miami.'

'Do they deliver stone crab?'

'Sure, stone crab and champagne. That's another promise.'

Thirty-eight

Making love was all that she imagined it to be. Lying tenderly cradled in Paolo's arms, Madeleine realised that she had fallen dangerously in love with this man. She watched his brown eyes, shaded with golden lights, gazing steadily at her. He brushed his palms against her nipples that were now relaxed. She felt the loss of sexual tension from her body. She sighed deeply. 'Happy, *amore mio*?' he asked. There was no anxiety in the question. He knew she was always happy in his arms, and he was calm and confident in his ability to please her. He was a good lover, and now Madeleine knew that, once having found this level of sexual pleasure, she was not going to be satisfied with less.

'More champagne?' Beside the bed there was a roll-away table littered with crabs' legs and various salads. Paolo reached over her and poured her a fresh glass. 'Here, darling.' He held the glass to her lips. She sipped the champagne.

'I could do with a bath before we go swimming.' She stretched lazily and gazed out of the window of the suite. Across the road the sea was blue and inviting.

They'd left New York behind in the sadness of the end of summer days. Miami felt like a young girl, with her arms open wide to welcome her guests. The waves rolled along the shoreline. There were tourists about, but not many. The hotel was exactly as Paolo had described it. Madeleine loved the big wide reception rooms, the little cordoned-off areas for people to sit and take tea, the long polished bar where they both had their first gin and tonics. She also loved their suite.

'Lana Turner once slept here,' the porter had proudly boasted.

'I wonder,' Madeleine said with a grin, 'if Lana Turner had as good a time in bed as we did?' She climbed out of bed to have her bath.

'Certainly not,' Paolo was laughing. 'She didn't have me for a lover.'

'*Certo*, darling.' If Professor Stanislaus could learn Italian, then so could she.

Later, lying on the flat white sunbeds, Madeleine was conscious of the sun beating down on top of her body. She was slightly brown from the summer, but she wanted to tan. She liked to be dark brown, but she was usually too impatient to lie in the sun. 'You're like a lizard, Paolo. It's not fair.'

'It's the Tuscan sun, darling. By the way, when I get back, my wife is coming over with the children for two weeks.'

The news stunned her for a moment. 'That's nice,' she said, trying to keep her voice steady.

'Yes, it will be wonderful to see the children. They will love New York. I'm planning to take them to the zoo.' Paolo lay back, smiling.

The zoo? How could he take his children to her favourite place? 'I must go in and have a swim, Paolo. I need to cool off.' Madeleine got to her feet and plunged into the surf. She lay spread-eagled on the water, tears streaming down her face. How could he be so matter of fact? How could he make love to her in his bedroom in New York, and then make love to his wife in the same bed? The thought horrified her. Her heart was racing and her stomach turning. Why did she mind so much when she had a husband who'd cheated all her married life?

The answer was that she had never loved Syracuse. Not the way she loved Paolo. Syracuse was a duty. She had married him, taken care of him, tried to please him, but at a very late stage she had realised that he was useless as a lover. Selfish men make bad lovers.

Paolo was not selfish. He was romantic and generous, and now she had to face the fact that his wife was coming to New York and would be sitting in the chair she had sat in.

She would be standing in the kitchen that she so loved. She would, worst of all, lie in the same bed where Paolo had seduced her so very willingly. She rolled over on her back and gazed into the very deep blue sky. High above, little silver bullets of aeroplanes were filled with Americans jetting off to England to eat English cream teas. They would return filled with English people coming to see Disney World and the wonders of the Floridian rainforests.

Why, oh why did Paolo have to be married? Of all the millions of possible men in the world, why did she have to fall in love with Paolo? She didn't know the answer to the question. She rolled on to her stomach again. Shit, she thought, that's ruined my day.

She walked up the beach towards Paolo, and she wondered if he'd broken the news to her this way so that she would have time to go off and absorb it. Probably. He had plenty of experience with women. She had none with men. Maybe what she learned from this is that with a married man there are no-go areas and this was one of them. You paid a high price for your happiness. The price was silence. A hurt silence, but a silence no less. She wondered if Allegro was all right. 'I must ring Hilary tonight,' she said when she lay down beside

Paolo. 'Of course.' He put a big brown hand on her back. 'Here, let me rub you with sun-tan oil.' She felt her spine arching as he expertly smoothed the oil into her skin. 'Oh, Paolo, we have all this lovely time together. What are you going to order for dinner?'

'I want to take you to a little fish restaurant I know down by the docks.'

'Wonderful. I'd love that.'

Sitting in the restaurant, looking out over the water, she saw something moving. 'Look, Paolo, what is it?'

'It's a manatee. Come, bring your drink, and we'll go and talk to it.' They walked down the thin wooden planking. Lying on its back was a little whiskered gentleman. He looked rather like a walrus, but he had a much fatter face. His flippers were crossed over his belly and he was gazing benignly at them. Dr Stanislaus? Madeleine kept the thought to herself, but could not suppress a smile when the manatee winked at her.

Paolo put his arm around her shoulders and pulled her to him. 'You make me so very happy, Madeleine,' he said. His voice was hoarse.

I wonder if his wife makes him as happy as I do. She didn't voice this thought. No-go area, the lights in her head blinked. Before now, the idea of Paolo's wife had been kept to the back of her mind. She had always held the whole idea of his marriage and his other life at bay. He had his life with her in New York, and somewhere, eight thousand or so miles away, was his wife and family. Now she would have to think about it because they were coming into her territory. She kissed him back, but he felt her withdrawal and held her at arm's length. 'You don't have to be worried, Madeleine. It's only for two weeks, and then they will be gone. You knew I am married.'

'I know,' she whispered miserably, 'but I didn't know it would hurt so much.'

'Ah, *cara*, you must grow up. You must learn to live in the real world. You can't always keep yourself safe from hurts and confusion. Come, let us go back to the restaurant and finish our wine and then the night is ours – yes?'

'Yes, Paolo.' She so much wanted every night to be theirs, but she also knew it was impossible. She had to share her man with another woman, and that was another price that had to be paid. As she climbed into their rented car, she wondered if the price was going to be too high for her. She didn't know, and she couldn't guess. Maybe that kind of stocktaking had to be done later. For now she was content that she would spend the whole night with her lover and wake up beside him.

'Hilary, how is Allegro?' She felt an anxious pang.

'She's fine. Do you want me to get her for you?'

'Sure, I'd love to speak to her.' She very much wanted to tell Allegro about the manatee. 'Allegro . . .' She could hear Hilary call to her daughter. Then there was a yell that sounded like Allegro answering back.

'She says she's playing in the garden and she doesn't want to leave her fort.'

'Oh, OK. I guess that means she's fine.'

'She is, really. Don't worry about her. Are you having a good time?'

'Yeah, marvellous, and I'll be so brown when I get back you'll be jealous.' When she put down the telephone she felt hurt. Allegro had always been her best friend, and now even she didn't want to talk to her. Life's a bitch at times, she thought as she left the sitting room to take a shower.

Thirty-nine

❧

'Are you always this erotic in the morning?' Paolo was leaning on his elbow, gazing at Madeleine with mild surprise in his sun-flecked eyes.

'I guess so. It is a little embarrassing to admit that first thing in the morning I always wake up feeling so horny that I think I'll burst.'

'You certainly do. I thought convent girls, nicely brought up like you were, had inhibitions?'

'Not this one.' She lay contentedly on her back. The sheets were twisted and damp with sweat from love-making. She threw her arms up over her head. 'Oh, Paolo, I feel so whole. So all in one piece, if that makes sense. I don't see how people can think that making love is like fast food. I think it takes time, like having a wonderful banquet, to really savour sex. For the first time I feel completely satisfied.' She lay with her eyes half closed.

'I'm glad, *amore*, that I was able to do that for you.'

'It was so marvellous to just wake up and reach for you and there you were ready to slide into me. We have another two whole mornings.' She stopped then. There was no point in saying anything about the weeks when he would be busy with his own family. That was the time she would be busy herself, with Edwina and Germaine. How many other women did that when the 'other woman' was in town? Probably all of them. She could also spend time with Hilary. She had such a calm, refreshing certainty about her. She talked in a clipped

English accent, but unlike Americans, she gave her information in short, sharp sentences.

'Shall we go swimming, *cara*?' Paolo stretched. She loved to watch his big shoulder-muscles writhe, his long, lean back contort. He had a handful of black hair in the small of his back. She liked to kiss that patch.

Madeleine rolled over on to her back. 'Let's make love one more time, and then I'd love to go swimming.' She curled into Paolo's stomach. 'There, you put your hand between my legs, and come into me from behind. It feels great that way.'

Paolo smiled, his mouth against her neck. For a little provincial American woman, she was amazingly inventive in bed. What a fool her husband must have been. Paolo knew he was on dangerous ground with Madeleine. He knew better than to fall in love with her. He guided her into an intense sexual climax. 'Ahhhhh, that was marvellous,' he heard her say.

Why does this woman affect me so intensely after so many women? I don't know, he thought. He lay against her sweating back. Maybe it's just she is so unspoiled. 'Here, darling, I have a towel for you for your shower, and then we'll go swimming.'

Madeleine jumped out of bed and walked towards the bathroom. 'Don't look,' she said. 'My stomach is horrible.'

'I love your stomach. It isn't terrible. It carried your child.'

'Yes, and after all that, the little beast can't be bothered to speak to me.' Madeleine got under the shower. The hot water poured over her. She washed her hair and then the water soaked her shoulders. She felt marvellous. She had not been so happy for a long while. Maybe the price one paid for living and loving was times like this when the whole world celebrated your happiness with you. Then of course there were the lows. The mean, dark red days when even worms turned on you. Everything was black, covered in sludge and mud. The sun refused to shine. Those were the days to take to your bed with a bottle of wine and an armful of good books. Madeleine knew all about those days; she'd had many of them living with Syracuse. Edwina's solution for getting rid of the black days was to pick up men and ball them.

Madeleine could always return her books to the library when she was finished with them. Edwina had to try to get rid of the men once the bad days were over. 'I'm having "one of those days", Madeleine.' It was Germaine's voice on the end of the telephone somewhere in the universe. If Germaine's black days weren't too bad, she'd be in Boston or New England. If it was a serious black event which was going to spread into weeks, she called from Norway or Iceland. Germaine always said she felt her blackest in Norway and Denmark. They really know how to be black in those countries.

Anyway, today was a happy day, and Madeleine picked up her swimsuit and pulled it on. She stared at herself in the mirror. She was pleased with her tan. She liked the way her eyes blazed when she was sexually fulfilled. She turned and gazed at her bottom. Still too large, but Paolo didn't seem to mind. She ran into the bedroom. Paolo was standing on the balcony, gazing out at the sea. She put her arm through his and stood wordlessly beside him. 'What are you thinking about?' she asked, breaking the silence.

'I was thinking that it is so nice to be here with a woman I like to make love with. This is a good hotel for lovers, is it not?'

'Sure, think how many lovers have been here. Now

we've been here.' She gazed at the gulls that were riding high on the thermals. 'Have you been in this hotel with other women, Paolo?'

Paolo put his fingers on her lips. 'Madeleine, you grow up now. You don't ask questions like that. Even if I had, I wouldn't tell you. My past life is past.'

'You should give lessons to Syracuse. He tells me every little detail. It's so boring.'

'Ah yes, but that is because he is a little boy confessing to his mother. I agree that it is terribly boring, but then he will always be a little boy.'

'What happens to men like that, Paolo?'

'Oh, they pick up women for a while, but then they get older and want younger women to reassure them that they are not getting any older. Usually they have no money because they have thrown away all their good opportunities.' He shrugged. 'Bah, they either find a woman who is willing to put up with their temper-tantrums, or they live alone and become bitter and sad. They rant at the rest of the world and the rest of the world ignores them. It is a sad condition to be so narciss-istic. Very spoiled, like a three-year-old child.'

'Well, that certainly describes Syracuse. I hope he finds a woman who will put up with him. I don't wish him any harm. I just want him out of my life.'

She wanted to talk to Paolo about her feelings now. How she couldn't imagine her life without being married to a man. How she was the sort of woman who had always seen herself as married. How it was perfectly natural for her, after they had made love for the second time that morning, to call down to room service and order breakfast for two. She for many years had always woken up deciding what Syracuse might like for break-fast. Even if she forgot to order dinner properly, she had been trained by her mother to take care of a man. The care you took of your husband was the most important thing in a wife's life. First you cared for him, and then for your children, and finally yourself. Now, in the new order of things, she felt a little lost. She no longer had all the fences created by running a big house, a staff and a family. Now she had a wide, boundless vista ahead of her, without a permanent man. She realised that this was yet another conversation she could not have with Paolo. He gave off the impression that he wished only for the two of them to live in the here and now. No past and no future. Very well, she would comply. 'Let's go swimming, darling.' She kissed him passionately.

'Yes, I think we must give the maids time to clean the room and change the sheets, otherwise you will have me back in bed again, won't you?'

'*Certo*,' Madeleine laughed. 'Race you down to the beach.'

Forty

❧

Their time together was over. Madeleine smiled at Paolo as he held open the door of the suite for the final time. She looked wanly over her shoulder at the now well-remembered rooms. She closed her eyes and pretended she was a camera. In her mind's eye she could see the rumpled bed. She could hear the cries and moans of delight, and long nights whispering thousands of loving thoughts. Her hands were still full of Paolo's body, her nostrils full of the animal smell of him after a night's love-making. The memories caused her to feel faint for a moment. She took his hand as they walked down the corridor. They were an acknowledged couple here in the hotel, and heads turned regularly as they walked past.

Madeleine realised how much she enjoyed being seen with Paolo. His tall, broad-shouldered presence comforted her. She felt safe with him. She had never felt safe with Syracuse. His fear was contaminating, and for so many years she too feared everything. In her ex-husband's world, all sorts of frightful and evil things might happen. He walked in a cloud and a miasma of terror. Soon those terrors would haunt her again, too, but for now she was confident and brown from the Miami sun. Her hair was shining and thick. It tumbled about her shoulders. She felt as if she had gained back ten years from her unhappy marriage. Why didn't I know I was so unhappy? she wondered.

She argued with herself constantly. Because you had nothing to compare your relationship to. You married nothing to compare your relationship to. You married the first man in your life and you took what he did for granted. Edwina at least found other moments of happiness. Germaine got out but you, idiot, stayed locked away in your unhappiness for all those years; when look what now lies before you. What? she asked herself as the aeroplane took off. What indeed? She gazed sideways at Paolo. His head was resting on the back of his seat. His eyes were closed. His long dark lashes covered his eyes and she wondered if he was thinking about his wife's arrival. She knew better than to ask him. She learned fast.

Allegro, she was pleased to see, was delighted to see her. She jumped into her mother's arms and said, 'Gee, Mom, you look great. Did you have a good time?'

'I did, darling, I had a wonderful time.' She just wished the ache in her heart would go away. Driving home, Allegro chattered incessantly, and Madeleine felt guilty when she packed her off to see Nanny Barnes and withdrew into the drawing room to have a gin and tonic. On holiday she had obeyed Paolo's dictum that Italian men drank only wine, but now she very much felt she wanted the comfort of the gin and the well-remembered fizz of the tonic on her tongue. She had drunk gin and tonic before she'd met Paolo, and she was not going to make the same mistake she had made with Syracuse. She had bent over backwards to accommodate all his neurotic needs. She had changed herself into a woman unrecognisable even to herself. Now, standing in the middle of her own drawing room, she gazed into the large mirror over the fireplace. 'Wow,' she muttered out loud, 'you look great.' Suddenly she cast herself into a big plump armchair and burst into tears. Why was falling in love so painful? Was it really worth this feeling of loss to be in love with Paolo? Wouldn't she have been better to just boot Syracuse out of her life and to live alone like a nun? She tried to summon Dr Stanislaus, but he refused to come. I can't interfere with your pain, he signalled. It belongs to you and can't be taken away. It's called consequences. You must feel pain to change. She heard his voice loud and clear.

'But if I can never have Paolo, what is the point of just experiencing pain?'

'You cannot have one without the other. No loss, no pain. No pain, no gain. Simple.' Abruptly he was gone.

The telephone rang. 'Hi, honey, how was it?'

'Great, but I feel absolutely miserable now, Edwina.'

'Sure you do. It's to be expected. When the bastards leave us we have to learn to take care of ourselves. I can't have dinner with you tonight and comfort you, I have to go to one of Scott's boring business dinners and play the silly little wifey. But I want a new mink coat for Christmas, so I'd better humour him. Germaine is in tonight, though. Why don't you telephone her and have a good moan? That's what girlfriends are for.'

'Edwina.' Madeleine's voice was hesitant. 'Paolo said his wife is going to be in New York for two weeks.'

'Sure thing, she often visits. After all, it is her apartment as well.'

'But it hurts, Edwina. I don't want to share Paolo with his wife.'

'Oh, do grow up, Maddie. You're such a child. She'll go after two weeks, and you can have him to yourself again.'

'Until the next time.' Madeleine felt like crying. 'I don't mind him being in Siena with his family, but I do mind him making love to his wife in our bed.'

'He was making love to his wife in his bed before he met you.'

'I know that, but I didn't think about that before. Now I do have to think about her, and I don't like it.'

'Wait until you hang about on street corners waiting to see her, and then you'll know you're really hooked.' Edwina was laughing.

'I'd never do a thing like that, Edwina. Never!'

'Oh yes you will, Miss Goody Two-shoes. You're no different to the rest of us. I got to go, honey.' Edwina blew Madeleine a loud kiss and put the phone down.

'You see, Germaine, I've been wondering if men are born with a selfish gene in their DNA that we women simply don't have. I know that it's in their nature to spread their seed as widely as possible so that the human race doesn't die out. That's understandable. But it's the way they live their emotional life I can't understand. For instance, the three of us women all talk about everything. Well, almost everything.' She remembered her refusal to discuss her sex life with Edwina.

'But Paolo, without actually saying anything, makes it very clear that he does not intend to discuss his private life with me, and even more does not want me to discuss anything about my life, except for what we are both doing together. So if I'm miserable about Syracuse, he doesn't want to hear about it.'

Madeleine was sitting at the dinner table, pushing around a salmon mousse. Upstairs, Allegro was tucked up in bed, talking to her friend the unicorn. 'Mom had a wonderful time in Miami. Look, she bought me this T-shirt. It's a unicorn, like you.' The unicorn tossed its silver mane. 'Goodnight, unicorn. Thank you for visiting me. I love you, unicorn.' Allegro closed her eyes and fell asleep. The unicorn leaned over the sleeping child and breathed his hay-scented breath upon her, and then he turned and, leaping into the air, he soared into the night sky. No good will come of this night, he cried. Huge tears rolled down his face for his favourite child.

Downstairs, Germaine was sitting at the far end of the table, listening intently. 'Darling, the truth about men and women is really very simple. The feminists got it all wrong. Men and women are two completely different species. Men have larger limbic brains than women. They live on a primitive level of eating, fucking and shitting. In that order.

'I once read a study of the gorilla. Man's closest relatives. They put a big pile of bananas in the corner of the male's cave, and then they let in a female gorilla on heat.' Germaine laughed. 'They watched the male try to decide which to do first. In the end he took the bananas, of course, and then he screwed the female. I suppose you can always find a female on heat, but his need to eat was primary.

'The little female tried to tempt him away from his bananas, and he hit her. She kept trying to play with him but he wasn't having any of it. No, Madeleine, if you want to survive in the world of men, you will have to toughen up a lot. They are ruthless and brutal.

'We told men that we wanted to muscle into their lifestyles and they just said OK. Took off their gloves, and now we are faced with men as they really are. No attempt at civilisation, just tooth and claw.'

'Oh Germaine, do you think it is really as bad as that?'

'I do. That's why I live on my own. I couldn't pander to that endless male need to be cared for by a woman. Look at Syracuse, out of your bed and into another. He wouldn't last five minutes on his own out in the real world.'

'I sometimes feel I wouldn't do too well, and I have a staff of people to look after me. I also have Mom and

Dad. It's so strange not being a couple with Syracuse any more, and then being a couple again with Paolo. I like being a couple, but then I don't like the price I paid for being with Syracuse for so many years.'

'Consequences darling, consequences. That's what life is all about.'

'Yeah, Dr Stanislaus said that there's no gain if I refuse to take risks with love. At least, I think that's what he was saying. If only I could be more like Edwina and not take things so seriously.'

'You wouldn't be *you*, darling, if you didn't take things the way you do. I've got to go now, but you stay just the way you are. Don't ever change. Edwina's great fun and I love her, but I also love your clean moral sense of outrage. Don't ever lose it.'

'It's that bloody convent, Germaine. Everything was so black and white. An action is either a sin or not a sin. There is no black and white in real life, though. Real life seems to be different shades of grey.'

'You're asking me? I don't know the answer to that one, Madeleine. All I know is that, for me, the American idea that "if it feels good, do it" was never a philosophy I could tolerate. I'm afraid human beings want to do things that are no good at all for their inner sense of harmony. When I am out of harmony with myself, I am out of harmony with the whole world. That's why I like the great Libyan desert skies and the simple people.

'There they are so in harmony with their inner worlds. Here it is all lost in the clutter of possessions and greed. Except, of course, your lovely house, which does feel so much more peaceful without Syracuse to pollute the place with his rage.'

'It does feel different, doesn't it? He took all his stuff while I was away and left me the usual cringe-making letter. I'm not reading any more of them, I'm just sending them back to him. I've made my decision, and Allegro says in one of her made-up songs, "I will live in the world of tomorrow." She makes up such beautiful songs. I love to hear her sing. She really is the oddest child, Germaine. But she's so happy and looking forward to going to England.'

Madeleine kissed Germaine goodnight on her doorstep. She watched the beloved, solid figure disappear into the cold night air. Madeleine shivered and wrapped her arms around her slender body. She had lost weight after a weekend of making love and eating heartily. What a way to diet, she thought as she climbed the stairs to bed. Her head was full of wine and remembrances.

Rule number whatever. Memories of making love with your married man is what you get to hang on to while he's with his wife and family. But at least they were great memories, she reminded herself.

Forty-one

Madeleine didn't expect to find it so difficult to concentrate. Usually when Paolo was in Siena, she waited patiently until he telephoned to say he was back. Now that she had the house to herself, they could talk on the telephone when he telephoned her. She, of course, could not telephone him, which left her hypersensitive to her telephone. She had already installed extra phones in the main rooms in the house, in case she missed him. The telephone and waiting for his calls were intravenous. Without them she felt she could not live.

She knew Paolo's wife's name, and that she was Sienese, but nothing else about her. She could have asked Edwina, but she preferred not to. She rather wanted to keep his life with his wife and children safely in a large bank vault.

However, now his wife was actually several blocks away in New York, things changed. She spent large parts of the day staring into space. Did Paolo fill his wife's arms with flowers? Did he laugh with her like he did with Madeleine? The bed bit she refused to consider. She hoped his wife had a permanent period while she was in America. A change of time-zone could bring it on, she knew that.

Occasionally Syracuse telephoned from a pay-telephone in a bar. 'Go away, Syracuse. I don't want to talk to you.' She hated the self-pity in his voice. 'Your new woman won't let you use the telephone from her house, uh? Sensible girl. I always thought the little nurse looked like a good match for you. Dad is taking my alimony out of your pay-cheque and cancelling your trips to Hong Kong and to Japan, so you'll have to say goodbye to your little bitches out there.'

'I don't see either of them any more, Maddie. Can't we at least be friends, for Allegro's sake?'

'No, Syracuse, you'll just manipulate everybody. You threw us both away. After your horrible spoiled behaviour, I now realise how many years of my life you wasted. It was like running a private madhouse. I was an idiot, but I'm free now.' She could hear the repressed rage in his voice, and she trembled for the little nurse, but then there were women just as tough as he was, and when the nurse had had enough, she was perfectly capable of throwing him out.

Just recently, when he'd come to collect Allegro, she'd refused to go with him. 'He's so boring,' she'd complained. Boring was Allegro's new word and she loved it. Privately Madeleine agreed with the child, but she tried to encourage her to go.

'You're cutting me off from my own daughter,' Syracuse whined.

'No, I'm not, Syracuse. She doesn't want to spend the day in a hamburger joint or in the park.'

'Lucinda doesn't like children, and she won't let me take her home.'

'You mean, take Allegro back to Lucinda's house? You don't have a home, Syracuse.'

'Why are you being so hard on me, Maddie?'

'Because I hate you, Syracuse. Because you are an ageing narcissistic exhibitionist. You're past your sell-by date. Don't contaminate my telephone.' She slammed down the receiver before he began his usual manic ranting. She'd heard it for too many years. The whole world had failed Syracuse Winstanley. There must be millions of American men like Syracuse. The boys of ambitious mothers, born with brilliant promise, who failed to live up to anything at all. So that's why Syracuse ranted. He was shouting in the dark. He was afraid of everything. Now secure with a lover who enjoyed being with her, she was able to feel less harshly towards him. Still, she was frightened of him. She always knew you could be beaten with fists, but she had not realised that a woman can be battered by words. That was the worst. At least after the long rants, had he hit her she would have something to show her parents.

Now she had to suffer her mother's sorrowing eyes. 'Mom,' she said a few days after the telephone call. 'If he'd broken my arms, you'd be furious with him, but he ranted and shrieked at me for hours on end and you seem to think that's OK?'

No, better not to play the 'friends' game with Syracuse. So often she'd seen women conned with that ploy. First the instant friendship, and then the whining just continued. Paolo never whined. He never made problems for her. When she was with him his attention was totally for her. She wondered if all Italian men were like that. She wondered again what he was doing with his wife at this moment.

One day, to her disgust, she found herself driving past his apartment on her way to drop off Allegro.

'This isn't the way to go to school, Mom.'

'I know it isn't, honey, but I just felt like driving a new way for a change.'

'You're not happy, Mom. I can see black lights all around you.'

Tears welled in Madeleine's eyes. 'I'm just a little confused, honey. I don't know if I'm doing the right thing.'

'Well, when you came back from Miami, you were all gorgeous gold and silver, so that was the right thing, wasn't it?'

'Bless you, darling.' She picked up the grubby, nail-bitten little hand that was resting on her shoulder and she kissed it.

Forty-two

ॐ

'I don't see why you are taking Allegro away for Christmas. Christmas is a family time. You and Hilary are in cahoots against Peter and myself. You've planned this so Peter and I have nowhere to go.'

'Don't be silly, Syracuse. You have your nurse and Peter has another woman. Why don't you celebrate Christmas with your loved ones?'

Paolo was going back to Siena to spend Christmas with his family, as she knew he must. That was the hardest part. How many women spent Christmas aching for their married man? Millions, she supposed.

After the visit of his wife, Madeleine had spent at least a month trying to break down her internal barriers. To make love again in the bed where he had lain with his wife was difficult. On the first few occasions she had been unable to let herself go and slide into the glorious glissade that swept her into their shared sexual universe. 'What is it, *cara*?' Paolo whispered anxiously.

'I can't explain,' she said, sitting up and wrapping her arms around her knees. She couldn't tell him that she, for the first time in her life, knew what jealousy was. It was a far, far worse feeling than anything she had ever read about in novels. Books did not describe the long-toothed monsters that whirled and twisted in her stomach. The tearing of her body until she believed she might die from the pain. The gasping and the retching over the lavatory at night. Sweating in her bed that soaked her and her nightdresses. If this is love, then I want none of it, she groaned, sleepless.

Some nights she stood motionless in front of her drawing room windows, gazing out into the blackness. She pondered on the well that Paolo had shown her. In that well, like still, deep water, lay tenderness. This was something she had never experienced in her relationship with Syracuse. He was incapable of tenderness. That, she knew, had always been missing in their marriage.

Paolo also sensed her inner world. The part of her that she kept hidden from everyone except Allegro. How odd that a six-year-old child could anticipate and sense, with her rare antennae, her mother's unspoken thoughts; but of course it was not odd. Allegro still had the clear vision of an innocent child. She was not barnacled with envy and hatred.

Dr Stanislaus had also become a cornerstone in Madeleine's life. His calm reassurance, that life was not at all what it seemed to be, sustained her. He was there to hold her elbow during the difficult days. He reassured her that there was a higher meaning to everyday, common hurts and woundings.

She remembered the day that Paolo's wife had been due to leave New York. Madeleine had been watering her plants. She'd been waiting with the usual aching uncertainty for the telephone call from Paolo to tell her that he was free again. Would he call? Did he still want her? All the questions of every mistress everywhere.

Did he ever wonder if she wanted him? Did he ask himself anxiously if she'd changed her mind and no longer loved him? Probably not. He knew the answers, as most men do everywhere.

Women give their whole heart in the affairs of love. That is their tragedy. Men rarely, and that is their tragedy. She felt like Ophelia. Slightly mad. And then she smiled. She could hardly drown herself in the thin trickle from her hose. She could save on the water bill and water her plants with her tears. Really, I am too ridiculous, she told her plants. Now Paolo is leaving for Siena, Hilary and I must make plans to have such a wonderful time in England that I won't have time to think about Paolo.

The problem was that the ache in her heart would not go away. Paolo had unleashed a whole new sensual side of her that had been closed down since the early days of her marriage to Syracuse. He was gentle but demanding in bed. He knew what pleased him, but above all he knew what pleased and excited her. The knowledge that he could intuitively meet her needs fired her into an excess of passion. Often they both lay gasping for joy on his bed.

'You are a marvellous lover, Paolo.' She hugged him.

'*E tu, cara mia.*' He lay there, smiling. It was their last time together before he left for Siena. He kissed her gently on her satisfied lips.

'*Amore mio,*' she whispered. She'd decided that Italian was the only language for love.

Forty-three

Sometimes the guilt of depriving Allegro of a father wore heavily upon Madeleine's shoulders.

'Don't be so silly, Maddie,' Edwina told her. 'That little shit of a husband of yours never did anything for Allegro except spoil her. He was never at school meetings with you. You were always alone. In fact, you did very little together, and if you were at a party with him, he ignored you almost totally. How much does he see of her now?'

'Not a lot, Edwina. She doesn't like fast food and he hangs out there all the time, probably looking lustfully at the waitresses. He looks dreadful these days. Like an overgrown spring chicken. He's into clothes that are much too young for him, and he's growing a beer belly. I wonder what the hell I ever saw in him.'

'Big lesson in life, darling, people don't change.'

'Yes they do, Edwina. I refuse to believe that people can't change, and for the better. Psychopaths don't change, that's all. Oh, they can make promises, and for a while they can put on an act; but really, in the end, they don't change. I'm sorry for Syracuse. He's scared now. He thought he'd run off to some big party, and he's learning that there is no party for him any more. Just a drab little life. Dad's cut out his foreign travel and he has to pay me most of his salary, whether he wants to or not. So I guess he's broke.' She laughed, and was surprised at the bitterness behind the laugh. She thought she was over most of the hurt, but evidently not.

Her long evening telephone calls with Edwina were her lifeline to reality. 'Still, I'm off to London next week with Hilary, and we are going to have a ball. Mom and Dad have booked us a suite at the Savoy for my Christmas present, and I'm really looking forward to travelling with another woman. When you travel with a man, you have to take care of them. Funny how a man will say, "Don't worry about a thing, honey, I'll take care of you."

'You think, wow, that's great, and then discover what he really means is, "Don't worry about a thing, honey, because I know you will take care of me."

'With Syracuse I had to vacate the bathroom as soon as he wanted to use it. Order his food. See that he had clean clothes. This time I'm only responsible for Allegro, and she's a joy to travel with. Unlike her father, she'll eat anything, and loves to see everything. I'm most looking forward to taking her to the Tate Gallery. By the way, I'm having dinner tonight with Germaine. Do you have any messages for her?'

'Yeah, tell her to spend Christmas with us. I can't stand Scott over Christmas. All he does is whine about his childhood, and resent the presents that Tarquin gets. Really, all men are such children.'

'Paolo isn't a child.'

'You don't really know Paolo, Madeleine. You only get the best of him, and that's a mistress's perk, you know.'

'That's true. I'll remember that when I'm missing him like mad. You know you were right. The other day when his wife was here, I passed by in the car; and then I had to lie to Allegro about our new route from school. Isn't that ridiculous?'

'Not really. You've had years of ill-treatment from Syracuse, and you're grateful to Paolo for picking you up off the floor and bringing you back to life. Affairs with married men are always painful. Don't get too used to the idea of being with Paolo. He may get bored, or you may decide you don't want to go on with the affair. Just take each day as it comes and get the best out of it.

'Most of the damage is done by women thinking that they want the same relationship with their lover as they have with their husbands, but Paolo can't be that to you. He can't go to Allegro's school with you. He can pick up the telephone and telephone you, now Syracuse has gone, but then he doesn't much like the telephone, does he?'

'No, he treats it with the deepest suspicion. He often just writes a note or, if he can see me unexpectedly, he leaves a bunch of flowers on my doorstep. Allegro doesn't really know anything about him, but she thinks the flowers are a present from her unicorn friend.'

'Wow, how very romantic of him.'

'Well, he is romantic and very Italian. I always thought all Italian men only loved their mothers, but he has a good mom. He loves her, but not too much. Still, I'd better go and get Allegro.

'I was just thinking last night that I don't think I could get married again. I'm getting so used to my own bedroom. All the time in the world in my own bathroom. I feel as if I've shifted away from an awful black hole of mourning, and I'm beginning to see a light.'

'I know what you mean. Scott is a bad-tempered bastard first thing in the morning. Take my advice. Find yourself a very rich man and live in one wing of his house.'

'Nah, I'll be rich and I'll stay single. Allegro is my top priority. I really must change my nail varnish. I think I'll choose a tangerine colour for London.' She blew

Edwina a kiss over the telephone. ''Bye, honey. I'll send you a postcard from the Savoy. I wish you were coming with us.'

'So do I, but Scott wants me to be here for the whole bloody boring business of the Christmas meal. I pointed out that we'd just finished eating an enormous turkey dinner for Thanksgiving, and now I have to cook the whole meal again four weeks later. I want to have fish or something different. But no, it's all got to be like Mom did it. Only his mom is a brilliant cook and I'm not.'

'Hire outside caterers, Edwina. Have the whole thing brought in and save your nail varnish. I've found a fabulous take-away, and when it's Cook's day off I don't do anything but pick up the telephone. Now I don't have to feed Syracuse, I have nails that are a permanently pretty colour.'

'Sometimes I think you're the luckiest bitch alive.' Edwina's voice was envious.

'I must get off the phone. You're right, I am the luckiest bitch alive.' Madeleine put down the telephone. She felt uneasy. As if she had left her friend in an uncomfortable place. I must quit bragging about my freedom, she decided as she ran for the door.

Forty-four

'I feel that Edwina is very jealous of my freedom some-times. I don't know why, but it makes me feel guilty.'

'Don't be.' They were sitting in the bar finishing up a plate of gnocchi with a Gorgonzola sauce. They both picked at the plate with their spoons.

How nice it is, thought Madeleine, to sit with Germaine and know that I can have a good gossip with her and she will never repeat it to anyone. 'Edwina has choices, you know, Madeleine. She puts up with that dreadful man for his money. On her own she couldn't live at the standard they share. Her attempts at interior decorating don't bring in much. For her it's just a jobby. Something to keep her interested. Something to get her out of bed. America is full of middle-class married ladies who have their "jobbies" to keep them off the New York iced tea. She compromises her life. It's very bad for the soul, compromising. It takes all the spontaneity out of life.'

'I know that. I compromised for years. But you don't know that you're doing it until you stop. That's the problem. Middle-class women live in mink-lined cages.'

'They do, and when they shake the bars they don't give off a warning rattle.' Germaine laughed. Her eyes lit up.

'You know what I love most, Germaine. Every day is a new day. I can make the decision to do anything I like. Before, it was always Syracuse first. Then whatever Allegro needed. Then the staff and their problems, and finally me.

'Now it's me first, then Allegro, and after that the staff. I wake up each day fresh and happy. Still get days when I feel lost and insecure, but then I remind myself how awful life was with Syracuse and I cheer up.

'Anyway, I didn't come here to talk about myself. I came to ask you to give me a wish list. I want to buy you something wonderful from Fortnum and Mason's. Mom is asking her personal shopper to look out some party dresses for me. What would you like?'

'Not party dresses, Madeleine. Not for me. I think I'd be very grateful for a pair of English-cut jodhpurs. I need them for my next trip to Libya.'

'OK, done. I'll get a pair myself. I'd love to ride again, and also to get Allegro riding. By the way, Edwina says would you spend Christmas with her?'

'As a Christian act of charity, I suppose I will. If only to protect her from Scott. What a bastard that man is. Ugh, he has voyeur's eyes. They are like cameras. He watches women as if he has X-rays behind his eyes that can take their clothes off. Quick, order another grappa and some coffee. I need a change of mood. I hate the way he farts whenever he feels like it, and yawns with his mouth wide open.'

Madeleine kissed Germaine goodbye and then left her at the subway. She liked the doughty, independent streak in Germaine. It was missing in Edwina, but then Edwina was so delightfully perverse. She would miss them both.

Forty-five

❧

She boarded the plane with Hilary and the children in the early hours of the morning. In her hand-luggage she carried a precious bottle of Brunello di Montalcino. Paolo had given the bottle to her after kissing her good-bye in his apartment. 'It's a 1985 *vendemmia, cara*. I want you to drink it for me when you are in the Savoy.'

'Oh, Paolo, would it ever be possible for us both to be there at the same time?'

'No, *amore*, you know it wouldn't be possible. I have too many friends who drink in the American bar. It's a favourite place for Italians. Most of the staff are Italian, and many of the chefs also, so we feel at home there. It is difficult for an Italian to feel at home anywhere but in Italy. Still, we can find places where we can be together. When you come back we will go away for a weekend.'

He sounded so detached. It was as if she was going away and that was that. She felt torn and wounded. 'Do you think about me, Paolo, when you are at home?'

She watched a slight cloud steal over his face. 'Yes, sometimes,' he said absently.

'I think about you all the time I'm away from you, darling.' She knew she shouldn't offer this piece of secret information, but the pain of separation made her feel desperate for a response.

'You shouldn't do that, *cara*, it will make you sad. Why be sad when we can usually see each other any time we want?'

She remembered their last love-making. How she'd

hugged him to her body. She stretched herself against him, wishing that she could merge into his flesh. She remembered how he moved inside her, and she was filled with an unholy feeling of absolute terror. Where did she catapult off to? She remembered how she fell again and again through dizzying gorges. Colours flashed and she felt as if she was burned by the kiss of a hot sun in the centre of her soul. Paolo's love-making freed her in a way she'd never experienced with Syracuse. Even as she floated, this time, gently back to earth, she knew she must always be with a man who could stretch her to these dimensions. Then she also knew that the man who was capable of that was in her arms now, and she trembled at the thought of losing him.

Sitting on the plane, she remembered how she sat wrapped in his towelling robe while he showered. The robe smelled of him. She looked at the tag inside. Of course, the robe was from Siena. 'Upim', it read. Everything in the apartment was from Siena. She looked up at the map over the bed. It was a picture of the delicate shelled Campo, the *duomo* and the *comune*. She knew them all after poring over her map and reading book after book about Tuscany.

She wondered now, as the plane pulled away, whether loving Paolo was too high a price to pay. Happiness with him was such a fleeting pleasure. Maybe the dreadful feeling of failure about her marriage made her feel more vulnerable than most at the thought of the possibility of losing Paolo. Though it was true, Syracuse could hardly be thought of as a loss. Still, it was the loss of an ideal; of a person he never actually had been. She knew she gave him expectations and ideals he could not reach. She had stretched out her maternal hand to help an orphaned young man. She herself, with her mother and father and her disciplined lifestyle, had obviously attracted Syracuse. He also saw a young and vulnerable woman who was at a loss in the world of aggressive masculine sexuality. He was canny enough to insinuate himself into her life. To play the friend, and then the handsome lover, and finally to take vows to protect her, renouncing all others. Well, she had already paid, and would pay for some time to come for that mistake, and now she was risking herself again. Sitting in the plane, she sighed at the memory of the moment, and then she smiled at Allegro, who had her nose pressed against the glass window.

'Happy, darling?' she said as they both watched the clouds tumbling by.

'Oh, Mom, just think: we're going to London!'

'Honey, I'm so excited! What shall we do first?'

'I want to dress in my new trousers and go to Harrods' toy department and then I want to have a real English tea like Hilary told us about. Muffins and cakes and cream and tea in an English tea-pot. That's what I would like.'

'And that's what you shall have, my love.'

Forty-six

❧

'I have only literally walked into my suite, Syracuse, and you are on the telephone. Can't you give us a few days to settle down?'

'I can telephone any time I want to talk to my daughter, Madeleine, and you can't stop me.'

Madeleine could hear the New York whine in his voice. It made her mad. She flushed with anger. 'I don't want Allegro to think I don't think of her all the time. You're trying to turn her against me. You're trying to win her away from me.'

'What's the matter, Mom?' Allegro ran to her mother in the drawing room. 'Gee, you're mad at somebody.'

'No, I'm not, honey. Here, take the phone, it's your father.'

'Hi, cup-cake, it's Dad. How was the flight?'

'It was great, Dad. We flew over mountains in a place called Switzerland. I know about that place because they make great chocolate and the stewardess gave me some. This is a great hotel. We have a bath, big like a swimming pool, and I can see the River Thames outside my bedroom window. As soon as we get changed, I'm going to go to Harrods' toy department. Dad, what do you want for Christmas? I forgot to ask you.' Syracuse felt a lump in his throat. At least somebody loved him.

'Nothing, cup-cake, just you come home to your Dad who loves you more than he loves anybody in the whole wide world. How big is my love for you, Allegro?' He imagined her little skinny arms stretched to their widest in her drawing room at the Savoy. He really should be there with her. It was most unfair, and typical of Madeleine's evil nature that she should boot him out and then try to turn his only child against him. He was glad he'd left the bitch. She was a total neurotic. He'd tried. He'd done everything and anything a man could do to make and to keep her happy, and in the end she had kicked his teeth in.

No, he was better off as he was, and when Allegro got back they'd go off for some fun together. Maybe the amusement park in Orlando: it would be warm enough. If her rich bitch of a mother could take her to the Cayman Islands, perhaps he could persuade Lucinda that they could take Allegro to Orlando.

'Honey, when you get back, would you like to go to Disney World in Orlando?'

'Sure, Dad, I'd love that.' Madeleine watched as her daughter's little feet danced with pleasure. There was a sour taste in Madeleine's mouth. Already Syracuse had managed to cast a shadow over the holiday.

'I'll ring you every night, cup-cake. Give your Daddy a big kiss down the telephone. One that will knock my ear off.' Allegro giggled and let loose some big, smacking kisses. 'I love you, cup-cake.'

'I love you, Dad, I love you lots.' She put the telephone down and grinned at her mother. 'Dad says he's going to take me to Disney World in Orlando. Oh Mom, isn't everything just great? Come on, let's get changed, and we can go off to Harrods. Jonathan,' she yelled. 'Come on, where are you? Where's Justin?' She opened the door between the two suites. 'Are you ready yet?'

'That was Syracuse on the telephone,' Madeleine said dryly in response to Hilary's raised eyebrows.

'Huh, well, that's no surprise. Wait until Peter starts. I bet he sends a big bunch of flowers. That'll impress the boys no end. Ahhh, Dad really loves Mom. When will she let him come home?' She frowned. 'The answer to that is when hell freezes over, and then I'll be skating on his face.'

'Don't you feel bad being so bitter?' Madeleine watched her friend's lined face.

'No, he made my life a living hell and I'm right to be angry. We English don't analyse everything to death like you Americans. We get angry cleanly and honestly. Peter can bugger off for the rest of his life. I'm going to live on this side of the pond, and he can live the other side. I'm not going to be the typical American single parent and live on my own in New York trying to struggle with the dirt and the violence. I'm going to build a life here in England, where women often live on their own and are respected for it.

'We have a history going back through the two world wars, where women were called spinsters. I had several aunts like that, and I grew up admiring their lifestyles enormously. I used to watch my mother slaving to take care of us and our father, and I swore I'd never get married. Idiot that I was, I fell for Peter. Still, I have the boys, and even those awful years with Peter made that worth while. Anyway, before the arsehole contacts the boys, let's go off to the toy shop. I love toy shops. I was so glad that I had two boys, so I could buy guns and knives.' She laughed.

'I might as well have had a boy,' Madeleine admitted. 'Allegro plays with nothing else but boys' toys. I did try and convince her to wear a dress to Harrods. But no joy. I'm afraid it's jeans.'

They climbed into Allegro's first London taxi. Madeleine sat watching her daughter's face. How like mine, she thought, looking at the opalescent light that radiated from her face in the dark interior of the cab. Madeleine had lost the battle of the dress, but instead of jeans,

Allegro was wearing her Black Watch tartan slacks with a dark green pullover that set off her rose-coloured hair. Her eyes were sparkling, and the green of her eyes matched her jumper. 'First time in London, little lady?'

The taxi driver beamed at her over his shoulder. 'Yeah, and we're going to Harrods to see the toy department. I got twenty dollars from my grandpa to spend.'

'You'll have to get that changed. We don't use dollars over here. What are you going to buy?' Allegro thought for a moment. A cornucopia of ideas flooded through her mind. 'I think – let me see,' she whispered to herself. 'I think I'm going to buy a whole set of soldiers. The kind that guard the queen. Do you know the queen?'

'No, I don't, but she's our queen all right, God bless 'er.' He smiled and glanced at Madeleine in the mirror. 'You got a beautiful little girl there.'

'Thank you,' Madeleine blushed.

'And 'er mother's not a bad looker either,' he told himself as he watched the happy little party of women and children rush into the main door of the shop. 'Pity about the war, though.' He still had a bitter memory of losing his first girlfriend to a big American bloke who had an unlimited supply of chocolates and silk stockings. Still – he put his foot down on the gas pedal – Maeve's a good wife, and he too had a beautiful daughter. The memory of Allegro's face haunted him for the next few days and, as he passed the Savoy, he kept an eye out for that wild-coloured hair and those blazing eyes. She'll make some man a cracker of a wife, he thought. Then he grinned. Life wasn't like that any more, but he wished her all the luck in the world. Sentimental old fool that I am. 'Look out, you bastard,' he shrieked at a passer-by.

Forty-seven

❧

'Madeleine has no idea how upset I am. She's a selfish bitch. I can't believe we were married so long, and she doesn't even care about how I feel. She is a cold, heartless woman, and I'm better off without her.'

'Sure, Syracuse, you are better off without her. Now could you just stop talking about her all the time? Quit whining – you bore me.'

Lucinda rolled off him and sat cross-legged on the floor gazing at him. 'Look, honey, she's gone. Forget her and get on with your own life. You're here with me now. Why don't you take me out dancing? I'm bored.'

'I'm too tired to go dancing, Lucinda. Why can't you cook dinner and let me watch the Chicago Bears?'

'Because I've been off duty and stuck here in the apartment. I want to go and get crazy.'

'We can get crazy all by ourselves after the match.'

'OK, but you got to smoke a joint, otherwise you premature ejaculate and that's no good for me.'

He very much wished that Lucinda would keep her brutally honest remarks to herself. Madeleine never complained like Lucinda did. 'OK, OK. Anything you say. What's for dinner?'

He really felt bummed out at the idea of smoking a joint. It made him feel soft and dreamy and out of control, and he hated to feel he was out of control. Besides, the weed made his throat raw. Why couldn't she just let him get on with making love at his own speed? OK, he came too fast, but that wasn't a sin. But he'd learned with Lucinda never to criticise anything she did. She had a scream that could stop turtles mating. He was terrified of her anger. Madeleine never screamed; she only wept and implored. Oddly enough, he now realised that Madeleine brought out the cruel side of his nature. The more he watched her tear-stained face, the more he wanted to kick her face in. Not literally, of course; he would never dream of striking a woman.

However, Lucinda had no such repressions when it came to hitting him. For a small, slender woman she packed quite a punch, and she was lethal with a frying pan. He learned to keep most of his comments to himself. Anyway, he got to watch the football match, and supper would be good. He sighed. Sometimes he wondered if Madeleine missed him at all. He rather thought not, judging from her cool voice on the telephone. Now she was in her suite in London. He knew it would be a long time, if ever, before he saw the inside of the Savoy. Still, he was young, and he was working hard. Soon he must find another job. He couldn't stand his father-in-law's restrictions. He was bored with New York. Very bored. He wanted his Mei Mei. The thought of her gentle, loving hands filled his eyes with tears.

Western women were the pits, he muttered, and went to put on the television. Damn Madeleine. He'd had life by the tail, and she had gone and ruined it. He wondered if she had a man yet. Probably not. No man would want to put up with her behaviour. Spoiled, that's what she was. Spoiled rotten by her loving, over-protective parents. He plumped himself down on the sofa and gazed bleakly at the threadbare carpet under his feet. He'd a quick vision of the beautiful Chinese hand-washed carpets in the drawing room, and then he settled back on the sofa with his six-pack beside him.

At least he could be himself with Lucinda. Drink his beer from a bottle, yell at the television, and slump all he wanted to. He was now who he really was. A red-blooded, all-American male. He grunted. Thank God, no more trying to behave like an English country gentle-man. In Lucinda's cupboards his English-cut suits were gathering mould. Out of work, it was jeans for him. Jeans and American T-shirts. Whatever had made Madeleine think he could become an Englishman? But then, when you are in love, you'll do anything to convince the woman you love that you'll jump stars and ride the moon for her. That's what love is all about, he thought as he switched on the channel. Soon he was watching the game intently. 'Atta-boy, stomp the bastards,' he screamed.

Lucinda came into the room and put a plate of steak and chips on his lap. She bent down and kissed him and handed him the tomato ketchup. Syracuse grunted his thanks. There's a woman who really knows how to look after a man, he thought as he bit into his steak.

Lucinda walked into the kitchen and wondered how long Syracuse was planning to stay. She had her eye on a nice little Chinese nursing assistant at the hospital. He had snake hips and a mean look in his eye that she intended to explore.

Forty-eight

'Edwina?'

'Hi, honey, how are you?'

'I'm fine, Edwina. We spent our first afternoon in Harrods' toy department, and now we're heading off to Hamleys. Allegro is in seventh heaven. She thinks London is all toy shops and roast beef and Yorkshire pudding. Listen, could you do me a favour?'

'Sure. What?'

'Can you remember exactly where Paolo's house is in Siena?'

'Why, Madeleine, you're not going to go and give the wife the once over?'

'Of course not, whatever gave you that idea? I was just looking at a map of Siena in a tourist book, and I wondered, that's all. I can't talk to him because he's in Siena, and I miss him so terribly. I didn't know you could feel quite so much pain. It's dreadful. I miss him so much more than I ever missed Syracuse. I don't miss him at all. He's whining down the telephone at Allegro. I just let him get on with it.'

'OK, Maddie, let me think. You walk up the road from the Campo. Walk right up to the top near the Feltrinelli book shop, and then you turn right down a very narrow road and it's the third house on the left. It has a big brass knocker and there are metal guards over the windows. You can't miss them. They look like music scrolls. Maddie, why are you tormenting yourself? I've done it enough times to warn you. Stay away from the wife. It just makes the hurt worse.'

'I will try, Edwina, but I feel as if I've got this knife in my chest when he's with her. It twists and turns and I can't sleep. Allegro lies there uttering her little baby snores, and I walk the room. I never loved Syracuse. I felt sorry for him. I felt guilty because I led such a wonderful, privileged life and he hadn't.

'If I'd known that falling in love with Paolo was going to make me crazy, maybe I'd have said no to him. But then I would have lived my life as Syracuse's wife, and that was awful. So I risked myself and now I am suffering the consequences. Oh why,' she heard the desperation in her own voice and it frightened her, 'does it have to be like that?'

'Because, honey, we only learn when it hurts. I've got Peter whimpering like a lost dog on my doorstep. Talking about Peter reminds me to ask, how's Hilary doing?'

'Not bad for the walking-wounded. She's written to Peter to tell him she's not coming back. I'm seriously thinking of doing the same thing. I've always wanted Allegro to go to school in England, and she's nearly seven now. I'm really not comfortable with the fact that Syracuse is going to demand loads of access rights.

'I don't want him to fill her head with all his nonsense either. The child's no fool. For the moment she knows he's with Lucinda, but before long there will be someone else. What do you think?'

'I think you should do whatever feels best for you. To live in England has always been a dream of mine. Don't worry about Allegro; she'll turn out fine. She's never been that close to Syracuse anyway. He was abroad so much of the time fucking. You could let your house and give your new life a fresh start. Anyway, Siena is closer to England, isn't it?'

'Yeah, but Paolo stays in the Savoy when he's here, and I couldn't visit him there. I won't see so much of him, but maybe that's no bad thing?'

'I think it might be just as well, Maddie. You should spread your wings. Date other men for a bit. Don't put all your eggs in one basket.'

'I'll think about that. It's difficult if you've found a particularly good basket. Anyway, how's Germaine?'

'She's fine. She tells me she's found a Libyan professor at her institute who takes her out for cous-cous and kebabs. So far it's platonic, and knowing Germaine it probably always will be.'

'Don't be too sure of it. I've always thought that Germaine would fall hard when she falls. Sounds good to me. Goodbye, Edwina. I miss you.'

'I miss you too. Bring me back the English tea and some after-dinner mints?'

'Sure thing.' Madeleine put down the telephone. She smiled a soft, gentle smile. Edwina knew her better than she knew herself.

After they moved down from London to Devon to stay with Hilary's people, Madeleine fully intended to slip across the Channel, go to Italy and wander past the house. She had to know where Paolo lived. Fire raged through her veins at the thought of catching a glimpse of him. She wanted to know everything about him. She realised that her fantasy of him was not fully fleshed out. What did his house look like? How did his wife look? Did his children look like her or like Paolo? Was his wife more beautiful than she was?

The exhilaration of being in London made her cheeks flush and her eyes flash. She felt indecently randy all the time. Maybe she could bump into Paolo on the Campo and persuade him to take her to a hotel? Maybe not. She knew with an absolute certainty that she would lose him if she in any way threatened his life with his wife and family.

No, far better to just go and look. To lean on street corners. To lurk in the passages that she now knew from maps of Siena. She imagined the city shaped like a honeycomb.

What held Paolo to his wife? Was it really love? He never discussed her or the children. It was as though they didn't exist. In the apartment there were no children's drawings. Nothing to suggest it was anything but a bachelor's apartment. But the wife and the children did visit it. What did he do with the discarded toys when they left? With the bits of ribbon pulled impatiently off ponytails? With rubber bands abandoned in the bathroom? Sindy dolls with bright scarlet shoes? All swept away as Paolo returned to being a bachelor and entertaining women in the apartment.

She wondered if she was the only woman now that went to the apartment. She couldn't even answer that question. Another rule. Thou shall not find out about your lover. Only that which he is prepared to let you know. Well, she would break that rule. She *would* find out.

'Allegro,' she called out for comfort and reassurance.

'Yes, Mom?'

'Let's go find Hilary and the boys and split.' She smiled at her daughter's eager face. 'Give me a hug, darling,' she said, gazing into her daughter's deep green eyes.

Forty-nine

Madeleine followed behind her daughter's dancing feet. Miles of Hyde Park, the zoo, the Tate Gallery flowed past her. She responded by smiling, inanely she sometimes felt, at the little group that housed her. Hilary, sensing something was wrong, tried to help her. 'What is it, Madeleine? What's happening inside you? You aren't really here. You're not listening to what we are saying or doing. It's like you're a robot.'

Madeleine couldn't bring herself to say that she was fighting an internal battle against ringing up her travel agent in New York and booking a ticket to Siena.

How odd, she thought, standing in front of a huge Turner painting at the Tate. Ever since I was a child, I've wanted my children to see this painting. Now, here we are, and all I can think about is a married man who might be in Siena or might not. She'd decided then and there to telephone Edwina and ask her to check on Paolo's whereabouts. Now she even used her friends in her efforts at spying on her lover. She felt dirty and ashamed. She felt driven, just as she felt sexually driven to make love to herself again and again. How could one man give her such intense delight? She felt ashamed partly because she shared her room with Allegro. Thank goodness they had separate beds; but still, after she had finished, she lay bathed in sweat and she could see Allegro's profile innocently asleep on her pillow.

No longer did she wonder if it was all worth while. It was far too late for that kind of thinking. She was enmeshed in Paolo just as surely as if she had been installed as a crankshaft. It was an odd image, but it had been brought on by the sight of a sleep-purring Rolls-Royce gliding past outside her hotel window. The suite comforted her. How many mournful lovers had stood where she often stood, gazing out over the Thames? Hundreds? She imagined a long line of deserted and abandoned women standing behind her, stretching through the history of the hotel. Only she was not abandoned. Paolo loved her very much. He had told her so in his lovely, lilting Italian. She assumed he didn't love his wife. Happily married men did not have affairs – or maybe she was being naïve? Maybe married men had it all. Happy marriages and affairs. It was different for women. Edwina was certainly not happily married, by any stretch of the imagination. Madeleine always imagined Edwina imprisoned by Scott, her blonde hair and one arm sticking out of the marriage, waving a yellow duster of surrender.

Only Hilary and she had tottered out of their respective concentration camps and were clinging to the wreckage that their escape had left. Doubts and lost promises and vows were strewn like a dirty heap of confetti on the paths behind them.

'I think the boys are much more relaxed now that I don't live with Peter any more. They are glad they don't have to put up with his mistresses. The last one was a dumb blonde.' Hilary smiled her slow, painful smile. They were sitting at the dinner table in the River Room. 'I know that's me trying to rationalise my guilt over depriving them of a father,' she shrugged. 'But then if I'd stayed, I'd have become an alcoholic to deal with the pain.'

'*Anche me*, me too. I was taking to the gin and tonics at an astonishing rate. I realised that we were only happily married as long as he was allowed to play. As soon as he had to get down to some serious work, and I had to devote myself to the new baby, it all stopped. He had a good act, but Mom saw through him far quicker than I did. I was a fool, I suppose.' A long sigh shuddered from her heart.

'Yes, we both were, Madeleine; but maybe we have learned something to our benefit.'

'I don't think I've learned anything. Hilary, could you do me an enormous favour?'

'I'll try. What is it?'

'Do you think I could pop off for the weekend and leave Allegro with you?'

'Of course, but where do you want to go?' Hilary looked startled.

'Well,' Madeleine looked shame-faced, 'I know this sounds crazy, but I want to go to Siena. I'm probably deluding myself, but I want to see where Paolo lives. I have this absolute passion to see his wife. I always swore I'd never do a thing like that, but there you go. All my life I've been the sort of person who says I won't do something, and then I go and do it.'

Hilary gazed fixedly at Madeleine. 'I have never had an affair, and only two lovers before I married Peter, so I'm not much use, but I'd find it terribly complicated to fall in love with a married man.'

'Believe me, it is.' Madeleine's voice was bitter. 'I'm planning to write a rule book about the whole miserable business. For a start I don't know if he's in Siena. I'm going to have to implicate Edwina. She'll have to check if he's in his apartment or not. Even if he isn't, he may well be elsewhere on business, and I can't ring his house in case his wife answers. I can't telephone his apartment because she could be there, or a friend of the family who would be suspicious if a strange American woman telephoned for Paolo. I suppose I could always pretend I'm the woman from American Express calling to check an item on his account. That's the sort of thing Edwina would do, but I'm no actress. I think I'll just go to Siena and quench my curiosity. At the moment I'm in such a turmoil, I can't enjoy the holiday. You know you can watch countries fighting each other on television, and bleed for the people and cry for the children, but what's going on inside me is invisible and it hurts so much I could die sometimes, Hilary.'

'I know that feeling, Madeleine. I feel as if I'm permanently walking on glass shards, my feet dripping with blood. Sometimes when we are walking on the pavement, I am amazed that there is no blood trailing behind me. You know, I often think we know so much about our external worlds, and very little at all about what goes on inside us.'

Madeleine nodded her agreement. 'Germaine is good that way. She sits in the desert and goes inside herself. I'm getting better. I feel as if I'm an iceberg with only the very tip of who I am showing; underneath all the water and the sludge is the real me, and that's what needs to get out.

'I've been held under water by trying to take care of Syracuse. He stood on my shoulders while I was drowning. He'll do that to any woman who'll let him, and I've got to learn for once that no man is worth drowning for.'

Hilary watched her friend and then she said firmly, 'You go, Madeleine. Even if he's not there and you just see his house and his wife, at least it will all become real to you. For now, so much of your love affair with Paolo exists in fantasy.'

'Paolo has never been interested in my life, my home, or anything outside the time I spend with him. Maybe all men are like that? They exist in boxes. I'm not sure whether, if I decide to live in England, Paolo will want me any more. I won't be his box in New York. He knows everything that I do because I tell him. I know nothing of his life. He tells me nothing. It all feels so odd. So uneven. But then Edwina says that's normal. Scott confesses all his affairs to her. Syracuse did that to me. I was his home-coming Mommy. My job was to listen, mop his brow, forgive him. Then he'd sail off to the next port-of-call.' Madeleine finished her coffee. 'Come on, let's go. With any luck the children will be fast asleep.'

'Fat chance,' Hilary laughed.

'Mom's downstairs having dinner with Hilary, and we're watching television.' Madeleine could hear Allegro's high, clear voice answering the telephone. Her mouth tightened. That would be Syracuse. She glanced at her watch. It was late. 'No, Mom doesn't have uncles, just us.'

Madeleine strolled into the drawing room. She took the telephone from Allegro's hand. She bent over and kissed her. 'Run along, honey, and watch your programme. Shut the door behind you.' She waited until Allegro had closed the heavy cream doors with their big brass handles. 'What the fuck do you think you're doing, Syracuse? Questioning my daughter about men in my life? Don't be so disgusting. Just because you fuck about, doesn't mean I do it.'

'You don't have to be so virtuous, Maddie. No men are going to be interested in you. You and your awful temper. What's the matter, are you on the rag again?'

Madeleine found herself shaking with anger. She would leave America and bring Allegro up in England. Far away from Syracuse and his whining, miserable little existence. If he could afford it, he could come and visit her. If not, too bad. Allegro was better off without him. She slammed the telephone down and left the room. She had options, and Syracuse had better remember that.

She put Allegro to bed, and then picked up the telephone in the drawing room. 'Edwina, do you know if Paolo is in his apartment?' she asked her friend after they'd chatted for a while.

'I saw him at a cocktail party the other day, darling. He's in Siena for the next week, and then he goes to the Far East on business for a month. Why do you ask?'

'I know you will think this a lousy idea, Edwina. I want to pop over to Siena and take a look at his house and his wife.'

'Sure it's a lousy idea, but we all do it. Go on and get it over with. It will either cure you completely, or make it worse. Either way you can't win. It's just one of the many steps for a woman who is in love with another woman's husband.'

'Thanks for understanding, Edwina.'

'I keep telling you, that's what girlfriends are for.'

Madeleine put down the telephone. Without my women friends, I might as well be dead, she said to a passing tug. The tug hooted in agreement. She crept softly into the bedroom and opened the bar. She collected a large gin and tonic and a packet of roasted peanuts. Why did the gin and tonic taste especially good in England? It was the tonic, she decided. It wasn't sweet like the tonic in America. Well, soon she would be living here, and she could have as many gin and tonics as her heart desired. The thought made her smile, and a small icicle melted in her heart.

Fifty

Once Madeleine was on the aeroplane she felt nervous. She was sitting in the front row of the business class. In her hand she clutched a glass of champagne for courage. In her bag she carried her pink tin with her Dutch cap. She needed all the serenity she could muster. Why on earth was she doing this? She didn't know, but anything was better than the painful scabs of wanting to know where he lived and with whom. She sighed. The passenger sitting next to her looked up sharply. He had been reading the London *Times*. He was elderly and he had half-moon glasses on the bridge of his nose. 'Are you in trouble, young lady? That was a very big sigh.'

'Not really.' Madeleine was pleased to be called a young lady when she felt middle-aged and baggy. 'I think I'm doing something most unwise.'

'Then don't do it.' He reminded her of Dr Stanislaus. He had the same kind of warm brown eyes. 'Why don't you tell a complete stranger what it is that you are about to do, then let me advise you?'

'All right.' Madeleine liked the idea of unburdening her soul to a complete stranger. 'You see,' she continued, 'I'm in love with a married man. I never really meant to do it, because for me it is a terrible sin to pinch somebody else's husband, but I guess I was getting out of my own unhappy marriage and I was clutching at straws. The thing is, I never thought things would get this complicated. At first we just met at his apartment and . . .' She stumbled with embarrassment.

302

'Go on, my dear. I'm used to listening to young ladies who are taking risks.'

'Well, I discovered silly things like you can only contact him when he feels like it. Your life is divided into little boxes. You have your life with your child and your home, and he has his and doesn't want to discuss anything personal. Of course, he is wonderful and romantic, but for a woman that's not all there is to life. He isn't there to kiss your finger better. I can deal with all the big things in my life, but it's the little ones that tear me up. Like pinching my finger in a door or having the lavatory blocked. Of course Mrs Poole, my housekeeper, can sort it out for me, but it's just not the same.

'I'm used to having a man around the house. Mind you, my husband was an awful shit, and now I've sort of got half a relationship with a married man.' She stopped, feeling like a dried up old spigot.

'So you're going to Italy to find him?'

'No, actually *not* to find him: he'd be furious. I just have this terrible urge to go and see his house in Siena, and I have to see his wife.'

'Oh dear, you have a very bad dose of being in love.'

'Is that what this is?'

'I'm afraid so, my dear. We've all done it. I suggest you turn right round at the airport and go home.'

'I can't. I really can't. I feel that if I don't do this I'll go mad.'

'All right, dear, but don't say I didn't warn you. Here, I'll give you my address in London, and when it all comes tumbling round your ears, telephone me and I'll take you out to dinner and offer you gin and tonics and sympathy.'

'Do you drink gin and tonic as well?'

'Definitely, and only Bombay Gin – it's the driest. I

have to take my tonic water to the United States. It's far too sweet over there.

'Look, we're about to descend. Would you like me to hold your hand?'

'I would if you don't mind. I'm dreadfully frightened of taking off and landing.'

'So am I, my dear, so am I.' He took her hand and held it lightly. 'My name is Vincent Heatherington. Here is my card.'

She looked down at the card in her hand. 'You're a judge,' she said, smiling.

'What a pretty smile you have, child. Yes, I'm a high court judge, and well used to women in love. I saw them almost every day when I sat on the bench. Love makes fools of us all, dear.'

'No bigger one than me.' Madeleine lost her smile.

'When you get older, you realise that falling in love is always painful. I lost my wife a few years ago. I did not think I would ever recover. Every time I hear the Elgar Cello Concerto, I think of the times we listened to that together.

'There is a bit in the beginning that is unbearably tender. She was such a kind and tender woman. They don't make women like that any more, I'm afraid. Once I married her, I never looked at another woman. Why should I bother? She gave me everything I wanted. God was very good to me. He really blessed me with my Janet. She was my pride and joy.'

Madeleine watched his face soften with the memories of their years together; memories to keep him warm in this cold and lonely world. She had already made one mess of her life with Syracuse, and now she was probably going to create another mess with Paolo. Still, this was something she was going to do. To take these steps down her own personal *via dolorosa*. She was used to the procession around the church at Easter-time. The bloodstained steps of her Lord. He who so perfectly understood suffering. He was abandoned and betrayed by every one of his disciples. He did not have Allegro. The one person on this earth who would stay beside her. She missed her daughter fiercely. 'I'll be back soon, darling,' she silently promised Allegro. 'Sooner than you think,' said the little voice inside her heart. It was one of the guardians. She didn't know which one. 'Shut up,' she instructed the voice. 'Mind your own business.'

Fifty-one

She checked into a hotel half-way down to the Campo. Her father had recommended it to her when she telephoned to say that, instead of her usual Sunday call from England, she would be taking a short break in Siena. She felt guilty at the enthusiasm in her father's voice. 'Your mother and I love that hotel, and I'm thrilled that you will be staying there. Do you want me to get my secretary to book it for you?'

'No thanks, Dad, I'll enjoy doing it myself.' She stood now with her Italian phrase book in her hand, trying to remember the words in Latin. The manager of the front desk was young and very beautiful. He had a graceful Italian renaissance look about him. As she wandered down the wide road that led to the Campo, she was entranced by the beauty of the strong Tuscan faces all around her. The well-dressed children with open, smiling faces. She wondered how many of them had divorced parents. Probably nothing like America. They still had a passionate attachment to religion.

As she left the hotel, her luggage safely ensconced in her room, she looked into the bright well-stocked shops. Around her the young people paraded. She envied the girls their fresh faces. Their slim, unlined necks and their light brown skin. Once too she had looked like that. She sighed, then she saw the book shop and her heart started to beat. She turned the corner feeling frightened and ashamed. Frightened because if she bumped into Paolo, what would she say? She'd rehearsed her excuses many times, but none of them sounded at all convincing.

She was wearing a large hat that covered her face and dark glasses. She was dressed in a self-effacing suit, and she just hoped for the best. She turned the corner and walked under the arch. She swung her handbag in a jaunty fashion, and then she saw the house. The scrolled iron window-guard was just as Edwina had described it. She stood stunned as the fantasy became reality. This was her lover's house. In there he had his wife and two children. In the eaves of the house he had made love to Edwina, a casual pick-up from the Campo.

Her own relationship with Paolo had flowed from the moment he'd offered Edwina a drink; now Madeleine stood outside his house, eight thousand miles from home, having abandoned her daughter in England.

All this, to stand like a rock groupie outside his house. I want to see what his wife looks like, she reminded herself. She stood for several minutes watching the house. She realised being a Sienese house, it would have a secret internal life of its own. Siena was famous for its secrets, Paolo had explained to her. No American porches with swings and neighbours over the back fence.

No, so far what she had seen of Siena made her think of a small, arm-wrapped city. Silent and secret. Only the occasional laugh of young lovers sitting on the beautiful petal-shaped Campo. She had gone straight to the Campo by taxi. It was just as beautiful as Paolo's description. Now almost overloaded with the beauty of Siena and the sight of Paolo's house with its door shut for ever against her, she felt tears falling down her face and she turned to go.

As she did, the door opened. She blinked. The tall figure was Paolo, and beside him stood a small, dark-haired woman. She was dressed in a tight-fitting flowered dress. Her hair was swept up in a chignon. She had expensive, high-heeled Italian shoes on, and around her neck she wore big expensive pearls. On her wedding finger there flashed a five-carat diamond engagement ring. Madeleine slipped into a deep dark arch. She stood in the shadows and watched. Frozen with terror.

'*Andiamo, cara mia?*' Madeleine's ears strained to hear Paolo's deep voice asking the same question he often asked her, 'Shall we go, my darling?' The words tore a jagged hole in her side. '*Sì, amore.*' The woman's voice was light and pleasant. Paolo put his arm around his wife and they walked past Madeleine, both locked into their own shared reality.

Madeleine watched them go, numb for the moment except for the jagged words that hung out of her stricken body. She watched them reach the top of the street, and then Paolo bent down, towering over his small wife and kissed her gently on the mouth. At that moment Madeleine felt the world go black. She swayed on her feet and felt herself being pulled into a vortex. 'Help me,' she pleaded to the guardians. 'Where are you, Dr Stanislaus?'

'Consequences,' he whispered in her ear. 'You knew he was married and you pursued your fantasy. This is the reality.'

'I know,' Madeleine clutched her side. 'But it hurts too much, this reality.'

'You created the events that led to the consequences, didn't you?'

'I wanted it all to turn out so differently,' Madeleine protested.

'Don't we all?' Dr Stanislaus said softly. 'Don't we all?'

Fifty-two

She didn't know how she got back to the hotel. She knew she made a fool of herself as she stumbled and wept her way up the steep cobbled road. Her Siena had fallen apart on her. She, this wondrous city of love, had been treacherous. She had betrayed all Madeleine's dreams.

'But then,' the guardians reminded her as they led her invisibly back to her hotel, 'you betrayed your lover's wife.'

Madeleine nodded, momentarily aware that not only was she howling and falling on the cobbles in her high heels, but she was also talking to invisible people. 'I thought in the end he'd love me enough to leave her, but he didn't.'

She heard gales of cosmic laughter. She saw for a terrifying moment thousands of women with their arms outstretched and their hair wild and stringy. She knew that these were the undead. The women who killed themselves for the love of a man. A crime punishable by never seeing the Light. A torment for all ages. 'There is no second chance,' they lamented. 'No man is worth dying for. It is the first law of love.'

Madeleine tried shaking her head to get away from them, but they persisted, filling the narrow streets behind her. They jostled and pushed the on-lookers. 'What about men who betray their wives?' she screamed back. 'What happens to them?'

'Nothing, they do not carry the life-force within them.'

'Who are you?' Madeleine felt them pushing against her as she struggled up the hill.

'We are the monstrous regiment of women and we have waited for you for aeons. Now you are one of us, and our only salvation is through your daughter Allegro.'

'Allegro?' Madeleine was aghast. 'My daughter?'

'She was born so that we could have another chance. We can leave the unmanifest and live in the real world. We will follow her and she will lead us to our salvation.'

Madeleine reached the door of the hotel and she turned to confront the host of women. Only one remained. A slim, beautiful girl. Her hair was cut in a page-boy style. Her eyes were deep blue and her voice was hoarse. 'I killed myself for the love of my husband. Allegro will save me. You were told that she had a special task on earth. Well, she has, and we will be with you always. When she is twenty, we will come again. Till then, take my word for it, you will heal. It will take a long time and you will be *ananthropos*, which is a Greek word meaning "away from men". Take small steps like a child and one day you will smile again. Goodbye, Madeleine, and remember we all love you.' There was a blink. A tiny tear in the silk parachute of time, and the women slipped through.

How Madeleine got to her room and on to her bed she never understood. For a very long time she lay staring at the ceiling. After a while she had no more tears to cry. She didn't know it was possible to exhaust a well of tears, but it was. Her eyes were dry and glassy. Her chest was tired from heaving great sobs from the bottom of her heart and pushing them into the world.

She lay still, spent and empty. She telephoned the room-service desk and ordered a pot of tea. English tea.

Then she picked up the telephone, finding it almost too heavy to hold.

'When is the next flight out of Pisa?' she asked. She checked her watch; it was late afternoon.

'The last flight for London has gone, *signora*. There is an eight o'clock flight tomorrow morning.'

'Good. Could you ring my travel agent in London and ask him to get me home on that flight – and could he meet me at Heathrow, please?'

Thank goodness Robert was not just her travel agent; he was also a good friend. Right now, that's what she really needed. She drank her tea. What was it about tea that was so comforting? She climbed into a hot bath and then she fell back into bed after taking a sleeping pill.

Sleep came in fits and starts. Nightmares all tangled up with broken women's bodies and Paolo's face. Had other women killed themselves for love of him? She didn't know, but she did know that for her, now that she had Allegro, suicide was not a consideration. Besides, she would heal and she would get stronger in the broken places, and above all she would now stay with Hilary in England until they could both function again in the place called the real world.

She felt as if she had been in a major traffic accident and had been badly smashed. She lay on her back, thinking about the monstrous regiment of women. Why should women be so punished and not men? That seemed really so unfair. But then life was unfair. Look at Syracuse. He got fed up with her and ran off to the little nurse. He had plenty of offers. There were his mistresses in the Far East. Still, did she want to be like Syracuse? No, of course not. He was always miserable and always whining. She was far better off as she was. The thought cheered her enough to crawl across the room and pack her suitcase. Standing up felt much too dangerous. She telephoned Hilary.

'Darling, I'm coming back tomorrow. Robert is picking me up at Heathrow. Have a very stiff gin and tonic waiting for me, OK?'

'Are you all right?' Hilary's voice was worried.

'What's your pain level from one to ten, Hilary?'

'Oh,' Hilary gave a short laugh. 'Eight out of ten, I guess.'

'Well, mine's ten out of ten and I'll tell you about it tomorrow.'

Then the sobs came back and hit her like a force-nine gale. She picked up the receiver again.

'Edwina,' she whispered down the phone. 'I'm sorry about the time differences. Are you asleep?'

'Oh, Madeleine, you've seen him, haven't you?'

Madeleine was nodding her head. She couldn't speak, the pain was too dreadful. 'Darling, I told you not to go. Are you OK? Do you want me to come over?'

'No.' Her words came out in short gasps. 'I'm all right, Edwina. I'm being picked up at Heathrow in the morning. I've got to get on with my life and rescue a monstrous regiment of women when Allegro is twenty.'

'Maddie, are you sure you're OK?'

'Yeah, I've just taken a sleeping pill. I'll ring you when I get home. Tell Germaine that I love her.'

'I'll do that, darling. You get to sleep; you will get over this. I crucify myself over men all the time.'

'I'll never, *never* get over it.' Madeleine fell asleep, mumbling into her pillow that was now wet with her tears.

Fifty-three

It was all very well comforting yourself, like Hemingway, with the thought that suffering could strengthen you in the broken places; but come to think of it, he didn't do too well himself, did he? She tried to smile, and then she realised that she felt as if she had two black eyes and every bone in her body was broken. She had never imagined that pain could be so physical. She had suffered in those years of living with Syracuse, and when he left she had minded the humiliation of his being seen at her friends' houses with his little nurse, but she had been so bowled over with her love for Paolo that she had not given her divorce much thought. It would go through in time, and time was something she thought she had. No longer.

The train meandered through the beautiful Italian countryside. It was so breathtaking that Madeleine pinched herself. Am I in a Sienese fresco? she wondered. It was very early in the morning and the sun was just lighting up the tips of the cypress trees. The cypress trees surrounded the cemeteries. Nothing grew under them. She knew how they felt. Both times she had been betrayed. Nothing good grew near her. But she wasn't asleep or dreaming; it was all real.

I'm so sorry I have to leave like this, she thought. I feel like a whipped cur with my tail between my legs. She sat in the clean little train, squashed against a big-bosomed lady with a very black moustache and a man on her other side who smelled of garlic and red wine. They had impressive, bony faces and craggy chins.

313

Across the way sat a youth with shoulder-length blond hair. He was so staggeringly beautiful that Madeleine tried not to stare. He had a slim Michelangelo face and Madeleine wondered if he'd just stepped out of a painting. She sat, unable to speak the language, and now with a sigh she acknowledged she would never need to. Her love affair with Paolo was over.

Sitting on the aeroplane, she decided to telephone Mrs Poole and Nanny Barnes and ask them to pack up the house and offer them a job in England. She had no wish, at this point, to return to the States, or to the house she had shared with the poisoned dwarf. Those awful, unhappy years were over. She need never speak to Paolo again either. She would just drop out of sight. Mom and Dad could come over and visit. Besides, she had sufficient money in her trust fund to survive and rent a place in the country near Hilary's people. It would do her good to get away from America and Syracuse's whining voice. This way he couldn't have much access to Allegro. That comforted her, and with a plan in mind, she felt she could face the rest of the day.

Day one was over. In her thoughts, day one had been unbearable. How she'd survived it she did not know, but the vision of all those women sustained her. She would help them. Whatever lay ahead, she knew that no man was worth dying for. She had seen the evidence before her eyes, and she silently thanked the guardians for letting her catch a glimpse of the future. She had a purpose in life now. No more wasting time with men. That was for Edwina to do. She could come over with Germaine and visit whenever they felt like it. She would not lose two of the most important people in her life. By the time she was picked up by her travel agent at Heathrow, the first hole in the broken vase that was her heart was mended. Now there were just the odd million or two pieces to find.

The drive into London was horrific. Robert took one look at her face and bundled her into the car. 'Do you want to talk about it?'

Madeleine shook her head. 'No,' she said. 'How's business?'

'OK, not bad for this time of year.' He drove smoothly and efficiently. 'Hilary is waiting for you in the suite. I'll just drop you, because I've got to run to the Foreign Office and deliver tickets for the Russian ambassador.'

'Thanks, Robert, that was really kind of you.'

'Don't thank me, that's what friends are for.'

Madeleine smiled faintly. How often had she heard that phrase? Thank God for friends, good friends. They were always there for her. Robert kissed her on the cheek and watched her enter the swinging doors of the hotel. Poor old love, he thought. Just got rid of one bastard, only to get involved with another. He sighed. It happens to us all, he reminded himself. Not just to women. All the novels his wife read so voraciously mentioned women's exclusive right to suffer, and to suffer loudly and often. We men get our hearts broken just as many times, but we suffer in silence. Then he smiled. He was lucky. He was married to a woman he loved very much. He was smiling as he left the cul-de-sac: she was cooking egg and bacon pie for him for dinner. On his way home he'd buy her a really nice bottle of wine. Life was sweet when you are happily married: he knew that now.

Fifty-four

❧

'Oh, Madeleine, I was so worried about you.' Hilary wrapped her arms around her friend.

'Are you OK, Mom? You look awful. All black around the edges.'

'I'm OK now, Allegro. I just had to take care of some business.' She hugged Allegro to her. She was her most precious possession.

'Did you get an answer to your question, Mom?'

'Yes, I did, darling, and it's all over. How would you like to live near Hilary in Devon? You can go to school here.'

'Really, Mom? Live in England and ride horses and go to a real English school? I'd love it!'

'That's a deal, then. Now you run along and play with the boys, and I'll talk to Hilary about our new life.'

'You see, Hilary, it wasn't jealousy or the fact that he made love to his wife; I could accept all that. What crippled me was the tenderness he showed her. I thought that belonged only to me. I thought he was unhappy with his wife. That's where I was such a fool. He wasn't unhappy at all: he just wanted to have his cake and eat it.'

'That's most men, Madeleine. You just have to grow up and get less romantic. Most of my friends know perfectly well their husbands have affairs and they just put up with it. I don't, but then I'm different. I might be shy and quiet, but underneath all that I can be very tough. Peter's lying and cheating me has come to an

316

end. Even if I feel sorry for the boys without a father, they are better off without a silent, bitter mother.

'I'm much happier, and this week in London has been brilliant for the boys. It really has. I can't thank you enough.' She stood in the window looking down into the green little garden. 'Here we are, two middle-aged women about to take on life as single-parent mothers. Who would have guessed it?'

Madeleine joined her. 'Darling, let's look at this as a great adventure. Tonight let's take the kids to the theatre next door, and then have dinner in the River Room. I'll order a special bottle of champagne. Well, I've lost an Italian lover, but I've gained a great deal of love for Italian wine.'

She smiled and her heart gave off a spark of light. I'll heal, she told herself. One day I'll be whole again.

'I'm not coming home, Edwina. I've talked to Dad and he's agreed to sell the house for me and send over my furniture. I want to start my life again in England, with no reminders of Syracuse or Paolo.'

There was a moment of silence. 'I can't help you, Maddie. There's nothing to be done about breaking up with a lover but to go through the pain. I'm here on the end of the telephone, and if you want me to come over I will, even if you just need me to hold your hand. Only time will really help, and it takes time, believe you me.'

'Did you know that Paolo really loved his wife when *you* slept with him?'

'Yes, darling, but I was only playing with him. I don't take married men seriously. I did the first few times, and then I thought, what the hell, I'll give them as good as I get. I've broken many a heart in my time.'

'Well I haven't, and I don't want to, ever. I wouldn't inflict this pain on my worst enemy.'

'By the way, Maddie, I saw Syracuse in full moan the other night at a party. He was on his own, without the woman, and trying to pick up young girls. It really was sad. He's having a mid-life crisis, only he's a walking crisis himself. He's furious that you're staying in England, and he's threatening to go to court. He's telling everybody that you deliberately left the country to deprive him of access to his daughter.'

'Sure I did. The thought of him getting his tainted hands on Allegro disgusts me. He can go and fondle all the women he wants. She doesn't miss him. Neither of us does, he was such a bad-tempered little bastard.

'We're leaving for Devon in the morning. We've had such a wonderful time in London, but it will be easier for me once I get into the country and can search for a house. Oh, Edwina, isn't life full of surprises? Still, if I hadn't gone to Siena, I would never have found out about Paolo, and I would have gone back home and gone on with an affair that could have lasted for years. I won't ever sleep with a married man again. I don't want somebody that belongs to another woman. I've tried it once and that's enough.'

'Try a toy-boy next,' Edwina giggled.

'What, and get landed with a gigolo? No thanks. I'm going to do nothing for a good long time. I'm going to enjoy myself once I get over my broken heart.'

'You'll get over it.'

'I will, but many don't, Edwina.'

'I know. A friend of mine killed herself over her man. Silly bitch.'

'We ought to have T-shirts that say "No Man Is Worth Dying For". I'd be the first to wear one.'

'So would I. I must go and get Tarquin, darling, so you take care, and Tarquin and I will be over to see you as soon as you have your house. Lots and lots of love.'

'And to you, Edwina.'

Germaine's telephone calls were full of sound, practical advice. She listened for hours to sobbing and wailing with an accepting patience that comforted Madeleine in a way that Edwina could not.

Allegro knew her mother was sad and, often finding her with tears running down her cheeks, put her arms around her mother and hugged her.

After two months of searching, with Hilary's help Madeleine found the house she wanted. It was Georgian. Built four-square facing a river. It had thick pine floors and all the windows still had their original Georgian shutters. 'Oreo,' she exclaimed clapping her hands. She walked around the four big upstairs bedrooms with Allegro behind her.

'Mom, I want this room for my bedroom. Is that OK?'

'Sure, honey.' She wandered down to the big kitchen. She felt sure she'd been in this house before. In another life, maybe? She knew where everything was. She ambled out into the two acres of garden. Over there, under the apple tree in the orchard, she knew she used to swing as a child. She had a flash of herself in a long grey dress with a white frilly apron over the dress.

'This is a lovely house, Mom. Can I have a pony?'

'You can have anything you like, darling. This is our new life together.'

'What about Dad? He's not coming here, is he? I don't want him in our new life. He's creepy.'

'When you want to see him, we'll go and stay with Grandma and Grandpa. That way you don't have to stay with him.'

'I'm glad. Lucinda walks around with no clothes on all the time. I don't like that.'

'I don't blame you, darling. Don't worry, we'll cope with your father together.'

A few moments later, Hilary drew up. 'Sorry I'm late, darling, but I got caught up in the traffic.' She smiled at Madeleine. 'I can see you found your house. Your face is blazing with joy.'

'Isn't it perfect, Hilary, and only two miles from your house and Allegro's school? You know, I'd always thought I'd send her to boarding school, but now I won't have to. She can have her pony in the orchard and I can do my gardening and grow all our own vegetables. Isn't it awful the way women give up all the things they love in order to please a man? I'll never do that again.'

As the sun set on the greens and pinks in the garden, Madeleine sat on the front doorstep with Allegro. 'Here's where I'll dream my dreams and get better,' she promised herself as she lightly kissed the top of her daughter's head.

Fifty-five

❧

She did telephone Vincent Heatherington, the man she'd met on the plane to Siena. His kind face had stayed fixed in her brain. She was pleased that he remembered her name after all these months. 'I am surprised you remember who I am,' she said, smiling, as she held the telephone to her ear.

'Oh, I would remember a pretty woman with an absolutely terrified look on her face. How did your little visit go?'

'As you said it would. It was an absolute disaster but,' she sighed and felt the sadness draining away for a moment, 'I'm getting over him now. Anyway, I wondered if I might visit you when I'm in London? I'm going up next week to meet a friend at Heathrow, and I would very much like to have lunch with you at the American Bar at the Savoy. It's my treat, of course.'

She knew it was unwise, but she was driven to that bar as the only place she knew of in England where Paolo might be staying. It was a long shot, but it was worth a try. He must have wondered what had happened to her. He had seen Edwina on many occasions, but he had never enquired after her. Another compartment, no doubt. The drawer of the filing cabinet to be shut on her. Another weeping woman laid to rest. 'I would love to see you. Thank you very much for the invitation. Shall we agree to meet before or after you pick up your friend?'

'Oh, before. Germaine is usually jet-lagged. I'll pile her in the car and hit the road for home.'

'Where are you exactly? When we met you were only staying in England for a holiday.'

'I'll tell you all about my new life when I see you. Is Friday the second of April any good for you?'

'Let me consult my diary. Ah, let me see: two divorces in the morning. Real stinkers, so I could do with a good lunch. I'll see you in the American Bar. Goodbye, my dear.'

'Goodbye.' She put the telephone down. She was still smiling. He was such a nice, kind man; she needed that for the moment. She sometimes felt that she would never trust a man again. She could hear Allegro yelling at one of her many schoolfriends. They were out in the paddock practising jumping. For now Allegro thought she was a horse. Oh, why did Allegro have to do everything so intensely?

Madeleine was now used to her daughter cantering around the house, shaking her great mane of hair. She drew the line at letting Allegro sleep in a loose-box with her pony Tristram Shandy. 'Absolutely not, Allegro. You're a girl, not a horse.'

'Pony, Mother, pony. I'm under twelve hands, remember?'

'Go and brush your hair, darling. You're beginning to talk like an English girl. Your grandmother will be delighted.'

'I don't want to go back to America. I'll miss my pony and my room and my cat.' They had recently acquired a tiny little ginger kitten that Allegro nursed devotedly. Mrs Poole didn't approve at all; she was terrified of cats, and could be found marooned on top of a chair in the kitchen, wringing her hands and begging Hilda Barnes to get the thing out of here.

Hilda was vastly amused by the turn of events, and made very little effort to rescue her friend.

Mrs Poole and Nanny Barnes had both been thrilled to return to England; they were devoted to Madeleine and Allegro, and despite their initial mutual animosity, were now inseparable. Cook had stayed behind in America, so Nanny Barnes did the cooking. As far as Allegro was concerned it was a turn for the worse. Nanny Barnes only cooked mince, blancmange, rice pudding and lumpy mashed potatoes. Madeleine did her best, but they often resorted to dinner in the local pub where Madeleine was made to feel at home.

When Madeleine walked into the American Bar on the Friday just before one o'clock, she was wearing a slim skirt with a black cashmere jumper. She had a long string of pearls around her neck. For once she had managed to wear gardening gloves while gardening, and she had painted her nails a pretty colour of pink. She knew that her toes were painted as well. She needed all the confidence she could muster in case he was there. For days she had imagined what it would be like if he were there, standing tall and handsome, leaning nonchalantly on the bar.

Would she dissolve into his arms? Probably. Or would she play it cool like Lana Turner and walk past him as if she hadn't seen him? She played the scene so often she exhausted herself. She lay in bed or in the bath talking to herself.

'Only mad people talk to themselves, Mom.' Allegro was irritated. 'I hate men, Mom,' she fumed.

'I know, darling. I think I am a little mad at times.'

'No, you're not, not since we got rid of Dad. You're much happier, and you dance to your music and you sing. You're much happier. Even though the man who made you happy has gone away.'

'How did you know it was a man, Allegro?'

'I listened when you were on the telephone with Edwina.'

She gave Madeleine a cheeky grin. Madeleine remembered the remark when she stood for a moment in the door of the bar, scanning the crowd. She stopped breathing. She felt as if time stood still. Everyone in the bar, mostly men, turned to look at this tall, graceful woman. The flow and chatter subsided for a moment, and then she felt the force of the men's lust hit her like a wall. She saw desire in men's eyes and she felt naked and ashamed. Once she had known hot desire in her own body and in her lover's body, but now she wanted none of it. She turned to leave and to run out of the hotel and into the safety of her car. She felt a hand on her elbow. It was Vincent. 'Come along,' he said cheerfully, and led her to a table at the end of the room. 'We'll sit quietly here until you have regained your composure. What will you drink?'

'A gin and tonic, please.' Madeleine could hear her voice shaking.

'Make that two gin and tonics,' Vincent said to the waiter.

'I guess I am a bit upset. You see, I hoped that I might see Paolo here. He's the man I was travelling to spy on in Siena.' She felt quite silly having to admit that she had been spying. It seemed so childish. 'Don't mind about me, Madeleine. I've been in love a few times, myself.' He was smiling at her with a twinkle in his eyes. 'Oh yes, I was quite a one for the ladies at one time.'

'I can believe that. But were you ever unfaithful to your wife?'

'Good heavens no, my dear. I loved her so completely that, once I was lucky enough to marry her, I was completely faithful. You see, no one could compare with her. I told you about her on the plane. She was so beauti-

324

ful. So witty and so wise. She cooked like an angel. Why should I look elsewhere?'

'Well, if you're the last faithful man in the world, there's still a chance for me to find another relationship.'

'You know, in my business I always ask the divorcing couple when they stopped talking to each other. Usually it's about three years into the marriage. They cease to speak, to share secrets. Competition grows between them instead of partnership. The friendship stops and then comes the divorce. So sad. So terrible for the children.'

'Do you have children, Vincent?' Madeleine almost felt she wanted to interview him. He seemed to be the only man who had been genuinely happy with his wife. Maybe he could teach her what to look for.

'Yes, I have three girls. Two of them are married and I have three grandchildren. Here.' He pulled out his wallet and took out the family photographs. The first was of a plump grey-haired woman who was obviously his dead wife. There he was in his back garden, sitting with two small children on a patterned rug under some tall pink hollyhocks. Madeleine smiled at him. 'You're lucky,' she said. 'So very lucky. I feel such a failure.'

'You'll be lucky again, my dear.' He patted her hand. 'You'll get over this chap, I promise you will. Next time, stay clear of married men. If they can cheat on their wives, they will cheat on you.'

Madeleine grimaced as she sipped her gin and tonic. 'I've thought about that,' she admitted. 'It's rule number three hundred and ten in my book.'

'Are you going to write a book? What a wonderful idea!'

'Actually I think I will, Vincent. I'll dedicate it to you as the only happily married man I know. What was your wife's name?'

'Her name was Janet.'

'OK, it's a deal. For Vincent and Janet. My book on how to survive an affair with a married man. Rule number I've forgotten how many now: don't hang about his bar hoping to see him.' She laughed. 'That way lies madness.' She felt the colour coming back into her face. 'Now let's order oysters. Lots of them.'

Fifty-six

When Madeleine got home she realised that she had not been joking. She settled down that night with an exercise book and began to write. Soon even Allegro couldn't drag her out of her study. 'Go away, darling, I'm writing,' she mumbled as Allegro came barging through the french windows.

'You always say that, Mom.'

'I know, darling.' She looked up from her yellow lined legal pad. 'I can't stop, Allegro. It's like a terrible compulsion. I've just got to get it all down now.' For months she had been immersed in her other world. It was a world full of real people. They were more real than the everyday people that filled her time with wasted words and emotions. She talked to her real people. She cried with them and for them. She rolled in her bed with grief when her favourite character had to die. The pain she felt was real, and oh, how healing it was.

She washed away the pain of Paolo in a tide of reminiscence. It was a novel, not a rule book, but it warned women who took what did not belong to them. It warned again and again that men were different to women. Women gave their all. Even Edwina stubbed her toes on man's inhumanity. Edwina liked to laugh and play tough, but even she at times exposed a raw, vulnerable side of herself where she had been lanced and bled like anybody else.

She finished the book a year later. Allegro was now eight and socialising a lot. She wrote the final line and sat back in a daze. Mrs Poole and Nanny Barnes had been wonderful during her labour. It was a labour more difficult than carrying and bearing Allegro. She felt like Sisyphus. As she wrote the words, 'The End', she felt an awful pang of loneliness. What would she do now that her obsession was over? No good sitting here staring at the manuscript. What she needed was an agent. She would telephone Vincent Heatherington. He knew a lot about the publishing world. 'As it happens, my dear, I have a great friend in publishing. She's one of the best editors in town. Just wait by the phone and I'll ring you back.'

Madeleine waited nervously by the telephone. After what seemed like ages, the telephone rang again. 'Her name is Susan Last and she'd be delighted to give you lunch in London any time you are free.'

'That's wonderful, Vincent. How about tomorrow?'

'Why don't I give you her telephone number and you can ask her yourself.'

Madeleine drew a deep breath and telephoned the editor. She had always thought of editors as semi-god-like figures. Maxwell Perkins with his wide-brimmed felt hat. She imagined them all to behave as he did. She'd never quite forgiven Maxwell Perkins for overlooking the writer Sherwood Anderson. He was a writer she treasured. His short story, 'Wings', had greatly influenced her writing style. Madeleine was obsessed by people's hands and their feet. She almost forgot to look at people's faces, except for a first peek at the eyes.

Paolo had such beautiful hands and feet. Long and slender. Oh no, she thought. Now I've finished the novel, I mustn't let him slip back into my head. She dialled the number and a loud, boisterous voice answered, 'Can I help you?'

'I am trying to speak to Susan Last who is an editor,'

Madeleine began shyly. 'I've been given her number by a friend of mine, Vincent Heatherington.'

'Oh yes, my dear, I've just finished speaking to him.'

'Do you think I could have lunch with you tomorrow? I've just finished my book and I'm anxious for someone to read it and tell me it's not all rubbish. You see, I've been writing for a year and I'm frightened it's no good.'

Susan Last smiled. She checked her diary and realised she would have to cancel her lunch with a major author. He was very firmly established; she understood how Madeleine – a first-time author – needed to see her now. 'All right, Madeleine. Where are you coming from?'

'I live in Devon, but I can get up for lunch without any problem.'

'Tell you what, my dear, I'll meet you in Covent Garden. There's a little Greek restaurant in Melvin Road. You can't miss me: I weigh two hundred pounds and I have bright red hair.'

'My daughter has red hair.' Madeleine felt comforted. Meeting new people was always very difficult for her, but she would ring Hilary and ask her to pick Allegro up from school. 'Wonderful,' Madeleine said gratefully. 'I'll see you at one o'clock with the book under my arm. I must admit it feels very much like giving away a child of mine.'

'Now don't you worry about a thing. I'm used to people's novels and I understand how you feel. I'll be gentle with it, and I'll be gentle with you.'

'Thank you.' Madeleine felt suddenly tearful. No one had been gentle with her for such a long time. Not since Paolo, and that had been a betrayal. Thank goodness she was out of all that now.

Automatically, Madeleine lifted herself from the chair and hobbled down to the kitchen. Really, she told herself, she must swim or ride. She felt as if she were crippled by the long hours of sitting and writing.

Even Syracuse seemed less of a nuisance. Now they had been away sufficiently long, he whined down the telephone less often. Even he realised that she was never going to live in America again. They had spent two months of the previous summer back in New York. Madeleine had been glad to get back to England. She was mostly bored by Syracuse. His self-pity disgusted her. Lucinda tried to be nice to Allegro, but she wasn't interested in little girls or horses, and Allegro's only passion was horses.

Madeleine was amazed at the discipline writing imposed on her life. She wrote six days a week, and then did nothing on Sunday but lie about and think of her book. Now she put on the kettle and wondered how many cups of tea she had made while writing the book. Thousands, she reckoned. She hobbled back to the library and wrapped up her manuscript.

She tied it carefully with gold string, and then carried it reverently back to her bedroom and slipped it into her capacious handbag. She straightened out her shoulders and stretched her neck. It was so good to be finished, but also sad. Paolo, hopefully, had been laid to rest. A gravestone had been erected over him. The epitaph read: Here lies Paolo. Tenderness was his downfall. She grimaced at the pain, but it was now more like a scratch. The sort one might have if accidentally handling a wild kitten. Now she must think about supper for Allegro. Thank goodness she was over her blood-lust phase and was pigging out on olives and french fries. She would fix American hamburgers and french fries. Mrs Poole and Nanny Barnes had gone to the cinema for the evening. Tomorrow she would be in London. She felt a trembling in her stomach. She knew first novels often faced a mass of rejections. Scott Fitzgerald papered a room with his. She could make the bathroom available for rejections, then she could lie in the bath and read them all. She smiled. 'Keep the faith,' she told Dr Stanislaus.

'Certainly,' he replied. Thank goodness he was over his Italian phase.

Fifty-seven

❧

Susan Last was as enormous as she promised. She had a cheerful, friendly face. 'Here you are,' she bellowed loudly, but her eyes were attentive. Madeleine relaxed. Here was a woman who could understand her. Since she'd run away from Paolo she had been hesitant and uncertain. Waving back at Susan, she made her way through the tightly packed tables, past people leaning forward, earnestly discussing politics and their novels. Pausing by Susan's table, she pulled out the solid bulk of her novel. 'It's called *Palio* for now, but I can always change it.'

'You mean after the *Palio* in Siena?' Susan took the book and hugged it to her.

'Yes,' Madeleine nodded. 'You see, when the *Palio* takes place twice a year, the husbands and wives go off to their own *contrade* and there are no questions asked on either side.

'Women in Italy are a lot more practical than we are. They know that their husbands have affairs and they do too, only the matter is never discussed between the couples.'

Oh dear, Susan thought. Another broken-hearted novel from yet another broken-hearted woman. She glanced at Madeleine's left hand. She saw a white strip in her tan where a wedding ring must once have been.

Madeleine laughed. 'No,' she said. 'The book isn't about my husband. He was just a boring little shit. It's about having an affair with a married man.' She grimaced as she had the day before when she'd finished the book. 'Writing sort of takes away the pain, if you know what I mean.'

'I do indeed. All great literature is about distilling the pain. Thank you for giving me the book. I promise to read it quickly and get it back to you with a reaction. I must warn you, most first novels are rejected, but even if I can't take it, I can give you some advice.'

Madeleine slipped into a chair. 'Thank you so much. I know I have a lot to learn.'

Susan leaned back in her chair. 'Now, my dear, do you have any questions to ask me?'

'Do you drink?' It sounded such a silly question, but she was dying for a gin and tonic.

'I do indeed. What would you like?'

'A gin and tonic, please.' Susan ordered two gin and tonics, and then consulted the menu. 'The lamb here is excellent, and so is the Greek salad. The olive oil is like green axle grease. I love it.'

'I had a Tuscan friend in New York; he has his olive oil and wine shipped from the Altesino winery in Buonconvento.'

'Whoever the friend was, he hurt you, didn't he?' Susan leaned forward. 'You are still recovering, are you not?'

'Yes, I am,' and she smiled at Susan. 'I couldn't write the way I do if I hadn't suffered pain. Someone told me to treat it like an old friend.' She didn't want to tell Susan about Syracuse, or about the monstrous regiment of women. Susan would think she was absolutely potty. Potty was such a good English word. '*Eh, basta*,' she said, picking up a piece of crumbly Greek bread. 'Life moves on.'

'So it does, so it does, and when you've lived as long as I have, you learn not to take men too seriously. Stick to your girlfriends for love and secrets, and use men.

They can be great fun in small doses, just like big children, which is all they are. Now let's get down to the serious side of publishing.' She laughed at Madeleine's face. 'Not books, you silly goose. Eating and drinking. That's what publishing is about. It's the most incestuous group of people in the world, but I love it. It's in my blood. You see, most of us had seriously awful families, so we hang on to each other like limpets. We curse each other and we gossip viciously, but just let any outsider attack any one of us and we shut the door tight. *We* can criticise, but outsiders do at their peril.' She laughed an enormous laugh that shook her pendulous belly. 'Another gin and tonic?' she said. Madeleine smiled. Writing for a living sounded like fun.

Madeleine went home and began anxiously waiting for the phone to ring. She found she missed her novel. It was as if all her friends in the book had packed their bags and left the house. How silly, she told herself several times a day: it's only a book. But she knew that was not true. It was a huge part of her unmanifest self. Deep within her psyche her people struggled to be heard. She found she had to write every day.

She wrote her diary every morning after reading the Bible. She particularly loved Isaiah and the Psalms, and then hypnotically she found herself beginning another story. The voices whispered in her ear and she took dictation. She could see her new friends standing in front of her. She saw them in colour like an internal film screen. She wanted no social life; just her books, herself and her household. She loved the silence of the country with a passionate intensity. She muttered the days and waiting weeks away, and then at last the telephone went and she knew without knowing that it was Susan Last.

'Well, my dear, you've written a wonderful book.'

Madeleine stood by the telephone, shaking with excitement. 'Do you really think so?'

'I know so, darling, and I'm going to buy it for my publishing house. Now you will need an agent. I have one in mind. She drinks too much but then we all do.

'She's called Stella Runion. I'll have her call you and then we'll get together. I shall come down to see you in a few days if that's all right with you?'

'I'd love that. I don't often have people here, and to tell you the truth it is lonely sometimes.'

'Right ho, Madeleine, I'll bring you some smoked salmon and champagne and we shall celebrate. I will tell Stella not to bring her latest perverted lover with her, and we shall have a women-only day. It's so much more fun.'

'I think you're right. In our house we are all women on our own. I mean my nanny and my housekeeper and Allegro my daughter. I don't think I'd ever want to share a house with a man again. You know, it's all over long before you think it is. They keep bumping into you as usual, but you start to mind. I used to stand in the kitchen and shake with fear. I can't stand their tantrums and their anger. Women are so much gentler and easier than men. Still, maybe things will change, but for now I am quite happy . . . You'll never believe it, Susan: I've started another novel.'

'You'll write lots of novels, darling, and I'll be there to help you. Expect a call from Stella. She's a good girl, even if she is a lush.'

Madeleine put down the telephone and hugged herself. She ran outside to look for Allegro. 'Darling,' she said, embracing her long-legged daughter. 'I'm a writer, a real writer. Susan has just accepted my book!' She whirled Allegro around. Allegro whinnied her approval.

'Edwina, I'm a novelist. My editor is Susan Last and

she's just this minute accepted my novel. Isn't that wonderful?' Madeleine felt her stomach churning. She was elated. She called her mother and her father and they too were delighted. 'We have a writer in the family,' her father said with great pride in his voice. 'Well done, darling.' He passed the phone over to her mother.

'Mom, after I finish any revisions that Susan might want, I'll bring Allegro over for a visit. You'd better clean out a stall for her. She's obsessed with horses at the moment, and she even smells like one. She's making no attempt at being clean. Bathtimes are a nightmare.'

'Just leave lashings of pretty bath-oil in the bath, and keep her in clean clothes. She'll get round to cleaning up when she's interested in boys.'

'I don't think she'll ever be interested in boys – you're probably going to be the first grandmother who has a baby stallion as a great-grandchild.'

'Darling, don't worry. You were always such a neat, tidy child. That's why you find it all so difficult. But we're proud of you, Madeleine. You've picked yourself up and dusted yourself down and after your divorce you'll find a man who will really take care of you.'

'No I won't, Mom. I don't want anything more to do with the world of men. They're all big babies, and I've had one of those. I have my books. I'll put everything I know into them. They won't hurt me. They won't be envious or jealous. They will sit on my shelves and mark the years of my life and all the things I intend to do. Life on my own as a single-parent mother is such fun. Allegro and I can dash off any time we like. We can get up when we feel like it, or stay up late and watch what we want to watch on the television. I don't think I was cut out for marriage. It was and still is an institution designed to service men. These days women don't want to service men like an all-night bus station, do they?'

'Well, I don't know about that, darling.' Dolly's voice was guarded. She didn't like to hear what she called her daughter's 'modern' attitude to men. 'I always believed in the iron hand in the velvet glove myself.'

'That's all very well, Mom, but I got beaten over the head with the iron glove. Syracuse was a bastard. Of course they don't start off like that, but pretty soon they take everything you give them for granted, and I suppose he's just past his sell-by date. Anyway, that's enough of him. I'm a novelist now, and I have to think of my new career. I'm just waiting for a call from my new agent, so I'd better get off the telephone.'

When the telephone rang again it was Stella, and she did sound drunk. 'Helloooooo,' she drawled. 'I'm Stella Runion. I'm known in the business as "The Ruin".' She laughed an asthmatic, cigarette-stained laugh and then she coughed. 'Won't last long at this rate, but Susan telephoned me and said you've written a fabulous book, so I'm offering to be your agent and soak Susan for a lot of money for you. I like to make my authors very rich. I get fifteen per cent worldwide. How does that grab you?'

'How much is Susan offering for the book?'

'Don't know at this point in time, but I'll call in a few other chums of hers and tickle the situation until we get a figure. There's no knowing at this stage, but I'll talk the book up all over town and then when I'm in America I'll do the same thing. We should do quite well for you. I'll reread it myself, of course.'

'Of course?'

'Most agents don't bother to read their authors' books. Neither do some editors, come to think of it. At least you don't have to sleep with me. I'm not Venetian in that way.'

'Not Venetian?' Madeleine felt a little like Alice in

Wonderland. Was there a whole new vocabulary to getting published?

'Yes, it's the old way of saying Lesbian. Very pretty, don't you think?'

'I guess so, I haven't thought about it actually.'

'Yes indeed, sleeping with your editor is de rigueur in some publishing houses. Most of publishing is done between the sheets. I just drink. I had a lover who can't get it up. He has to sit and watch me put on my make-up. It reminds him of his mother. Most things remind men of their bloody mothers.'

Madeleine felt a headache coming on. This was a very weird conversation. 'Don't worry, I'll get Susan to arrange a visit and we'll come down. D'you have gin?'

'Yes, I have lots of gin, don't worry. Susan says she'll bring smoked salmon and champagne.'

'Very good, and I'll just bring myself and my emphysema.' She laughed a very juicy laugh, and Madeleine put down the telephone. 'How very peculiar,' she remarked to herself, and walked off shaking her head.

Fifty-eight

❧

Madeleine heard the sound of a large and powerful car come up the drive. The engine roared up to the house. Alarmed, Madeleine and Allegro dashed to the front door, closely followed by Nanny Barnes and Mrs Poole. Astonished, they watched Susan Last decant her voluminous body out of the red Mercedes and stagger with her arms full of food to the front door. Behind her, limping, Stella Runion had a heavily bandaged foot. 'Fucking fell over I fucking well did.'

Madeleine didn't know whether to clap her hands over Allegro's ears or shake Susan's proffered hand. She could feel Nanny Barnes and Mrs Poole shaking with indignation. 'Well,' she heard Mrs Poole's loud, sibilant whispers. 'Is this what the poor little mite will learn with her mother as a writer? Artists! Pah, all filthy dirty and no knickers.'

'Shhh, Mrs Poole,' Madeleine whispered nervously. 'Besides, they do wear knickers.'

'No, I don't,' Susan said amiably. 'Never wear the damn things. Nothing worse than twisting your knickers. That's what I say to my damn managing director as he falls through our office door first thing in the morning. It's these damn secretaries. He can't keep his hands off them.'

'I have a friend in New York who is married to one of those problems.' Madeleine decided that she might as well try and have a conversation, even if it was taking place in her front hall.

A great avalanche of sound descended upon the house

as Susan burst into a fit of laughter. She clutched Stella and then she coughed again. 'Aren't you going to invite us in, dear? I'm exhausted and I must pee. Don't want to do it in your front hall. That would never do.' She gave a quizzical look at the older women's scandalised faces. 'Sorry, m'dears, but I live on my own and forget that I can be offensive. No offence meant, my darlings. Now where is your loo?'

'This way,' Mrs Poole said rather faintly. She tried not to touch Susan, who grinned and filled Mrs Poole's arms with the champagne and smoked salmon.

'Gin,' Stella gasped. 'I'm done-for without gin, and I've emptied my flask.' She waved a pigskin-covered drinking flask at Madeleine. Madeleine rescued the empty bottle and handed it to Allegro, who was watching the proceedings with her eyes alight with excitement.

Nanny Barnes hurried after Mrs Poole. 'Marjorie, I have an awful feeling that this is the end of our lives as we once knew them.'

'Fiddle-de-dee, Hilda. We have to do our best to protect our little lamb. Madam has gone quite definitely doolally tap, if you'll pardon the rather common expression.'

There was a loud flushing from the downstairs lavatory. How did Susan manage to make so much noise? Madeleine wondered. Was it her larger-than-life character? Possibly, but it was endearing. She would have to have a private talk to Allegro about language. But she feared it was probably too late. 'Fucking hell, the back of my dress went down the loo and I'm all wet. Never mind. Have you got a towel I can sit on?'

'Sure thing,' Madeleine called back. 'Just come to the sitting room and I'll find something for you to sit on.'

Madeleine dived into the kitchen and surprised Nanny Barnes and Mrs Poole, who were in a huddle, plotting. 'Give us a towel, Nanny Barnes, please.'

Nanny Barnes's eyebrows shot up. 'Surely that dreadful fat woman hasn't had an –' Here Nanny Barnes paused for a moment of delicate silence. 'Had an accident?'

'She's probably infected the lavatory with her germs. I'll get the Dettol.'

'Don't be silly, Mrs Poole. She's just had a real accident.'

'Where I come from, having an accident means wetting your knickers.' Nanny Barnes sniffed self-righteously.

'Oh, both of you stop being such spoilsports. I want lunch served in half an hour, please.' Madeleine swept out of the kitchen feeling quite annoyed. Here were her artistic friends from London, and Nanny Barnes and Mrs Poole were behaving like old hens.

She ushered the two women into the drawing room and watched Allegro trailing after them, hoping for dirty words to fall from their lips. Stella was trying to light her cigarette with a shaking hand. 'Fucking cunt,' she addressed the cigarette amiably. 'Silly little sod, stay still will you?'

'Allegro, I think you should run along and play, dear. Perhaps you could have lunch with Nanny Barnes and Mrs Poole?'

'Dear little girl you have there. Where's the husband?'

'I dumped him. He's in New York.'

'It figures. I'd dump any man from New York. Does he whine, you know, in that high-nosed way?'

'Sure, all the time.'

'Well done, then, for getting rid of him. Any man in your life now?' Susan leaned forward for the answer.

'No,' Madeleine said shortly. 'Never again. I've had men probably for ever.'

Stella laughed and drew on her cigarette. 'Darling, you'll do it again. We all say we won't, but we do. Look at the mess I'm in. Can't live with him, can't live without him. Ha! That's why I drink. Speaking of drink, where's the gin?'

'Oh, sorry,' Madeleine dashed to the drinks cabinet. 'What's for you, Stella? Gins all round?'

Madeleine made three stiff gins and handed them around. 'Here's to the success of your book, darling.' Stella raised her glass.

Susan lifted her glass. 'Bottoms up,' she said, grinning. 'With knickers of course?' She stared at Madeleine. 'Your little *ménage* is really very traditional. I mean, with a nanny and a housekeeper. I shouldn't let anybody in publishing know about that. We're going through one of our left-wing phases. You know, you have to pretend the little Vietnamese that creep round their mansions are paying guests, and buy cheap wine from Sainsbury's, and never eat anything from South Africa because you're contributing to apartheid.'

Madeleine sat looking perplexed. 'Are you sure about that? You're not just joking?'

'No, I'm deadly serious. If you don't do what we all do, you'll be sent packing with your tail between your legs. I told you when we first met. Publishing isn't about selling books any more than selling oil or baked beans. It's all a big game played by men. They can't hit us over the head with clubs and drag us off to caves any more. So they put a suit over their furry hides and go and sit in boardrooms. It's all still tooth and claw, darling. But don't you worry, we'll keep you safe. Both of us are very fierce women. Now let's get down to business. What's for lunch?'

Much to Madeleine's surprise, they spent ten minutes discussing a few changes to the book, and then went on talking endlessly about publishing. As she listened, she wondered if she'd ever get all the names straight. It all sounded very frightening. Words like mergers, takeovers, floors, bids. None of it made any sense to her, but as she drank her wine, she relaxed and enjoyed the sheer good humour of the two women.

After coffee, they filtered back into the sitting room and to more gin and tonics. At five o'clock, Susan got to her feet and, swaying precariously, she announced that she and Stella must find their way back to London. 'Gin is such excellent stuff for driving,' she announced loudly.

'Are you sure?' Madeleine never drank if she were driving. 'Shouldn't you stay the night?'

'No, I'm a home bird. Besides, I have five stinking cats and a smelly old dog to feed. Come on, Stella, let's hit the road.' They shuffled out of the house. Susan roared her farewells down the hall at a terrified Mrs Poole and Nanny Barnes. As the car left the drive, Madeleine found herself asking God to please see both safely back to their respective homes. Her head was spinning from all the unaccustomed gin. She went outside for some fresh air. She stood in the driveway and then she heard the unmistakable sound of Allegro saying in an exact imitation of Stella's voice, 'Fucking cunt.'

'Allegro,' she said severely. 'You are not to say the f-word or the c-word ever again.' Then she had to laugh. Too late, she thought. Allegro's hooked.

Fifty-nine

'If you do write a bestseller, don't expect that you'll be liked.' Susan was sitting in her chair behind her desk in the office, smiling at Madeleine. 'In fact, sweetheart, you'll probably be hated. The problem with writing a novel is that everybody and their aunt think they can do it – very few can. I can see that you have an enormous inner world. I found it absorbing in your book. That's the first thing that excited me. A truly original way of looking at things. You're a very internal writer. Women tend to have much larger internal worlds than men. Unless you think of homosexual writers like E. M. Forster. He was in close touch with his feminine side and it showed.

'Years ago I was working with a beautiful woman author who wrote like a dream. I discovered she was from a very abusive and violent background. As a child she escaped from that world into her own internal world, which she built as a bulwark against what was happening to her.'

'What happened to her?'

Madeleine could see tears in Susan's eyes. 'She killed herself. Or rather publishing killed her. It's a brutal business, my dear. A very brutal business. I'll keep you safe, don't you worry.' She grinned. Madeleine knew Susan, as her publisher, was as tense as she was over the auction of her book in America.

'Oh dear, you make it all sound so sinister.'

'It is sinister, darling: don't be so naïve. Where there are large sums of money and a lot of talent for making it, the worst side of people comes out. The bitch god-dess, fame, has ruined many a writer and an editor. With fame and money, the writer – and often even editors, for God's sake – begin to think of themselves as stars. What a load of rubbish. The book is the star, and the rest of us, from the art director down to the sales manager, are the team, including you as the writer. I'm here to see your book through the works and to keep your feet on the ground.' She grinned. 'End of boring lecture, darling. Let's see how Stella is doing with the auction.'

Susan picked up the telephone and took a swig of coffee. 'Gin and coffee mainlined.' She dialled and obvi-ously got Stella. 'Great, there's a floor bid in New York.' She spoke out loud to include Madeleine. There again was the mysterious term 'floor bid'. Whatever it meant, it was now an important phrase in Madeleine's new life. Susan put the telephone down. 'It's good news,' she was beaming. 'Northrups have put down ten thousand dollars. That means that they have secured the right to the last bid. Now we sit back and wait to see what the other publishing houses decide to do.' She let out a sigh of relief. 'At least we know that you have ten thousand dollars secured. For a first-time novel that's a fair price.'

Susan sat on her chair drumming her fingers. Madel-eine felt pure adrenalin pouring through her veins. Well, at least someone had put in a bid. She had been terrified that no one would make an offer. She rather wondered now if she could take the rejection of writing.

So far she had been lucky, but from reading exten-sively about writers' lives, she knew that rejection was the norm. She had taken her two failures at relationships very badly. Writing had become her therapy, and had restored her sense of worth. She dreaded being told even in her fiction she was a failure.

She had always been oversensitive. Syracuse had

scolded her on so many occasions. 'You have been born with too few skins,' had been one of his favourite jibes. 'You have no sense of self,' was another. No wonder women fell apart at the seams.

Watching Madeleine's face, Susan realised that she would never be one of those writers that delighted in the publishing game. No, Madeleine would be one of those writers who best stayed at home and let Susan get on with the cut and thrust. For Susan and for Stella, the whole business was a perpetual high.

'Darling, why don't you go home and play with Allegro? This is going to go on until the wee small hours of the morning. You can't really go on sitting here wringing your hands and looking as if you are about to keel over. Leave it to your Aunty Susan and your Aunt Stella. I promise we'll pull something out of our knickers.' Madeleine nodded faintly. She kissed Susan goodbye as Susan reached for the telephone.

Funny, she thought as she drove towards Hammersmith. In this business, money, power and sex are all fused. No wonder it's so ruthless. She thought about her new book, and all the people introducing themselves to her. Maybe she so loved writing because she could people her world with those that she loved. Even if many of the people in her book did dreadful things, she could understand why they did them, and then she could still love them. It wasn't true of real life, she discovered to her cost. Still, she had a bid for her first book, and that gave her an enormous sense of elation. I'm not a total failure. She braked as she spotted a toy shop, parked the car and went inside.

Once in the cheerful, reassuring world of children, she felt safe. She picked up a little portable doll's-house. The kind you could close like a suitcase and put in your pocket. She stood looking at it, marvelling at the kitchen and the stairway that climbed prettily to the bedrooms. She put it down. As usual she would be buying it for herself; Allegro would look at her scornfully if she came back with it. No, another little pony with long blond hair and a comb to comb its mane. She chose a blue one. Allegro didn't like anything pink. 'Too girly,' she'd say, and her nose would wrinkle like a dried prune.

She drove back to her house, glad that she lived in Devon. For her Devon was the most beautiful county in England. When she'd first arrived she had rushed about this tiny island called England. She had gloried in the fact that Scotland was available to her in a few days.

As she drove, she dreamed of those first few frightening and confusing months. Places like Tintagel Castle put her back together. Her fragile inner sense shook most of the time that first year. Now she was going home a writer. A woman who could lift her head high after so many long years as a failure. She was going home to her family and her house, leaving behind two friends. Her publisher Susan and her agent Stella. They had made her feel stronger, so much stronger, in the broken places.

Sixty

∾ৡ

After ten hectic years and one brief love affair, Madeleine found she needed to take time to think about her life. Why she hadn't done so before seemed odd to her. Allegro was now a beautiful eighteen-year-old girl. So much of Madeleine's life had been poured into her books, she had forgotten how to live.

For four years she had refused to have anything to do with men. Then she'd met James and had a happy, carefree love affair for a year. He left his socks on the floor of her bedroom, and she threw him out. Since then she'd stuck close to Hilary, who was happily married again. Madeleine wished her well, but the drug of aloneness had bitten deeply into her soul, and she didn't want a full-time man, or any man for that matter, in her life.

Edwina visited, as did Germaine. Edwina's main concern was that she was menopausal, and she moaned endlessly about whether she should stuff herself with artificial hormones or not. 'If Scott gets it up, we do it, but these days it's rare.'

On one of her visits, Edwina eyed Madeleine across her kitchen table. 'What do you do now, Maddie, as you are the nun that has none?'

'I mind my own business, darling. Besides, I'm grateful that I don't have to take care of a man's prick any longer.' Madeleine was surprised at the anger in her voice. The question flew straight to the raw, empty part of her heart that still missed making love with Paolo. She sat with a bottle of Brunello di Montalcino di Altesino. She chose the 1975 vintage.

Now she was an expert on wine. She consulted her shipper, who was the one bond she kept with Paolo. The Altesino winery in Buonconvento was where he ordered the wine they drank together. She knew having the bottles in the house made her ache, but it was the only part of Paolo she could hold on to.

Sometimes she wondered if she should have disappeared without trace. Was there anything left to say between them? Now she would never know the answer, but she had broken no universal law except the one which said, Thou Shalt Not Take That Which Is Not Yours To Possess, and she had paid the price. How many other women in the world felt as she did?

Did he ever think about her and the times they spent together? Her one-year lover left her blank with the knowledge that, however much he tried, his love-making never reached the innermost depth of her soul. She remembered how she had felt that passion like that she had felt with Paolo could not be a sin. But then, if it was not, why the retribution? Why the fall from grace, when before she saw him with his wife, the world was a beautiful place filled with glowing colours?

She was at a wedding with Hilary and her husband. 'Look at the bridegroom, Madeleine. Isn't he dishy?'

'Hilary, don't be an asshole. Those dishy-looking men are totally useless. They spend all their lives in front of a mirror. We married men like that. Remember?'

Allegro was at that wedding, surrounded by a huge crowd of admiring men. Men of all ages. She was largely oblivious to their attentions. She was playing hockey for the county, and was also a good cricketer. She had no time for men, and said so loudly.

'I'm John Bartlett. I am reliably told that you two pretty women live locally. I've just moved into the area, so I'm trying to meet people.' He had nice kind brown eyes, and the sort of Englishman's skin that goes pink when they think lustful thoughts.

Madeleine had read somewhere that men think of sex once every six minutes, and she wondered if he would go pink in the next six minutes. He didn't and John, she decided, must be rare. 'He's nice,' Hilary whispered hopefully to Madeleine as they followed John into the marquee for the wedding luncheon. Hilary, ever hopeful on Madeleine's behalf, didn't understand how cynical Madeleine had become.

Now, sitting over her bottle of wine with Edwina, she remembered the struggle she'd had with several men to get them to leave her alone. 'You know, Edwina, in the beginning I tried to make friends with men. Except for Vincent Heatherington, who remained a rock in my storm, I find it impossible. Why do I attract such absolute bastards?'

'Because, sweetheart, they take one look at you and know you'll do whatever you are told. Now you know our new rule? You don't agree to say anything, not even good morning to a man, until I rush over and check on him. I have a friend called Caroline. She's a private detective; she'll run a check for you.'

'It gets to something when you have to check the bastards out with a private detective.'

'Sure it does, but Caroline was telling me before I left New York that she had a client who was told by her lover that he had a private yacht and loads of money, and when she ran a check he was living out of a rented van.'

'What has happened to men these days?' Madeleine could scarcely believe her ears. Edwina blew a puff of cigarette smoke into Madeleine's face. 'When men don't go to war with each other, they declare war on women.'

'Well then, we'll just have to declare war back.'

Madeleine frowned. 'That's a girl, Maddie, and if you don't do it, Allegro sure will. Tarquin's really smitten with her.'

'He's wasting his time. She seems to have no interest in men. You know, I'm not sure of the reason why. I get all guilty and ask her and she just smiles and pats me on the back. "Shit, Mom," she said last time I asked. "I'm too busy with my women's movement." She is involved with a group of girls she was at school with, and they have formed this corporation. They have all vowed to be millionaires before they are twenty-five. They have also vowed to have no boyfriends and only to recruit women.

'I explained to Allegro that the no-men rule was against the anti-discrimination laws, but she says any men who tried to join them would be quietly terrorised until they were only too pleased to leave. I think she's probably right. They are all terribly fierce young women. I wouldn't want to cross Allegro when she's angry, and as for her friend Amy . . . She has a black belt in everything, and was born and raised in Harlem. Nothing frightens her.'

'Talking of New York, I'd better pack, Maddie, and we'll run for the plane. Scott will be back tomorrow, and he'll be in a foul mood if I'm not there.'

Poor Edwina, Madeleine thought as she put her on the train. She remembered too those awful days when she used to have to hurry home to fix a drink for Syracuse. Now he was almost phased out of her life. Allegro refused to have anything to do with him. 'Boring wimp,' was her comment after his last phone call. 'Who needs a biological father anyway? I'd rather pick my own.'

'Who would you pick then?' Madeleine was curious. At least there was one man on this earth that Allegro liked. 'Vincent Heatherington and Hilary's husband, Bruce. Their auras are fine.'

'Just as a matter of interest, Allegro . . .' She had returned from putting Edwina on the train, and found Allegro sitting in the kitchen.

'Shhh, Mom, we're constructing a bridge between the manifest and the unmanifest with the help of the Crowley pack of Tarot cards. It's quite a dangerous thing to do, so please don't talk about it to anybody.'

'Darling, are you sure you know what you're doing?'

'Yeah.' Allegro's tone was laconic. Madeleine knew that Allegro and her friend Amy were immersed in the unmanifest world with Dr Stanislaus, and she kept herself with her friends in a tight circle, but she was shocked to hear this new idea. 'Darling, I certainly won't tell anybody. Who is there to tell now Nanny Barnes and Mrs Poole have retired? I'm alone in the house.'

'I mean Edwina; she talks too much. Germaine knows all about it, and now it's time for you to be told. Here's what we plan to do. Do you remember all those women you saw when I was little? They had all killed themselves for the love of a man?'

'How did you know that, Allegro? You were so young.'

'I know far too much for this life, Mom.' Allegro suddenly looked very vulnerable, and Madeleine reached across the kitchen table and hugged her.

'Does it frighten you?'

'Sometimes, Mom. I came to do this thing, and I accepted my gift when I was quite little. We intend to build a fragile bridge for the women to cross from the unmanifest into the manifest, which is our world. Then, though they cannot ever fall in love again, they can finish what they set out to do in their careers before they fell in love and died.'

'That's wonderful, Allegro. Are you sure you can do this?' Then Madeleine sat still and she remembered the small, slim woman who'd told her why Allegro was sent. 'Of course, Allegro, I had completely forgotten. A woman told me you would grow up to change the world. Now I remember.'

'You didn't forget, Mom. You were made to forget. Our brains don't forget anything. They are super-computers. We just don't know how to use them properly. Yup, often I *am* afraid. It's lonely sometimes, but the other alternative is to live what other people call "real life", and believe-you-me that's even lonelier. I have the whole universe to myself. I can transport myself to different parts of it. Oh Mom, it's all so beautiful. What an enormous universe the Light created. How perfect it is. How totally harmonious it is.' Her voice trembled with emotion. 'How can people not see the Light, or recognise the divinity of love? That's why I won't waste my time with human emotions. We in our group wait until we find the other half of ourselves for union. There is no union without communion. That's a lesson this world must learn. All those women who have passed centuries in the undead never learned that. Isn't it awful?'

'I guess so, darling. I'm not sure what it all means, but I trust you.'

'You can, Mom. Don't forget, Dr Stanislaus is on our side.'

'I won't forget, Allegro. I often talk to him and he's so funny. He says I have a two-time married face, but he won't tell me when or who. Still, somewhere out there is a man for me. I tell him it has to be third-time lucky, but then I'm so used to living on my own that I'm in no hurry.'

Later that night, with Amy and Allegro upstairs, building their bridge, Madeleine sat with a glass of wine

353

in her hand. Edwina informed her that menopause had completely killed lust in her life. I wish I was so lucky, she thought. Fortunately, in her dreams, she often went back to her days and nights with Paolo. Although upon waking she was relaxed after her erotic dreams, she cried. Tears of love and longing for what could never be. She sighed and heaved herself up. She wandered into the library. There was a new book on neuro-biology she wanted to read. Now she had all the time in the world, she found she was fascinated by neuro-biology. The whole universe in our heads, she mused, and then she became absorbed in the book.

Allegro was tired. The bridge had materialised. It had been early in the morning when the last woman had come over. She was sitting in her office drinking a cup of much-needed coffee. They had been arguing about sex. 'Yeah, but can you pleasure yourself with your own mouth, Allegro?' Amy was stretched out on the sofa in Allegro's office and was grinning at her.

'No, it can't be done. You must be joking, Amy?'

'No, I'm not. Watch me.' She tumbled on to the floor, then she lay on her right elbow. She raised a long, elegant black leg and hooked it behind her head and then she leaned forward. 'See,' she said. 'It's an old Indian trick. You release your spine. Easy, and it's far better then fucking men. They're all so clumsy.'

'Not all of them. I've been reliably told that a few men are worth the trouble they cause. The main problem seems to be that once you let a man into your bed they think they own you. Nobody owns me.' Allegro was just about to celebrate her first million pounds and her twenty-first birthday at the same time.

Across the road, Gabriel, known as the black angel, sighed. 'I don't know how she does it.' His office block was opposite Allegro's glass tower. 'Sometimes I feel those women are all witches. How do they manage to capture the stock market across the world and never seem to put a foot wrong? Allegro's a spoiled bitch, but Amy?'

Boyd, his business partner, laughed. He was a big man with wide shoulders and a tendency to gather fat around his waist. 'Amy raped me in my own flat.' Gabriel shook his curly brown locks and his famous mouth pouted. 'I can't look at her in the face to this day.'

'I'd stay well away from both those ladies, Gabriel. If we men think we're a bad lot, we're nothing like as bad as that lot over there.' He watched as a string of young, stunningly beautiful women piled out of the opposite building, heading for their business lunches, Filofaxes in hand. 'My, oh my, where does Allegro find them?' Gabriel moaned. 'Not a wrinkly among them. All of them so beddable.' As he watched, he noticed yet again that there were women from practically all parts of the world. They moved with a firm step, almost as if they were in an army. They walked with their arms around each other, talking and laughing, barely glancing at the people who passed by. Men whistled from the building site across the way. One look from Allegro, who was leading the exodus, quelled them instantly. 'Shut up, shit-faces,' Amy screamed at the men. They stood uncomfortably on their scaffolding, at a loss for words. Amy laughed sourly. 'Can't take it when we dish it back to you, can you?' There was a deafening silence.

Sixty-one

❧

Gabriel Lawrence sat in his office, half watching the coming and goings in the building across the street. He thought mostly lustful thoughts when he wasn't thinking about money.

Silken sweep of thighs, long legs slightly open. Moist soft mouths. Hummocks of breasts with dark nipples. He preferred dark nipples, and he knew that Allegro would not have dark nipples with that colour hair. Still, he would forgive her. He was in a strange state over Allegro. He couldn't ever remember feeling like this before. On the one hand she terrified him to death, and on the other he wanted to have her in the worst possible way. He'd never really recovered since she'd slapped him in the face at a banquet after he'd playfully tried to slap her bottom.

'I was only playing,' he'd said, aggrieved. He blinked his eyes in memory of the pain. That woman could pack a punch. He leaned forward in his chair and then he picked up a pair of field-glasses and watched Allegro arriving in her pink Rolls-Royce. 'So tacky,' he snarled in irritation. He knew he couldn't afford a Rolls-Royce at any price. His wife, or rather his ex-wife, had thrown him out of the marriage for bed-hopping. 'I love only you, darling,' he'd yelled up at the window. She'd thrown his clothes and his suitcase down on top of him. 'Fuck off,' she'd yelled. 'Don't come back, you bastard.'

Now, several years later, he shook his head at the memory. 'I don't know what's got into women these days.' The other morning he'd taken his ex-mistress

Amelia out to lunch for a long session of let's remember. She'd arrived after not bothering to telephone him for six months. She had been wearing a fearsome three-piece suit with a tie, and her hair was cut short. There was quite a lot of let's remember; mostly a review of all his faults. Then he'd tried to pay and she had refused to let him. She had taken out her wallet. He'd been amazed at the credit cards she had. All of them platinum. He'd been angry he had none. His bank manager had repossessed them all. It wasn't fair. Amelia was probably balling her bank manager. Life was really unfair.

When he'd recounted the story to Boyd, his business partner, Boyd had disagreed. 'He probably isn't bonking her. My bank manager is so frightened of these New Women that he hides under the desk and gives them everything they ask for . . . It's an absolute lie put round by women journalists that there is such a thing as a New Man. We're all the same wimps we always were. It's the New Women. I thought I'd married the bossiest woman in the world, but phew, these women are terrifying. Stay away, is all that I can advise.'

'I can't stay away, Boyd,' Gabriel had mourned. 'I'm addicted to pussy.'

'I don't know any man who isn't. I think I'd rather be gay; at least men are kind to each other . . .'

'You know, that's it.' Gabriel was talking out loud. There was nobody in the office to hear him, and he knew all the male executives in their offices also had field-glasses, and no doubt also confided their most intimate thoughts to their desk blotters.

He watched intently as he saw Allegro climb out of the car and her chauffeur open the door for the other passengers.

'That's Allegro's mother.' He whistled softly. Not bad looking. A little wrinkly, but then wrinklies are so

357

grateful for it. Maybe he should try and make a pass at her. That would upset Allegro, and the thought of upsetting Allegro pleased him. He smiled. His dimple quivered and he put his face in his hands. 'Ah,' he sighed. Allegro. She'd broken many a man's heart, and no one had broken hers yet. He was doing his best, but so far with very little result. Maybe he'd send her a big bunch of roses. Red and dark and true. Show her he could be romantic and not just a boor. He picked up the telephone. 'Get me the flower department of Fortnum and Mason, please,' he barked. The man who ran it was an old friend of his, and had seen him through many an affair. Discretion came easily at Fortnum's, where the hampers left the hamper department smoothly. The light cane baskets sat well in the boot of a car. Ah, the women he'd had on his black and green tartan blanket. They seemed to get delightfully randy at the mere sight of the Fortnum and Mason crest.

In Gabriel's opinion there were two types of women. Fortnum women, who were bred like race-horses. Allegro belonged in that class. Or women like Allegro's mother. They were stayers in this race of life. They shopped at Harrods. Allegro's mother would bother to go to Harrods to shop. Allegro wouldn't waste her time. She'd pick up the telephone. Send round the Rolls and it would all arrive in beautiful boxes. On the whole, Gabriel thought he liked Fortnum women best, but the Harrods women were better cooks.

Allegro, he knew because she'd told him often enough, couldn't boil water. He picked up the telephone again. 'On the card for the flowers,' he told his secretary. 'Please could you invite Mrs and Ms Winstanley to dinner at my place at eight. Make it Monday.' He needed to have people to dinner on Monday. He hated Mondays. If anything went wrong, it would go wrong

358

on a Monday. Also, the weekends could be lonely if everybody was in the country. Gabriel hated the country with a passion. All those turding cows. Smelly goats and ducks. The only good duck was a dead duck as far as he was concerned. He began to plan his menu. He would spend the evening flirting with Madeleine. He grinned hugely at the thought.

Gabriel sat at the end of his dining table, gazing first at Allegro and then across the table at Madeleine. He was quite surprised that Allegro had agreed to come to dinner at all. She had received his bouquet and signalled her disapproval of his kindness by tearing the bunch of flowers to bits on the pavement outside her skyscraper in full view of all his employees. 'Fucking grow up,' he'd screamed down at her. 'You bastard,' she had screamed back.

He'd withdrawn from the window, his face red with fury and exertion. 'One day I'll get that bitch across a bed, and then I'll show her who's boss,' he said loudly. Inside he knew that, if he ever got into bed with her, he would never be the boss in any situation with Allegro. Her mother, however, looked far more amenable, and she was quietly glowing in the candlelight.

'Madeleine,' he said, leaning forward and dimpling. 'Tell me about your life now.'

'My life is very quiet, Gabriel.' She smiled at him, thinking what a handsome man he was. Allegro was so adamant about having nothing to do with him. 'He's cunt-crazed, Mom. Just leave him alone.'

'Darling, don't be so fierce,' is what Madeleine said when she saw the invitation. 'I'd like a night out. I've always found him such good fun.'

'OK, if you insist. I'm wearing steel knickers. Anyway, I've got to come; he'll pounce on you if you go alone.'

Now, watching Gabriel flirting with her mother, Allegro felt uncomfortable. She knew that her mother had been living quietly and in almost solitary confinement in her house, and she hoped very much that she would be able to resist Gabriel's long-practised charms. She watched as she saw a great warmth emanating from her mother towards Gabriel. The colour was timorous and shimmering.

Gabriel radiated a great deal of gold. But then he would, the bastard. Money was all he thought about. Money and sex. She wished she were back in her bedroom with Amy, sitting on her bed, constructing another bridge with the help of the Tarot cards. Amy would be over later in the night so they could open the bridge and help the undead over into this manifestation.

Now she was quite used to talking to Dr Stanislaus, who often appeared. There was another unmanifest called Rollo. He'd been French in his last life, and he had a lovely accent and a terrific sense of humour. Now the army of women was increasing hugely. She was thinking of expanding her business.

She had recently bought a huge block of flats, and they were converting it into a luxury high-rise block. All women builders, architects, and plasterers. She enjoyed watching them go up, and then seeing the lights light up at night in the windows. The new manifestations had been given the right to design their own bodies. Their past lives were erased once they crossed the bridge. Most of them designed themselves between the ages of eighteen and twenty-five.

They were a gorgeous-looking crowd. The city was buzzing with excitement as the girls took on as many men as they pleased. They were safe from falling in love. Only Allegro was free to fall in love. Amy preferred to pleasure herself so she was out. Allegro, after she'd seen what her mother had been through twice, knew she would never fall in love with a man. Love is for fools, she told herself, and then she willed herself to return to the conversation.

'Do you ever get lonely, Madeleine?' Gabriel leaned forward, with sympathy oozing from every pore. 'Yes, I do sometimes, but that's a price I pay willingly for being a writer. It's a lonely business for all of us. It has to be, otherwise you don't get anything written. I don't think people ever quite realise what an effort is involved in writing a novel. It's like Sisyphus. I roll the stone a bit higher up the hill every day, and hope it's not going to roll back on me. Believe me, I am exhausted after a day's writing, and just want to sit back quietly by my fire and digest the next day's work.'

Gabriel grinned at Allegro. 'Well, you certainly aren't a chip off the old block, are you?'

'Nor are you, old bean,' Allegro retorted with an emphasis on the word 'old'. She saw her arrow strike home, and she smiled sweetly at him. 'Do tell, darling, are we having our mid-life crisis yet? You know, the male menopause? After all, you're well past the big three-O, aren't you?'

'If your mother weren't here, I'd turn you over my knee and spank you. You're a spoiled little brat, Allegro.' He felt an achingly sharp pain in his shin, and it took him a minute or two to realise that she had kicked him with her steel-tipped bovver boots. 'Your daughter just kicked me,' he roared at Madeleine.

'I'm so sorry, Gabriel. Really, Allegro, you're much too old to kick people.' She leaned forward and took Gabriel's hand. 'Allegro has always had a problem with her aggression, you know. Dr Steckel, her childhood psychiatrist, said it was all my fault because I was much too gentle with her.' Madeleine sighed. 'I know I failed, but I really can't get upset over things, and she was such a dear little thing.'

The dear little thing smiled sweetly at Gabriel. He got slowly to his feet and tried not to limp into the kitchen. Once there, he moved over to the sink to examine the damage. There was a neat indentation where Allegro's foot had connected with his shin. 'Blast,' he cursed, as he now hobbled about the kitchen, collecting the pasta for the main course. He had made an exceptional sauce. Even Allegro must enjoy it, but she would probably die rather than admit it. Why, oh why did she have to be such a bitch? Still, he was getting on well with Madeleine. He returned to dining room, put down the tray and handed round the plates. 'Smell this, Madeleine,' he said, putting the bowl of pasta and sauce under her nose. 'Have you ever smelled anything like it?'

Madeleine's eyes met his, and he saw with a shock an electric bolt of pain rip across her face. It was as if her face for a second fell apart, and the vulnerability of this lovely, elegant woman touched him deeply. 'I'm sorry, Madeleine. I didn't mean to stir an old memory.'

'Don't worry, Gabriel. I know you didn't mean it. Anyway, how could you know? Yes, I do know only one sauce that smells better than this.' There was a moment's silence. 'It was a long time ago now.' Then she smiled. 'Here, Allegro, let me fill your plate.' Gabriel realised that Madeleine blamed herself for Allegro's dislike of men.

Gabriel watched the dark-haired woman lean over her daughter. How much guilt did Madeleine carry for the sadness she had brought into the life of her daughter when her heart was broken? These sorrows impinge not only on the lovers, but the fall-out irradiates the whole family. Was the man who cut Madeleine's heart in two Allegro's father? He rather thought not. On the few occasions when the subject of her marriage came up between them, Madeleine had always been light-hearted about the years she'd spent with her husband. No, this must have been some other man who, along with the damage he'd caused Madeleine, had also infected Allegro. Often, as Gabriel knew to his cost, the child nearest to the mother is as badly affected. He had divorced his first wife, and still carried the guilt for the damage he had inflicted on his daughter. He'd become aware far too late that he had been the first man in her little life, and not only had he betrayed his wife with his affairs, but also his daughter. His wife was able to look after herself, but his tender daughter was not. He helped himself to his pasta and the sauce.

'Well,' he said, filling the wine glasses. 'Here's to a new effort at being friends with Allegro. Darling, can't you make-believe that I'm your brother or something? I don't want to quarrel with you.'

'No, you just want to fuck me, like you do all women.'

'Allegro,' Gabriel tried to address her with quiet dignity, 'why must you be so basic about everything?'

'Because that's how it is. Don't think I don't know how you and Boyd talk. Boyd's always sure that any woman who doesn't come running after him is a frigid bitch. Well, Amy taught him a lesson, and you too for that matter.'

'She did indeed,' Gabriel tried not to look pained. 'But can't all of you just lay down your arms for once?'

'No, not until men down theirs. We've tried to be nice. We tried to have equal relations with you, and all we got was kicked in the teeth. Now we're fighting back.' She grinned.

'What does that actually mean, Allegro? Do you mean you have an organised plan? Other than terrorising the city with your women-only financial empire?'

'Wait and see, dear boy. Just you wait and see. If you forgive me, I just have to slip away in order to do some more terrorising. I'm sure Mummy will give you a hand with the washing up. She's very good at it. Mummy, make sure he doesn't get his hand up your skirt. Goodnight, darling.' She kissed her mother gently on the cheek. 'I don't suppose I get a goodnight kiss,' Gabriel pleaded. 'I only cooked the dinner.'

'Of course you do, my darling boy.' Allegro leaned over Gabriel and kissed him long and deeply on the lips. Her mouth was soft and gentle. Her breath smelled of rose petals. Her little tongue slid for a second between his lips, leaving him almost incoherent with longing. 'Allegro,' he whispered, trying to stay her fleeting figure. 'So long, Gabriel, and good hunting.' She laughed and danced her way out of his house.

'Well,' Gabriel began shakily. 'Your daughter is quite something.'

'She is indeed,' Madeleine agreed, wondering what he'd say if he knew about Dr Stanislaus and Allegro's future plans. But that was not for men to know. For the moment Madeleine was enjoying sitting in this pretty bachelor's house. There was an early autumn fire in the grate of the room next door, and the promising smell of coffee to come. 'I'll help you wash up, Gabriel. It's early yet, and I don't want to go home.'

'I know that feeling. Sometimes I wish I could say to a guest, "Couldn't you just stay until it's my bedtime?" But that sounds so childish. There is something so sad about an empty house when a guest leaves early. There are those hours of silence, which I fill with music before getting ready for bed. I always make myself a cup of Ovaltine. What about you?'

'I get two digestive biscuits and a cup of tea and dunk them in the tea. Then, of course, there is my hot-water bottle. I take that everywhere with me. It's an old boarding school habit.'

'Let's take our coffee into the drawing room and sit by the fire.' Gabriel was really enjoying this evening. Madeleine was a warm and pleasant being in his house. He liked the way she smelled and the way she moved. She had a peace and a serenity about her that calmed him. There were no hidden agendas with this woman. No sharp edges that might prick him and leave him dripping blood on his lonely bedroom floor. 'Do you want to tell me about the man who broke your heart?' he asked gently.

'Not really, Gabriel. Partly because it was a long time ago and I'm as healed as I'll ever be. I think the scar tissue remains for ever, but I have rebuilt my life and I'm happy. I've always believed that life gets better as you get older, and you bring to it your experiences and wisdom.' She laughed. 'Of course, I still make mistakes, but I don't get so upset by them. I've learned not to take myself so seriously, and above all I have learned to love my own company.'

'I wish I could learn that. I don't like to be alone.'

'Well, Gabriel, you will have to learn to be alone. It is a treasured condition. Before we were bombarded with television and music players, children learned from a very early age to read a book or to wander off into fields or cities to explore for themselves. Now, unfortunately, they sit parked in front of their television sets,' she smiled. 'Allegro was different. She was far too active. She was off from a very early age, and she too loves her own company. We're both strong and independent women.' Madeleine drained her coffee. 'Are you ready for bed now, or do you want to talk some more?'

'Just to ask if you ever see yourself in a relationship again?'

'Yes, darling, but I never finished the one I had. One day, when Allegro is married, I will go and find him. I need to put a debt right. I ran away without ever giving him a chance to explain. That was cowardly of me.'

'Allegro married? You'll be a hundred and two before that happens.'

Madeleine smiled at Gabriel. 'When Allegro gives her heart, it will not only be for ever, but to a man who is worthy of her. I will see to that.'

Gabriel flinched at the uncompromising message in Madeleine's eyes. They said, 'Hands off.' He stood up and said gruffly, 'I'll go and get your coat.' There was a lump in his throat. He had wanted her to say, 'I would like you to be that man.' He was torn between a feeling of ridicule towards himself and a wish to take this wise woman into his arms and hold her. Wise she might be, but she was much too vulnerable for her own good. As he slipped on her coat, he did take her into his arms for a brief moment. She relaxed against him and he felt her trembling. 'I haven't been held by a man for a long time,' she said, smiling into his face. 'And I'm glad it is you, Gabriel.' She kissed him gently on the cheek, and he was surprised yet again that evening to feel tears smarting in his eyes.

He closed the door behind her, and led her down the stairs. He took her to her car and tucked her carefully in. It was a long time for him since he'd felt safe enough from attack to venture to exercise the old male prerogative of escorting a lady to her car. He stood on the pavement and watched her drive away. She waved a black-gloved hand at him in the driving mirror. He waved back.

Sixty-two

❧

'Are you really telling me that Allegro and Amy are going to take that monstrous army of women to join the big-hair brigade in New York?' Boyd's voice shook with horror and disbelief. 'The world will be changed overnight if they all get together. As for those Amazons on the Japanese Stock exchange . . .' He tried to pretend his shuddering was just a joke, but had he but known it, Gabriel was doing his best to maintain his own composure.

'I had dinner with Madeleine, Allegro's mother, last night. Allegro left early to plot with her women, and I found it such a relief to be with a woman who was just happy to have a cup of coffee with me and to help me with the washing up. We had a lovely time talking; it's been years since I haven't had to worry about how to get the woman into bed if she wanted to. Or, if she didn't want to, how to cope with the rejection.'

'Same here,' Boyd said gloomily. 'I mean, about the getting rejected bit. It's far harder to get a hard on if you don't really want it and all you really want is a goodnight cuddle and a kiss on the cheek. I don't know what the world's come to, I really don't. Anyway, my wife's night for a bridge party tonight. She plays killer bridge, and I'm not that good, and she screams at me in front of our friends. You know, I think American women have become far more aggressive in recent years.'

'Of course they have.' Gabriel nodded his head. 'It's

because we live in a patriarchal society and we oppress them.'

'But I don't think I oppress my wife. I bought her a huge house. I pay the mortgage. I pay the kids' school fees. I pay for the groceries and the holidays. How do I oppress her?'

Gabriel wrinkled his marble-smooth brow. 'Well, I don't know exactly, but I know we do because that's why my wife left me. That and of course I had affairs. She did, too, but that was different, or so she said. She said I had no right to interfere with her need to explore her own bisexuality. Do you see?'

'No, I don't see. When my wife decided she had to get a job, she pottered about interior decorating and they upped my tax bracket. So I paid so that she could work. If that's oppression, then I give up.

'I'll buy you lunch, Gabriel, and maybe we could get smashed?'

'OK, you're on. I have to leave for New York tomorrow, and all the big hairs will be on me in a flash. They must have some kind of radar. Maybe it's in their ovaries. You know, I'm sure that they have a whole set of organs going to waste because they won't have sex with men, and that they've converted them into radar sets.'

'That is definitely a sexist remark, Gabriel.'

'I know, Boyd, but I've never been politically correct and I never will be, thank God. It's a form of fascism as far as I'm concerned. Now come along, you genitally disabled male, let's go and have some lunch.' They left the building feeling quite pleased with themselves. These secret meetings revived their self-confidence.

'Bastards, complacent bastards,' Allegro said under her breath. She switched off the microphone that was under the carpet in Gabriel's office. Amy was smiling at her furious face. 'Don't worry, Allegro, we've got them running scared. Let's cable that remark of Gabriel's to New York. June and Debbie are expecting him in their offices tomorrow morning.'

'Boy, I wouldn't like to be in his shoes. I even feel a little sorry for him. June's one hell of a big hair.' Amy grinned. 'Serves him right for being rude about our wombs. I wonder if we could link our pheromones with our photons and shoot the particles of light around the earth? I must speak to Virginia. She came over the bridge two nights ago. She told me she was the first woman to win the Nobel prize for physics. Of course, she didn't get it. Her lover claimed it and he got it.'

'Even Nobel prize winners die for men? You'd think they'd be more intelligent than that.'

Amy shrugged. 'Darling, the cleverer a woman is, the more likely she will be to attract bastards. Men are cruel, and they like destroying that which they cannot understand. If a man can't steal your talent, he'll try and kill you for it.'

'Mom is still so vulnerable. I was watching her last night. She is far too innocent. I hope Gabriel leaves her alone. If he hurts her I'll kill him. I should have killed the last one, but then I was too young to protect her. I still feel enraged when I remember how she cried, and think how many years it will take her to get over the damage, if she ever will.'

'She'll get over it, Allegro – eventually. But it wouldn't hurt her to have a fling with Gabriel. He's good in bed.'

'I thought you said he was lousy?' Allegro felt hurt. They always told each other everything.

'I frightened him, that's all. He'll put a light in your mother's eyes.'

'No, he won't,' Allegro's tone was curt. 'If he does try it, I'll scratch his eyes out.'

'My, aren't we in a snit today? Come on, let's get some snifters out and drink some brandy and wait for June's reply.'

When the cable arrived, both women chortled. 'Leave him to us.'

'Boy, I'll sleep well tonight,' Allegro rejoiced. Amy's eyes were brimming with adrenalin. 'Knowing that Gabriel is going to suffer in June and Debbie's hands is an orgasmic pleasure.'

'You sadistic bitch.' Allegro punched her friend on the arm.

'My father taught me well,' came the chilling reply.

Gabriel was jet-lagged. He had spent the journey sitting in the first-class compartment resisting the advances of a New York big hair who had nothing to do with the stock market. 'Oh no,' he groaned as he felt her hand steal into his lap under his blue blanket. He turned his head to look at his supposedly sleeping partner and he could see no expression on her face.

He had the reading light on and was trying to catch up on his figures for his meeting in the morning with June and Debbie. They were both notorious nit-pickers and he didn't want to be caught floundering. He could already hear their New York nasal whines, which seemed only to belong to the big hairs.

They said things like, 'Surely, Gabriel, you must have realised that you needed to customise the overview you took in the last meeting? I mean, you didn't change your point of view? You seem to us to be severely mentally challenged.' Gabriel could not follow half of what they said. He knew it must be his fault, because his former wife had pointed out often enough that everything was the fault of men. He learned long ago to take the line of least resistance. To agree to every word and to grovel and drivel until they took pity on him. Not June or Debbie; they were merciless in the face of his discomfort.

By now the hand seemed to have taken on a life of its own. He pressed the bell for the stewardess, hoping to chase it away. As the stewardess swayed down the gangway, the hand withdrew. He sighed with relief and ordered a whisky sour. His head throbbed from the long lunch with Boyd, at which they had promised each other that they would launch a men's movement that would wipe the monstrous regiment of women off the face of the earth.

'Death rather than dishonour,' Boyd had hiccuped as they'd hugged each other goodbye. 'Get in touch with our feelings,' Gabriel had yelled as he'd poured himself into the taxi to Heathrow. '*À bas* the bitches.' He had last seen Boyd trying unsuccessfully to negotiate a lamp-post. He'd given up and peed on it. Gabriel had rolled about the taxi laughing. The sight of Boyd in his three-piece suit, his bowler hat jammed over his ears, and his black umbrella hooked neatly over his arm made Gabriel hysterical.

Now this was no laughing matter. Big hair sat up in her seat. Her massive thighs encased in jeans embraced a seemingly pregnant belly. But her hanks of Medusa-like grey hair belied the possibility. She had a face like a Christmas pudding and more than a trace of a moustache over her liver-like lips. Gabriel felt quite faint.

He tried to remind himself that he had made passes on aeroplanes on several occasions. Try as he might to rationalise the situation, though, which was what he'd been trained to do by his wife, it was no help at all. He desperately wished he could retract his willy into his body. He read that Indians could do that at will. He promised himself lessons as soon as he got home. Maybe all men should take lessons. A sort of bolt-hole for testicles and willies. He drained his drink. The hand came back. It was not a gentle hand. It felt like a hand that had been accustomed to milking cows. In spite of himself, he felt his penis rise. Accustomed to choice, the damned thing had a life of its own.

His mind plunged in horror like a stallion on a training rein, but the adversary between his legs continued to grow. In desperation he rang the bell again. The stewardess came down the gangway. 'Yes, sir,' she said testily. Everywhere was a deep silence. Most of the plane was asleep and he was being a nuisance. 'Bring me three whisky sours, please.' He wanted to say, 'Please help me, I'm being sexually harassed,' but he couldn't. Men don't get sexually harassed – only women.

They could stand with tears welling in their eyes, recounting their terrible adventures, and be rescued. Other men only roared with laughter when Gabriel tried to recount his terrifying ordeal with Amy. 'Lucky bastard,' had been the standard reply.

Well, Gabriel didn't feel lucky now. He threw back the first whisky sour while the hand continued to treat the favourite part of his body like a teat. The second whisky sour tasted better, and he began to feel a warmth spreading between his legs.

He decided that the only way to get through this was to lie back, enjoy it, and think of England. It had always been good motherly advice for women. He finished the third drink and then relaxed. The climax was pleasant. He gazed at the woman next to him. 'Why did you do that?' he asked in all innocence.

'You looked like such a wimp when you came,' she said, gazing into space. Gabriel wanted to cry.

'Do you do that to all men?' he asked, curious.

'Mostly they don't mind.'

'Well, I did. I'm human, you know.'

'No you ain't. You're a man, aren't you?'

'Sure I am, but I do have feelings.'

'No you don't. All men are bastards, and all men are rapists.'

'Gee, you must know my wife. She's got one of those banners in the hall.' He was angry now.

The hand reached for the bell for the stewardess. 'This man,' said the face covered with big hair, 'is bothering me.'

'OK,' said the bored stewardess. 'Get moving, buster.'

Gabriel sighed and picked up his suitcase. It was all very Kafkaesque; he'd never understood his books either. 'I'm coming,' he grumbled. 'Take no prisoners.' He followed her disapproving back down the plane to the back seat of the front cabin. Anyway, he comforted himself. At least I'm safe now. Maybe I should hire a big bodyguard when I get home. That thought comforted him.

Sixty-three

~ঽ

June and Debbie sat behind their twin desks, peering at Gabriel as if he were something out of their trash-can behind the office block. He felt like something nasty. His eyes were gritty with lack of sleep. He felt unwashed and he was indeed unshaved. Big hair had monopolised the first-class lavatory.

'It must have been the shit of the century,' he'd mumbled at her as he'd left the plane.

She had scowled at him. 'Fuck off, dickhead,' she'd said by way of a farewell.

'Ah, the romance of the maiden.' He had tried to smile at her, but then he'd found himself walking as fast as he could down the tarmac and ducking into the door of the airport, hoping she was not going to come along behind him and smash him to the ground.

Now, as he sat looking hopefully at the two women in front of him, he just wanted mercy. He promised himself that, from now on, he would treasure women – all women. His days of dashing about bedrooms seducing women were over. Not because he had suddenly been converted to the ways of the moral majority, but because it was just too bloody dangerous. In the old days, the only thing to fear was the inopportune arrival of a husband or lover. That just added spice to the game. No, nowadays women had become malevolent creatures. Far more dangerous than men. Gabriel believed that men just wanted to fuck and eat, or the other way round, with time for a cigarette in between. Women, he had observed, plotted. They sat in their little spider's web of intrigue and knitted out scenes with a pair of poisonous knitting needles.

'Hello, darlings.' He thought he'd try the casual approach.

'We're not your darlings,' June and Debbie glared at him. 'All right, if you would please get out your papers, we can begin this business meeting at once. You're ten minutes late, and for us ten minutes aggregates at three hundred dollars of time. If you are late again we shall have to fine you.'

'Hey, hang on.' Gabriel was furious. 'Being ten minutes late isn't a crime.'

'It is in New York.' The two women unrolled a huge poster, and then Debbie stood up and turned the poster round so that Gabriel could see it. Her salt-cellars and her whole body shook with rage. Gabriel blinked and then he shut his eyes. Oh no, he was still on the plane and this was a nightmare. Gingerly he opened his eyes again. It was a nightmare, but it had now become a daymare.

The poster had a picture of himself naked, with a pink ribbon tied around his prick. Above his head was a portion of his conversation with Boyd. The poster read: 'OK, I have to leave for New York tomorrow. All the big hairs will be on me in a flash. They must have some kind of radar. Maybe it's in their ovaries.'

'Did you say that, Gabriel?'

'I was only joking, honestly.' They both turned to gaze at him. 'Well, if you must behave like a male chauvinist pig, you'll have to be taught a lesson. By tomorrow night this poster will be up all over New York. By the time you return to England, various billboards will be plastered with it during the night. Some of the alternative magazines, including *Spare Labia*, are willing to carry it. You will indeed be infamous. What do you think of that?'

'Not much, actually, now that you are kind enough to ask. I think it's a jolly rotten way to behave.'

'Well, we think it's time you learned to respect women.'

'But I do respect women. I have always loved women. That's been my problem. I've loved them too much. But I promise I will reform. I'll say chairperson, womanhole, anything you like, as long as you don't put out that poster.'

'Too late. It's been agreed upon by the sisterhood.'

The two of them sat down. Gabriel wondered if they were joined at the hip. The royal 'we' was unnerving. Only the queen of England was allowed to use the royal 'we'. But then the big hairs thought they were royal anyway.

'Let's get down to work.' June mouthed the words with disgust. Her face glistened with triumph. They both sat on their skeletal shanks and opened their big black shiny briefcases. The kind that executive women rammed into men's backs as they pushed them off buses in London, in the Metro in Paris, and biffed men coming out of taxis. The world had definitely become a very dangerous place for men, Gabriel decided.

The meeting went on interminably. At one o'clock the women sent out for tuna-fish sandwiches. They arrived in a big, fluffy, tasteless mound. 'I ordered one for you,' June said with an attempt at a smile.

'Er, no thanks, I had a huge breakfast on the aeroplane.' His stomach was sticking to his spine, but he could not possibly manage to munch his way through such a pile of debris. He'd tried an American hamburger once and his stomach had rebelled.

As soon as he could get out of here, he would go to

his favourite little French restaurant and have a soothing meal with Madame Julliet. She would understand him. Why, when New York had some of the best food in the world, did the great American middle classes eat such appalling food? Why, when the shops were full of delicious clothes, did the big hairs dress like old bag-ladies?

June and Debbie were wearing patched Indian skirts. Black sweaters and sneakers. They had watery, mean eyes. A slash of scarlet lipstick completed their outfits. At three o'clock the women had finished talking. American women could not stop talking. Not the women he met in the shops and the streets, or those who took care of him in hotels. They were warm and good-hearted but these executive women never used one sentence when they could use three. It gave him a terrible headache. Usually, by the time they had laboriously climbed to the top of the argument, he'd forgotten the question, and they would have to begin all over again. 'But what's the point you're making?' He was desperate by the time they came to the end of their meetings. He'd drunk far too much coffee. They had been swilling beer from the bottles as usual, and their breath across the office desk smelled like a beer factory.

The onions in the sandwiches caused Debbie to burp loudly. Gabriel tried to ignore the noise. June cackled loudly each time she erupted. Gabriel was glad to get out of the office and into the streets, where the real, decent people of New York went about their business. He telephoned his old friend Henry. 'Please come and rescue me,' he said desperately.

'What's the matter, old bean? You sound distraught.'

'I'm not distraught. I'm terrified the big hairs are after me.'

'You mean the sisterhood? I say, you do need help. Where are you?'

'I'll meet you at Madame Julliet's restaurant. I'm going straight there to order a decent meal and a good bottle of wine. Big hairs live like pigs.'

'Tell me about it, brother, I have to live here.'

'Then we'll have to do something about it.'

'You're braver than I'd ever be, Gunga Din.'

'I'm not brave. It's bravery born of desperation, which is the coward's way out.'

'See you, Gabriel.'

'Thanks, Henry.'

'Don't thank me, that's what pals are for.' Henry put down the telephone. You could always rely on your men friends, unlike women. He whistled for a cab.

Sixty-four

'It's not true that men only talk about sex.' Gabriel's forehead was lined with worry. He tackled his plate of grilled chicken. 'I talk about other things sometimes, don't I, Henry?

'I talk about wine, I suppose, and eating. Pizza first or after. Of course, there's always the delicate psychological problem. If you light up too soon after, she might think there was something wrong with her performance.'

'Have you noticed how many of our friends have to do all the cooking?' Henry asked. 'Women whine that men don't want commitment. Why on earth would a man want to have a woman in his life who can't cook, can't clean, and is usually lousy in bed because she's too tired doing big deals and won't make love? Thank goodness Monica is different.'

'Tomorrow I'm going to be the laughing stock of London and New York. Why I sounded so desperate is that June and Debbie had a poster printed of me naked with a pink ribbon dangling off my willy. What really hurts me,' here Gabriel cleared his throat, 'is that they've made it look smaller than it is. That's a really low blow.' He sat there looking like a spaniel. His face drooped. His eyes gazed mournfully at Henry.

'There's not much you can do about it, I suppose.' Henry put a hand on Gabriel's arm. 'You could try and get an injunction restraining them from putting it out, but it's a bit late for that.'

'Bitches,' Gabriel spat. 'Now I want to get together with some like-minded men and go after them.'

'Do you think that's wise? After all, you know what women are like when they're crossed – and these aren't even women. Allegro and her sidekick Amy at least have a sense of humour, but the New York big hairs? Wow, I'd just go off into the country and hide until it blows over.' Henry tried to smile encouragingly at his old friend.

'Allegro has a motto. No Man Is Worth Dying For. Well, we need a motto of our own. Hands Off All Women. Let them beg for sex. We will refrain from all amorous encounters with women until they agree to lay down their arms and lie in ours with love.'

'Gabriel, you really are an incorrigible romantic. Women'll never lie in men's arms for love.' Henry was laughing now. 'Women want certain things from us and we get sex in exchange.

'While women are bearing their children, men get short-changed with sex because there's nothing sexy about bringing up children. I should know, I have three kids. Half the time the house smells of baby sick and shit. We both work hard, and if she doesn't have a headache, I do. But we are good friends, and we soldier through together. The day will come when we can be alone again, and hopefully our lives will resemble the lives we had before we had the children.

'Sometimes I get desperate, and look at my wife who is worn and tired; but then both of us adore the children. So we give each other a goodnight hug, and get some badly needed sleep. Monica is not part of the war between men and women. She's a good wife and mother and I love her.'

Gabriel smiled. 'You're a lucky bugger, Henry.'

'No, I'm not, Gabriel. It's not a matter of luck, but

of commitment. I had years of uncommitted sex. It's like bad wine; all you're left with is a hangover. At least you can throw the wine bottles away. Those women hang on like leeches. They seem to think that dropping their knickers for you is a lifeline to forever. None of them was worth a second thought until I met Monica. Now I know what love is, and a happy marriage, I'm fine. Actually, I watch you running around with your tongue hanging out, and I feel quite sorry for you.'

'So you won't join my movement?'

'Sure I will, Gabriel, but I'm on the side of the millions of decent women who get a raw deal from men. If anything I'm on Allegro's side. Your war is not with her but with the big hairs.'

'I know my war is not with her, Henry. I love Allegro. At least, I think it's love. Do you get a dreadful pain here?' Gabriel pressed his hand to his chest. 'If you are away from Monica, I mean? I do when I'm away from Allegro, but she hates me. Her war is against me. It's very personal. I wish it weren't. I've even invited her mother to dinner, and a man can't get more serious than that. In fact, I think I'm half in love with her mother. She's so gentle and sweet. When I get back I think I'll telephone her and ask if I can go and stay with her until this is all over. As you say, it would be wiser to go underground until the poster thing is over.'

'Do that, Gabriel. I've got to go back to the office. Take care, old chap.' He stood up and slapped Gabriel on the back. Gabriel winced. Why can't men kiss each other like they do in the Mediterranean? he wondered.

On the way back to the hotel he bought himself a bottle of women's hair-dye. He couldn't possibly sit on an aeroplane and wonder if the people around him had seen the poster. It would be just too terribly embarrassing.

Once in the hotel, he barricaded himself into his bathroom and read the instructions carefully. He pulled out the plastic gloves and then washed his hair and applied the liquid carefully. He put the plastic cap on his head. He went into the bedroom to lie on the bed and wait for the moment when it could all come off. Then he should have blond hair and hopefully no one would recognise him. He wondered as he flipped through the hotel menu if he could sue June and Debbie for falsifying information about his prick. He'd always been proud of it. He'd also always slept with it safely in his hand. He had nightmares of it detaching itself from his body and going out to have adventures of its own. In fact, the nightmares were so real he used to wake screaming from his sleep. For dinner, before he caught the plane, he intended to order a good bottle of wine so that he could board and go to sleep.

He forgot to check the time. He washed off the dye and shampooed his hair. He gazed at himself fearfully in the mirror. Yes, indeed his hair was now a fabulous colour of ash-blond, but his black eyebrows and his dark chin looked distinctly odd. He sighed. How do women do it? he wondered. They put all that stuff on their fingernails and wobble about on high heels. Now, if he'd been a woman, he'd have loads of women friends to telephone tonight. He could discuss his new hair-do and get expert advice. He could fill the room with their whispery, gossipy giggles. Because he was a fellow, he'd have to dine alone.

All of his men friends in New York were hurrying home to wives and partners. Men just didn't have a support group like women did.

If a man was unattached, he could always go home to his mother. Gabriel did not have a mother. She had died of cancer many years ago. He felt cosmically lonely in the hotel bedroom. He felt his eyes filling with tears and he reached for the telephone. Thinking about his mother reminded him of his evening with Madeleine.

'Madeleine?' he said. 'I'm in awful trouble. Do you think you could help me?'

'What on earth's the matter, Gabriel? You sound miserable.'

'How did you know it was me?' Gabriel felt distinctly more cheerful. Madeleine must really have liked him to remember his voice so clearly.

'Of course I know your voice, Gabriel. It's very distinctive and I'm good on voices. What can I do to help?'

Those words were like gold in Gabriel's ears. 'Can I come and stay with you tomorrow? Those horrible women in New York are putting out a beastly poster about me, and I'll be the laughing-stock of the entire financial world.'

Each time he heard that phrase which had been running about his head all day, it sounded more and more dreadful. 'It's a huge poster with me with no clothes on with a ribbon tied around my . . . well . . . um . . . my John Thomas.' John Thomas sounded less crude than willy. He winced as he heard Madeleine shriek with laughter. 'There's nothing to laugh about, Madeleine.' He felt hurt. He'd thought she at least would not make fun of him.

'I'm not really laughing, Gabriel. No, I'm really not. I'm sorry,' she said, dissolving into hysterical giggles again. 'What on earth are you going to do?'

'Hopefully come and hide with you.'

'Of course you can. I've got my agent and my editor coming for the weekend. I haven't seen them in ages, but you'll like them. Come, by all means.'

'Do you think you could possibly come and get me? I know it's a lot to ask, but the idea of a train with all those people who might recognise me . . . I mean, I feel paranoid already.'

'Of course. What time are you landing?'

'At eleven o'clock in the morning. That's really wonderful of you, Madeleine. And could you bring a blanket, just in case I have to run for it? Hopefully no one will notice me. I'll wear a hat and dark glasses and turn my coat-collar up.'

'Oh dear me, what an adventure, Gabriel!'

'It's not an adventure, Madeleine. It's me naked, and they've made my John Thomas look much smaller than it really is.' He could hear Madeleine rocking with laughter at the other end of the telephone. 'How would you feel if it were you, Madeleine? I bet you wouldn't be laughing.'

'I would if they made my bum look smaller than it is. I'd be dancing. Don't worry, Gabriel. You'll have the most famous dick in the world. Maybe you'll become a famous film star?'

'Not with a shrunken willy, I won't.'

'Oh darling, don't worry, I'll take care of you. What's your favourite food?'

'Toad-in-the-hole. I drink whisky sours.'

'Right you are. I'll see I'm all stocked up. I'll pick you up at eleven tomorrow morning. Don't worry about a thing.'

Easier said than done, Gabriel thought as he put down the telephone. Still, he felt much comforted. She'd asked him what his favourite dish was. Toad-in-the-hole. All that lovely thick Yorkshire pudding with the sausages stuffed into their holes, peeking out, begging to be eaten. Then there was all that thick brown gravy. He was going to order dinner before boarding the plane and, who knows, tomorrow he might see Allegro again. He hadn't asked Madeleine about her. Better to lay his plans carefully.

Sixty-five

Madeleine left messages for Allegro, asking her to make Susan and Stella comfortable while she went up to London, though she didn't tell Allegro why she was going. Making them both comfortable meant lashings of gin. She made stuffed crab vol-au-vents to line their stomachs, and realised that it had been a number of years since they'd both found the time to come down for the weekend.

London high-living seemed to be one huge whirlwind of a party. Madeleine tried the party circuit, but the famous faces that she saw on television in her own home intimidated her. She no longer went to parties, preferring to make her vol-au-vents in her kitchen; she also saw Susan and Stella infrequently in London by themselves.

Over the years she had watched the grey settle into her hair and the lines arrive around her mouth. Her thighs were no longer taut and she mourned the loss of her elastic skin. But, even as she mourned, she realised she had gained immeasurably in self-confidence. She was still very shy, and found it hard to let people into her inner world, but she was now much stronger in the broken places. As she confirmed this thought to herself, she finished putting fresh basil on the vol-au-vents.

She was through with the cut-and-thrust of real life. She had no need for that. Unlike so many of the people in that world – who had so quickly become friends when she became famous as a best-selling author – she bled real blood when she was knifed. For far too long she had been knifed too often.

As she drove up the motorway to collect Gabriel, she thought about Germaine and Edwina. You can throw away husbands and lovers, but good friends last for ever. She smiled at the clear blue sky. Gabriel sounded as if he'd got himself into a right pickle. She laughed out loud, then she wondered what he would look like naked. She stopped at the tobacconist on Chiswick High Road and she saw a group of teenagers on their way to school, giggling over a magazine. She walked into the shop and asked for a copy of *Spare Labia*. 'You're lucky, my dear, this is the last copy in London. What a hunk.' Madeleine paid for the magazine and refrained from opening it to find the poster of a naked Gabriel. What if the women realised that she was on her way to collect the hunk? She ran to the car and sat in her seat, giggling. She could now torment Gabriel all the way home.

She stood by the barrier, craning her neck. Where was he? Then she saw him. There was no mistaking the tall figure with the wide shoulders. She realised that part of her attraction to this man was that he reminded her of Paolo. If only she were collecting him. She shrugged and cast aside the thought. It could not be. Gabriel was wearing a homburg pulled low over his face. He wore a grey mackintosh with the collar covering most of his face, and the biggest dark glasses she'd ever seen. Even bigger than the ones she'd bought in New York to begin her affair with Paolo. She touched the glasses. She wore them to this day. A constant, painful reminder, but she couldn't throw them away. They had shielded her from so many curious faces. They had sat on her nose faithfully through seas of tears and swells of sobs.

Gabriel saw her through the pushing crowds and waved his briefcase. She waved back and waited. Good, he was here, and all in one piece. He hadn't been torn to pieces by a mob of big hairs at the airport in New York. 'Have you seen your poster?' she asked while he hugged her fiercely. 'Yes,' he groaned. 'There was a big one at Kennedy airport. I sat in the plane with my hat and dark glasses on the whole way back. Thank goodness nobody noticed me.' He gazed about furtively. 'I'll get even with June and Debbie, just you see.'

'Come on, darling, I've got my agent and my publisher at home and they'll be well into the gin by the time we get back. I love them both to distraction. Allegro is taking care of the toad-in-the-hole.'

'Oh dear, Madeleine, if she knows it's for me she'll spit into it. It's not nice to think that the whole sisterhood hates me.'

'Allegro doesn't hate you, Gabriel. She doesn't have much time for men, and I can't say that I blame her. These days, if a man has an idea, he forms a committee. If Allegro has an idea, she does it all herself and gets on with it.'

'I don't know where she gets all her energy from,' Gabriel yawned.

'Women have always had a great deal more energy than men. We are designed to take care of the world in the long term. Men can only work in short bursts. Women are far more evolved than men. We use far more of our higher brain functions, if you think about it.'

'I don't think about it. I'm exhausted. Do you mind if I go to sleep?'

'Be my guest, darling.' Madeleine was grateful for the silence. She wanted to think about her new book. The characters were slowly coming to life. Various of them were talking to her, and a fight had erupted because her male hero was jealous of the time she was spending taking dictation from his female protagonist. 'You're always listening to her moaning about me,' he accused Madeleine.

Madeleine laughed as she drove the car. Other drivers must think I'm mad, talking away to myself. 'I don't spend more time with her,' she answered. 'At the moment I need to listen to what she has to say. You'll have your turn shortly.'

Madeleine always loved this part of the novel. She never knew what a new day's writing would bring. Often dripping with sweat, and exhausted after a day's hard writing, she would sit in a heap in an armchair, glowing with the pleasure of it all.

If it had been a particularly exciting day, she would pour herself a large gin and then raise it to the god of writers. 'To the light,' was her prayer; and then she would go and cook herself a delicious meal. Today, for dinner with everyone, she planned fresh artichokes with a green basil mayonnaise, followed by the dreadful toad-in-the-hole; but it would make Gabriel happy.

Men were such children when it came to food. Gabriel's sleeping body reminded her rather too forcibly of Syracuse, snoring his life away beside her. All these years wasted in sleep. She was glad that part of her life was over. Never again would she let a man get his foot over her doorstep or into her bed. The price was just too high. Except for Paolo? 'Go away, Dr Stanislaus, and catch a mouse,' she snorted.

Madeleine could hear Stella's voice as she entered the hall. Gabriel staggered in behind her, carrying his suitcase and still half asleep. 'My goodness, Gabriel, we've just seen your willy on television. There was a dinky little black patch over it.' Stella greeted Gabriel with gales of drink-sodden laughter. 'Here's to the most famous willy in the world.' Susan's bulk shook.

Allegro sashayed into the drawing room, a poster

dangling from her hand. 'Look at this, Gabriel; it must be the smallest willy in the world.'

'My willy is not the smallest in the world. It's quite big, actually. Do you want me to show it to you?'

For a moment there was a frozen silence. 'I don't think that will be necessary, darling,' Madeleine said gently. 'We'll take your word for it.' Gabriel looked so vulnerable that Madeleine went up to him and put her arms around him. 'Come on, sweetheart, let's take your things up to the bedroom.'

'Thank you, Madeleine. At least somebody around here is sympathetic to my plight.'

'We'd show a lot more sympathy for your plight, as you call it, Gabriel, if you showed more respect for the plight of women.'

'But I do respect women, Allegro. I meant that remark on the poster as a joke. I love women, I honestly do, and so do my friends. I even have a friend who is happily married and he's faithful to his wife. He even loves his children. Can you imagine that? Ghastly, dirty, snotty things, kids, and he loves them.'

'Come along, Gabriel.' Madeleine chivvied him up the stairs. 'When you've had a wash and a brush-up, we'll go downstairs and we'll have lunch.'

Much later that night, Allegro heard a feeble scratching at the door. 'What is it, Gabriel?' she said sighing.

'How did you know it was me, Allegro?'

'I've got X-ray eyes,' she replied.

'I don't want to make a pass at you, Allegro, honest. I just want to show you my willy – it isn't small. It's really quite big, actually.'

'Go away, Gabriel. I believe you, I believe you. Go back to bed.'

'I only want to show it to you, Allegro . . .'

'Go to bed, Gabriel.' She heard him shuffling down the hall, and she fell asleep with an affectionate smile on her face.

Sixty-six

≈

'Bloody marvellous! The whole country's laughing at my willy.' Gabriel had spent the rest of the night, after shuffling away from Allegro's bedroom, pouring his heart out to Susan and Stella.

Now, at twelve o'clock the next morning, he was unshaven and hungover. Still, he managed to look wonderful, Susan thought. Pity she wasn't younger or she'd pull him. Maybe she should offer to take him to Holland for a book fair. She was bored by book fairs and she had plenty of friends going who would be interested. Most of them were fairly jaded with what was available; a bit of new blood wouldn't do any harm. She smiled at Gabriel. 'I don't think everybody's laughing at your willy, Gabriel. I think women are just enjoying a good joke. After all, if it had been a poster of a woman, nobody would have noticed.'

'Well, I'm going to get them back. I'm going to consult with my friend Boyd and we'll come up with something lethal.' He crossed his legs protectively.

'Hey, Gabriel, seen yourself in the *Morning Argus*?'

'No, and I don't want to.' He held out his hand for the newspaper. Allegro was wearing an old T-shirt that emphasised her pointed breasts, and a tight pair of jeans. Her hair was tumbled around her shoulders, and as usual she wore no make-up.

Those two would make such beautiful babies, Susan thought, watching them together. But there really was no point in such sentimental meanderings. Allegro just wasn't interested in men.

'Ouch, Allegro. Don't pinch me, you beast.' Gabriel rose to his feet. 'If you pinch, poke or punch me once more I'll smack your bottom.'

Allegro stuck out her tongue. 'You'll have to catch me first,' she yelled.

'OK.' Gabriel started to move and Allegro struck him a glancing blow on the arm before taking off for the french windows. The grass was cool under her feet. She felt the wind pull back her hair. Running like this on a chase was thrilling. She could hear Gabriel crashing along behind her. She pulled away, laughing boisterously. Oh shit, she thought. He's catching up. She could feel the earth shaking under her feet as he pounded along behind her.

Usually men were never able to outdistance her. Only Amy could run as fast as she could. Now she could hear Gabriel's heavy breathing, and then she felt his hand reach her arm. 'Got you,' he said triumphantly, and he floored her. She lay under him, too puffed to speak.

'Fuck off,' she finally managed. She bit his hand savagely. Gabriel screamed. He turned her over on the grass and hit her hard on her bottom. He held her face down on the grass and hissed, 'I said don't hurt me you arsehole.'

He turned her back over again, still keeping her pinned to the ground. 'Let me go,' she said, squirming. Tears were beginning to form in her eyes. Gabriel looked down at her face. 'Allegro, you're frightened of me, aren't you?'

'No I'm not.' She spat at him.

'Yes you are. You're scared I might make a pass at you.'

'Let me up,' Allegro said in a slightly less belligerent tone.

'Listen, Allegro, I don't go round forcing myself on

women who don't want me. I don't need to do that. I've got far too many women in my life already.' He rolled on to his back and she sat up. He lay stretched out, chewing a piece of grass. 'What I really need,' he said reflectively, 'is a friend. A woman I can trust and moan to. Why can't we just be friends?'

'I don't know about that, Gabriel.' Allegro was sitting beside him. He could feel her body was poised for flight, but she was still there. 'I've never had a man for a friend. Amy says there is no such thing as a friendship between a man and a woman.'

'Well, if there is no such thing, why don't we invent the first great friendship? I've always envied the way women tell each other all their secrets. Will you tell me all your secrets? Men don't ever admit to anything, except the sizes of their watches and their cocks.'

Allegro was studying Gabriel's face. 'All right, but first you must tell *me* a really big secret.'

'All right,' Gabriel thought for a moment. 'I go to sleep with my willy in my hand in case it drops off at night.' He felt himself blush furiously. Allegro was grinning. 'I knew you'd laugh,' he said helplessly.

'Actually, I'm not laughing. I think that's rather sweet. Let me see, it's my turn now. I have a Winnie-the-Pooh hot-water bottle. It goes everywhere with me. I have toys in my briefcase that nobody knows about. Not even Amy knows that I play with toys.' It was her turn to blush. 'Gabriel, do you have a Noddy car?'

'I do indeed, and I have Big Ears. All the Noddy books are by my bed. You know, Allegro, I think we could be friends.'

'Honestly, no sex, just friends?' Allegro looked at him questioningly.

'Sure, Allegro. Pax, OK?'

'Pax, Gabriel.'

'Race you back to the house, Allegro.' She was off and he followed. She's like a little oak leaf, he thought. So very much more vulnerable than he'd ever realised. He felt a protective surge of warmth for her. She needed taking care of. Madeleine took good care of her daughter, of course, but that was a woman's way of caring. For a man it was different. He wanted to wrap a blue cashmere blanket around Allegro. To waft her on to the front seat of a big Rolls-Royce. To see that she was never cold or hungry. He arrived at the house both surprised and delighted with his new-found friend.

When they both arrived back at the house, Stella noticed their pink and smiling faces. 'Made it up, you two? For a while I thought you were going to kill each other.'

'Nay,' Allegro grinned. 'Gabriel and I are going to stop the war between men and women. We're going to be the first plank in the bridge that brings both sexes together again.' She thought of her other bridge. That twinkling, gossamer edifice that spanned the chasm that gave the unmanifest women their right to eternity.

'It is time,' she heard Rollo whisper, 'that you extend your hand. Good girl, *chérie*.' Allegro could hear her mother talking to her friends.

'You think it's all right to be friends with a man? I won't end up getting hurt like Mom?'

There was no answer to the question. Allegro remembered she had to live her future. There was only one way to find out if she and Gabriel could be friends, and that was to try out the friendship.

She helped Madeleine pile Stella and Susan into their car. 'Good luck with the writing, Madeleine.' Stella coughed her way into the passenger seat. Allegro handed her various bulky packages and a bag of fruit from the orchard. 'Come to any conclusions yet?'

'About the war of the sexes? If I did I'd have no more novels to write. Novels depend on the battle between the sexes; I sometimes wonder how much we novelists are responsible for all this bloodshed.' She leaned through the window. 'Susan, do watch your smoking, darling. I'm worried about your chest.'

'Don't be, Madeleine. I'm at an age when sex is no longer my main vice. So if I do pop off it will be the cigarettes. Mind you, I preferred it when I had sex as well.' She sighed dramatically.

'Come off it, Susan.' Stella butted in from the driving seat. 'It's not age that stops you feeling horny. It's lack of interesting men. Men crumble and get old so much earlier than women. We retain all our interests and men lose theirs: that's the problem.' She smiled at Madeleine and her voice grew soft and affectionate. 'Take care of yourself, darling. I always hate leaving you in this God-forsaken green forest. I'm sure you're more lonely than you let on.'

'No, actually I'm not. If I am lonely it's more of a cosmic loneliness. I would feel that anywhere. You can be with people you love and talk all night long, but then they go and you're back with the silence.

'Without that silence I couldn't write. I couldn't hear the voices in my head. Usually I wander about the house or sit on the doorstep staring into the forest. I'm lucky because both of you understand what a delicate thing a novel is. It's like a developing baby; until the baby is born, anything can kill it.

'Sometimes I'm so strung-out it's terrifying. Anyway, I'd better let you go. When I'm in full flood about writing it's like talking about a drug. It's an all-consuming passion.'

'Madeleine, we do understand. If you need a voice on

the end of the telephone, I'm there twenty-four hours a day for my writers, and so is Stella.

'Before I leave, I must ask you, Madeleine,' Susan leaned out of the window and whispered at her. 'Is there any chance that Allegro might ever fall in love with Gabriel? They look so wonderful together.'

'I don't think so, Susan. The fact that they came back this morning and are being civil to each other is a first. It would be nice, wouldn't it? He's such a nice young man, even if he is a real heart-breaker. He's very good for me because he reminds me that I'm still young enough to find myself a good lover. Maybe I'll come up to London and find a man who'll be a part-time lover and not leave his socks on the floor and make a mess in my bathroom.'

'A man who doesn't make a mess in the bathroom? Chance would be a fine thing, Madeleine. You give me a ring and come up and we'll plan a day to ravage London.' Stella put her foot on the accelerator and they took off.

Madeleine walked quietly back to the house. She sighed as she reached the doorstep. She did love the company of her agent and her editor. But now she would spend the evening cleaning up the sitting-room. Picking up piles of cigarette stubs. Remembering to check the guest bathroom: Susan usually left butts in the sink. Stella's gin glass was garlanded in the usual bright red lipstick. Madeleine smiled as she went into the bathroom. There *were* butts in the sink.

Both women were so alive and so vital. They were at an age when bits and pieces of the machinery of the body started to go wrong. They lived lives that made doctors blench. But they were survivors in the war. Susan was the calmer of the two. Whether it was her bulk that slowed her down and made her take life more easily, Madeleine didn't know.

Both had independent careers from when they left university. Neither married, though they were notorious for their many love affairs. Stella, Madeleine knew, had been in love for a very long time with a married publisher. He died, leaving her bereft. Bereft: it was a word that now held so much meaning for Madeleine. Like the tearing feeling of her head when she'd left Paolo in Siena.

Sometimes it felt as if it almost hadn't happened, but then she knew it really did. The wound was so deep that it kept her away from men and celibate. She could not and would not risk that kind of passion again. She often comforted herself that at least she knew what passion was.

She felt stronger now than she had ever been, but she was deeply suspicious. Not bitter like Stella, or resigned like Germaine. Just careful. She wore her dark glasses constantly when she was out of the house. Even as she teased herself by calling herself a wrinkly, she still attracted men. It irked her sometimes, but at other times she was glad. To be anonymous, which was Germaine's condition, was for Madeleine frightening.

To walk down a busy road and have no one catch your eye. This did happen on occasion, and then she felt invalid, scrubbed off the face of the earth. Women, for most of their lives, have a child or children around them as they walk. Children verify that you exist. Otherwise you might just be a spectre. She had Allegro. Allegro, with her shining, exuberant life ahead of her.

She could hear Allegro shrieking with laughter in the kitchen. The little cloud of depression, which had surrounded her since the two women had left, lifted. She picked up the glasses and walked towards the kitchen.

'What are you two laughing about?' she said, smiling.

'Gabriel is just telling me about his meeting with June and Debbie in New York. They were in an awful mood with him. But then, if you're a woman in New York, you've got to be tough. I reckon the worst men in the world hang out there.'

Gabriel shook his head. 'I think it's not New York that's the problem. It's the fact that it attracts the wannabes from all over the world. California is much more laid-back. New York seems to draw all the manic violence that exists in America. I've seen hustlers from Santa Barbara leave the hot beaches and the coconut palms to try and make it up there,' he shrugged. 'It's not a place to be without lots of money to insulate yourself, unless you find dying exciting.'

'For women, nowhere is safe any more. I find that frightening. Even London is becoming so like New York. Amy and I travel on the underground. I don't worry when I'm with Amy, but by myself I do. I have a black belt in judo, like Amy, but now men hunt in packs and I wouldn't stand a chance. I'm afraid I wasn't brought up like Amy; I just don't have a real killer instinct.'

'I'm glad to hear that,' Gabriel smiled a wry smile. 'You see, you women told us not to be chivalrous any more. I don't think women ever understood the concept of chivalry, and how much it is necessary to instil it in men. We don't have your gentle, benign, maternal instincts. Our instincts are to ravage and spread our seed as widely as we can. To collect what rightly or wrongly is ours, and to take it off to our caves and breed our own little armies which are called families. You can't educate that out of us. It's in our genes.'

'We soon will be able to change men's behaviour medically. With gene-altering we could turn all men into pussy cats. Or we could even clone from ourselves and breed a world full of women.'

'Would you really like that, Allegro?' Gabriel sat looking adoringly at her. Madeleine stood at the sink, washing up. She was interested in her daughter's answer.

'Actually, not really, Gabriel.' She wrinkled her nose. 'Amy would love it, but I like the few men in my life, like Vincent. And,' she said shyly, 'I think I quite like you.'

'Really?' Gabriel felt a warm glow cover his soul. 'Do you mean that? You're not just joshing?'

'Gabriel,' Allegro was back in her armour again, 'we need to stop gossiping and decide what we are going to do about your nude posters.'

'There's nothing to do. I shall go back to the office tomorrow. Get horribly teased, and by Friday the media will be on to another scandal. I'll sit up late at night with Boyd, and we'll think of something dreadful to do back.'

'Don't,' Allegro said. 'The smartest thing is to totally ignore them both. After all, it was my fault. I bugged your telephone.'

'You what, Allegro?' Gabriel was horrified.

'Sure, women are better than men ever are at espionage. I've bugged your phone for months. You do say the dirtiest things to women, you know, Gabriel.'

'You shouldn't have been listening.'

'I know, but it was such fun. Now you know, do I have to give up listening?'

'I'll have my office swept clean of bugs tomorrow. Allegro, you must promise me that you won't do that ever again. Besides, I've taken a new vow to respect women. I shan't be making any more of those kind of phone calls.'

'Good. Now that we are friends, let's call a truce

between the sisterhood and yourself. OK, Gabriel?'

Madeleine smiled as they left the room, hand in hand. She was glad that Allegro had found a friend in this man. She was pleased that he'd stayed in her house long enough to rekindle her desire to find another man. For so many years she had been internally frozen. Now she could look forward to a new future with confidence.

She also very much hoped a real truce could be called with the sisterhood. She knew Allegro would try.

All night long, Dr Stanislaus bothered Madeleine in a dream. 'You must go back to New York,' he said.

'Why should I?' Madeleine asked. 'I'm going to London for a fun weekend.'

'I can't tell you why, I'm just warning you. Your presence is needed,' and then he faded away. After a six o'clock haunting by Dr Stanislaus, Madeleine got fed up. 'Oh, do go away you silly little man, I'm going to London to have dinner with Vincent, lunch with Gabriel, and to spend the night with Amy and Allegro. I intend to have myself a wonderful time. Don't be a spoilsport.' She rolled over firmly, and ignored Dr Stanislaus's angry hooting. It's just my conscience giving me a bad time. Reverend Mother making me feel guilty. She fell asleep again, and when she awoke the next morning she had forgotten the whole episode.

Sixty-seven

❧

'Where am I?' Bella Battenburg arrived across the bridge, shaking and trembling.

'You're back on earth, Bella. Don't worry, we're here to help you.' Bella collapsed into Amy's arms. She was a big woman, but beautifully built. She was wearing the clothes she must have worn when she had played Tosca and had fallen to her death. She had a low-cut dress, with leg of mutton sleeves swathed in black ribbons. The skirt was full and she had matching tiny pointed shoes. Her hair was golden and very long. She had wide blue eyes with very, very black eyelashes. A straight little nose and a full pink mouth. She tried to smile at Amy.

'I'm so afraid,' she whispered.

'There's nothing to be afraid of, Bella. We're here to help you. You opted to come back and relive your life so that you can finish what you did not do. It's a really good decision. You haven't redesigned yourselves like the others.'

'No, I suppose I haven't. I couldn't really, you see. I so much wanted to sing Tosca. I don't remember what happened,' she saw Amy exchange a look with Allegro, 'I can't remember, but I must sing the whole thing and then I must hear the applause. I want to sing Tosca and to be the best there ever is, was, or will be. That's been my ambition ever since I was a little girl.' Her blue eyes were blazing.

'And you will, Bella. You will. I'm Allegro, and together we women will help you do it.' Amy put her arms around Bella's shoulders and moved her on through to the sitting room, where a crowd of brightly dressed women stood chattering.

Once they were alone, Allegro said, 'It's OK, Rollo, you can go now. Bella is safely across. Pick up the Tarot card of the tower on your side of the bridge, and bring it to me.' She knew he must not take the final step off the bridge, because he was in the unmanifest. His electrons would disintegrate, which would be a true death. Then his particles could be sucked through the wormholes in the universe. She held up the card of the lovers to protect him on his visit. She held the card steadily as he walked slowly towards her on the shimmering bridge.

'Allegro?' he said, his voice trembling. 'I have something to ask you.'

'What is it, Rollo?' Allegro was curious. She had never heard him use that tone before. Their relationship had always been light and teasing. 'Allegro, trust me on this and try to understand. I want to escape through the wormholes. One day when I ask you – even if I have to beg you – will you drop the card so I can escape?'

'But Rollo, you'll disintegrate. Dr Stanislaus told us all about that.'

'Yes, but what an adventure. Can you imagine being spread out in space? I'm a scientist by trade. I have always wondered what it might be like on the outside of the whole universe.' He gazed at Allegro, his big brown eyes pleading with her. She stared back at him and then she saw and felt the excitement beating in his aura. She watched as he moved towards her. He was an exceptionally good-looking man. Slim and elegant. His long slender hands were stretched out to her.

'How would you find your particles to put yourself back together again?'

'I know how to do that, but I don't want to reassemble my particles. I want my protons and my electrons to remain free. The first whistle is for all of those women who want to reassemble themselves in the universe. I don't want that. There is a second whistle which lets all the markers in the particles know that they can remain scattered. That's me. The second whistle. When you let me go free you'll hear my two whistles and you'll know that I'm where I most want to be.'

Allegro was mystified but thrilled. 'What does it feel like to be disintegrated?'

'I'll show you in the next few days. Trust me.'

'I'll always trust you, Rollo.' The force of her answer surprised Allegro.

'Take the card of the sun out of your Tarot pack. Hold it up; I want to kiss you.'

Allegro leaned into the sparkling lights that surrounded the bridge. He let his lips touch her for a moment. Allegro felt a flash of many-coloured lights. An immense expanse opened in her chest. Rivers of water splashed through her. 'Oh, Rollo,' she sighed, 'that was wonderful.' He smiled gently at her, his eyes alight with amusement. 'I do not think you have kissed an unmanifest before?'

'I have never kissed any man before,' she corrected him.

'Ahh,' Rollo grinned. 'My little bird, no wonder your heart beat faster. I must go now, I can hear the guardians calling. Do not talk of this matter. I will tell you more the next time I escort more of the unmanifest.' He bowed formally to her and then he blew a fairy kiss across his palm. He walked back slowly, one hand holding the narrow rope. As he walked, the bridge disintegrated behind him until he was a small golden dot in the blackness.

Allegro looked down at the three cards in her hand. 'Don't be silly,' she said, looking at the card of the lovers. 'It was just a kiss,' but she knew it wasn't just a kiss. If kissing made her feel this way, then maybe it was something she should pursue?

The next few days were frantic. Bella was in a bad way. Madeleine and Allegro took her to see a colleague of Madame Winona's in Eton Place. Although Bella could not remember her past she was twenty years old and shards of desperation still clung to her. Through the channelling she was able to move from her terrifying past into the present moment, and she smiled when she recovered her true self. 'I feel as if I am new-born,' she said, smiling at Madeleine.

'In a way, you are.' Madeleine was moved. Here she was, giving advice herself, when for so many years she had needed Edwina and Germaine and anybody else to advise her. Working with Allegro. Moving among the women who were now mending the broken nets of their lives, Madeleine felt intensely alive. 'You know, Gabriel, I've lived such an introverted, selfish life. I didn't know what was out there.' She waved her hand in the general direction of the real world. She sat, listening to Gabriel recounting his battles with the big hairs, and she realised she was bored. 'Gabriel, all that doesn't matter.'

'Why not?' he said truculently.

'Because those women are only a tiny handful of people who feel they are powerful. Take them away from their little ivory towers, and what have you got?'

'Ugly women,' Gabriel grinned.

'Don't be silly, that's not the point. I'm spending the weekend with Allegro and Amy and we're doing something that really matters. We're helping women come to terms with their past. That matters to us.'

'You mean, doing good works, like my aunts? Jam-making. Women's Institute stuff? Oh, Madeleine, I thought you were less suburban than that.'

'Gabriel, I am deeply suburban. I like making jam. I like cleaning what's mine. I like my home and my garden and I don't want to see a man in my kitchen. Yes, I'm deeply suburban if you like. Anyway, I must go now. Please don't get up. I have to go and make some more jam.' Madeleine got up and left the restaurant. Once outside, she hailed a taxi and sat in the back seat feeling pink and pleased with herself.

When she got back to the flat, she found an exhausted Amy and a tired Allegro. 'We've turned off the plug to the telephone. I don't want Bella disturbed. She is sleeping now, and hopefully when she wakes up she will be OK.'

'All right, darling, I'll go out and find a telephone. I need to tell Vincent that I can't see him this weekend. I've just had a row with Gabriel. Not a big one, just a mini-fuss.'

'Good for you, Mom.' Allegro looked at her mother's flushed face. 'Fighting with Gabriel is good for you. You should do it more often, Mom. It makes you grow a thicker skin.'

'Vincent, darling, I can't come and visit. I'm too busy working with Allegro and Amy.'

'That's all right, Madeleine. I'll miss our chats, but telephone me the next time you're in London.'

'I feel so odd, Vincent. It's as if something is happening and I don't know what it is.'

'Don't worry about it: it's called indigestion, Madeleine.'

'I suppose you're right. I'm always so frightened of everything, I can't believe I can have a few days of happiness without paying for it with a disaster.'

Madeleine came back and fell asleep. Amy found Allegro lying on the floor beside Bella's bed. She slipped a pillow under her head and covered her with a blanket.

Allegro looked so defenceless asleep that tears came into Amy's eyes. No one would ever know how much she loved Allegro. How she lived for her and would die for her if necessary. She smiled at herself. You silly romantic fool, she scolded herself. That won't be necessary. She left the room and sank wearily into a big black bean bag. There was a contented silence in the flat, and the four women left their mortal bodies to join hands in the dream world.

Sixty-eight

'You see, since I've renounced all women I don't have a social life at all.' Gabriel's voice was plaintive. 'I didn't realise quite how much of my life was spent in the pursuit of women.'

'Well, can't you just take them out to dinner without wanting to take them to bed?' Madeleine sat back in her chair and tried not to laugh. She hadn't intended to see Gabriel again, but she'd bumped into him lurking outside the flat. She accompanied him to a restaurant in Pimlico. She was aware that she looked as if she were out to dinner with a toy-boy, but she found she didn't mind. Gabriel always attracted a lot of attention wherever he went. He seemed unaware of the effect he had on the women in the restaurant, and oblivious to the scowls from their jealous partners. 'Oh, Madeleine, it really is difficult. Yes, I could take a woman out for dinner, but these days they insist on paying half, which I simply can't have. Then they want to come back to my flat for coffee and then, well, um . . .'

'A leg-over?' Madeleine giggled. 'Come on, Gabriel, since when were you embarrassed by the word fuck?'

'Since I gave up doing it. Boyd says not doing it is saving him a lot of money but ruining his marriage. His wife is not used to having him home all the time. He says he minds less than me, but then he doesn't need it so much.'

'I was married for a long time to a man who couldn't do it. He hid the fact by having a mistress in Hong

Kong, one in Japan. Oh yes, then there was a German one, and then of course, his little nurse.'

'Didn't that hurt your feelings?' Gabriel automatically took her hand. He held it tenderly and gazed with practised sincerity into her eyes.

'Don't be silly, Gabriel, I'm much too long in the tooth to be taken in by your flirtatious ways.' Madeleine disengaged her hand. 'No, actually it didn't hurt terribly. It did at first, but then I was really glad to have him out of my hair. He was no good in bed anyway.' She watched as Gabriel's eyebrows shot up in surprise. 'Don't be fooled, dear boy. Many a woman knows how to please herself in different ways. We women are far more sexually versatile than men. For men, sex can be a very crude release of tension. Not for us. For us it is an infinite and never-ending ecstasy. That's why I have remained uninvolved. I had that one brief relationship all those years ago, and I won't settle for less.'

'But whoever it was hurt you deeply. I can see it in your eyes and in your face, Madeleine.'

'Yes, he did, but I don't regret it. My love for him deepened me and made me stronger and more sure of myself. Now I know who I am and what I am worth. I won't make that mistake again. Maybe you have to be deeply wounded to realise that you may not take that which is not your own.

'Maybe we must realise that men and women do look at love differently. Women are nothing like men. We share a chromosome, that's all. On the whole we are a far more noble species. We can love anybody and everything altruistically. We share what we have and take care of others quite naturally. Certainly men do the same, but only under certain circumstances. Usually only if they are sexually engaged with a partner, and then if you're lucky they'll take care of you and yours.

Allegro is doing well. She is my main concern. That and . . .' She frowned. '. . . I'm worried about my father. I'll telephone when I get back to the hotel.'

'Allegro is certainly doing well. Her horrible friends are persecuting me. I see there is an all-female block of flats going up at the end of my road. Their business is recruiting women only. If we men tried that, there would be an outcry. Sexist Male Chauvinist Pigs would be on banners all over the country. It's not fair, Madeleine. It simply is not fair.'

'Look at it this way, Gabriel.' Madeleine finished her coffee. 'Life has been unfair for women for far too long. Now the boot, so to speak, is on the other foot.'

'I'll say.' Gabriel finished his wine and motioned for the bill. 'I vividly remember Allegro's steel-tipped boots. But what are we fellows supposed to do?'

'I don't know, darling, I'm only a writer. Now, if you would take me back to the hotel. That's where I was going before you highjacked me. I'll offer you a totally chaste nightcap.'

'Sure thing.' Gabriel pulled back her chair and watched Madeleine snuggle into her coat. The waiter smiled at her as she wrapped her garment around her. How grateful she is, thought Gabriel. What on earth has happened to the world of women that they all stomp about in boots like men? He put his arm around Madeleine's waist. Her body was lithe under his hand. He enjoyed escorting her across the floor of the restaurant. She was at that certain age when a woman is at the height of her power. She carried herself with dignity. Thank goodness she had no use for plastic surgery of any kind. Gabriel put her into his car and headed for her hotel.

As she came through the revolving door, the man behind the desk approached her. 'I'm afraid, madam, there've been calls for you all evening. Your mother says could you call her back, it's very urgent?'

'Thank you.' Madeleine held her voice steady, but Gabriel could see the panic in her eyes. He followed her, running up the steps to the lift. Then he held her gently and felt her heart beating against his chest. 'Shhh,' he comforted her. 'It will be all right.'

'No, it won't. I should have checked yesterday. I knew something was wrong, but I was so excited about coming to London I was careless. Please God,' she prayed out loud. 'Let nothing have happened to Dad.' Gabriel heard the note of panic in her voice. They left the lift and ran up the seemingly endless thick-carpeted corridors.

Madeleine opened the door of the suite and ran in. She made for the writing desk by the window. She stepped over little drifts of telephone notes that had been slipped under her door all weekend. They lay like snow on the carpet, silently reproaching her. A message light blinked ominously at her. 'Mom,' Gabriel heard her say in a low, urgent voice. 'Is Dad all right?'

Gabriel watched her mouth tighten and then the colour drained from her face. 'In a coma? I'm coming right now.'

'I'll take you to the airport,' Gabriel said. Madeleine nodded and disappeared into the bedroom to pack. Gabriel stood by the window and watched the river sliding by. It was dark and the bridges, lit by fairy-lights, looked magical; but now he knew that Madeleine's father was in a coma in New York. More suffering for a woman who had suffered too much.

'Try ringing Allegro,' Madeleine shouted from the bedroom. He tried but the telephone was always engaged. 'Get me on to an aeroplane and then go back and find her. She's taken the telephone off the hook.

We were working.' Madeleine came back into the room with her suitcase and her passport in her hand. 'Quick, let's go. I'll get the desk to arrange the ticket while we are on our way to the airport.'

'Goodbye.' Gabriel gave Madeleine a last kiss and waited for her to go through the gates. He watched her figure disappear; he wished he could go with her to hold her hand, but he had to find Allegro.

Later, he stood outside the flat, looking up at the empty windows. He tried the bell but no one stirred. Then he banged on the door. 'Allegro,' he shouted, 'it's me. Open the door.' He could see lights snapping on as the neighbours awoke. 'Come on, Allegro, open up.' Soon a window opened above his head. 'What do you want, Gabriel?' It was Amy, and she was not in a good mood.

'I've just taken Madeleine to the airport. Allegro's grandfather is in a coma.'

'Oh, dear.' There was genuine sorrow in Amy's voice. 'You'd better come on up, then.' He heard the sound of the dead bolt being released. He pushed open the door and bounded up the stairs. He pushed past Amy and walked into the sitting room. He gazed uncomprehendingly at the woman in a long robe lying on the bed. She was so stunningly beautiful. He then gazed at the floor where he saw Allegro sprawled fast asleep.

'She's exhausted,' Amy explained. 'I'll wake her. Allegro,' she shook her shoulder, 'come on, wake up. Gabriel's here.'

'Gabriel?' Allegro opened her eyes and stared at him. 'What on earth are you doing here?' Gabriel dropped down on one knee. 'I've got some bad news, Allegro.' He put his arm around her shoulder and pulled her into a sitting position. 'I've just taken your mother to the airport. It's your grandfather. He's in a coma. He's had a stroke and I need to take you to catch the plane, OK?'

He held her thin, trembling body. 'Oh no,' she whispered. 'I knew something was wrong, but we were too busy with everything else for me to think about it. Now it's too late.' She gazed for a long moment over Gabriel's shoulder. 'I'm going to be too late, I can see that now.' She could see her grandfather hovering over his body in a room in a hospital. He was lying in bed, plucking at his chest. 'Mom will make it, but I won't.' She could see her grandfather trying to breathe. 'His soul is already trying to escape. Take me to the airport, Gabriel. Amy must stay with Bella. She can't come with us.'

'Don't worry, Allegro,' Gabriel said quietly. 'I'll take you to the airport, and if you need me I'll take you to New York.'

Amy watched them leave with a terrible ache in her heart. 'I understand only too well,' she said to Gabriel's retreating back. 'You love her as much as I do, and it's no use.' At least Amy hoped it was no use. Now was no time to be jealous. She didn't want to add that suffering to the agony of loss she was feeling at this minute. She sighed and went into the kitchen to make coffee for Bella.

Sixty-nine

❦

One of the things Madeleine had learned in the broken places was to take disappointment calmly. The depths of her suffering had been as if she had boarded a Nautilus submarine and travelled deep into her own universe. There she'd met Death and Suffering, and shaken both by the hand. 'Why,' she asked Death, 'are you always portrayed as a man?'

'Because women are the givers of life.' He smiled at her. His smile was ghastly.

'Suffering,' she said, taking the proffered hand, 'why are you always portrayed as a woman?'

'Because,' Suffering said, her beautiful face filled with pain, 'we allow men to make us suffer.'

When she'd resurfaced, Madeleine had made a vow: no man would ever cause her to suffer again. Now, sitting by her father's bed, she held the hand of one man who had loved her steadfastly all her life. Maybe there was only one man in her life. Her father. Now he was slipping away from her and back into the light.

He was not quite unconscious. She could still feel a slight pressure from his fingers. Then he raised his right hand and began to pluck at his chest. Dolly leaned over her husband, tears dripping off her nose. 'Can you still hear me, honey?'

'Talk to him anyway, Mom.' Madeleine pressed her father's time-worn hand gently. 'I love you, Dad, and I'll miss you,' she whispered. 'Allegro will be with us just as soon as she can.'

She knew with a desperate certainty that, instead of

going out to dinner with Gabriel, she should have gone back to her hotel and telephoned home. Yet again an attractive man had distracted her. This was the first time she'd been to dinner with a man on her own for many years, and look what had happened. The straitjacket of her vow tightened its grip on her body. 'Serves you right,' Reverend Mother whispered.

'Please God, let Allegro arrive in time. She'll never forgive herself if he dies before she gets here. I'll never forgive myself . . .' She paused and then she leaned over her father, gazing into his vacant eyes. 'Dad, Dad,' she called. 'It's me, Madeleine. Remember the Changing of the Guard in London? Remember the polar bears in London Zoo?' She saw a flicker of warmth in his face, and then he reared up so suddenly that he nearly hit her face. He sat bolt upright in his bed with a big smile on his face.

Madeleine looked at her mother in fear. Instinctively they reached for each other's hands. 'It's all right, Dolly. It's all right!' he shouted joyously. 'I can see the light. It's shining. Take me home, please.' He pleaded with an unseen being. 'I'm ready to go.' He stretched out his arms and then he fell back in the bed.

'He's gone, Mom,' Madeleine said quietly. She put her arms around her mother's heaving shoulders.

'He was such a good man, your father. Never a cross word between us . . .' She sobbed in her daughter's arms. They called the nurse.

'Don't cover his face,' Dolly said. 'We will wait with him until his granddaughter arrives.'

They waited as the room grew darker. Mother and daughter held hands across the bed. Her father's body slowly got colder and colder. 'So this is your touch, Death?' Madeleine acknowledged his presence. 'You are the taker of life. We sit here and we suffer and we grieve.

We mourn and then we go and get on with life again. I've been here before too many times. But at least I was in time to say goodbye to him.'

Allegro arrived in the middle of the night. She walked into the room with red and swollen eyes. 'I was with him, Mom, it's all right. I helped take him home to the light.' She kissed her mother. 'It was me he could see when he called out. He went joyfully, and his mother was there to greet him. You should have seen him run into her arms.' Allegro was crying. 'The human side of me is going to miss him very much. The spiritual side of me knows that he has had a wonderful passage and we were lucky to have known him in this lifetime. He has finished what he came to do, so he can stay in the light if he wishes. But knowing Grandpa, he'll want to come back again and make another happy family.'

She smiled through her tears. 'Gabriel is outside. He insisted on coming. He's been quite useful for a man for once. Come, Grandma, we'd better go home.'

'No, I'll stay here with Grandad. When they bring the coffin I'll bring him home with me until we bury him.' Dolly sat down again, a small, determined figure.

'No, Grandma, you take Mom home. She's all done in. I'll sit vigil with Gabriel. We'll bring Grandpa home to you, I promise.'

When her grandmother had left, supported by Madeleine, Allegro looked down at her grandfather. She kissed him on his forehead, and then she passed her hand over his eyes and they closed. Now his face lay serenely on the pillow.

Allegro remembered her grandmother kissing her grandfather before she left the room. 'It's just goodnight, darling,' she had whispered. 'I'll see you in the morning.'

'We always said that to each other.' She had looked

at Allegro. 'What happens when he's not there to say good morning to?'

'You'll say good morning to him anyway, Grandma. He'll always be with you. People don't die. Their empty bodies are like envelopes, which they leave and then move on. This is the hard bit. This life all weighted down with a fleshy envelope. He'll be hurling himself about the universe. It's like skiing, but without the cold.' She found herself enveloped in the moment she was describing. She vaulted out of the hospital, high into the clear, colourless ether of time. She was suspended. Then she surged forward in a huge rush. Backwards, free of all atoms. Free of all particles. She glissaded up a prism of light. She broke into all colours of the spectrum. 'This is fun,' she heard herself shout.

Then she was disappointingly back in her body. That, she told herself, is what Rollo was talking about. Free in the universe. Not tied by manifest or the unmanifest. Perfect freedom. Yes she would help Rollo go free.

Now she must sit and wait with Gabriel until they came for her beloved grandfather's body. She would take him home as she had promised.

Seventy

~&

Allegro was surprised to find that she needed consoling. Amy, her only real consolation, was in London. Her mother and grandmother had left the hospital and were no doubt comforting each other in her grandmother's house. Now she sat beside her dead grandfather and ached.

Her human side was in pain. This was the second heart-break in her life. Her first had been watching her mother over the months and then the years suffer over her love affair with that Italian man. Now she thought of him with fear and loathing. Even though the memories were from her early childhood, time had not dimmed her anger.

Her own father she thought about rarely. The one man who loved her was now lying so quietly beside her. The human reality of death struck her between the shoulders and she put her head down on the bed and she sobbed.

She had no idea how long she had been crying in between sleeping. She felt a hand on her shoulder.

'I'm here, Allegro. I thought it better to just sit and wait until you've had time to grieve.'

'Thank you.' Allegro raised a face swollen with pain, and Gabriel winced as he saw the eyes tight shut from the force of the tears. 'I can't see,' Allegro whispered.

Gabriel bent down and gently lifted Allegro into his arms and carried her to the bathroom. He took her grandfather's flannel, grey with age, and carefully wiped her eyes with cold water. 'Is that better?' he asked.

'Yes,' Allegro looked at herself in the bathroom mirror. 'I look terrible,' she said. She found herself blushing. 'What an idiot I am. I know in my head that he's just moved on to another place and that death comes to us all, but my human side is hurting, Gabriel.'

'I know it is, darling, but you'll get over it. Remember that you will become strong again in the broken places. It's your favourite quote.'

'I know I will, but I shan't see him again for a very long time. I can't go after him into the unmanifest because I'll hold him back with my will and that would be selfish. I have to wait until I go over and then I can be with him again.' She was sobbing.

'I don't know about those sort of things, Allegro, but I do believe that we are all eternal.'

'You do, Gabriel?'

'Why are you so surprised, Allegro? Not all men are dumb bastards.'

'Oh, Gabriel, how can you say you're not a bastard? You've had hundreds of women.'

'Allegro, don't be such a child,' he said the words gently. 'There wouldn't be any naughty men if there weren't naughty women, would there? Anyway, I've reformed, Allegro. I explained all that to your mother. Boyd and I have given up chasing women.'

'No, really?' Allegro sat bolt upright in his arms. The look of astonishment on her face made him smile.

'Yes, honestly,' he agreed.

'How does that make you feel?' Allegro was curious, and for a moment forgot her dead grandfather in the next room.

'Very boring. Chasing women was a full-time occupation, in between working and eating. When we get over the funeral I'll take you out to dinner and confess everything. A man must have at least one woman to whom he can tell the truth. The sort of thing one doesn't tell one's mother. If I had a mother.'

Allegro slipped out of Gabriel's arms. She tiptoed back into her grandfather's room. She could see her own aura light up the gloom of the room, and then a yellow light from her fingers gently stroked her grandfather's face. She sat down on her mother's vacated chair and then she waited.

Gabriel sat across from her, and eventually fell forward into a deep sleep. She smiled at his face on the bed. The eyelashes were swept across his cheeks. His straight nose twitched in a dream, and she realised that she felt attracted to the shape of his mouth. His lips were full and sensuous. Perturbed by this, she got to her feet and leaned over Gabriel and gently touched his mouth with her lips. She drew back, surprised at the warmth of his mouth.

Beside her lay her dead grandfather. She now touched his hand. He was colder than the Alaskan tundra. How strange is the difference between life and death: just that the live man is breathing in chestfuls of air, whereas the breath that is life no longer filled her grandfather's body. The warmth of one filled by the breath, and the loss of warmth in the man who was dead.

She stood now in the room, feeling guilty that she, Allegro, of all women, could feel the first stirrings of sexual interest. No, the first stirring had been her kiss with Rollo. 'Remember,' she could hear Amy's voice now, 'all men are bastards. All men are rapists.' She felt uncomfortable with these thoughts scrabbling about her head. She reminded herself of the women who had come over the bridge. They had killed themselves. But then the judge in her head: 'They made their choices, they chose bad men.'

'What about the man who so badly hurt my mother?'

'Again,' chorused the jury, 'your mother made her choice and got hurt.'

Allegro sighed. All this human being stuff was just too adult for her. She preferred to climb back into her fortress where she had a secret garden. To go and sit by her rippling, shining stream and play with her fish.

Seventy-one

৽১

Madeleine felt it was weird to be back in New York under these tragic circumstances. As much as she longed to go and stand outside Paolo's apartment, this time she told herself she would not. Now she could think about him without pain. The hurtful years lay in the past, and she remembered with a warm, nostalgic glow their wonderful times together. She held her tongue with Allegro. Still guilty of the damage she had done to her.

For Allegro, New York was still her favourite city after London. After the funeral, she began to feel herself coming alive again. She telephoned Debbie and June. 'Hey, I'm in town for the next few weeks. Shall we get together?'

'Sure thing, Allegro. We're having a meeting of the sisterhood tomorrow night at our place. Come around eight and bring a bottle.'

'I've got the dark angel, Gabriel, with me. Can I bring him?'

'He'll be mincemeat if I ever see him again,' growled Debbie.

Allegro grinned at the phone: she loved teasing the big hairs. 'OK, I'll come by myself.' When Debbie and June got heavy it made Allegro giggle. They took hating men very seriously. She made a mental note to bring a big bottle of sweet white wine. Galileo is what they all drank. Gallons of it. She imagined a whole long row of big, heavy, sweating women in ranks along the main room of the loft. Cigarettes dropping from their lips and hands around bottles of wine or beer. She grimaced at the thought, but then it wasn't at all like that. Usually the sisterhood meetings had women from all over the world. Allegro had never had time to attend these meetings when she visited her grandparents and her father. The invitation excited her.

'I'm going to see June and Debbie tomorrow, Gabriel. They said I can't take you with me.'

'I should think not,' Gabriel said nervously. 'Wild Algerian women wouldn't drag me anywhere near those big hairs. Henry says he feels quite faint whenever he comes across one of them in his office.' Gabriel shuddered. 'They take male hormones with their toast in the morning.'

'Darling, we don't need male hormones. Women's hormones are much stronger than men's. In fact, *you* have to have extra hormones to make you function as men. We are complete from birth.' She knew the remark was completely illogical, but she enjoyed the puzzled look on Gabriel's face. He was so irritatingly logical.

Gabriel looked at Allegro, radiant in the sunlight. What a pity she was off men. 'All right,' she said. 'I'm off to see what I can buy in the way of clothes for a big-hair night out.' She bounced up to Gabriel and kissed him. He held her for a moment too long, and then he looked down at her. 'Don't you ever think about sex, Allegro?'

'Sure I do, but then I have lovely wild erotic dreams. My world is so alive, and I can invent the perfect lover for myself. I don't need the real life thing. The bad breath, the snoring, the funny smells in the loo. Men smell very different to women.' She sniffed at him. 'You smell nice, Gabriel. You smell like honey and fresh-baked brown bread.'

'Thank you,' Gabriel was pleased. 'Nobody ever told me I smelled of honey and brown bread before.'

'Anyway, Gabriel, you shouldn't be thinking about sex. You've given up, remember?'

'How can I forget? I can't stop thinking about sex, it's all we men do. I wish I were French and then I could do it all the time. Their wives just put up with their husbands' infidelities. You almost never see a French man with his wife. He escorts his mistress about the place, and leaves his wife to attend to the home and the children. Very sensible, too, I think. Wives should neither be seen nor heard.'

'Oh, Gabriel, you're such a big softie. One day you'll find a woman and you'll be faithful until the day you die.'

'The way I'm going, I'll be dead before I meet her,' Gabriel grumbled. He was enjoying his conversation with Allegro. 'Don't go, Allegro. I'm scared to go out in New York on my own.'

'You, scared? All six foot three of you?'

'Allegro, you have no idea how scared men really are. We're scared shitless all the time.'

'Don't worry, little brother. I'll take care of you.' He watched Allegro dance down the stairs and out of the house. He leaned against the window and saw her wild strawberry hair form a halo in the wind around her head. 'Look after me,' he mumbled. He very much wished that she would.

Allegro had put herself off-limits for him. He knew that, and he respected her for it. 'Bloody lucky lover she had, even if he is all in her imagination.' He had a go at imagining himself in the arms of a beautiful, pneumatic mistress, but he couldn't.

Seventy-two

❦

Allegro very much wished Amy was with her. Even with her steel-capped bovver boots and her black leather jumpsuit, she felt insecure. Amy never even knew what the word insecure meant. She just scowled at people whenever she walked into a room, and everybody backed off.

Allegro put her head around the door of the loft. From the street there had been big red arrows pointing up the stairs. She'd climbed for ages, and her feet were hurting her. On the walls there were posters depicting women doing unpleasant things with guns and fists. Why, oh why, Allegro thought for the umpteenth time, must women be so aggressive in New York? Why can't we be more like the Italian women? They had their men sewn up. When the Italian contingent arrived for big-hair meetings, they all had freshly manicured nails and glossy hairstyles. They smelled of Femme and Givenchy. They flashed their big brown eyes and waved their hands. They were such fun to be with. She felt a heavy bout of doom and despondency descending upon her shoulders. 'Why am I doing this, Dr Stanislaus?' she said out loud.

'So that you can undo some of the damage you did in your last manifestations. You were a man that time.'

'Of course, how silly of me,' Allegro felt sarcastic. 'I'm to be punished for something I don't even remember I did?'

'My dear child. You do not remember what you did, but in this life the opportunities are offered again. It is up to you to take them and live your life now with a good heart.'

'You're right, Dr Stanislaus. OK, I'll do this with good grace.' She heard voices in a far room and she walked across the bare boards of the loft. She followed the voices until she stopped, blinded by naked bulbs that hung from the ceiling. They swung backwards and forwards, casting strange shadows on the crouched women who had formed a circle on the floor.

Allegro stood for a moment quietly surveying the scene. Why, she wondered, did women naturally form circles on the floor when they were together? Men were much more inclined to sit on chairs in straight rows or around a table. She much preferred the women's way of doing things. 'Hi,' she said to a woman, who sat cross-legged on the floor next to her. She paused to listen to what a very big hair was saying.

'It isn't just that men oppress us. It isn't just that they beat us in our homes and in our streets. They rape us,' her voice reached a hideous climax.

'I don't think any man would dare rape her,' Allegro whispered to her neighbour. She was relieved when the woman giggled. She looked at the face of her neighbour, and could make out a tiny pointed chin: the woman was obviously from the Chinese or the Japanese delegation. Big hair paused and glared at them both. 'How are you oppressed in China, sister? There is supposed to be no oppression there.'

'My name is Chieh Chieh. I am from the fifty-second commune. My husband and I work in the fields alongside other couples. When the day comes to an end, we women go off to our houses to make the food, and the men take their time coming back. I say to my husband this is oppression, he should help me make the food, but honestly . . .' She struggled for words. 'He is a terrible cook and a nuisance in the kitchen.' She ended in a wild burst of giggles. Around her, women were nodding and agreeing.

'Your husband is showing you negative passive aggression. He, by not helping you in the kitchen, is failing to share the workload. He is making your kitchen your concentration camp, and he is the warder.'

'But I love my husband, and my kitchen is not a concentration camp. It's a very pretty kitchen. I don't want to eat his food and he is not a warder, he is just very clumsy and he stands on my foot.' She burst into tears. 'Anyway, I miss him, and I don't see why he couldn't come to this meeting.'

'Good for you,' Allegro whispered.

'Americans make terrible tourist visitors to our country,' Chieh Chieh grumbled under her breath. 'Ugh. They are meat-eaters and they smell bad. Not all Americans I mean.' She gazed apologetically at Allegro. 'You're different.'

Allegro smiled. 'Let's get out of here and find a decent restaurant. I've done my duty and I want out.' They crept away from the ring of talking women.

'We're near my mother's favourite restaurant. Let's grab a cab and go.' She whistled down a passing cab. Once inside, Allegro looked around the place. This was the bar where the Italian man used to take Mom, she reminded herself. Then she shook herself clear of the memory. Mom's OK. She's getting over Grandfather's death. Soon they would be out of here and back in London with Amy and her friends. She wondered how Bella was getting on. She was due to sing her first concert today.

'Tell me about love in China, Chieh Chieh.'

'It's no different in any country, Allegro. Have you ever been in love?'

'No, I don't think so. I'm beginning to think about it though. It seems to affect everybody at some time in their lives. It must be a bit like measles. There is a man in my life; his name is Gabriel. He's like a big brother to me. I like to look at him. He has a beautiful mouth, but he is terrible to women and I can't forgive him for that.'

'There are no conditions to love, Allegro. You either love him or you don't.'

'How do you know what love is? There are so many kinds of love. Dad was a mean, ruthless little shit to Mom. Her lover Paolo was, she says, wonderful and romantic, and she fell in love with him, but he was not in love with her. I watched her go through such agony that I decided that love was not worth it. I'd rather live by myself and keep my love for myself. At least that way I can never be hurt.'

'Allegro, life is about taking risks. Here I am in New York. I'm with a deputation from Beijing. I should be in a conference, but I sneaked away to see what was happening to women in New York. There were some really nice ones in that meeting house. But just a few women, like the one you heard talking when you came in, ruined it for many. She would not be allowed to say those things in my country. She would be denounced and forced to confess her arrogance in China.

'Of course, we do have some of the old guard that shout and scream, but they are old and we ignore them.

'Our men treat us well, and if they do not we can denounce them to the party. Then they must explain why they hit us or bullied us, and they are punished. On the whole our men treat us well. I love my husband. Here.' She took from her pocket a photograph and gazed at it wonderingly. Allegro felt a stab of envy.

What did this man have that made Chieh Chieh light up like a Christmas decoration?

Allegro handed back the photograph. 'He looks lovely.'

'I know. We have been married for two years now, and we hope to have our child. Making babies is fun.' She giggled loudly and put her hand over her mouth.

'I'll bet it is,' Allegro had a sudden vision of lying in Gabriel's arms. She blushed. 'Come on, let's order some wine,' she said gruffly in her best male voice.

'OK,' Chieh Chieh smiled. 'One day,' she said, 'you will fall in love and then you'll understand everything I'm saying.'

'Don't bet on it, sister. Too many women have died from it.'

'Choices, Allegro,' Dr Stanislaus said in her ear. 'Women have choices.'

Seventy-three

❧

'Allegro, don't you want to kiss me?'

'No, Gabriel, I don't want to kiss you.'

'Most women want to kiss me. Why don't you?'

'Because kissing is like swapping spit, and I don't want to do that.'

'I promise it's more fun than swapping spit. Please just try.'

'Oh, Gabriel, you promised you were going to stop all this sex stuff, didn't you?'

'I know, but now there's a war on between men and women. Men said they'd stop sleeping with women, and women just don't seem to care. It's not fair, it's really not fair.'

Gabriel's lower lip hung out like the edge of a cliff. Allegro laughed and skipped past him. He reached out to grab her, but she dematerialised her body and danced away. 'How on earth did you do that?' he demanded.

'Easy-peasy. I learned to do it as a child. I used to make Nanny Barnes fall over when she was annoying me. All children can do these things if they listen to their guardians. Unfortunately, most children grow into adults and lose their magic. I won't ever grow up. I'll always be able to do things other people can't do.'

Ever since Gabriel had climbed into the aeroplane with her, and unconditionally given her his support during the death of her grandfather, she had been aware of tiny silken strands of gold webbing floating from her body to his. At this moment she was attached to his wrist. Often she tugged at the strands, trying to pull herself away, but they would not budge. She didn't like the feeling of being attached to another human being, except for her mother and Amy.

'You're falling in love with him,' Amy said crossly when she complained. They were waiting for the last of the women to cross the bridge, and tonight she was going to have to decide whether or not to let Rollo escape from the unmanifest into the universe. Now she knew how blissful an experience it was, she very badly wanted to go with him. 'Don't be silly, Amy,' Allegro said absent-mindedly. She didn't want to argue with Amy, she just wanted to think about Rollo. 'Chieh Chieh explained what love felt like, and I don't feel at all like that. Gabriel is such a silly idiot. I can't take him seriously.'

'You are in love, Allegro.' Amy could feel the affection in Allegro's words.

'How do you know that?'

'Because I've been in love,' Amy replied. 'It hurts,' she said, her voice trembling as she guarded her secret very tightly.

'Oh, darling, who hurt you?' Allegro's huge eyes were immediately concerned.

'Nobody you'd know,' Amy gave a short, harsh laugh. 'I'll get over it.'

'There, you see why I don't fall in love. I don't want that sort of pain. I saw Edwina when I was in New York, and time hasn't been kind to her at all. Her face-lift's slipped and she looks permanently agitated. My Mom's old friend, Germaine – she's also my godmother – looks fine. She's aged like old wood. She has a lovely warm patina to her face, and her body is soft like a dormouse. She doesn't bother with men either. Sensible woman.'

Allegro checked her watch: five minutes to twelve,

she noted. 'OK, I'll lay out the cards.' She held the card of the lovers in her hand yet again. It all looked so marvellous in the card. She heard Rollo's soft voice in her ear.

'When I walk back along the bridge tonight, take out the card of death and dying and hold it up to my face and then I can let go of this unmanifest body and fly. Will you do this for me?'

'Yes, Rollo, I will. I want to come with you, Rollo.'

'No you don't, *chérie*. You have something to finish down there.'

'But I don't want to lose you. I think I love you. Ever since I felt your mouth on mine, I've been thinking about kissing you, and I have never wanted to kiss a man in my life.'

'That's because we were lovers in the past, Allegro. I kept coming back to you to try and change you. I've loved you every eternity; you were so wanton and so stubborn. But there is an event in front of you, and if you do this thing properly, one day we will be reunited in eternity. You will hear me whistle twice when I am free.'

'Oh, Rollo, I love you and I'm going to miss you terribly.'

'This will just strengthen you for what is to come. You know how to work and now you will learn how to love. Be of good courage, *mon enfant*. Keep the faith in the light.' For a moment he shone in her face. The bliss of the light enveloped her.

'Good heavens, Allegro, you look as if you have a light bulb inside you.' Amy was astonished.

'I know, Amy. I've just found out what love is. It's like a very bright, warm light, and it switches itself on and then you feel all happy and tingly.' She hugged herself. 'It's such a wonderful feeling, Amy.'

'I know.' Amy's voice was subdued. 'Look out, Allegro, they're coming.' The soft white light crept from one card to another. Then the bridge of lights began to grow. Allegro always felt tearful at this point. She saw Rollo's figure begin to manifest at the far end of the bridge. Now she hung in space with Amy.

Rollo crossed the bridge with the women behind him. He stood gazing at Allegro. The love in his eyes wrapped her in a cocoon of warmth. It was cold in that emptiness of space. The women moved on past in various states of distress. Allegro had learned by now how to switch off her emotions. They would be well taken care of on earth. They had an efficient service of care-takers, and highly trained women therapists, who took care of the feelings they brought with them. Bella, all the rage in the opera world, was a shining example of what a woman could do to restore her past.

Now she just looked at Rollo and felt a very tiny nascent stirring. 'Yes,' he said, smiling down at her. 'That's what love feels like. Now you let that feeling grow, and wait until you feel it with a real, manifest man.'

'It won't be the same as I feel about you.'

'No, it won't, darling, but you will find your happiness.'

'Will I have to grow up?'

'Allegro,' he was laughing. 'There's not much chance of that.' She leaned into the unmanifest. 'Kiss me again, Rollo.'

He took her in his arms and he kissed her with passion. 'Oh, Rollo, that felt wonderful.' She was breathless. 'I think I'm going to like kissing.'

'Well, you get some practice, darling, while I'm gone.'

'I will,' Allegro promised earnestly.

Rollo turned and walked back across the bridge.

Allegro pulled out the death card and, as he turned, he raised his hand to salute her. 'Goodbye, my beloved,' he shouted. She saw his particles of light disintegrate and fly like sparks of a fire, upwards. They were coloured like many bright boiled sweets. Then, in a second, she heard a loud, joyous whistle, followed by a second piercing whistle. She stood with tears running down her face. Amy hugged her.

'I'm not asking you what that was all about, because I know it's none of my business, but are you all right?'

'Yes, I guess so, Amy. I've loved Rollo for so many aeons it hurts when he goes, but he's free, Amy. Oh, you don't know what it's like to be free of both the world manifest and unmanifest. It's the best feeling in the world ... Come, let's take the women to the big house and settle them in. Bella and Mom are waiting to welcome them. Bella is so pleased with herself. It takes away the pain of losing Rollo. I'll be pleased to see her.'

'Welcome, all of you.' Allegro straightened her shoulders and dried her eyes. No one would guess she was dying inside. No one, that is, except for Amy. 'Come on, Allegro, we'll take them home and then we'll go out and find an all-night bar and get smashed.'

'Sounds like a good idea to me.' Allegro grinned.

Seventy-four

❧

The war between men and women dragged on, and Allegro was drawn into it. Sometimes she felt guilty that she took so much pleasure in Gabriel's attentions. She sneaked over to his flat in the dark to have dinner with him and giggle.

Even though Rollo had not been her lover in this manifestation, she realised that she felt his loss very keenly. Sometimes, late at night, before dawn touched the London sky, she stood outside on the balcony of her little flat and gazed up at the sky, hoping for a sign from him.

During the weeks and months that followed, Bella sang in all the major opera houses in the world. No men dared attend the concerts. They were not invited.

The physicists and chemists among the women discovered a new pheromone which drove men away from women. Women were trained to produce it in all cases of danger from men. This gave women protection, and the threat of rape retreated.

Amy was delighted with this new foul-smelling pheromone. She strode the streets, streaking unsuspecting male passers-by with her fingers. She laughed loudly when the men sniffed and then sniffed again. They ran down the street, gagging and retching. 'You are a beast, Amy,' Allegro told her.

'I know, but men have had all their way for far too long. Now it's our turn.'

*   *   *

Edwina was over for a visit with Madeleine. 'What are you doing for sex these days, Gabriel?' Edwina was hoping he'd make a pass at her.

'Not a lot, Edwina. I'm in the forefront of the war against women. I do talk-shows with Boyd. We're being interviewed tomorrow by Dr Donella Rose. She's got a face like a buried hatchet and talk about big hair. The stuff's all over her. Ugh. Coils and coils of lank grey hair. She smells permanently of that dreadful pheromone that drives men mad. Amy keeps telling Allegro to smear it all over me. Allegro, bless her dear little heart, won't do it. It smells like the deadliest, most rotten meat you've ever smelled, and it takes weeks to go away. Trust women to behave like skunks. That's what they are, Edwina – skunks.'

'Get back to the question, Gabriel. I'm not interested in your politics. What do you mean, not a lot?'

'Not a lot of sex with women. Not any, in fact.' Gabriel was really rather tired of explaining himself. After all, women gave up sex all the time. His wife closed down more times than British Rail. Now, because he'd given up sex, he had to explain himself all over the place – including to incredulous male journalists – that he was off the whole thing.

Not having sex with women saved him a lot of money. Chasing women was extremely expensive. Gabriel reckoned he could afford two Caribbean holidays a year and go skiing at Christmas for the price of remaining chaste.

'What do you do with your time, then?' Edwina was horrified.

'I jog, of course, lots and lots of jogging. Look, Edwina, feel my muscles.'

Edwina leaned over and felt his chest. 'Not much good

having bulging pecs, Gabriel, if nothing else is bulging.' She gazed at him speculatively. 'You don't feel like taking a rain-check on chastity while I'm in town?'

'No, Edwina, I'm sorry, I can't. My reputation is at stake here, and I'm a man of honour. I know it's come late in the day, but I've discovered chivalry. I'm practising it on Allegro. I open doors for her and park her car and carry the shopping. All those things my father taught me, but I could never practise because by the time I discovered women and sex, women said they didn't want that sort of thing.

'Allegro does though,' he sighed. 'She's so funny and so beautiful. I'd marry her tomorrow if she'd have me. But she's got her reputation to think of as well. She's on the other side. It's a sort of Romeo and Juliet situation, don't you think, Madeleine?' He turned to her with a wistful expression and Madeleine smiled fondly at him.

'I could stand under her window reciting, "Allegro, Allegro, wherefore art thou, Allegro?" Only I'm afraid that awful bitch Amy would dump a bucket of something disgusting over my head. I just lurk around at night sometimes and watch her when she comes out on to the balcony and gazes at the stars. She's missing a man called Rollo, the bastard. If I ever get my hands on him he'll be sorry.' Gabriel frowned and tried to look fierce, but merely looked as if he had eaten something that had disagreed with him.

'I don't think that'll happen. I mean, I don't think you'll ever find Rollo.' Madeleine laughed. 'Allegro will get over missing him. They've known each other a long time, a very long time. Hopefully Allegro will return your feelings.

'She needs a lot of space, Gabriel. She hasn't had the experiences you've had, and I'm afraid I didn't help.'

She smiled at Gabriel who was sitting on the sofa in her living room. She really had come to love him. She enjoyed their times together with Allegro. The three of them talked the night away. Allegro had really accepted Gabriel as a friend, and Madeleine knew, without saying anything, that Allegro was mortally afraid of losing his friendship.

Making him a lover instead of a friend was a risk Allegro was unwilling to take. For now he was the only man she could trust herself with, since the death of her grandfather.

Often Madeleine watched her daughter staring at Gabriel with a question in her eyes. Allegro never took the war between men and women as seriously as the big hairs. She had not joined the war out of sad disillusionment with the world of men. She had had a good relationship with her grandfather, so she knew that friendship with a man was possible.

She really was loyal to her friend, Amy, who had no reason not to distrust men. Amy's father had been violent and sexually abusive. Besides, the army of women was now all in place. Many of the women had expanded their spheres of interest and moved into the Third World, where they were teaching contraception and how women could take control of their own lives.

Now that it was proved that women no longer needed men, they were far more able to abandon their own dependencies and take their lives into their own hands.

It was a heart-lifting time to live, Madeleine thought. Of course, there would always be the Edwinas of the world, who had soft centres like marshmallows for men to feed on. Now even she was rare. Madeleine grinned at Edwina, who sat at her table lusting hotly after Gabriel.

Recently she'd had a postcard from Germaine in Libya. 'Who'd have thought we would see such a revolution in our lifetime?' it read. 'The women here are fantastic. Bella came out and gave a concert. A very moving moment. Love, darling, Germaine.'

'Are you expecting Allegro this evening, Madeleine?' Gabriel nonchalantly checked his watch.

'Oh, Gabriel, you know she always comes on a Friday night for supper. Yes, I am expecting her. Come on, you lay the table for me, and by the time you've done that, she'll be here.'

'OK.' Gabriel jumped to his feet. 'What's for dinner?'

'Curried chicken.' Madeleine smiled at the expression on his face.

'That's my favourite meal, after toad-in-the-hole.' Gabriel sounded incredulous. 'All week I've been living on beans and soup, and tonight I come here and you are making one of my favourite dishes. Madeleine, I love you.'

She found herself scooped up into Gabriel's enormous arms. 'Put me down, you oaf,' she shrieked. 'Put me down.'

Gabriel carried her into the kitchen and dumped her on to the floor. 'If Allegro won't marry me, will you?' he said, throwing himself down on one knee and grabbing the flowers on the kitchen table. 'I've got to have both of you in my life. I can't live without your toad-in-the-hole.'

'Darling, I'm far too old for you, but if you wait patiently, Allegro will probably find her way into your arms. Just wait, and don't be so impatient.'

'I'll be so old I won't be able to go down on one knee by the time she makes a decision. Time's passing us by, and I want to have a son ... or a daughter,' he said hurriedly, remembering his political correctness.

'Don't be silly, Gabriel. You don't have to say you want a daughter if you don't. I'm not interested in all

439

this p.c. rubbish. Of course you want a son. I wanted a daughter, and thank goodness that is what I got. Men don't realise until they have a daughter just how frightening it is for them to have to rear a girl child. They know and understand a boy child; they were once a boy child themselves. But a girl, that's an entirely different matter. Men are afraid of women, anyway, and terrified of their daughters.' She grinned. 'Can you imagine what it's like for a man when his daughter has her first date?'

'If I had a daughter, I'd kill any boy that looked at her.'

'Yes, well, quite, Gabriel, that's the problem in a nutshell. Men have to learn they don't own or control women.'

'It's difficult to be a man these days. On the chatshows, I'm so frightened of saying the wrong thing that I tend to say what the big hairs want me to say.'

'Why don't you stop being a wimp and say what you want to say?'

'Because being a wimp is much safer. If I say what I think – and believe you me, I have tried – women spit at me on the street and threaten to hit me.'

'Gabriel, no darling, the forks go that way.' Madeleine wrested the forks out of Gabriel's hand. 'There is no hope for women until men can lay the table. If you want to gain Allegro's respect, you'll have to start behaving like a real man, and stand up for yourself. Otherwise you're in danger of becoming like so many American men. A WUS.'

'What on earth is a WUS?'

Madeleine wrinkled her nose. 'A WUS is a cross between a wimp and a pussy. That's what most men are these days.'

Gabriel paused and looked at Madeleine. 'Do you think I'm a WUS, Madeleine?'

Edwina strolled into the kitchen. 'Of course you're a

WUS, Gabriel. All men are WUSs now; that's the way we women like them.'

'I am not a WUS, Edwina, and anyway, I wasn't talking to you, I was talking to Madeleine. I am a man, aren't I, Madeleine?'

She smiled gently at him. 'I think you have been a WUS, Gabriel, but you also have excellent potential for being a really lovely man, and when you do come out of the closet and behave like a real man, Allegro should be the first to recognise the new one. Her grandfather was a real man. My father was a mature and loving man, and that's what Allegro is looking for.'

'You got it, Madeleine.' Gabriel looked determined. 'Is there any green tomato chutney to go with the curry tonight?'

'Yes, of course, Gabriel. Would I give you a curry without green tomato chutney?'

'No, you wouldn't, Madeleine. That's why I love you so much.'

Ah, men, Madeleine thought. They don't get their minds much above their bellies, and Gabriel was no exception.

Seventy-five

❧

'Mom, do you think you're always going to live alone?'
Allegro was holding an autumnal bunch of chrysanthemums for her mother. They had big sunburst cloud
faces. She loved the tightly curled baby-fisted petals in
the middle of the flowers. She buried her nose in the
warm yellow of the stamens. She sniffed and sneezed
loudly as the pollen filled her nose. 'I think so, darling.'
Madeleine wasn't really concentrating on the question.
'There, how does that look?' She paused and tried to
balance the colours of her flowers from her flowerbeds.

Whenever she was asked about her future, which
seemed to obsess her friends, she went on to automatic
hold. Hilary was the most obtrusive. She positively
dripped with the joys of marital love. Why, Madeleine
wondered, did it upset so many people that she preferred
her own company? Surely it must be quite obvious that
women artists couldn't afford to be married; unless, of
course, they found a paragon of virtue. The problem
with a paragon of virtue is that he would probably be
dreadfully boring. Anyway a p. of v. didn't exist in either
sex, except for those bound for sainthood. 'Allegro, darling, I will once more answer your question. I have
everything I need. I love my house, my garden, your
horse that you never ride. My paddock, the orchard,
the apple trees, and above all my peace and quiet. Why
would I want to share all that with a man who will
want feeding and grooming just like your horse?'

'For love, Mom. Not even if you fell in love?' Madeleine was about to say, especially if she fell in love, but she heard a note in Allegro's voice she'd not heard before. 'Maybe not for myself, darling. I've reached an island in my life where I don't want to risk what I have now. I've learned that people do change. Now probably more than ever before. I don't change. I still dislike television and most machines. I still cook with chopsticks even if the kitchen is full of the most wonderful machines you bring me. As for computers and faxes, a pox on the lot of them. Which reminds me, you're going to have to send off some faxes for me. Why don't you run upstairs and do it now, before Susan and Stella arrive? I must sort out the ice-bucket: they'll be desperate for a drink after the long drive.'

'But Mom, you didn't really answer the question.'

'I know, darling, but you haven't asked me the right question, have you?'

'Darn you, Mom, you're so very perceptive. You know me so well.'

'Sure, darling, and you want to know if it's OK to risk loving Gabriel?' She raised her eyebrows and watched Allegro, who was dithering by the door.

'I guess so. I feel so confused, Mom. One minute I think the whole thing is really silly, and then in another moment I want to throw myself into his arms. Why is life so difficult?'

'Because relationships between men and women have become confused. Your grandmother was protected by a very strict code of chivalry. I think that before King Arthur introduced the idea of the age of chivalry towards women, things were very much like they are today. Then, for a long time, men and women knew the rules and how to approach each other. Now it's just confusion, with men grabbing what they want and then throwing women away.

'This is just my opinion, but I think that for men to

live without any attempt at chivalry is dangerous. Their lives are spent in tooth-and-claw competition with other men. They don't know how to operate for the common good like we do.' Madeleine sighed. 'As for you, my darling, if you think you love Gabriel, go to him and talk to him honestly. Tell him what you think love is all about. See if it is something you can share together.'

'You know, Mom, I think my first rule is that he has to give me all of his heart. I don't want all of his soul. I think for both of us it is as well that we have parts of our souls that stay forever inviolate. Otherwise I might get cannibalised like you did when you gave everything you had to that Italian man all those years ago. You had nothing left when you put him out of your life. You had to begin all over again.'

'I know that. Those first few years alone with you were terrifying, but slowly I rebuilt my life and now I'm glad, funnily enough, for the experience. That much intense pain and suffering has left me with a very peaceful centre in my soul. I'm confident that I'll never lose that again. Sure, Allegro, if a man did come into my life that I could love, I'd be happy, but I am too selfish now and set in my ways to live full-time with a man. Unless,' she laughed, 'unless I make so much money with my next book that we could buy a mansion. I could live in one end of the house, and he could live in another. I would have the key to the drawbridge, and could pull it up whenever I wished to be alone.'

'OK, Mom, I'll send off those faxes for you. I'll be down in a minute to help.' Madeleine stood in a trance. She remembered a little tiny girl lying in her arms with her bright pink hair. She realised she was seeing a vision. Not of the past, but of the future. The child was her grandchild. 'Oh, I do hope so,' she whispered out loud.

She heard the flutter of feathers. 'Whyever not?' she

heard Dr Stanislaus hoot. 'Whyever not?' Then she heard Susan's car coming up the drive.

'I'd even be prepared to be faithful to her.' Gabriel was shaving. 'I'd never look at another woman again in my life.' He was addressing his shaving mirror. He felt so virtuous that he had even put the top of the toothpaste back on and wiped the hair from his chin off the wash-basin. 'I'll have to clean up my act first.' He looked around the bathroom. He saw a desolate sea of socks and grey dishevelled bath-towels. 'I'm going to ask her to marry me. No more waiting around.' He picked up the bath-towel and wrinkled his nose with disgust. 'It smells of mould,' he remarked to the wall. 'Anyway, I'm off to buy her a bunch of flowers.'

'Edwina, I really think Allegro is going to get engaged to Gabriel.'

'Do you, darling? I do hope he's good in bed.'

'Oh Edwina, don't you ever change?'

'No, but she should check out the goods before she marries him. Look what happened to you . . .'

'I know that, but Gabriel is not at all like Syracuse. Nobody is quite like Syracuse.' She could laugh about it all now, but still not about Paolo: that was different.

'Germaine? What do you think about Allegro marrying Gabriel?'

'I think he'd make her really happy, Madeleine. What do you think about it all?'

'I would be really happy, Germaine. But then, how does one ever know about these things? Are you OK, Germaine?'

'I'm fine, Madeleine. My little dispensary is growing nicely. I am surrounded by little children. They have

445

such happy faces. I remember when I first arrived and they were so wan and thin. I'm perfectly safe here. Nobody wants to rob me or hurt me. I realise that I lived in terror in New York. I was afraid of what men could do to me. How are you, my darling?'

'I'm fine, but I want to ask you for advice.' Madeleine knew that Germaine was the only friend she would trust with her secret. 'I'm thinking of writing to Paolo in Siena and telling him that I want to see him again. I know you must think I'm mad after all these years, but I feel I need to lay that particular ghost to rest. How does that sound to you?' Madeleine waited anxiously for the reply.

'I think it's probably a good idea, Madeleine. We all need to put our ghosts to rest. Go ahead and do it. I think you need either to put him for ever out of your life, or find that you still love him. Either way, not doing anything about it, just living your life wondering about him, leads to negative energy.'

'That's great, Germaine. I'll do it. I'll write to him and see if he's willing to see me.'

'You know, Madeleine, when I lie on the floor of the desert and I see the blazing stars over my head, I wonder how people are unable to understand the force of the light. I am so aware as I watch the comets shooting across the sky that I am part of this huge, intelligent universe. It's so easy here in the desert to believe in the oneness of everything because, as I am alone, I have the time to really see it all. I think that's the source of my happiness. If I am part and particle of everything that occurs in the universe, then there is no such thing as loneliness, only aloneness, and that is different.'

'I've been thinking about that when Allegro asks me about my living on my own. Also, I am aware that if Allegro genuinely falls in love with Gabriel, we must remember that all the women who are now manifest will be able to go into the universe. I've held that secret for a long time. Only you and I knew about it. I have to deal with Dr Stanislaus, who is getting very impatient with Allegro, who's dithering about whether she is in love or not. I've told him he has no right to push her.' Madeleine laughed. 'Dr Stanislaus is still impatient. I've threatened to pull his tail feathers out the next time he manifests as an owl; he's very proud of his tail feathers.'

'I trust Allegro will do what's right for her, Madeleine. We both know she was specially called. You go ahead and write that letter. Do you know his address?'

'I know his old address. I'll send the letter there.'

'Goodbye, Madeleine.' Germaine's voice sounded far away.

Madeleine put the telephone down and walked to her writing desk.

'Dear Paolo,' she began. 'I don't know if this letter will reach you. Allegro, my daughter, is marrying a very nice man. I'm thrilled for her and for myself. I know this sounds odd. A voice from a very distant past, but I would like to see you again.

'If you would like to see me again, I could come to Siena for a long weekend, and maybe we could just talk.' She carefully used the word 'just'. She continued to write. 'I feel I owe you an apology for running away. I am not the sort of person who usually runs away, and I feel I owe you an explanation. I will wait for you to reply.' She signed and sealed the letter and walked down the drive to her postbox. She hoped the stamps were sufficient. Part of her hoped the letter would not arrive and there would be no answer, but then she wasn't at all sure about anything any more, except that her daughter would marry Gabriel. That made her happy.

Seventy-six

❧

'What on earth made you think I might want to marry you, idiot?' Allegro blushed furiously. 'You promised to be my best friend, remember?'

'I am your best friend, Allegro. I want to marry you and then we can be best friends for life.' Gabriel was sweating. 'Rather like blood-brothers, only we'd be blood-sister and -brother,' he said lamely.

'Oh, Gabriel, I can't marry you. Amy would be furious. She hates you and she's my best friend.'

'I'm not marrying Amy, darling. I'm offering to marry you.'

'I'll have to ask Amy first.'

'OK, ask if you must, but at least let me kiss you.' Without waiting for a reply, he pulled her into his arms and kissed her soundly.

Breathlessly, Allegro came up for air. 'Gabriel, I didn't even say yes.'

'I know you didn't, but you had to be persuaded, didn't you? Now that wasn't at all bad, was it?'

'Well,' Allegro wiped her mouth. 'No, not really, I suppose.'

'So could we do it again?'

'No, we couldn't, Gabriel. I'm going to find Amy and talk to her. She'll know what to do.'

'Sure she will, and I'll get to be a monk for the rest of my life.' Gabriel's face was the picture of sorrow.

'You'd stay faithful to me for the rest of my life even if I didn't marry you?'

Gabriel nodded. 'I'm really in love with you, Allegro.

I've never felt this way before. It's you and nobody else ever again. I'll forswear all women if you'll marry me. I promise.' He put his hand over his heart. 'Please think about it.' He put a dozen red roses into Allegro's arms. He had been clutching them defensively all through the conversation. 'And I bought you a box of chocolates.' He handed over the box and watched Allegro tear off the top. 'Oh goody,' she crooned. 'My favourite.'

'Can I have the chocolate with the walnut on top: that's my favourite?' Gabriel reached into the box.

'No, you can't have the one with the walnut: that's my favourite.'

Gabriel tried to tear the silver paper from the chocolate.

'That's my box of chocolates, Gabriel. You gave it to me.' Allegro tried to wrench the chocolate out of his hand.

'I paid for them,' Gabriel protested.

'Fuck off, Gabriel. There, see, we're quarrelling, and we're not even engaged.' She took off at high speed across her mother's lawn.

'I wouldn't marry that ravening brute if he were the last man on this earth.' Allegro threw herself into a chair.

'Well, darling, he probably will be the last man on this earth, the way things are going. Don't marry him if you don't want to, but watch out, he's a very attractive man, and you might lose him to another woman.'

'Fat chance, he's stuck on me.' Allegro grinned. 'I'm going to enjoy giving him a hard time. Anyway, I'm off to see Amy, so tell him I've dropped off the face of the earth and to go fuck himself if he can manage to do that.'

'I'll tell him you've left for London,' Madeleine said

diplomatically. 'Darling, if I go away for a long week-end, will you take care of the house for me?'

'Sure thing, Mom.' She looked at her mother's face and she knew to ask no questions. There was a yellow aura around her mother's shoulders that made her realise that her mother had unfinished business on her mind. She smiled and kissed Madeleine. 'I love you lots, Mom.'

'I know you do, darling, and that's what makes my life worth living.' She watched Allegro attempt to run down Gabriel on her way out of the drive.

There was a look of pure astonishment on Gabriel's face as he shot into the hall. 'That daughter of yours tried to run me down.'

'I know, I saw her, but she missed, didn't she?'

'She's completely mad.' Gabriel was puffing.

'You'll have to get fit if you want to deal with Allegro, Gabriel.'

'I can see that, but how do I stay alive?'

'With difficulty,' Madeleine said with great feeling, remembering her early days with her tempestuous daughter. 'With great difficulty,' she repeated. She rejoiced at the sound of her own laughter. It sounded so free.

Seventy-seven

&

When a letter did arrive from Siena, Madeleine felt a huge sense of relief. She opened the letter with a shaking hand. 'Cara Madeleine,' it read. For a moment she felt faint: she could hear his beloved voice again. For so long she'd blocked it out, but now she could hear it. 'I would love to see you again. I often wondered what happened to you. I respected your decision to fall out of my life. I can only tell you that your absence left a deep hole.

'Five years ago my wife died, and now I am alone with the girls. I am pleased to hear that Allegro is going to be happily married. My girls are both at the University of Siena. One studies Political Science, and the other Biology.

'Do telephone me when you are ready to visit, and I will take you to lunch on the Campo.' Madeleine smiled. She felt her heart give a huge sigh of relief. Of course she was sorry his wife had died. No, she wasn't. 'Well, I ought to be,' she admonished herself.

After so many long, lonely years, she knew she couldn't wait to be with Paolo. She had to finish her novel before she left for Siena. She wanted Allegro and Gabriel to have made a decision about their future together. She wanted to be with them when Allegro formally made her wedding vows. Then, and only then, could she go to Paolo and see if they had a future together.

A few days later she picked up the telephone to call Italy. It was seven o'clock in the morning in England,

and Italy, she knew, was an hour ahead. Paolo had always got into his office by eight o'clock.

'*Pronto*.' It was his voice. Uncurious, businesslike.

'Paolo,' she said. 'It's Madeleine.'

'Madeleine? What are you doing?'

How very Italian. What are you doing? So practical. 'I'm doing very well, Paolo. How are you?' She knew this was an inane conversation, but her heart was beating so hard in her chest she could hardly speak. 'Paolo, I'm so glad you want to see me. I'm so sorry I ran away, but I got frightened.'

'That's all right, darling. We'll talk when you come to Siena. When do you come?'

'As soon as my daughter's married. Knowing Allegro, once she's made a decision it will only be a matter of days before she acts on it, so I expect to know in the next week or two, and then I will telephone you. Is that all right?' Madeleine knew that her voice was ridiculously anxious.

'I await your call, Madeleine.' There was a silence and then Paolo said, 'I am wishing to see you, Madeleine.'

Another silence and Madeleine heard her voice saying, 'Ohhh, Paolo, it's been so long.' Then, afraid that she might cry, she put the telephone down gently. Only then did she cry. Long, lonely sobs of anguish. She walked around her drawing room with her arms wrapped tightly around her body to comfort herself, and then she put on the kettle to make a soothing cup of English tea.

It took exactly four weeks for Allegro to make up her mind. 'You know, Mom, quite apart from the fact I do love Gabriel, I am thrilled that all our women can now go back into the universe if they want to. Bella does. She says she's now finished her need to sing to audiences on this earth, and she wants to move on to what she calls the harmony of the universe. The closest humans can get to hearing it is when you hear and see the Northern Lights. Also, sometimes they sing in the middle of huge storms and hurricanes. I must say, if I didn't have Gabriel, I'd really want to go with her. Imagine being part of some celestial choir.'

'Yes, darling, it must be wonderful, but you couldn't take Gabriel with you. Anyway, I want grandchildren.'

'How many, Mom?' Allegro was laughing.

'At least six, darling.'

'OK. I think I'd be rather good at being a mother. As long as Nanny Barnes and Mrs Poole promise to come out of retirement for the first few years.'

'I expect they would. You can ask them. They will come to the wedding.'

'So, Mom, you're telling me I should get married?'

'No, Allegro, I'm ordering you to get married. Gabriel is a good man and he'll make you very happy.'

'Mom?' Allegro took her mother by the shoulders and looked into her face. 'Has something happened that I don't know about?'

'Yes, darling. Don't ask any questions, but I will tell you after you're married.'

'Oh, I hate secrets, Mom. Tell me now.'

'No, Allegro. It's so wonderful I want to keep it to myself. You know, it's like when you know where the Easter egg is, and none of the other children can find it. It's sort of thrilling to have a secret like that.'

'Oh, Mom, you'll never grow up either.'

'Writers don't have to, Allegro. They live in their own world. Now, you run along and organise a date with Gabriel.'

'Actually, I came down to say that we thought next Friday would be a good day, and then he's taking me to Little Cayman for a fortnight's honeymoon. I think that's a marvellously romantic idea. He knows how much I loved the place as a child.'

'He is romantic, and you're lucky, darling.' She looked at her daughter's glowing face. We came through it, she thought to herself. We came through it all with love.

Madeleine stood beside Allegro in the little chapel in the village. The place was crowded and she saw Nanny Barnes beaming at Allegro. Beside her was Mrs Poole in a ferocious black hat. Even Amy was there, in her New York black leather training suit. She wore a large, bright red map of Africa around her neck. She was smiling, which was a relief to Madeleine.

Allegro was wearing a pink silk dress. She wore high heels and white silk stockings. In her hand she carried a small posy of pink gardenias. That was Gabriel's idea. Beside her he stood very rigid and silent. His two aunts were in his family pew, and one rather moth-eaten uncle. Madeleine longed to hold his hand: she could see how frightened he was.

Allegro was smiling. Madeleine was so glad that she seemed to be totally happy with her decision. She kept looking shyly up at Gabriel, and he looked down at her with such a gentle warmth in his eyes. Madeleine felt as if she were drowning in happiness. The local vicar, who was thrilled to be marrying off his little hoyden of a parishioner, held out his hand. 'Wilt thou have this man . . .' The familiar words left his mouth and were carried to the waiting women. They, in ranks, stood around Bella in the deserted opera house in the City. Long ago this building had been closed down for lack of funds, but now it was to fulfil its last function.

There was a silence in the room. No one moved. Bella could feel her body straining to hear the words being said in the chapel in the country. The women watched and waited and then they heard a faltering voice say, 'I will.' It was all over.

There was a sudden rush of wind. The sound grew as the women were lifted through the roof. 'Follow me,' Bella screamed. 'We're coming,' was the great chorus.

Back in the peace of the chapel, all was silent. Suddenly there were two sharp whistles. The vicar jumped. 'What was that?' he said.

'Nothing,' Allegro said. She reached up to kiss her new husband. Nothing at all. She grinned at her mother. 'I kept the faith,' she said.

'So did I,' answered Madeleine. She kissed her son-in-law.

'Now, Mom, tell me your secret.'

'I'm going to Siena to see Paolo, darling.'

Allegro hugged her mother. 'You're sure you'll be all right?'

'I'm sure, darling. I'm very, very sure.'

Morningstar
Erin Pizzey

There are only two ways to get away from Michael Morningstar – die or move abroad. Michael Morningstar is an enigmatic man. No one knows quite who he is, or how he got the fortune he spends, but the women who pass through his hands pay a terrible price for their folly . . .

But perhaps in Nina, Michael Morningstar has met his match. Bright and beautiful, she attracts him from the first – attracts him so much that he wants her in his house and in his bed. And then he wants to humiliate and destroy her. Bribing his way into the world of charitable social causes which Nina inhabits, he slowly draws her into his net. But he did not anticipate her strength – and, above all, the fact that someone would kill rather than see Nina harmed . . .

A tantalizing and sexy novel from a powerful storyteller.